Melting THE ICE

BETH BOLDEN

AUTHOR NOTE

Melting the Ice and the Portland Evergreens series take place in the wider Beth Bolden universe: a universe that is more inclusive and welcoming than our own.

In Beth-world, the first professional athlete to come out of the closet was Colin O'Connor (*The Rainbow Clause)*, and after this happened, approximately ten years ago, there have been numerous players, coaches, and even owners who are living their best queer life freely.

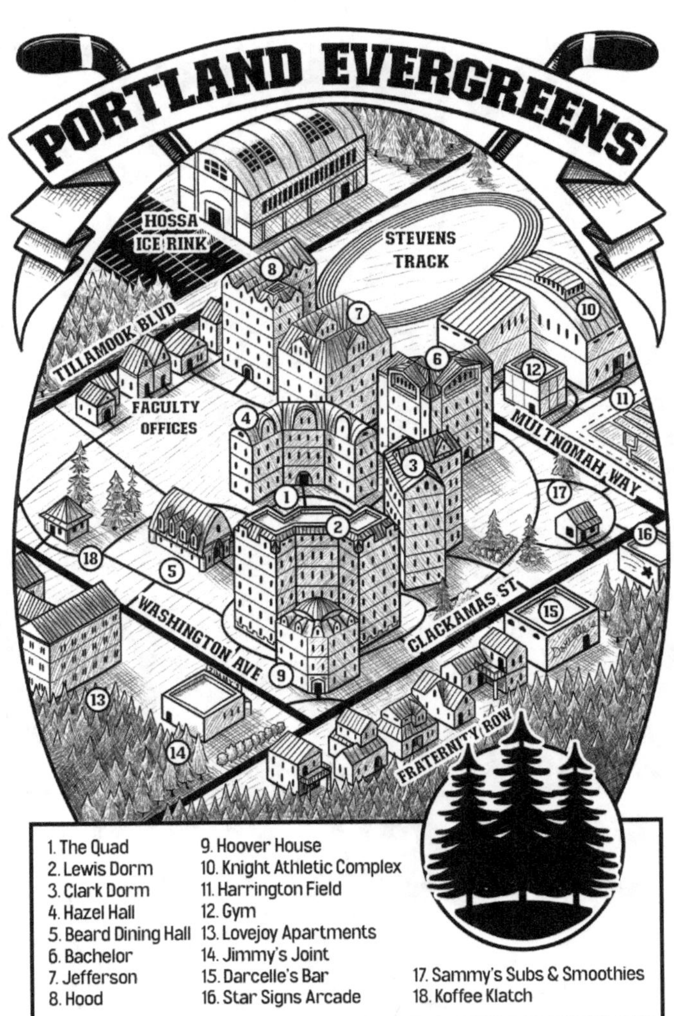

PORTLAND EVERGREENS
HOSSA ICE RINK
STEVENS TRACK
TILLAMOOK BLVD
FACULTY OFFICES
MULTNOMAH WAY
CLACKAMAS ST
WASHINGTON AVE
FRATERNITY ROW
1. The Quad
2. Lewis Dorm
3. Clark Dorm
4. Hazel Hall
5. Beard Dining Hall
6. Bachelor
7. Jefferson
8. Hood
9. Hoover House
10. Knight Athletic Complex
11. Harrington Field
12. Gym
13. Lovejoy Apartments
14. Jimmy's Joint
15. Darcelle's Bar
16. Star Signs Arcade
17. Sammy's Subs & Smoothies
18. Koffee Klatch

CHAPTER ONE

Brody Faulkner jogged up the stairs to the apartment, telling himself that the two flights were no big deal and he wasn't even going to be upset about lugging groceries up them in the rain, because he and Ramsey, one of his friends on the Evergreens, the Portland University hockey team, were *finally* sharing a place together.

No more weird roommates who didn't understand the crazy schedule collegiate athletes had to keep, or who looked down their noses at protein shake stains on the kitchen counters, pull-up bars in the doorway, and the never-ending, impossible-to-eradicate-completely smell of old sweat pervading the place.

Ramsey probably wouldn't have been his first choice of roommate—he was a little bit of a loose cannon, *but* when push came to shove, he was a good friend and an even better hockey player—but Brody hadn't minded because Ramsey had to be better than the other guys he'd roomed with before this, his junior year.

Brody's first indication something was wrong was the pot full of half-dead plants sitting next to the door.

First, if Ramsey was staying here, they would one hundred percent be totally dead, because the guy had never met a planter he didn't want to pee in.

Second, there was a football lying in it, resting in the dirt right next to the bedraggled plants.

Ramsey famously hated every sport that wasn't hockey.

He wouldn't touch a football with a ten-foot pole.

But maybe he *would* pee on it.

"You okay, honey?"

Brody glanced down the stairs and saw his mom, box in hand, one of Brody's duffels slung over her other shoulder, straight dark hair tucked behind one ear, a concerned look on her face.

"Oh, I'm . . ." *Worried because Ramsey is Ramsey.* "I'm fine."

"You just stopped there. On the third step from the top. Thought maybe you might've felt a . . ."

"My knee is fine."

His knee *was* fine.

The doctors said he'd totally recovered from his season-ending ACL tear last year and that he'd be as fast as ever on the ice.

But mentally trusting the knee had surprisingly not come so easy.

There were some moments he still struggled with the worry that it would just give out again.

Today wasn't one of those moments, ironically.

"Oh, good." Tish glanced up at the doorway. "I didn't know Ramsey was into plants. Could use a good watering, though."

"He's not. He's really not." But Brody didn't get any more words out, because the door opened then, and that definitely wasn't Ramsey filling the empty space, shoulders nearly brushing both sides of the doorframe.

"You must be Brody," the guy said gruffly, shoving too-long chestnut hair behind his ears. "Hey, I'm Dean. Dean Scott."

"Dean?" Tish asked hesitantly. Brody could feel her eyes on him and knew that he should've told his parents that he could move in without their help.

Ramsey wouldn't have given a shit if his parents drove up from Northern California to help him move in. Okay, he would've *definitely* given Brody crap about it, teasing him about being a first grader needing his hand held on the first day of school, but it all would've been good-natured, because Ramsey liked his parents, too.

But this was a stranger.

Named Dean.

Brody unstuck his voice. "Where's Ramsey?"

The huge mountain of a man sighed and crossed his arms over his chest. A big, broad chest. Brody knew his way around a weight room and could tell this guy spent a *lot* of time in one. Clearly an athlete of some kind.

Then there was the football in the planter. And the Evergreens logo printed, with "football team" underneath it, on the T-shirt currently plastered to all of Dean's muscles.

Not just an athlete, but a football player.

Brody wanted to find Ramsey and wrap his hands around his neck and choke him slowly until his eyes bugged out and he laughed so hard he couldn't breathe.

"Ramsey didn't tell you." Dean's resignation was punctuated by another sigh.

"Apparently not. Let me guess, he's not living here this year."

"He...uh..." Dean scratched his scruff-covered chin. "Said he got a better offer."

"Well, that's rude and well..." Tish trailed off, and Brody looked over at her. They exchanged a look. "Very much like Ramsey," she finished.

It did sound just like Ramsey.

That didn't mean that Brody wanted to choke him out any less.

"Then yeah, I'm Brody." Brody shifted the box he was carrying and held out his hand. Dean shook it, and Brody got a brief impression of callouses and strength, before Dean was motioning him into the apartment.

It was tiny, and even tinier with Dean in it.

That was going to take some getting used to. Brody hadn't felt small in years, but Dean made him feel practically doll-sized.

"Apartment came furnished, but I brought a few things, and it seems like you've got some stuff," Dean said. "I've been here a few months already—I'm on the football team."

Right. Football season started way before hockey did. In the summer? Brody wasn't sure; he didn't spend much time thinking about football. He wasn't actively against it, not like Ramsey, but it was easy to get absorbed in school and practice and games and forget that there were other sports teams on campus than just the hockey team.

"Right. I'm...I should call Ramsey."

Dean's gaze narrowed. Like he was suddenly worried. "You had your heart set on rooming with him?"

Well, *no*, not exactly. Not with Ramsey the person. But Ramsey, the known entity.

This Dean was a stranger. A nice enough stranger, Brody supposed, but Dean was supposed to be *Ramsey*.

"No, not exactly—"

But Dean didn't let him get the explanation out. "Well, *I'm* glad you're here. It's hard for me to afford this place on my own."

Brody met Dean's intense glass green stare. Told himself not to feel ashamed of his parents' Porsche SUV downstairs, his brand-new car in the parking lot, the new things his mom had insisted on buying that she was currently setting on the old, worn linoleum kitchen countertop.

Both his parents were successful doctors. He'd been lucky to never hurt for anything that money could buy. Hockey wasn't the cheapest sport to get involved with, but he'd never worried about the costs associated with it—and Brody knew just how privileged that was.

"I . . .uh . . ." Brody hesitated. "I'm sure it'll be fine." He didn't really want to live with Dean—but then when he thought about it, had he wanted to live with Ramsey, either?—but it would probably be fine.

The guy seemed decent.

"Good," Dean said, with a firm nod. "You guys need any help bringing your stuff in?"

"No, I think we've got it—"

"Hey, Brody, what's this football?" His dad walked in, salt-and-pepper hair gone more salt than pepper, gleaming under the fluorescent lights, his brown eyes taking in every inch of the worn furniture, blank white walls, and the scuffed vinyl flooring.

"It's Dean's," Brody said, gesturing towards the big man. "My new roommate. Dean, this is my dad, Roger, and my mom, Tish."

Brody gave Dean credit. He greeted them each with a grave smile and a quick handshake, even though Brody had already figured out that the guy wasn't the most social creature on the planet.

He'd be quiet, if nothing else.

But Brody would still be wringing Ramsey's neck for letting him show up without having any clue that he'd bailed and found some new guy to take his place.

Brody would definitely be adding an extra layer of shit that the new roommate was a football player.

It didn't take long between the three of them to get Brody's stuff moved in. He hugged his parents goodbye and then walked back into the apartment, more than ready to get unpacked and settled in.

The bedroom next to Dean's was small but functional, with a double bed at least, instead of the regulation twin. The apartment had been listed as "mostly furnished," including the beds, and so the larger bed made sense because Brody couldn't imagine Dean fitting on a twin, anyway.

The bathroom was between them, again small but adequately sized, with a big tub that Brody already knew was going to alternate between soaking him and his equipment.

Toby, the Evergreens' equipment manager, did a great job of taking care of stuff, but Brody liked to be a little more hands-on. Wash some things himself.

Brody was halfway through unpacking his clothes when a voice startled him.

"So, you brought your parents to move-in day."

Brody looked up from one of his half-empty duffels, surprised. For a big guy, Dean even *moved* quietly. His comment wouldn't have been unexpected coming from Ramsey, but he was surprised Dean would bring it up, especially considering they were basically strangers.

Roommates, now, but *still* strangers.

Thanks for fucking nothing, Ramsey.

"Uh, yeah," Brody mumbled, willing his cheeks not to flush with embarrassment. He was twenty-one now, supposed to be a grown-ass man who didn't need his parents, even acted like they didn't exist. Certainly not like he *needed* them, still.

"Huh," Dean said. That wasn't exactly judgment in his expression or his tone, but it wasn't *not* judgment either.

Brody honestly wasn't sure what it was.

Maybe Dean always had that kind of closed-off face.

"You yell at Ramsey yet?" he asked next.

Brody might have to revise his previous opinion that Dean was going to be a quiet roommate, because that was *two* questions he'd asked now, clearly making an effort to create a conversation and some kind of camaraderie—if not a friendship—out of nothing.

"Not yet," Brody admitted.

He'd been waiting until Dean left or until he went out, because there were things he wanted to say that he didn't want the other guy to overhear. It wasn't *his* fault that Ramsey had apparently changed his situation without even bothering to tell Brody.

Maybe Brody could've told him *nevermind, I'll find someplace else,* but then there was the fact that Dean had clearly mentioned the expense of rent, and he'd been suddenly and acutely aware of never worrying about where next month's rent was coming from.

His parents' checking account, that was where.

"He a good friend of yours?"

There was a third question.

Brody looked up and decided that if Dean was making this kind of effort, he should actually reciprocate.

"No, but we play on the hockey team together."

Dean nodded. "That's what he told me. You're what . . .a . . .uh . . ."

"Defense," Brody supplied. He looked Dean up and down. "And you're . . . a handy wall that the offense has to throw around?"

"Something like that," Dean said, chuckling under his breath. "A linebacker. Edge rusher, actually."

"Are they usually your size?"

"No," Dean said. "But it's what makes me good. I'm big, but I'm fast."

Of course he was. He'd probably never gotten injured either, not seriously anyway.

Brody stopped himself from rolling his eyes. It wasn't Dean's fault, either, that he was a prime specimen of athletic ability or that Brody was already feeling anxious about getting back on the ice.

Not that it *would* be his first skate. He'd skated plenty since his knee had healed. But not officially. Not in front of their new-old coach.

New, because he'd just been hired to take the Evergreens over.

Old, because he'd coached at Portland U for years, before he'd left for the NHL.

And now he was back, and Brody would've probably been anxious about their first practice anyway, but now that he was going to do it under Gavin Blackburn's watchful and notoriously expert eye?

Well, that wouldn't be intimidating *at all*.

"I'm afraid I don't know much about football," Brody admitted.

"And I know jack shit about hockey." Dean cracked another smile. "But I think we'll manage to stay out of each other's way well enough."

If Brody thought that pronouncement was a little weird—after all, why was he hanging out here, trying to make conversation if he wanted them to only co-exist?—he didn't say so because that would only make things *weirder*.

"Yeah, sure. But you know . . .uh . . .feel free to use any of the kitchen stuff my . . .uh . . .mom brought. The blender and stuff."

"Your parents those helicopter types?"

Well, they were rich, sure. But they didn't own a fucking helicopter. "No," he said. "Owning a Mercedes isn't the same as a helicopter."

Dean stared at him for a long moment, then threw back his head and straight up cackled. "Not that they *own* a helicopter, are *they* helicopters?" Dean made a circling motion around his head. "Like they don't leave you to your own shit."

"Oh, no. No. Actually no." Brody internally winced at his triple, no doubt very obvious, denial. "I just . . .we're close. That's all." *No, it's not cool. I know that.* He didn't mind it when his teammates and friends or even Ramsey gave him shit about it, because they knew him and loved him, and *got* it. But this was some big stranger, three days of beard on his face, looking wary and together, like he'd laugh in the face of any parent who tried to help him do *anything*.

Who didn't *need* a parent to carry some boxes to the second floor; who certainly didn't *want* them to.

"That's cool."

"But yeah, I'm sure she overdid it." Brody's wince was not internal this time, much to his embarrassment. "Someone else should get to enjoy her zeal."

"Zeal, huh?" The corner of Dean's mouth tilted up, not quite in a smile, but in something. "You a lit major?"

He shook his head. "Biology."

Dean's eyes widened. "Fucking serious? You're a *science* major?"

"Yeah." He was used to everyone thinking he was crazy at this point. The jock who also happened to be a nerd. "You?"

Don't say you're a physical education major, don't say you're a physical education major . . .

Those guys were always the worst, the type who rarely bothered with class, and would graduate just because they were bound for the pros in whatever sport they played.

Even Ramsey was in Communications, though that was mostly an excuse for him to send DMs to hot influencers and spend too much time on TikTok.

"Physical education, but don't say it." Dean was outright grinning now. "I actually go to fucking class."

"Are you the only one who does?" Brody asked.

Dean shrugged. "I don't give a fuck what anyone else does. Just me. I want to get a good education, have options, before I go to the NFL."

Brody supposed he shouldn't have been surprised by the matter-of-fact way Dean said it, like it was inevitable, not even a question. He knew the football team was good, that a lot of their players got drafted into the pros.

And if Dean was as good as he claimed he was . . .well, maybe it *was* just a fact that he'd be going to the NFL.

"But shit, I know how it sounds," Dean continued. "I know most of those guys are useless. And you're in biology. *Fuck.* Why? Aren't you going to go pro?"

"Actually, I've already been drafted. Third round, by the Hurricanes."

"Oh. But you're still in college?" Dean's forehead crinkled, the way so many people's did when Brody tried to explain why some hockey players entered the draft and then returned to play in college.

"Yeah, it's a developmental kinda thing. And I want to finish my degree. My *parents* want me to finish my degree. So we're in agreement, at least. But yeah, eventually, I'll move on." To what . . .well, Brody knew he was being deliberately nebulous. He was supposed to want to play professional hockey. He was supposed to be thrilled he'd been drafted. He *had* been thrilled.

He wanted to play—but when his knee had failed him last year, everything had changed.

He'd started to worry. To wonder.

There was no denying he'd had his future laid out for him from his early teenage years, and it was always what he'd wanted, what he'd worked so hard for. His only rebellion had been his major, the science classes he enjoyed too much to stop taking, but now, suddenly, with too much time on his hands, he'd started to think.

Ramsey would have told him thinking was a bad thing, and Brody shouldn't hurt his brain by doing it too often, but he hadn't been able to help himself.

It hadn't helped that his mother kept dropping hints about medical school. She meant, of course, that he could do it *after* his professional career had ended. She had no idea that he'd started thinking about doing it *now*.

Well, he didn't know what the hell he was gonna do. Brody was hoping a light bulb would switch on and he'd *know*, but so far, that hadn't happened.

Instead, for right now, he wanted to focus on getting back on the ice. Hoping his knee would hold him the way it was supposed to.

"Well that's cool. I never want to stop playing football." Dean hesitated. "And I guess you don't gotta worry about money, no matter what you do."

"No," Brody admitted. So much for the guy not noticing their expensive cars or the new Vitamix blender in its packaging, sitting on the kitchen counter.

"Figures," Dean said, but he didn't sound annoyed, more resigned.

He didn't need to say the opposite was true for him. It was obvious.

"So that's why you play, huh? The NFL? Getting rich?"

Dean shot him a look full of disbelief. "That wrong, somehow?" he demanded to know.

"No. No, of course not. Everyone's gotta do what they gotta do," Brody rambled, horribly aware that he'd stepped in his own shit despite being fully aware it was there.

"Right." Dean turned to go.

"Listen," Brody said, "I didn't mean it like that. There's nothing wrong with doing that."

Dean gave him a fleeting smile, all teeth. "I know that, pretty boy."

"Hey, I'm not—"

"Rich boy, then."

Brody realized then, before he could argue back that he wasn't pretty, he was a *hockey player*, and a damn good one too, that Dean was teasing him.

"Then I'm gonna call you big guy."

"Yeah, never heard that one before," Dean said, but he was smiling with genuine amusement now.

"Bet you haven't," Brody retorted.

He *wasn't* just pretty, he still wanted to argue. He had a brain. He was more than just the thick, wavy hair he'd inherited from his mom, and the impeccable bone structure from his dad. And he certainly didn't have *their* money, either. Not yet anyway.

But he'd been around long enough to know when a guy was giving him a hard time and when he was teasing, and with Dean, it was clearly the latter.

"Hey, I gotta run to practice. But good to meet you, pretty boy," Dean said, flashing him one final grin before he turned towards his own room.

Brody finished unpacking, not that it took very long, because it felt like all he wore most of the year was either shorts or sweats, and one of the many Evergreens T-shirts he owned.

He'd sent a text to Ramsey telling him they needed to talk, and the answer came through right when he was finishing up.

Jimmy's. Ten minutes.

Brody grabbed his wallet and keys and headed out, walking the block down the street to Jimmy's diner, which was open twenty-four hours and was one of the hockey team's favorite places to hang out.

Ramsey was sitting in the back of the diner in a booth, leaning against the cushion. "Hey, man, good to see you," he said, rising and pulling Brody into a hug which he only resisted for half a second before finally giving in.

"What the fuck," Brody said, as he slid in opposite him. "You just sprung a new roommate on me without even bothering to call? Text? Facebook messenger me? Even send out some smoke signals?"

"Oh, that," Ramsey said.

"*Oh, that,*" Brody retorted. "Like it's not a big deal!" He paused. "Hey, wait, what did you think I was pissed about?"

Ramsey waved a hand. "Ah, nothing. No big deal. So you met Dean, huh?"

"Of course I met Dean." Brody rolled his eyes. "I showed up today and he was there. Not you. What happened?"

"Had a different offer I had to consider," Ramsey said. The waitress approached then, and they ordered. Brody got the chef salad—Ramsey shooting him a semi-concerned look—and then added a plate of Jimmy's famous french fries.

"*What* different offer?" Brody demanded once she'd left. "And don't you dare say it was a better one."

Ramsey Andresen was one of the few seniors on the Evergreens, and to say he was wild was an understatement. Brody had discovered very quickly that whatever he expected out of Ramsey was the opposite of what might happen.

Usually he'd have a good time anyway; it *always* worked out, so it was hard for anyone to stay mad at him, but this whole last-minute roommate switch was a whole new level.

But Ramsey just shrugged. "I think this is gonna work out better for us all," he said. "Dean needed a place, and you needed a roommate you could rely on."

"Wait, you *know* Dean? He's a—"

Ramsey grinned. "Yeah, we won't hold it against him, alright?"

"*I* don't give a shit if he plays football," Brody said.

"Exactly."

Brody rolled his eyes. "You still could've told me."

"No, 'cause you would've thrown a fit. Like a melodramatic twelve-year-old."

"Not fair," Brody said.

"Listen, Faulkner. We'd have made each other crazy. You know that. I'm making you crazy right now." Ramsey leaned forward, grinning. "Are you gonna deny it?"

"You're making me crazy because you switched roommates on me!"

"Do you not like him?"

"He's…he's fine. He's…" Brody trailed off. "He seems like a decent enough guy. Quiet, probably."

"You'll like that. And think of all the rumors you're gonna save yourself, from everyone who would've assumed we were hooking up."

"I'm not—"

"Yeah, but I am, and let's face it, this face is kinda irresistible."

Brody supposed Ramsey *was* good-looking, if you swung that way, which he didn't. Ramsey swung *every* way, which was fine, Brody hardly held it against him, but even if he'd been interested, he wouldn't have wanted to be just another notch in Ramsey's bedpost.

Which…that was another point.

"Guess those excellent noise-canceling headphones I bought aren't going to come in handy after all," Brody said, beginning to understand why Ramsey had decided this for both of them. Eventually, Brody might've gotten pissed at him.

Like if he felt like hosting someone the night before a big test, for example.

Or more than one someone.

"I feel like I should defend Dean's honor and his prowess in the bedroom, but I'm gonna be honest, he's even more of a nun than you are."

"I—"

Ramsey leaned forward. "If you were gonna say you hook up, don't even bother. I know you don't really, and it's cool, man. Not a requirement. Just saying. A total waste, yes, but still cool."

"Thanks," Brody said dryly. Then suddenly, it occurred to him why Dean might've called him pretty boy. Had he been flirting with him?

"Don't worry about Dean, either. If he hooks up, I certainly haven't heard about it. That guy actually goes to class." Ramsey shook his head like he couldn't quite believe it.

"Ramsey, *I* actually go to class."

"Exactly. You two are meant for each other. A match made in roommate heaven." Ramsey grinned. "You can thank me now."

"I'm not gonna thank you," Brody grumbled. "You could have *told* me we weren't a good match. You definitely could have told me about Dean."

"Yeah, and then what would you have done? Gone off and found the next worst person. You're smart, yeah, but only book smart. Don't got a clue in your head about practical matters."

Brody wanted to argue with him but it was clear Ramsey believed that was true, so what was the point?

He changed the subject, instead.

"You excited about practice tomorrow?"

"Coach Blackburn! Yeah, he's gonna be fun to play for." Ramsey seemed unconcerned that the coach with one of the most celebrated histories in Evergreens history was now back at the school and leading the team.

No pressure or anything.

Of course, if Ramsey *ever* felt the strain of expectations, he certainly didn't show it. He was the epitome of grace under pressure, not even acting like he could overcome it but that it simply didn't exist at all.

"Yeah," Brody said. Wishing, not for the first time, that he could be more like Ramsey. He could emulate him, but he wasn't really like him, not deep down, not underneath.

"How's the knee?"

"Fine."

Brody tried to keep his voice level. *Normal.* Was pretty sure he had, but then Ramsey gave him a hard look and tilted his head.

"You said that weird. All high and anxious. Is it really fine?"

"Of course it is. I had months off. Months to rehab it. I'm .. .I'm good. I swear."

"But you're still freaking out about it." Ramsey said this matter-of-factly. So matter-of-factly that it was hard to deny, because what was the point?

Brody sighed. "It *is* fine. But yeah, I'm a little nervous, I guess."

About the knee. About everything else.

"You don't trust it yet." Ramsey's voice was shrewd now.

And man, Brody loved Ramsey, but he *hated* how he could see through even his best lies.

Now that he thought about it, there was no way he wouldn't have ended up hating the guy if they'd stayed roommates.

"I will," Brody said.

"Yeah, you will. You'll be good. I think we got a real shot this year, maybe even win the conference."

"You think?"

"You *don't* think Elliott, Mal, and Ivan aren't a fucking dynamite line?"

"They are," Brody said cautiously.

"And with Finn at goal, you don't think we've got a real shot?" He gave Brody one of his cockiest grins. The one that lured practically everyone to his bed. "And then there's us. Best defensive pair in the conference."

The waitress brought the food, saving Brody from answering—or from saying what he really wanted to say. Which was: *don't jinx it before the season even starts.*

"You really gotta learn to relax. Unclench. Or something." Ramsey said this as he shoved three french fries in his mouth.

Brody grimaced. "How do you get *anyone* to go to bed with you?"

"My huge dick," Ramsey said, waggling his eyebrows.

"You're a fucking Neanderthal," Brody said.

"But that's the best kind," Ramsey retorted with a wild grin.

CHAPTER TWO

Brody leaned down and tightened the laces on his skate for the third time.

"You doin' okay there?"

Glancing up, he saw Zach, the new assistant coach, standing in front of him, arms crossed over his chest.

He wanted to like Zach, but the truth was, Zach was only slightly less intimidating than Coach Gavin Blackburn, who was the winningest coach in Evergreens history, and who had only now come back to Portland after a successful, if short, stint in the NHL.

The only reason Zach wasn't just as ridiculously intimidating as Coach Blackburn was that 1) he was young, maybe only a handful of years older than some of the seniors on the team, and 2) he'd been a player here himself, playing for Blackburn during his first coaching stint.

"I'm fine, knee's fine," Brody said automatically. If he said it enough, maybe he'd finally believe it.

Zach crouched down in front of him, his blue eyes serious. "Didn't ask about your knee. I know Coach got the all-clear from your PT."

"Right." Brody felt like something—possibly any one of his hidden fears—had been exposed. "It isn't my first time back on the ice, you know." He hated how defensive, how *afraid,* he sounded, but he couldn't help it.

He was kind of a wreck. And not even the fun kind.

"Maybe not your first time on the ice, but Coach B and I know you're gonna start out at your own speed, whatever that is," Zach said quietly.

"Alright."

Zach put a hand on his knee. "You got this, Faulkner. I promise."

"Thanks," Brody said and pushed himself up off the bench.

His knee felt more than fine. Frankly, it was probably stronger than it had been before the tear. Both his surgeon and his PT had come highly recommended and he'd spent what felt like a very long spring and summer doing all the strengthening exercises they'd recommended.

He'd already done his stretches, loosening up his muscles, and there was nothing to do but to face his anxiety—and the ice just outside the locker room door.

"You comin', Bro?" Elliott, the sophomore forward, stuck his head just inside the locker room door.

"Yeah," he said, trying not to look like he was procrastinating, but then what the hell, they all knew him too well, even Elliott, even though they'd barely gotten to play together before his injury. "I'm coming." And then because he felt like he *should,* Elliott's young, uncomplicated face waiting there patiently for him, he stood and walked over to the door and actually managed to get through it.

"This year is gonna be fucking sick," Elliott chattered, listing out all the reasons. All the guys and girls he was going to sleep with. All the frat parties he was going to attend. Normally, Brody might've cautioned him to include *some* class and practice time in amongst all that, but he was too caught up in his own shit, which Elliott probably knew.

Which Elliott was probably trying to distract him from, come to think of it.

Brody wanted to smack him and hug him.

"You gotta go to class, too, you know," he said as they approached the opening in the boards.

"You're no fun," Elliott said fondly.

"I'm plenty of fun," Brody retorted. Not thinking of how just yesterday Ramsey had compared him to a *nun*. Everyone was a nun compared to Ramsey—and Elliott too, for that matter, who was making a real effort to follow in Ramsey's footsteps, but without some of Ramsey's natural panache—but that didn't mean Brody *actually* was.

Elliott shot him a skeptical glance and Brody was just about ready to tell him exactly the last time he'd had plenty of fun—every summer, he and Liz, a friend who lived down the street that he'd gone to high school with, always casually hooked up at least once—when he realized that with Elliott distracting him, they'd made it to the ice and he was skating, as easy and freely as he'd ever skated before.

"See?" Elliott said, grinning. "Not so bad."

"Ugh," Brody groaned. "Did everyone know?"

"That you were hiding in the locker room? Of course not."

Which meant—*yes*.

Ramsey skated up to him, flicking the puck over with his stick, and Brody grabbed it easily. They'd been partners for two years now, and it came naturally to play with him.

Once he'd gotten here, he realized how much he'd missed it, how much he'd craved that feel of flying over the ice, stick in his hand, his teammates around him, Ramsey at his shoulder, always right where he needed him if he looked.

Maybe Ramsey had been right after all. Maybe being room-mates would've been a disaster; maybe it would've ruined this.

"Hey! Let's circle up!" A tall man, still fit, with dark hair and a few threads of silver running through the temples, walked out onto the ice, stopping in the center of the rink.

He was Gavin Blackburn, both the old and *new* coach of the Portland Evergreens.

Zach was trailing behind him, but he'd put skates on, and was weaving in and out, blades cutting deep into the ice, making it clear that while he was a coach and a grad student now, he still had the moves.

"I'm Gavin Blackburn, your new coach," he said. Up close, Coach B had grooves in his forehead, fading dark circles under his eyes. He looked like he'd been through a war compared to the photographs of him a few years ago, before he'd left Portland to go to the NHL.

He'd only coached there for a few years, before leaving abruptly in the middle of the season when his wife, Noelle, had unexpectedly fallen ill and then even more unexpectedly died.

There'd been lots of talk that he'd never return to the ice, that he was finished, that he was holed up in a remote cabin in upper Michigan and refused to leave. That he was becoming a grief-stricken hermit.

But now he was back.

What had pulled him out of his hole, Brody wasn't sure, but he seemed determined to be present, in any case.

If the rumors of his thick black beard had actually had any truth to them, they didn't now, because he was clean-shaven, gray eyes meeting each and every player as they came to a stop around him.

"Zach here likes to call me Coach B, so that's fine," Coach said. "I think we've got a talented crew here, but I think your old coach was a little too free and easy with the rules. Just so you know, I won't be. I expect your best, on the ice and off."

Elliott mumbled behind him.

He wasn't going to be very happy about that. He might be an absolute demon during games—deserving of joining Mal and Ivan on the first line—but he hated practice and rarely exerted himself. And class? Well. If he even went, that was an unusual—and rare—step in the right direction.

"That means," Coach continued, "that we're going to be taking practice very seriously. Especially these first few weeks. I expect you to show up ready to work." He motioned to Zach. "Zach is gonna lead you in the drills, and I can't say I won't strap some skates on at some point. I gotta stay young somehow."

"Oh, you're young enough, Coach," Ramsey called out.

Coach didn't quite break into a smile, but it was far enough from what seemed to be his typical sternness that Brody considered it a win. Though he wasn't sure if Ramsey would.

Ramsey liked to charm everyone and was usually very good at it.

"My youth—or what's left of it—isn't up for debate," Coach said. "But your fitness is. Let's run some drills."

Zach proceeded to run them through a bunch of drills, starting with crisscrossing the ice, going both forward and backward, over and over again.

Brody's knee protested a little at first, but he'd put his brace on, and the more he warmed up, the better it felt. Still, he was shaking sweat out of his hair by the end of that one.

Next, Coach led them through some shooting drills.

Finn traded off with their other goalie, Dominic, and they skated up, sending shots their way.

Finn was young and maybe a little nervy, but he faced them all head-on and seemed to do just fine in the moment.

He'd transferred mid-season last year, and Brody had liked what he'd seen of the guy, but he also worried because the goalie's NHL pedigree might mask either mediocrity or anxiety—or both.

Four or five drills in, it seemed like Coach B wanted to find out if anyone had spent the summer on the couch instead of in the weight room. And it seemed that maybe a few of them had. Brody decided he was lucky he wasn't one of them. But by the time practice ended, even he was feeling sweat run down his back, damp underneath his practice jersey.

"God, that was tough," Finn said, wiping his face with his jersey as they staggered into the locker room.

"Don't tell me you spent all summer sunning yourself in Europe," Ramsey retorted lightly. "I saw plenty of pics of you out where, on your dad's beachfront property in Italy?"

Finn frowned. He didn't seem particularly happy that Ramsey had noticed that. Well, they'd *all* noticed, and it wasn't like Finn could possibly pretend that his dad wasn't Morgan Reynolds.

He didn't even try.

But he was frowning still.

"Yeah," Finn said shortly. "That's where the house is. Positano."

"Nice," Ramsey said. "No hockey rink there, though."

"I spent plenty of time in the gym," Finn argued.

"Right, of course you did," Ramsey said smoothly.

But Finn's color was up and there was clear exhaustion on his face.

Well, at least he wasn't alone. Everyone looked pretty beat. Probably what Coach B had intended for their first practice, to set the tone.

At least, Brody thought, as he stripped out of his equipment and headed towards the showers, his knee felt good.

He'd make sure to ice it later, just to make sure, but it had held up, exactly the way it was supposed to.

"Hear you've got a hockey player roommate," Wes said, tossing the ball back and forth between his two big glove-covered hands.

Even in Portland, notorious for its temperate and rainy climate, the Evergreens played football outside. Most quarterbacks avoided gloves, but Wes always practiced with gloves, and never played without them.

He was one of Dean's best friends on the team. Probably one of his best friends, period, since he didn't exactly have the extra time on his hands to go around making friends.

If they weren't in his classes, on the field with him, or at his job, he didn't have a chance in hell of getting to know anyone.

"Yeah," Dean said. He wasn't a guy who spoke up a lot. It always surprised him that he and Wes had gravitated to each other, because Wes was friendly and talked to *everyone*. But for the last three years, he always seemed to end up right back at Dean's side.

Without Wes, he'd probably be totally alone.

Mom didn't give a shit about him—never had—and wherever his father was, Dean didn't want him to crawl out of the hole he'd hidden himself in anyway.

He was just fine on his own, but he *was* grateful for Wes' friendship, nevermind that he didn't understand it.

Wes nudged him with an elbow. Tossed him the ball, and Dean nimbly plucked it out of the air. For a linebacker, he had pretty good hands. Not as good as Wes' maybe, but Dean's hands were there to give him the push he needed to destroy whatever lay in his path.

And he was *really* fucking good at that.

"Am I gonna get more details than just a single word?" Wes asked, the corner of his mouth quirking up. Clearly amused, and not annoyed, by Dean's reticence. Three years of friendship and he was no doubt used to it by now.

"Yeah, he's a hockey player. Name's Brody. Just moved in two days ago. Don't know him, so that's all I've got to share."

"And this is the guy Ramsey set you up with?"

Dean opened his mouth to argue with the *set you up with* addition, even though yes, it was technically true. It just didn't mean what Wes was implying, with his waggling eyebrows and knowing look. But before he could, Wes sighed.

"Yes, I know, he didn't *set you up* with him. Just facilitated a roommate arrangement." Wes shot him a limpid smile. "That un-romantic enough for you?"

Wes just wanted everyone to be as happy as he was, with his longtime boyfriend.

Dean didn't believe that kind of happiness wasn't for him, necessarily, just that by the time he got around to romance and love and the white picket fence, he didn't know if it would want *him* anymore.

He didn't know anyone who honestly managed to have it all. Something always lost out, and Dean wasn't going to let that be anything that mattered to him. Anything that he'd worked so goddamned hard for, all on his own.

"Yes," Dean muttered. "Anyway, he seems like an okay enough guy. Quiet. Biology major, if you could believe it."

"Really? He want to be a doctor?" Wes wondered.

"Says he was drafted. Can you believe hockey drafts them so young and *then* they go back to college? So weird. But I think he's not sure. He's a freaking biology major and his parents are both doctors." Dean shook his head. Brody hadn't said it, but he'd caught the clear hesitation on his face when they'd discussed their futures. Dean couldn't imagine anyone having that possible future within their grasp and rejecting it. Of course, he also couldn't imagine having not just one wealthy parent but *two*, and never worrying about where his next meal was coming from or if he could scrape together rent money this month or if he was going to have enough money for football fees that year.

Going through life unconcerned about what was possible.

Brody *wasn't* a bad guy, but Dean didn't understand him at all. In fact, he'd needed to shove down a flare of jealous resentment half a dozen times since he'd moved in.

It wasn't fair, because it wasn't Brody's fault that Dean's dad had taken off when he was a newborn, or that his mom was a waitress who had never really wanted him in the first place. Or that there'd never been enough money to go around.

Maybe he'd have been a hockey player, too, if he'd been able to afford the costs. There'd been a rink in town, and a team, and the coach had made overtures, but money was too tight, and so instead, he'd played football, which was cheaper. He'd clawed his way up with his sheer size and the raw talents he'd honed through too many two-a-day practices into skills that could translate into a new life for him.

He was only a season and a half away from that new life, and he wasn't about to fuck it up now.

"You work too hard," Wes said, worry flashing across his eyes.

"Don't tell me you're gonna suggest I start skipping classes now, like half the team does," Dean retorted, keeping his tone light and casual.

"I'm not," Wes argued. "But you're just so . . .hyper-focused. It's not good for you. You need to get out. See people. Do things."

"I do all of that."

"No, you worked all summer. When's the last person you dated—"

"Wes," Dean interrupted with a warning. Tossed the football back. "We've talked about this."

"I'm just saying, you can't meet anyone if you never go anywhere. And don't tell me there'll be plenty of time for that later. There's time for that now."

"So you say," Dean said.

"Come on," Wes said, changing the subject, tugging on his arm. "Practice's starting, and I know how fucking serious you are about practice."

It wasn't just him, Dean grumbled to himself, as he jogged over to where the defense was gathering. Wes worked hard, too. He was getting scouted just the same as Dean was. There'd been half the NFL at their first two games of the year, and it didn't look like that would be changing any.

Dean was on track to set some records in their conference for tackles and sacks, and Wes had never thrown the ball better. Overall, the Evergreens were pretty good this year, though Dean wasn't delusional enough to think they could challenge for a national championship. No, if he wanted a ring, he was going to have to get it once he turned pro.

And he had every intention of doing just that.

Dean unlocked the door and shut it behind him with a swift tap of his foot.

He was tired, exhausted, really, but his mind was still churning.

Not just with his regular worries of money and class and grades and practice but with the news that his prospective agent had brought to him about the scouting data.

Apparently some teams had the same worry Wes did. That he was too intense. Too focused. That he'd crack up, once he got into the NFL, and the pressure became too much.

He wouldn't.

He *couldn't*.

Dean didn't have a very good imagination, but he couldn't imagine having one great enough to think that after he'd been gifted this chance—through all this fucking hard work—that he'd screw it up.

He walked into the living room, thinking he'd throw a frozen pizza into the oven and shove it in his face while reading his chapters for tomorrow's classes. But before he could, he spotted Brody, sitting on the old stained sofa, ESPN turned down low, a bag of frozen peas on his knee and a frown on his face as he scanned something on his tablet.

He could possibly keep his head down, escape to the kitchen and then his room, and not even bother Brody, but with Wes' warning echoing in his head, he changed his mind.

"Hey," Dean said, walking into the living room and dropping his duffel bag onto the floor next to the couch.

There was only the couch—not even a chair—so there was nowhere to sit but next to Brody.

Dean knew he was big so he kept his body plastered to one side of the medium-sized sofa.

"Hey," Brody said, glancing over at him.

His eyes were warm brown, a little darker than the honey Dean liked to put in the tea he pretended he didn't drink in the evenings to try to cycle down after one of his very long days.

"Your knee okay?" Dean said gesturing towards Brody's makeshift ice pack. "Hurt yourself at practice?"

"Not this time, anyway. I tore my ACL late last season. Had surgery. Spent the summer in PT."

"And the ice?"

Brody shrugged. Dean hadn't known him very long, but anything the guy seemed to do—from whipping up a protein shake to carrying boxes to brushing his teeth—seemed graceful and purposeful, so he could already tell that he was awkward about this.

About his injury.

"I'm making sure there isn't any inflammation. I figure better safe than sorry." Brody looked almost embarrassed now, like he'd been caught doing something that he shouldn't have been.

But Dean *got* Brody's worry. Better than probably about anyone else.

He was terrified an injury might derail his plan and his chances just when he got right up to when he was going to deliver.

Maybe Brody didn't have to worry about what his future looked like, but it would still be terrifying to have the hazy possibility of it, right there in front of him, and then lose it.

"I could probably use some ice too. I think there's a few ice packs in the freezer, if you want to use them." They were cheap since Dean had picked them up at the dollar store, but they had to be better than a bag of frozen peas.

"You've never used peas?" Brody smiled, unexpectedly, and it was so bright it was hard to look at him. Dean barely ever noticed people's looks—because what were *looks* going to do for him, long-term?—but the *pretty boy* nickname he'd given Brody felt both still accurate and not quite accurate enough.

He wasn't pretty; he was actually kind of beautiful.

Whoa. Where did that thought come from?

Dean pushed it away, because he didn't understand it, but even more because he didn't have the time or the energy to deal with it.

"No?"

God, it felt like he'd been broke forever, but he'd never been forced to turn to the frozen vegetable aisle to reduce inflammation.

"They're the best. The way they shift and you can adjust them exactly around the area is just . . ." Brody grinned again. "Just fucking awesome."

"I'll have to try them sometime."

"I bought about twenty bags," Brody said with a slightly embarrassed wince. "So feel free to help yourself. Just don't eat them, okay?"

"Noted," Dean said, leaning back onto the sofa. He could relax; he *should* relax. Wes was probably not wrong about that. "What are you reading?"

"Syllabuses for tomorrow. I already got my books, but you know if you don't read the syllabus ahead of time, you're always fucked," Brody said. Then paused. "I guess not if you're taking physical education, though."

Dean didn't think, he just did, smacking Brody lightly on the arm. And that arm was surprisingly firm. For a hockey player, he had some real muscle tone going on.

"Hey, some of us aren't gibbering idiots," Dean retorted.

"Of course you're not."

"Some of us aren't crazy enough to take a science major, either," Dean said.

"Truth," Brody said wryly. "So, are you gonna tell me how you know Ramsey?"

"Ramsey?"

"Yeah. About six foot three? Hockey player? Blond hair. Big blue eyes? Takes basically nothing seriously?"

"I mean I *know* Ramsey, I just . . .what do you mean, how do I know him? I don't really know him. I know *of* him, of course. But I was surprised as anyone when he called me up and told me he'd found me a place to live this year."

"Huh." Brody leaned against the back of the couch.

"I think he knows Wes, the QB on the football team. Who's . . .uh . . .my friend."

"Oh, he hooked up with Wes, then."

"Actually, I don't think so. Wes has been with the same guy since high school."

Brody shot him a knowing smile. "Then they've definitely hooked up. Probably with Wes *and* his boyfriend. That's Ramsey's favorite: being a temporary third in a committed relation-ship."

"Oh." He didn't know what to say.

Dean knew people did that. Knew they enjoyed sex—otherwise, why do it? But he couldn't imagine it. Of course, in the best of circumstances he wasn't a fan of sharing. But if he actually met someone he really wanted and really loved? They'd own him for life.

Though maybe . . .if Dean ever ended up with someone like that, and *they* wanted it, he was pretty sure he'd give them whatever they asked for, gladly.

"It means he never needs to settle down," Brody said.

"I . . .uh . . ."

Brody laughed. "Ramsey told me you were more of a nun than even me, and maybe he wasn't wrong."

Dean wasn't a *nun*. He just . . .well, how did people have the time and energy to devote to sex?

His right hand in the shower was plenty fine *and* plenty efficient, thank you very much. Much like earlier today, at practice, Wes always moaned about how that wasn't good enough, that he must need *more*, but Dean couldn't say he was dissatisfied with the arrangement. It kept his attention focused on what mattered: his future and the years-in-development plans that were slowly, *finally*, beginning to unfold.

"I'm not—"

"I know," Brody said before Dean could try to explain. "Ramsey just doesn't understand anyone who isn't him."

"Right," Dean said. Even though he already had admitted that he didn't know Ramsey all that well.

"Guess I don't gotta worry about you bringing home girls—or guys?" Brody hesitated over the word, raising an eyebrow. "At all hours of the night. I would've had to with Ramsey. Maybe he had the right idea after all."

"It's girls," Dean said, though he couldn't even remember the last time he'd been with one. High school?

"Me too," Brody said. "But if it wasn't, it's not like I mind, you know? I got lots of friends who are queer."

"I'm good friends with Wes, and he's gay," Dean offered, though he wasn't sure before this moment he'd have called Wes a *good* friend—even if he was pretty sure Wes would've called *him* one.

"Yeah, sometimes I wonder, am I missing something? But I don't know." Brody shrugged charmingly.

"Yeah," Dean said, because he didn't know what else to say. "But yeah . . .uh . . .I think it's working out okay with us? As roommates?"

Brody's smile was blinding. He really was incredibly attractive—if you were into that, which Dean had *just* said he wasn't, so it was bizarre how his brain kept sticking on that particular fact. "So far so good," he said lightly. "You haven't pissed me off yet. It's hard rooming with people who aren't athletes—"

"They don't understand," Dean agreed. "Honestly when Ramsey told me about you, I thought you'd be perfect."

"Aw, only roommates a few days, and you already think I'm perfect." Brody fluttered his eyelashes as punctuation to that ridiculous sentence, and yep, he had long curling eyelashes, over those sweet brown eyes. They were the kind of eyelashes that Dean would expect on a girl, except that it was obvious that they were on a guy. There was Brody's definitely muscular build. His broad shoulders. The shadow of light brown scruff dusting his jaw.

"You haven't clogged the toilet or left a dirty dish in the sink, plus there's that sick blender your mom brought," Dean said gruffly. "Oh, and you gave me that tip about the peas."

Brody patted his knee approvingly. "You're pretty okay, too. Maybe someday I'll get used to how goddamn big you are. How tall *are* you, anyway?"

"Six foot five," Dean said, trying to keep the frustration out of his voice.

But clearly he'd failed because Brody asked, "I'm confused. Is that a bad thing?"

"For a linebacker, yeah."

Brody's jaw dropped. "They want you to be *taller*? Seriously?"

"No, no," Dean said, and he was chuckling now, amused even though this wasn't a subject that he'd ever laughed about in his life. "That's kinda tall for a linebacker, actually."

"The NFL is weird," Brody declared.

"Yeah, kinda. I guess. Don't tell me the NHL doesn't have ideal sizes for every position. What do you play?"

"Defense," Brody said. "And yeah, I guess. None of the scouts have ever brought up my height so I suppose I'm *not* too tall." He eyed Dean again, from his sock-clad feet to the top of his head. "Unlike some people."

"So you're gonna go pro, huh? Cause you were drafted?" Dean asked because he was genuinely curious about someone who'd had all these gifts practically *given* to him, and he was still hesitating. He hadn't missed how the last time they'd discussed this, Brody had been nebulous and then changed the subject.

Brody shrugged. "Yeah, I mean, I *should*. I always wanted to, but then I got injured last year and I'm . . .well, wondering now. I could play pro hockey *or* I could do something else, discover what else I can do, what difference I can make in the world."

Dean shook his head in disbelief. "You're really gonna throw being drafted away?"

"I don't know what I'm going to do yet." Brody's tone was crisp and defensive.

"I'm gonna get drafted and make it to the fifty-three man roster, my first season," Dean said gruffly, more than a little surprised at how Brody was un-sticking his normally reticent tongue. He'd only ever felt as comfortable this easily with Wes. Nobody else had ever managed to get under his defenses so easily. Or get him to talk so quickly about himself. About the things he wanted.

About all the plans he held so close to his chest, picking over them obsessively until they felt worn at the corners.

"Yeah? You got a guarantee or something?" Brody's question wasn't rude; it was more inquisitive. Curious.

Dean could see, easily, how he could be a scientist. That he'd want to deep dive into something and figure out exactly what made it work the way it did.

"No. There's no guarantees." He'd give anything for that not to be true, but it was. "But it doesn't matter. I'll do anything they want, be anything they want, to make sure that happens."

Brody stared at him, and for a brief, horrible moment, Dean was worried he'd exposed too much.

"You're that committed," he stated, rather than asked.

"Yeah." There was a part of him that wanted to say why, but he never shared that. He hadn't even told Wes why he worked harder than pretty much any guy on the defensive side of the ball or why he was so desperate to have his name called during draft night. And if he hadn't told Wes . . .well, he might feel comfortable with Brody, but he barely knew him.

Brody nodded. "I get it."

"You do?"

"I did, actually. I was like that. And then . . ." Brody gestured to his leg. "I wish I *still* did. Maybe I'll find it again. I don't know. All I do know is that I want something like that, something to feel so passionate about. I love hockey, I do, but it's not the same. Which is why I haven't made any decisions yet." Brody made a face. "I wish I had a little of that certainty you've got."

"You're a good player, you can't just give up on that," Dean said, which was stupid to say, because he wouldn't know a decent hockey player from a bad one, but when Ramsey had brought up his friend Brody who needed a roommate, unexpectedly, that had been one of the questions he'd asked.

Why had he even bothered? The truth was, he hadn't wanted a partier or a guy who didn't take his shit seriously, and if a guy was a good athlete, at this level, then he had to work at least a little at it. He couldn't get by on pure natural talent. Not anymore.

And when Dean had asked, Ramsey had only nodded, one of the few times he'd been serious in the conversation, and it was clear he'd meant it.

"Oh, am I?" Brody teased, nudging him.

"I can tell." He paused. "And I asked Ramsey."

Brody burst into laughter. "You're such a poser. I love it. You ever watch hockey?"

Dean shook his head.

"Well, I know jack shit about football. So we'll just agree that we're the best, okay?"

Dean knew he was the best, anyway. He wouldn't ever settle for anything else. But he nodded anyway. Why? For the same goddamned reason he kept talking to Brody when he should be eating dinner and reading his chapters for tomorrow. He just *liked* the guy. He made him feel comfortable in his own skin, and basically, nobody had ever made him feel that way.

"Sounds good to me," he said. He stretched out his legs, bumping them up against the cheap coffee table. "I should eat something. Read my chapters for the first class tomorrow."

"And he does his homework, too," Brody marveled. "Do the rest of the guys in your classes drive you insane?"

"If they don't come to class, if they don't respect the professors, if they don't do the work, then they don't even exist to me," Dean said.

Brody nodded, respect gleaming in those sugary eyes. "I get it," he said. "If you want to study out here, I'll turn the TV off. I've got some reading to do, too. It's gotta be more comfortable out here on the couch than at the little desk in your room."

Dean almost agreed. After all, Brody was one hundred percent correct. The desk was tiny and cramped. He often studied in the library because of that.

But he didn't say he'd stay out here, because if he did, he had a feeling Brody would crack him open like a nut, and he didn't know how to avoid that.

Or what to do with the desire to just let him do it.

Instead he shook his head. "Nope, it's alright. I don't mind. Quiet's good for me, anyway."

"Hey it's all good. I get it," Brody said, with a nod of approval. "You gotta do what you gotta do. I respect that."

And Dean had a feeling that he actually did.

CHAPTER THREE

BRODY GLANCED UP AT the clock, butt shifting on the bench, and knew, right before the opposing coach made the sign, that they were going to pull the goalie.

Coach B knew too, had probably known it was going to happen even before Brody did. But he *had* realized it, right before it happened, so he was ready. Ramsey was too, and the moment it happened, they were over the barricade, swapping out with the other defensive team.

Out of the corner of Brody's eye, he watched as Ramsey circled around the left side of the ice, and the rest of the line gathering up, everyone watching as the Cougars' best two forwards shifted the puck back and forth between them.

But Brody and Ramsey weren't the best defensemen on the Evergreens for nothing.

They had this handled.

At least Brody sure fucking hoped they did.

They'd held the Cougars to only one goal, and they'd scored when he and Ramsey hadn't been on the ice, a stray puck that one of the Cougars' forwards had slipped right past Finn's skate.

It had been overall a good performance, Elliott scoring on an absolute sick breakaway goal, and Mal adding another.

It was their third game, but it seemed the team was gelling in the exact kind of way Coach G kept pushing for.

Probably through all the intense practices that he'd led.

They'd come together because they didn't really have any other choice.

Brody would respect Coach for that if he wasn't so exhausted.

But it didn't matter how fucking tired he was. They had three minutes left, and they'd need to keep them scoreless to finish the Cougars off.

Ramsey was on the Cougars' highest scorer, Brody doing what he did best, which was to cover the corners, hoping that his pressure would be enough that they'd waste too much time to take too many shots at Finn.

Brody could see him now, eyes glued to the puck, gloved fist clenched around his stick, ready to react instantly the moment any of the Cougars made a move towards the goal.

But they didn't, passing the puck around, the time ticking down one long second after one long second.

It had already been a fucking eternity of a game, he was so tired, but he was going to give it his last effort, to pull out this win.

Brody certainly wasn't going to let them score *this* way and grab a victory from the jaws of defeat.

Not if he had anything to say about it. Sweat dripped down his forehead and down his back. He'd been gradually working his way up, with his skating, and he already could tell when he checked the stats of this game, he'd have the most minutes played since last season.

Since his injury.

His knee ached, but it didn't feel all that different than the rest of him, frankly. It *all* fucking ached.

But it didn't matter. He was gonna make it happen anyway.

That was when the forward, the one Ramsey had been shadowing, cut over sharply, and the puck slid to him, a quick little pass that Brody nearly missed, but he was tracking it.

But Finn had missed it, and in a second, everything was going to be over.

All the forward needed to do was flick the puck behind Finn's back and they'd be tied. Going to fucking overtime.

But Brody wasn't going to let that happen.

He pushed off, not even thinking in the moment that it was off his bad knee, the one he still didn't quite trust yet, and skated harder than he'd skated all game—all *season*. Pushing hard, he hit the crease, and slid in front of the puck, right before the forward could flick it in.

It bounced off his stick, and Ramsey grabbed it with his, and sent it back down the other way, clearing it all the way to the other end of the ice.

The Cougars chased after it but it was too late.

The last seconds ticked off, and the game buzzer sounded.

"Shit, man," Ramsey said, breathless, panting as he skated over to where Brody was still perched, on the ice, lungs working hard as he tried to catch his own breath. "You fucking saved that goal."

"Yeah," Brody said.

"Glad you did," Finn said, but there was a ghost of worry in his face.

Like he was already beginning to blame himself.

Brody knew they'd have to deal with their goalie's attempts to blame himself for every little mistake—but for right now, he just hoped that Finn and the rest of the team took the win.

"Great work out there," Zach said, slapping backs as the team filed in through the tunnel, heading to the locker room at the end of the game. He paused in front of Brody. "Sick play there, man. I loved what you did there."

"Thanks," Brody said. There was no denying it. Every time he stepped onto the ice that little frisson of worry slid down his spine, the concern that when he needed it most, his knee was going to fail him, but when it had come down to it today, it had carried him.

More than carried him.

It had given him the strength and the push he'd needed, when he'd needed it most.

But the best part was that when the moment had come, he hadn't hesitated.

He'd just expected it to hold him, and it had.

"Great fucking game," Ramsey said, collapsing onto the bench next to Brody. He pulled off his gloves and tossed them overhand into the equipment bin for cleaning.

"You too," Brody said.

"Party tonight at Gamma Sigma," Ramsey said. "You better be there."

"Aw, a *party*," Brody complained as he bent down, unlacing his skates. "I'm worn out, man."

"You sound like you're a hundred and one, not twenty-one," Ramsey said, a gentle reprimand on his face.

"Well, I *feel* like a hundred."

"You'll get a second wind. Seriously, you're coming. You've ducked out on the last two."

"My classes are murdering me, that's why," Brody said. Nevermind hockey. He'd not regretted his science major more than he did right now.

"Not surprised," Ramsey pointed out dryly. "You're coming anyway. And while you're at it, bring Dean with you."

"How do you even know he's free?" Brody said, forgoing arguing about his schedule, instead focusing on the one thing he *could*, which was Dean's somehow crazier schedule.

"They're on bye this week so he's home," Ramsey said. "How do I know this and you don't?"

"We don't see each other all that much," Brody admitted.

"Well, you gotta change that. Guy needs more friends."

Brody rolled his eyes, but he nodded too. He *could* agree with that.

"Fine, I'll see what I can do," Brody said.

He finished shucking his gear, took a shower, and then headed back to the apartment he shared with Dean.

The whole way home he expected to see that Dean wouldn't be there, after all, because he so rarely was. If Brody had been home more himself, he might've assumed that Dean was avoiding him on purpose, but he knew how much busier the other guy's schedule was, because he *worked*, too. What seemed like at least twenty hours a week, monitoring the gym that the college maintained for the general population.

Brody had run into him a couple of times on his way to the weight room reserved just for the sports teams, but they hadn't done more than exchange semi-friendly waves.

After trudging up the two flights of stairs—he *did* regret those, in the end—he unlocked the front door of the apartment, and to his surprise, Dean *was* there, on the couch, sprawled out, with one of the Marvel movies on TV.

"Hey," Brody said.

Dean glanced up. "Oh, hey," he said. "Good game? I saw you guys won."

"Yeah. It was, actually. We're coming together, I think."

"I'm glad for you guys," Dean said, giving him a swift smile that told Brody he meant it. And frankly, he'd looked up their game schedule *and* was keeping tabs on their wins and losses. Brody might've believed Dean's distance meant that he didn't give a shit, but he kept being proved wrong, over and over again.

He was beginning to think Dean didn't know how to be a *friend*. And how to tell that friend that he totally gave a shit.

It was that realization that pushed him to say, "Ramsey's going to the Gamma Sigma party tonight. Invited me."

"Yeah?"

"And you," Brody added. "Apparently we've both been working too hard."

For a long moment, Dean didn't say anything. Just looked at him, that brain churning away. For a guy who didn't say much, there was a lot going on in his head. Brody had learned that much about him, even in the handful of conversations they'd had since moving in together.

"That isn't a lie," he finally said.

"Then you're gonna come?"

"Don't know. Frat parties aren't typically my kind of thing."

"Mine either," Brody said wryly. "Come with me and keep me company."

Dean gestured down, at the pair of gray sweatpants he wore. "I'd have to get dressed."

"Just throw some jeans on," Brody suggested.

Dean raised his eyebrows. "You think I can go to this frat party in a worn-out T-shirt with a hole under the armpit?"

Brody looked him over. The shirt *was* clearly old, the fabric washed a hundred times and clinging tightly to his biceps and pectorals and stomach. He looked . . .well, if he'd been into that, it would've been a wet dream-worthy sight.

It was kind of wild how Dean didn't realize how attractive he was. But it was clear he had *no* idea.

"I think you're fine," Brody said.

"Alright, well, if I'm *fine*," Dean teased. He pushed himself off the couch and disappeared down the tiny hallway. A few minutes later, he was back, a pair of jeans maybe as old as the T-shirt clinging to his thighs.

Brody's mouth went dry and he looked away.

He couldn't explain why Dean's body was affecting him this way. He'd seen hundreds of guys naked in the showers over the years. Maybe more. And his brain had never caught on thoughts of them.

One of Dean's big hands ran through his chestnut hair. "Am I presentable now?" he asked.

"Uh, yeah."

Dean nudged him as they headed out the door. "Maybe I'm not pretty like you, but I think I'm not *that* bad looking."

Brody nearly tripped down the stairs, and only at the last second, Dean caught him, one of those big hands wrapping its way around his waist and tugging him back.

Pulling him against his bigger body.

Brody's breath went out in a harsh *whoosh*.

"You alright there?" Dean asked.

"I . . .uh . . .yeah."

"Good," Dean said and released him.

They made it down the stairs without any further difficulties and turned down Washington Avenue towards frat row.

As they walked, Brody tried to consider the problem—was it even a problem?—from a scientific angle. A *safe* angle.

Maybe he'd have been better off showing up at the frat without Dean and dealing with Ramsey's crap than he would be spending the evening with the guy.

It would probably have been the safer option. Because something kept teasing at the corners of his consciousness. Images of Dean, every time he'd seen him, flickering through his mind.

Dean blending up a protein shake in the morning, eyes sleepy and hair mussed and wearing only a low-hanging pair of athletic shorts, ripped abs on full display.

Dean with only a towel wrapped around his waist, hair dripping onto those broad shoulders.

Dean in the weight room, demonstrating a move to a simpering blond girl clearly angling for more than just a lesson, muscles bunching and relaxing as he went through the reps.

Dean, leaning towards him on the couch, those crystal clear green eyes so amused. So open. Surprised, even, like he hadn't expected to laugh with Brody and he liked it anyway.

Brody didn't want to think about why it was that he was so hyper-fixated on the guy. Or why the memories he kept catching on were these particular ones.

He wasn't stupid.

Clearly, maybe Ramsey was right and it *had* been too long since he'd had sex, if his *very* male roommate was able to turn him on.

"You're being quiet," Dean said.

"Pot, kettle," Brody said.

Dean chuckled. "That's fair."

"Just thinking I haven't seen much of you around," Brody said. Maybe if he saw more of Dean. Saw more of Dean's potentially bad habits and got to know him a little better, he'd snap out of this.

"Been busy. Told you I'd be a good roommate. Best roommates are absent roommates, right?"

"I guess," Brody said. "I just don't want you to think you have to avoid being at home, just because . . .uh . . .we weren't always going to be roommates."

"Nah."

"'Cause I like you just fine. Maybe even more than Ramsey." He knew Ramsey better, that was for sure. But could he like Dean more? Well, if his uncooperative mind—and dick—were any indication, he sure could. Because he'd never, not in a million years, ever been tempted sexually by Ramsey.

"Aw, that's sweet, pretty boy," Dean teased.

Brody tried to tame his flush. "Just the truth."

"I like you just fine, too. You're better than anything else I'd end up with by accident or necessity," Dean admitted. "And that's not just because of that crazy fancy blender your mom bought."

They turned down Clackamas and there on the corner was frat row, people already spilling out of the houses onto the ragged front lawns, noise echoing in the night from at least half the houses on the block.

"It's this one," Brody said, gesturing at one of the houses in the middle with the front door open, multi-colored lights and music pouring out of the gap.

"You really sure about this?" Dean asked skeptically.

Brody got it. He didn't really want to go to this party, but what was the alternative? Sitting at home, alone? Going over one of his lab reports? He was a college student. *Some* fun should come with the territory.

"No, but we're going in anyway," Brody said with determination.

"Alright then. Lead the way, pretty boy."

Brody flashed him a hard look and Dean flashed him back an easy grin.

"That's annoying," Brody told him as they walked up to the front porch.

"But true," Dean retorted.

And yeah, as they entered the house, packed with people, they were all staring at the pair of them with the kind of hungry gazes that weren't so hard to interpret.

"You want to hook up with any of those . . ." Dean scratched his neck, looking vaguely uncomfortable with the attention as they headed towards the back of the house, where Brody knew the bar was. "Puck bunnies? That what they call them?"

"Yes and *no*," Brody said.

"Me either. I'm not into being wanted for my accomplishments."

"Just your hot body?" Brody said it before he could even think about it, could dream of taking it back. Of leaving it unsaid.

Because Dean *did* have a hot body. Straight or not, that much was kind of a certifiable fact.

Dean gave him a startled look.

"Hey, you call *me* pretty boy," Brody retorted weakly.

"True," Dean said. Shot him a conspiratorial smile. "Guess we're both hot, then."

"Guess so."

Not that he wanted to acknowledge that fact. It was pretty fucking inconvenient and Brody didn't have the time—or the inclination—to want to unpack it.

They finally hit the back of the house with its bar, and sure enough, there was Ramsey, flirting with a girl and a guy both, flashing them one of his easy *let's hook up* grins.

Brody rolled his eyes. "Ramsey. See you're already working it," he said.

To Brody's surprise, Ramsey actually turned away from the pair and greeted both him and Dean with hugs.

Dean looked vaguely uncomfortable with it, but he didn't push Ramsey away.

Probably because he was too surprised.

"Glad you two both made it. I thought you'd be too comfortable growing into your couch to come out," he teased lightly. "Grab a drink. A girl. Enjoy yourselves."

"We're good with the drink," Dean said. He rooted around in a cooler and pulled out two beers. "You good with this?" he asked, showing Brody the label.

"Yeah," Brody said.

"But first, before you escape into some dark corner to talk very seriously about your bright futures," Ramsey said, pointing at the table that they'd set up like a makeshift bar. "Shots."

"Ah—" Brody was about to argue, to say he didn't really want to take shots, but Dean said instead, "Sure."

Surprised the hell out of him, but when he met Dean's eyes, he just shrugged. Like he'd given in because it was easier than arguing with Ramsey.

Which *was* generally true.

Ramsey poured out three shots of tequila from a bottle he grabbed from his own personal stash.

"This isn't watered down, unlike the rest of this," he told them with a shit-eating grin as he gestured at the rest of the bottles sitting on the countertop.

Dutifully, Brody licked the salt, downed the tequila, and then sucked on the wedge of lime Ramsey handed him.

Most definitely did not watch as Dean did the same.

"Oh, come on, one more," Ramsey persuaded.

"You tryin' to hook up with *us*?" Dean asked with a straight face, but Ramsey just burst into laughter.

"Oh," he said, "*oh*, I'm *so* glad I found you, Scott. You are an absolute fucking delight."

"Thanks, I think?"

"It's a compliment. Take it," Brody said, patting Dean encouragingly on the shoulder. "He doesn't give those out very often."

"And in honor of it, one more," Ramsey said, a mischievous grin plastered across his face.

"Fine, fine," Brody said.

The second shot went down even easier than the first.

Dean licked his lips as he tossed his lime wedge into the trash. "Damn, that's good stuff," he said.

"I know. You're welcome," Ramsey said smugly, handing them back their beers. "Now go forth and enjoy yourselves. Dance. Drink. Find someone to flirt with. Or God forbid, someone to hook up with."

Brody opened his mouth, ready to argue that he didn't *need* to hook up with anyone, fuck you very much, *Ramsey*, but before he could get any of it out, Dean wrapped one of those huge hands around his forearm and was dragging him out of the kitchen.

"Sure thing," Dean said, calling back, and Ramsey just cackled with amused laughter.

"You shouldn't encourage him," Brody grumbled as they headed back to the living room.

Dean hadn't let go of him yet, his grip was firm and Brody was trying to pretend it wasn't sending sparks shooting though him.

That's just the tequila talking.

Except that he wasn't sure it was, entirely.

"He's harmless," Dean said.

"You say that until somehow he's invited someone to your bed and you don't even know them and God only knows what they expect from you."

"Would he do that?" Dean frowned. "Did he do that to *you*?"

"No, no, I'm just saying, *would* he? Maybe. I wouldn't put it past him. He seems determined to get me to . . ." Brody trailed off, staring up at Dean's concerned face.

And wasn't that a fucking trip? He was six feet tall, and he had to look *up* at Dean. Brody didn't think he'd ever get used to it.

"You're good just as you are," Dean said.

The sparks had moved down from his arm and seemed to be pooling in the base of his stomach now, with the two shots of tequila.

Brody didn't drink much, and if he did, he usually just grabbed a beer. He took a long sip of his now. It wasn't going to clarify anything, but the booze did help him pretend all of this didn't exist.

"Thanks," Brody said. He thought about saying something else. Something like, *you ever think about it? Not girls, but guys.*

Because he was pretty sure he was thinking about it now.

Dean tilted his head. "Oh, there's Wes and his boyfriend." He gestured at a tall blond man in a T-shirt and jeans like nearly every other guy here, and the shorter guy trailing after him, holding his hand and wearing, to Brody's surprise, a suit complete with bow tie *and* matching pocket square.

"Wes," Dean said, greeting him. "And Marcus. Good to see you."

"Oh, stop pretending and come hug me, you big lug," the shorter man said, dropping Wes' hand and pulling Dean into a hug. "It's been too long. I never see you during the season."

"We're a little busy," Dean said. He turned to Brody. "And this is my roommate, Brody. Wes, of course, and his boyfriend, Marcus."

Brody shook Wes' hand and then Marcus', giving him another quick glance.

"I know," Marcus said, chuckling under his breath, "it's a common question. What's a fine guy like me doing with this one?" He elbowed Wes in the side. "Someone who wouldn't know good tailoring if it came up and bit him in the ass."

But it was clear from the looks they exchanged—fond, with just a lingering bit of heat—exactly what they were doing together.

"Oh, you love me," Wes teased.

"What's not to love?" Marcus retorted with a soft smile.

"How did you two meet?" Brody asked.

"See?" Marcus pointedly asked. "He wants to know, too. To answer your question, it was in high school. We got assigned the same project our sophomore year. I was not amused."

"The dreaded group project," Wes inserted, but he was beaming, like just hearing Marcus tell this story lit him up inside.

"Yes, definitely. I did dread doing it with you, because I expected that I'd be doing *all the work*."

"Hey, I might've been a jock, but I'm not a complete idiot," Wes argued playfully.

Marcus smacked him lightly on the chest. "Nobody ever said you were. Just that jocks like you might expect someone . . .discerning like me . . .to handle the whole thing."

"Did you?" Brody asked.

"Oh, no, I wouldn't let him. I made him work for it. I made him work *for me*," Marcus teased.

"He sure did." And Wes didn't look upset about it at all; he looked enthralled.

"To answer your question," Dean said in a low voice, "yes, they're always like this."

"It's a good thing you're cute," Marcus proclaimed.

"Oh, we all know how cute you think he is. You know how many nights he's been caught sneaking into Wes' room during away games?" Dean shot the pair a knowing look. "You are *not* subtle."

"Not in the least," Marcus agreed.

"Wes here is gonna get drafted and end up a starting QB in the NFL," Dean said.

"And what about you?" Brody asked Marcus. "You look like you're going places."

"You know it. Law school. Wherever this lunk gets drafted to."

"That's impressive." Brody was undeniably impressed. He spent so much time around the guys on the hockey team, most of whom were just happy to get good enough grades to stay on the team and graduate on time.

There were the students in his bio classes, of course, but it often felt like they were on a different planet than Brody. Certainly, even though Brody was smart and pulled in great test scores, they kept him apart. Talked about him like he was some kind of aberration they didn't know how to categorize.

"It is," Wes agreed.

"And you're not worried at all about this?"

Wes and Marcus exchanged a long glance full of certainty and unconditional love. "Not at all," they said, nearly at the same time.

"Come on," Marcus said, winding a hand around Wes' neck, "let's go dance."

Wes didn't fight, just went, following him like his whole life was wrapped up in the man with the gorgeous brown skin and limpid dark eyes.

"Yes, they *really* are like that all the time," Dean said when they were out of earshot.

Brody finished his beer. Noticed that Dean had, too. "You want another?" he asked.

"Sure," Dean said, "but I'll come with you."

"Aw, don't want me to leave you alone. Worried you're gonna get swarmed as soon as you're alone?"

Surely Dean had noticed all the girls, in clusters and in packs, ringing the living room, eyeing him. Eyeing them.

"Of course not," Dean blustered. But Brody knew.

"Maybe they think we're here together," Brody teased. "And it's keeping them at arm's length."

"Whatever's doing it, I'm happy about it," Dean admitted, following him into the kitchen. Brody grabbed two beers from the cooler and wiped the condensation off with the hem of his T-shirt then flicked the tops off, handing one to Dean.

He didn't have abs like Dean—did *anyone* have abs like Dean?—but he didn't miss Dean's gaze snagging on the flash of bare stomach before he dropped the fabric back down.

He didn't know what they were doing. They weren't even friends, really, so how could they be anything more?

Nevermind that they'd both told each other they were straight.

"Not looking to hook up tonight?" Brody asked.

It would be easier—would make *everything* easier—if Dean ditched him and found some girl who would pant over him the way Brody was trying not to.

But Dean just shook his head. "Nope," he said. "There's always strings and who's got time for that?"

"Not you," Brody agreed. He didn't think he knew anyone busier than his roommate.

"Exactly."

Brody tilted the neck of his beer bottle, tapping it against Dean's. "To not hooking up with anyone," he said.

Dean grinned. "You not doin' it to make Ramsey crazy?"

"I'm not doing it because I don't want to. I . . ." It was hard to explain. Especially hard to explain to the guys Brody knew, especially the guys on his team. None of them understood his reticence. His dislike of casual relationships. His need to be comfortable and familiar with someone before he got naked with them. "I don't really want to, that's all."

"Understood," Dean said quietly, and Brody thought he maybe actually did.

"Thanks," Brody said, meaning it.

"'Course. Who am I to judge? I work all the fucking time. And when I'm not working, I'm at practice, or in class. I've got no time for anything else."

"Why is that?" Brody asked.

Dean's expression went wry and he took a long drink of his beer. "Let's just say that my parents aren't both doctors. Or that either of them are actually involved in my life."

Brody wasn't surprised; he'd observed enough about Dean's life to realize that he'd grown up very differently. But he still felt a pulse of sadness. Dean was a great guy, with such a bright future. One he'd apparently fought for on his own.

"Yeah," Dean continued, suddenly looking awkward. "I don't talk about this much."

"I understand." And even though Brody knew his situation had been like night and day from Dean's, he *did*.

They were both lone wolves, fighting for what they wanted, for what they needed, in a world that didn't always understand them.

A world that assumed that with Brody's face and his hockey prowess that he'd want to have sex with as many people as possible. A world that assumed every kid who got this far, with this bright of a future ahead of him, had two supportive parents.

Out of the corner of his eye, Brody saw Finn walk in, a far-too-bright smile plastered across his face, eyes dark and a little haunted.

"Hey, one of my teammates just showed up, and I wanted to talk to him real quick. You okay here?"

"You gonna abandon me, Faulkner?" Dean teased in a low voice.

"Just for a minute," Brody promised.

"It's alright. Take your time. I get it. I'll go find Wes and Marcus, make sure they don't get carried away in a dark corner."

Brody headed Finn off before he hit the kitchen—and the booze.

"Hey," he said to the goalie, "great game today."

Finn shot him a look, bleak and tinged at the edges with something ugly. The something that Brody had slowly been growing more and more concerned over.

There was a desperation to be good, to be the *best*, baked into Finn's DNA. Maybe Brody couldn't fix it, couldn't take it away, but he could try to make it easier to deal with. Show Finn that he understood the pressure, too.

"They almost won. If you hadn't saved that goal—"

Brody interrupted him, putting a reassuring hand on his arm. "But I did. That's what I'm there for. You don't have to handle the whole defense on your own, Finn. That's what we're there for."

"But—"

"You weren't out of position, even."

"I didn't see the puck." Finn's voice was heavy, nearly dripping with that particular kind of pressure that only he could put on himself.

Brody hadn't been sure that he had seen the puck. Had worried that he hadn't, because of exactly this problem. "We've won two games and lost one, barely. We're getting better. And we can't do that if you melt down every time someone *almost* scores." He tried to keep his voice calm. Even. Soothing.

But Finn didn't look particularly soothed. "I'm not *melting down*. I'm trying to be good. I'm trying to give the team what it needs."

What the team needs is for you to cut yourself some fucking slack.

The problem was Finn would never believe that, and they could thank Finn's father and his storied NHL career for that.

"You are," Brody said. "I promise, you are."

"Who appointed you team cheerleader?" Finn asked, and before Brody could respond to the venom in his voice, he sighed with resignation. "God, I'm sorry. Forget I said that. You're just trying to help. You *are* helping."

Brody wasn't sure he really was, but he was going to keep making the effort. "Good. That's all I'm trying to do. You don't have to shoulder the whole burden of the defense. We're a team out there. Remember that, okay?"

"Okay." He looked a little better. Less self-destructive anyway, and Brody supposed that was all he could ask for.

"Don't drink too much either, or do something I'd regret."

"Why do we have to use *you* as a standard?" Finn teased. "Why can't I use Ramsey instead? Or Elliott?"

"Because Ramsey's antics aren't for amateurs, and someday Elliott is going to learn that too, the hard way," Brody cautioned.

"Don't worry. I'll take care of myself."

"Just make sure of that, okay?" Brody said.

"It's alright, Dad. I've got this."

Brody rolled his eyes, but he let him pass, Finn moving to the kitchen. He'd text him in the morning, make sure he *was* okay.

When he returned to the living room, a group of girls had indeed pounced on Dean.

It wasn't surprising. After all, he was a tall hunk of a man, and on the football team to boot—and if all the chatter was to be believed, heading to the NFL. He was basically an irresistible temptation to anyone who was into hooking up with jocks.

One girl with long blond hair tossed it playfully and looked up into Dean's eyes.

Brody might've left him alone, thinking that maybe he was doing the guy a favor, but the tense line of his back and his shoulders and the blank expression on his face made it clear that he wasn't happy about this situation.

It would be mean not to rescue him, especially when he'd promised not to stay away too long.

Brody approached and without thinking too hard about it, slid an arm around Dean's taut waist and leaned into him. "There you are," he announced loudly. "I thought I'd lost you."

Dean glanced down, and for a second, the rest of the room seemed to evaporate in the intense look in those green eyes. Clear and opaque both, like glass.

"I'm right here," Dean said and tucked an arm around Brody too.

"Oh, *oh*," the blond girl said, like she was just beginning to realize. "You should've said you were here with someone."

"Maia, you didn't let him get a word in edgewise," her brunette friend teased. "Come on, let's get some drinks."

Brody let go of Dean the moment they were out of sight, but he didn't miss how Dean's touch lingered for just a second longer.

He ignored how it lit him up inside. That was so much easier than thinking about it. Considering what it might mean.

"You ready to go?" Brody said. They'd put in their time. Had a few drinks. Talked to people. Surely Ramsey would count that against their hermit status.

"Yes," Dean said gratefully.

CHAPTER FOUR

The cool night air helped to clear most of the fuzziness from his brain. Dean didn't drink often, and when he did, he rarely touched hard liquor.

But the tequila had gone down so smooth, and it made his usual social awkwardness feel less present.

He'd actually managed to relax, at least when Brody was next to him.

Dean didn't know if Brody was feeling the booze, but as they walked up the stairs to their apartment, Dean could sense he was just as relaxed.

When they walked in, though, Brody didn't head to his bedroom. Instead he detoured to the kitchen and came back with two more beers. "Come on," he said. "I'm too keyed up to sleep. Let's watch something."

Dean, who'd thought he was tired, decided that the evening had been fun enough and chill enough that he didn't want it to end either. It turned out he actually *liked* hanging out with Brody.

He settled down on the couch with the beer as Brody scrolled endlessly through the options on Netflix.

"Just pick something, man," Dean teased.

Brody shot him a hot look. It hit him hard, searing around the edges. Dean didn't understand it, was afraid that he knew what it meant.

What the sparks that had lit him up meant, when Brody had come back from talking to his teammate and had wrapped his arms around him, tilting that pretty boy face up to meet his gaze.

"What do you want?" Brody asked, but instead of waiting for his answer, he tossed the remote onto the couch.

It was easy enough—but harder than he'd expected—to be honest. "I . . .I guess I don't know," Dean said.

Brody flopped back. His hair was mussed, his brown sugar eyes soft.

"Me either," he said absently, but he didn't seem particularly worried about it. For a moment, neither of them said anything, and anxiety rose inside him. What should he do? What should he say? He wasn't used to just sitting in companionable silence with someone. He wasn't used to sitting in silence *period*. He was always moving, always doing, usually forced to by his circumstances.

But it was a bye week. There was no game tomorrow. He didn't have to get up early for work. He could sleep in. In fact, he could *sit* here now, and there was nothing pressing he needed to do but listen to Brody's steady breathing.

"You ever thought about it?"

Brody's question broke the silence.

"About what's on Netflix?" Dean was confused.

"No. No." Brody waved his hands around him. "Like, we were talking to Wes and Marcus and they're so freaking happy.

And I thought, well, maybe it's not that I can't find someone I like, that I really like, that maybe I'm . . ." He hesitated. Like he didn't want to say it out loud, not until he *had* to. "Maybe I'm looking for the wrong kind of thing."

Dean's mouth went dry. "Like the wrong sex?"

He wished, almost the moment the word escaped him, that he'd said *anything* but the word itself.

Sex.

Brody swallowed hard. Dean could see it, watched as his Adam's apple bobbed with the forceful motion. "Yeah," he said.

Because now the word, the *idea*, was hanging in the room, thickening up his lungs and *God*, Brody's eyes were really so pretty. All of him was.

Maybe he wouldn't have been even thinking it if he hadn't drunk any tequila, but now he was, and he couldn't shove that thought back in the box no matter how much he kinda wanted to.

"So, yeah," Brody said wryly, a flush creeping up his cheekbones. "You ever thought about it?"

Dean realized he'd been silent for probably way too long. Maybe to Brody, he looked panicked, like he couldn't wait to escape back into his room and away from this awkward conversation.

"Forget it," Brody said, suddenly, pushing himself upright. In a second, he'd be off the couch and gone, and nothing would be right between them after this.

Or maybe it would go back to the way it was, just two guys who'd had a few drinks who were wondering.

But then it occurred to Dean that Brody was being honest. Not only that, but he was laying his insecurities and worries and thoughts bare. While Dean was still trying to figure out what *his* were.

Wes would tell him that if someone opened up to him, it was only the right thing to do to reciprocate. To at least make an effort.

"No," Dean said and reached out, tugging Brody back down to the couch. He went easily, and Dean knew he should let go, but he didn't.

He told himself it was so Brody wouldn't try to escape again, but the deeper truth was that he liked touching him.

"No, you haven't?" Brody didn't frown. But his expression went blank.

"No, we're not forgetting it," Dean clarified. Then paused. Tried not to stutter. "As for your question, uh, no, well, um, maybe."

He'd never been good with words, but plain and fucking simple, he'd never been worse than he was right now. Tongue-tied and mind racing with a hundred things he could say, but nothing seemed to come out.

"So you haven't. With a guy," Brody said. His gaze had taken on a speculative tint.

Dean shook his head. That much he could do.

"Me either," Brody said.

He had a feeling what Brody was going to say, and before he could, he managed to get out, "But we could always try it."

"Now?" Brody looked shocked, and Dean had a sudden, terribly heart-stopping worry that maybe he *hadn't* been about to suggest that.

"Uh, yeah. I mean, if you don't want to, with uh . . .*me . .* .nevermind. I shouldn't have—"

Brody raised a hand to his face and touched him, five fingertips pressing into his cheek, and Dean stopped in his tracks, words scrambling in his mind then disappearing entirely. "Stop me, if you don't want me to," he said seriously, and like hell Dean was going to.

He was curious.

And something more, too.

Brody leaned in a fraction and then another fraction, like the closer he got, the more he expected every moment that Dean *was* going to stop him.

But Dean didn't, and finally their mouths met.

It was a brief, quick kiss. One brush of their mouths together and then Brody was pulling back. Of course, that didn't matter, because the single touch had been enough to yank Dean's eyes wide open.

Not only had he *not* hated it, he'd liked it. Even the bristle of Brody's scruff against his own hadn't turned him off. His hands itched, because he wanted to reach out and touch. Wanted to tug Brody right back.

Brody's eyes fluttered open, and it was clear he hadn't hated it either.

But had he *liked* it?

It suddenly occurred to Dean, a horrible, swooping feeling in the base of his stomach, that maybe his lack of experience was a turn-off. Maybe he wasn't a very good kisser. It wasn't like he'd done it that many times. Or cared that much when he *was* doing it.

But he gave a shit now.

If that was the *only* chance he was gonna get, it should have been a good one, he should've—

All his uncooperative thoughts screeched to a halt when Brody murmured, "What did you think?"

"What did *you* think?" *Don't say I'm a bad kisser, that you didn't mind that I was a guy, but that I sucked, that I could've done better. I* can *do better, I promise.*

"I . . .I think I liked it," Brody said softly.

"Me too." Dean could hear the gravel in his voice. He hoped Brody wouldn't hear the desperation—and he hoped he would, too.

"Do you think we should . . .uh . . .do it again? Just to make sure?"

Dean cleared his throat. "We could. You know, for science?"

"Exactly. Can't do an experiment just once."

"You're the bio major, so I guess you'd know."

"We gonna just keep talkin' about it or *do* it?" Brody teased, eyes glinting with amusement.

Dean decided that was enough of an invitation, and this time, it was him who leaned in, pressing his mouth gently to Brody's.

This kiss was a little longer than the first.

It was definitely nothing like kissing a girl; soft but not really so soft, at all. But that didn't change the way Dean's blood fired as he fit his mouth carefully and deliberately over Brody's.

Brody tilted his head, to find a better angle, and their lips slid together, searching and retreating.

He tasted like beer, and something else, something unexpectedly sweet.

Dean's blood was pounding now, and he curled his fingers into himself, so he wouldn't reach out and touch Brody the way they kept wanting to. Then Brody reached over and hesitantly put a hand on his shoulder, squeezing once, briefly.

Arousal flared inside him. He wanted that touch everywhere, sliding lower down across his chest, his stomach, then lower still. He wanted to feel Brody's hand around his cock.

Dean sprang back, suddenly, and then regretted it. Only because he wasn't kissing Brody any longer. But he'd stopped because that thought had fucked him up. He didn't want Brody to touch him like that. Or did he?

Oh, he did.

"Well, that . . .uh . . ." Brody stumbled over his words, and it made Dean feel a little better. Maybe he wasn't the only one feeling unmoored by the direction this evening had taken.

"What is it about science experiments? Don't you need to repeat everything three times?" Dean could hear the plea in his voice. Didn't even care anymore if Brody heard it, too.

"You're a physical education major," Brody whispered, but the corner of his mouth was quirking up. The mouth Dean had just been kissing.

The mouth Dean wanted to *keep* kissing.

"Yeah," he agreed. He knew jack shit about science, only that he needed this experiment to not be over because it felt like it had barely begun.

Even when Dean had broken their kiss before, Brody still hadn't let go of his shoulder. Now he curled his fingertips into his T-shirt, and Dean felt his touch through the worn cotton. Tugged him closer, with just that touch. And Dean went, because he couldn't do anything else.

They met in the middle, and this time the kiss wasn't hesitant and it wasn't so gentle, either. It was sure, and then Brody's other hand reached to pull him even closer. Dean went, and hesitantly touched Brody, too, fingers brushing his shoulder, then his sternum.

Brody's T-shirt was newer, the fabric thicker, and Dean wanted more, wanted to feel the warmth of his skin, and so without even thinking, he tugged down the collar and *God*, he'd never mistake this for touching a girl and that didn't even matter. Brody's skin was soft and hot. The ripple of muscle beneath his fingers. Tough and vulnerable at the same time, an intoxicating combination that Dean hadn't even known he craved until this moment.

Brody groaned, deepening the kiss, and Dean swore he felt his tongue, just for a split second, but enough of a touch that his blood lit up, his cock throbbing in his jeans now.

He wanted him. There was no point in shying away from it or pretending otherwise. And Dean was pretty sure Brody wanted him, too.

Abandoning his exploration of Brody's exposed skin, he slid his hand down and curled it around his waist, and with barely any effort, shifted him backward, against the old, worn out pillows that flanked each side of the couch.

Brody froze for a second, and Dean worried he'd over-stepped. They were being careful, still, *mostly.* Their kisses were still only PG-rated, even though the thoughts flying through his head were increasingly X-rated.

But he didn't want to scare Brody away. He didn't want to scare *himself* away.

Brody lifted his mouth and Dean was more than a little relieved to see he was panting, T-shirt rising and falling with his breath, all that brown sugar in his eyes nearly swallowed up by his big black pupils.

"This feels good," Brody said.

Wrong.

You're so wrong.

It feels fucking amazing.

"Yeah," Dean said.

"We could . . .uh . . .keep doing it."

"I want to." *I want you. As crazy as it sounds. As crazy as it seems.*

"You're not—" Brody paused, chewing his bottom lip, red and wet from Dean's mouth. *Let me do that. I wanna do that, to you.* "You're not drunk, are you?"

Dean realized it had never occurred to him that any of this was happening because of the handful of shots and the two or three beers they'd drunk over the course of the party and then after returning to their apartment. He was more relaxed, sure, and less up his own ass. But that might also be because he genuinely didn't have anywhere else he needed to be, and that was an intoxicatingly freeing feeling.

But maybe Brody was. Maybe that was why Brody had suggested it in the first place.

Shit.

"No," Dean said. "Are you?"

"No, no," Brody said hurriedly. "*No.* I just . . .maybe I was a little tipsy when we got back here. Like calm. Relaxed. But not—not like that. That's not why I said anything, I just wanted to make sure—"

"No, I'm not drunk," Dean agreed.

God, he'd just been about to tuck Brody underneath him and really kiss him, to make out with him and touch him and he hadn't even double-checked that he wasn't too drunk to consent.

Of course, he hadn't *seemed* drunk, but the possibility sobered Dean up anyway. Brought him up short.

"Oh good. God, sorry, the thought just occurred to me, but obviously, someone like you, someone your size . . ." Brody laughed, self-consciously, gesturing up and down Dean's body. "A couple of tequila shots wouldn't be enough."

"No," Dean said. "But I should've—"

"Stop. *No,*" Brody interrupted, his voice firm and sure, before he could go down that road. "I want this."

Good. Me too.

He could've said the words; probably *should've* said the words.

Instead he kissed Brody. No hesitancy. No holding back. Poured everything he didn't know how to say into it.

Like dry kindling, Brody caught fire and kissed him back, fiercely, tongue slipping into his mouth. Then suddenly, they were making out, and Dean was losing himself to the push and pull of their mouths, to the feeling of Brody's hands skimming over his body. His chest, his shoulders, his stomach, his thighs. Feeling nearly every inch of him.

Every inch but one.

Not that he was averse to *just* kissing, but his dick was so rock-hard in his jeans, he felt like he might spontaneously combust if Brody touched him—even by accident—or if he *didn't* touch him.

But Brody kept studiously ignoring it, fingers skating around his cock so deliberately it had to be on purpose.

There weren't many thoughts left in Dean's brain—or much blood, honestly—but he reminded himself that they could just do *this*, mouths moving together, hot and easy. That was fine.

Hadn't he just told Wes a few weeks ago that sex was kind of overrated?

Sex did not feel overrated now.

Sex felt like something he craved so badly he thought he might cry if he didn't get it.

No. No. It's fine. You're just gonna enjoy this, exactly the way it is.

He trailed his hand down Brody's back. It was strong and firm with muscle, and Dean wanted more. Without even thinking about it too hard—or thinking about it at all—he slipped his hand up Brody's shirt, reveling in the feel of his skin, all those muscles shifting underneath his touch.

Finally, he'd mastered his self-control enough that he was okay—more than okay—with just touching Brody like this, and having him touch in return, fingers digging into his shoulders, when he stopped, suddenly. He pulled back an inch, practically panting in Dean's mouth.

"You like this?" he asked.

It was probably going to expose him if he said the truth, but Dean felt flayed bare by the look in those molten caramel eyes.

He couldn't have said he didn't, even if he'd wanted to.

And he didn't want to.

"Yes." His voice was so low, so rough, he barely recognized it.

Brody's fingertips skated down his cotton-covered chest. Dean wanted to feel it, skin to skin, wanted to revel in his touch in a way he couldn't yet.

Yet.

"Me too." Brody's admission was soft, naked.

His touch stopped short of the fly of his jeans, where Dean's cock was pulsing, as hard as he'd ever been.

So much for the belief he wasn't attracted to guys. He didn't think he'd ever been attracted to someone the way he was to Brody—and it had snuck up, the truth of it not revealed until they'd kissed for the first time.

"Do you want—" Brody stopped abruptly, swallowing hard. Dean couldn't help it, anymore. He reached up and nipped at his Adam's apple, sliding his mouth to his neck, not caring about the stubble there, almost liking it *more* because of the roughness. Definitely loving it because of the long, liquid moan Brody made as Dean's teeth found the tendon in his neck and nibbled there.

Maybe he wasn't as bad at this as he'd worried, because Brody sure seemed as into it as Dean was.

Then, finally, Brody's hand moved lower, just barely brushing where Dean wanted him so badly. Dean's cock twitched, unbearably eager for more of that pressure. "What about this?" he asked.

"Yeah. But only—"

Dean didn't get the rest of the word out, because suddenly Brody's whole hand was there, palming him through the thick material of his jeans—jeans he was seriously regretting right about now—and it felt like his whole body lit up with the touch, and if he'd had any words, they were gone now.

Lost—and they were never coming back.

He didn't think, couldn't think. Instead, he slipped his hand lower, right down the sleek, muscular curve of Brody's ass, and pulled him in, and down, trapping his hand around his cock and finally feeling Brody's own.

He was just as hard as Dean was, and that was a revelation all in itself. Dean had been pretty sure, but there was no *pretty sure* about the hard length pushing up against his own.

Surprise and pleasure bloomed in Brody's eyes, and that was all Dean could take before he was reaching up and pulling him back down to his lips, their mouths meeting in the hottest kiss of his goddamn life.

Nothing had ever felt as good as this.

It was the easiest thing in the world to get carried away. To get lost in the way Brody's mouth slanted, hot and ready and wanting over his, tongue brushing against his own, and their hips moving together, a rolling movement that was rough and delicious.

The pressure was almost enough, and Dean wanted more. He dug his fingertips into Brody's ass and pushed him harder. Brody groaned in the back of his throat and a second later, he was trembling above him.

Oh my God.

Dean broke the kiss and watched Brody shudder to orgasm on top of him.

Gorgeous.

He'd needed just a little more pressure, a little more *anything*, to follow him, but Dean wasn't even disappointed he hadn't gotten it, because it was so hot watching Brody fall apart like this.

His eyes fluttered open finally, and they were hazy with pleasure. But before Dean could ask, *oh God, what now*, Brody was slipping down between his legs, down to the floor, fingers wrenching open Dean's jeans and shoving them down unceremoniously.

He barely got a hand around Dean's underwear-covered cock before he was coming too, shuddering as the waves of ecstasy hit him hard.

"God," he groaned as it finally began to end.

"Yeah," Brody agreed.

There was no question about it. He'd been so eager, only a moment before, but now he was looking down, at Dean's bare legs and his come-soaked boxer briefs like he hadn't thought any of this through—and he was doing it now.

"That was . . ." Dean trailed off. He'd never been great with his words, and this situation had eclipsed any capacity he'd ever had for them.

He'd never expected any of this.

Certainly, he'd never *asked* for it.

He'd just wanted a decent roommate who helped with the bills and was willing to exchange some friendly small talk every once in awhile when their paths actually crossed.

Well, his and Brody's paths had just tangled up together.

Brody stood. He was looking anywhere but at Dean's face. In fact, it seemed more like his gaze kept catching on Dean's softening dick.

Like he couldn't quite believe he'd touched it.

Or that he'd wanted to.

Dean didn't know whether to pull his pants up, but finally, he decided, what the hell, and did it. Awkwardly. He was going to need to take a shower. Frankly, Brody was going to need to as well.

But before he could suggest it, Brody started talking—or more like, he started panic-rambling. "Well, that was a thing. That happened. Just now. I don't know—I didn't expect that to happen. We just . . .I just . . ." He snapped his mouth shut. "I'm going to take a shower."

"Right, uh, yeah." Dean didn't know what to say either. He was sitting there with his jeans up, but unzipped, hanging open, kind of like his stupid mouth. He should say, *it's okay, I didn't expect that either—but really, I promise it's okay.*

But he didn't. Probably because he didn't know if he even believed it would be okay. He didn't know if he even liked guys—sure, he'd liked *that*, but maybe it was just . . .the relaxation? Or the booze? Or the fact that he couldn't remember the last time he'd come with someone else touching his cock?

Yeah, you weren't just relaxed. Or drunk. Or horny.

Of course, just because it was the truth, resonating inside him, didn't mean it was any easier to say out loud.

So he didn't.

"It was just . . .a thing. Don't worry about it." *And don't worry about it, if you wanna do it again.*

But Brody didn't look like he wanted to do it again. He looked like he wanted to panic and then throw up.

"Really?"

"It's . . .yeah. Don't worry about it," Dean repeated. It didn't sound any more convincing than it had the last time he'd said it. *Stupid.*

"Don't . . .worry . . .about . . .it?" Brody's voice was creeping upward. "We just . . .*I* just . . ."

"Yeah." They couldn't hand wave it away, not with come cooling in their underwear, and an undeniably red patch on Brody's neck, no doubt a result of Dean's scruff.

"It was just a science experiment, right? You were just testing a hypothesis." *Don't say what the hypothesis was, don't say it out loud, 'cause if you do, he's gonna go to pieces, and you don't want to be responsible for that. You don't have the bandwidth for it, either. You know you don't.*

"Right, okay." Brody was pacing now, up and down the tiny living room. "Yes. Just an experiment."

Don't say it was a damn good one either.

"That's all you gotta worry about."

"Alright." Brody flashed him a grateful smile. "I guess I'll go take a shower."

"You should. I . . .uh . . .I'll get in after you." Dean paused. Wondering if he should say something else. *Worrying* that he should say something else. Maybe something like, *hey, it's all good, you're not really queer, 'cause nobody got naked and nobody touched a bare naked dick.* But that was ridiculous, even in Dean's head. "Uh, don't steal all the hot water?"

It was the only thing he could think of to say, but clearly it hadn't been the right thing, because Brody's face shuttered closed after that.

"Yeah," he said shortly and turned, walking towards the bathroom. Dean heard the door close and then the water turn on.

He still didn't move though.

On the TV screen, Netflix asked him if he was still watching.

He clicked the power off and groaned, falling against the back of the couch.

It wasn't that *he* wasn't freaking out too. He kind of was. This was unexpected, but Dean had never been the kind of person to shy away from unpleasant truths. And was this really unpleasant? It sure hadn't been only a few minutes before. It had felt like the most natural thing in the whole goddamn world.

So, he wasn't as straight as he'd thought.

He could accept that.

He felt less comfortable about the fact that the person who'd awakened those feelings inside him was Brody.

His roommate.

His hockey playing roommate.

On the surface level, they had nothing in common whatsoever, and it wasn't like Dean had time to dig down beneath and see if he could find something worth holding on to.

He'd told the truth. It had just been an experiment, and now it was over.

Brody ducked his head under the hot spray of the shower and tried to figure out what the fuck had just happened.

Sure, he'd been noticing Dean. And not just his body, which was a prime physical specimen. But he'd been *noticing him*.

And, his uncooperative brain added, *it was your fucking idea to experiment in the first place.*

It had been. He'd been certain, almost one hundred percent positive, that the first kiss would've told him everything he needed to know. That he wasn't attracted to men. That he didn't want to kiss them or touch them or have sex with them.

Well.

That ship had fucking sailed, right out of the fucking harbor, never to return.

Brody scrubbed a hand over his face.

He knew he'd freaked out after, that was undeniable, but then Dean had been so low-key about it, so chill, like he wasn't into doing it again, that he wasn't all that interested, as fun as it had been, so he didn't know what to do now.

If Dean had looked regretful or particularly worried about Brody's panic, then maybe he might have gotten out of the shower and knocked on his door and said, "Shower's free, I saved you some hot water, and would you like to make out again sometime? Sometime *soon*, maybe?"

But he'd been casual about it, like it was no big deal, it didn't really invite a second experiment.

Brody knew he was going to need to forget about it. Maybe not the truths the evening had uncovered, because once those were out of the bottle, there was probably no putting them back, but the idea that Dean was up for more.

That was disappointing, sure, because it had felt *damn* good, the kind of full-body release it felt like he was always chasing, always craved, but never seemed to get.

But he'd get over it.

He'd *need* to.

He finished scrubbing himself mechanically, ignoring the pulse of desire he felt when he cleaned his dick, making sure he got all the sticky residue. Dean had been so fucking solid underneath him, so strong and controlled, and yet his kisses had been wild, uninhibited, his body putty in Brody's hands.

Shit.

Sure enough, he glanced down, and yeah, he was half-hard again.

"Don't go there," he told his uncooperative dick. "We're not going there."

He'd mostly forced his body to cooperate by the time he opened the door, towel wrapped around his waist.

Truthfully, Brody had been half-expecting—maybe half-hoping—that when he emerged from the bathroom, Dean would be there, hovering around the doorway, and he'd say something like, "Oh yeah, let's do it again. Right now. Naked this time."

But the hallway was dark, and there was a tiny light underneath the closed door that led to Dean's room, but otherwise . . .there was no Dean, apologizing or propositioning him or anything else.

Brody told himself he wasn't disappointed, but as he shut his own door and he collapsed onto the bed, *alone*, he kinda thought he might be.

CHAPTER FIVE

"WHAT THE HELL, FAULKNER?" Ramsey called out from behind Brody's right shoulder. "You totally just fucking missed the puck."

Sure enough, there it went sliding by, right across center ice, because Brody hadn't caught it on his stick, and shot it over to Finn.

That was a rookie mistake. An issue he and Ramsey hadn't had since they first started playing together. It would've been bad in a game, but this was just practice.

Of course, with Coach B in charge, practice was no longer *just* practice.

"You distracted?" Zach skated over, concern etched across his features. "That's the second puck you've missed today. Is it your knee?"

"No, I'm fine," Brody said, waving away his worries. "Knee's fine."

He didn't want to talk about why he was distracted.

It wasn't just adjusting to this new reality where he was undeniably into guys—into *Dean*—but also the new reality where he saw his roommate even less than he had before.

As he'd lain in bed two nights ago, he'd finally heard the shower flip on and then five minutes later, shut off. Dean's door shut behind him.

The next day when Brody had stumbled out of bed, Dean had already gone. At least he'd thought he was. His bedroom door had stayed shut, but there'd been evidence that he'd been up early and left already, dishes rinsed and stacked in the sink.

They hadn't even seen each other since it had happened, and Brody kept trying to pretend he wasn't going out of his mind with the fact Dean was clearly avoiding him now, but he *was*. There was no denying it, considering that it was now Monday afternoon and he hadn't seen hide nor hair of Dean since Friday night.

Not only had his absence been even more glaring than before, Brody had an uncomfortable inkling that part of the fault lay with his freakout.

"Alright," Zach said, nodding. "Let's try this again."

They ran through the power play kill play Zach had outlined, and this time Brody forced his attention onto the ice—away from all the shit that was bothering him.

"Better," Zach called out from his spot near center ice. He was standing with Coach B, whose expression was opaque and unreadable. He didn't offer much in terms of feedback—he seemed to rely on Zach for that, instead—and Brody thought maybe that was what made the team feel different this year.

Coach's stoic blankness.

Sometimes Brody felt like he was the same, a mirror that everything just reflected off, and nobody saw what was roiling away underneath.

"Again," Coach said with a sharp clap. And then, after they'd run through it, Brody's legs and lungs burning with exertion, he said, "Again."

Nothing else.

It didn't seem to bother anyone else, this difference. Just him.

The Evergreens were still good; they *had* to be with the stacked roster they carried. They'd still won all but one game, but it *felt* different.

Maybe it wasn't the team; maybe it was *him*.

Brody pushed the thoughts away, because this wasn't the time or the place for them, but just because he didn't think about it didn't mean that those thoughts didn't still exist, lurking around his brain, and the moment he came off the ice, pushing his sweaty hair back from his face, they came rushing back.

He *wasn't* having the same kind of time he used to have on the ice. That much was obvious to him.

It had used to be his sanctuary, and now he couldn't stop himself from agonizing over all the uncertainties, even when he skated.

"You. Me. Sammy's," Ramsey threw over his shoulder as he finished getting dressed after showering.

"I'm—"

"You. Me. Sammy's," Ramsey repeated firmly. "Then you can go off and do whatever it is your head's into."

Brody wanted to claim it was homework and classes, but he knew that wasn't all it was.

Still, he had no intention of discussing what had happened on Friday night with Ramsey. He'd go and they'd eat and then he'd retreat back to the apartment with an excuse he had homework to do, and maybe then . . .maybe he'd finally see his roommate again.

"You're being super weird, even for you," Ramsey said, as they sat in Sammy's, drinking protein smoothies and eating Italian subs after a long, wretched practice.

Brody knew he should deny it, but he was tempted, even for a half a second, to confess why he'd only been paying half-attention to anything for two days now—because the other part of his stupid brain was still stuck, back on the couch in his apartment, watching as Dean shuddered to orgasm under his hand.

And the part that wasn't obsessing about that? Was obsessing about all the questions he couldn't seem to stifle about his future.

"I'm not," Brody said.

But he'd known Ramsey would bring it up, especially after practice.

"You totally are, and I just can't figure out why. It can't be your knee. It seems to be holding up just fine. You told Zach it was fine."

"It *is* fine," Brody said, realizing that he'd barely even *considered* his fucking knee in the last two days. Practice had come and gone and he'd only thought about it when Zach had brought it up.

Between that fact and his lack of focus during his classes today, maybe that should've been enough to convince him that Dean's absence was a good thing.

But it wasn't, because Dean's silence was driving him crazy.

It wasn't fair of him, because they'd certainly never promised each other anything, even friendship, nevermind anything else, but he wanted Dean to feel the same way he did. Like his skin was too tight for his body.

"Then what's up, man?" Ramsey questioned, leaning forward, his elbows on the table. "Is it Dean?"

"No . . . no . . . of course not . . . why would it be Dean?" Brody stuttered. "I barely see Dean." *Which is at least half my fault.*

"Just wanted to make sure I don't have to kick his ass," Ramsey said.

"For being a shitty roommate?"

Ramsey nodded.

"No, he's actually—" Brody cleared his throat. "He's great." *So fucking great.*

"I thought you barely saw him," Ramsey said shrewdly.

"Exactly." That was the safest answer Brody could give.

Ramsey nodded absently. "You left the party early on Friday."

Brody wasn't sure if this was Ramsey's attempt to change the subject and catch him off-guard or what, but he couldn't possibly know that he hadn't changed the subject at all.

Right?

Right.

"Yeah, we did," Brody said, attempting a very casual tone.

Nobody knew what had happened between him and Dean. He couldn't imagine Dean talking out his mouth about it, and well, Brody certainly hadn't told anyone about it. He *could* tell Ramsey about it; he couldn't say he hadn't considered the possibility.

He was one of his best friends *and* he was proudly pansexual. But Brody wasn't particularly proud of the way he'd panicked in the aftermath and then chickened out again when faced with the possibility of talking to Dean about his freakout. He didn't think Ramsey would be hard on him about it, or give him shit, but he might be conciliatory. Patronizing. Ultimately disappointed. And Brody didn't want to face any of that. His own thoughts were bad enough without adding Ramsey's to the mix.

"We? Of course you left with Dean."

"I didn't leave *with* Dean . . .uh . . .like *that*," Brody clarified before he could snatch the words back.

Ramsey leaned in. "Oh? Is that the way the wind's blowing? You're into Dean?"

"Oh, for God's sake," Brody complained.

But Ramsey wasn't stupid, not nearly as stupid as he let a lot of people believe, and he'd scented blood in the water.

"You're crushing on Dean."

"No," Brody said, and he was fairly certain that wasn't a lie.

"You had sex with him, then. How was it? Is he—"

"No," Brody repeated. Trying to convince himself that wasn't a lie, either. After all, he hadn't seen Dean naked. He'd seen more of Dean coming out of the shower before that night than he'd seen *that* night. He hadn't even touched Dean's dick, not really.

It wasn't sex. It had just been . . .an experiment.

That was all.

"Oh. Well, damn. I was so sure that was it. You had sex with Dean and it fucked you up." Ramsey sounded disappointed.

A different kind of disappointed than Brody had expected.

He felt a pulse of guilt because he had kind of lied. Sort of, anyway.

He'd certainly misled Ramsey, whose only crime was being a good friend to him.

"I . . . ah . . . well," Brody admitted. "We might've . . . had a bit of a thing. Not even a thing. A thing implies that it was *something*, like an actual official occurrence and it wasn't. Not really."

Ramsey raised a blond eyebrow. "Then what the fuck was it?"

"An experiment," Brody proclaimed and then realized how stupid that sounded.

Ramsey must've agreed, because he rolled his eyes. "So y'all were just experimenting? Two bros wondering what it feels like? Must've been pretty earth-shattering 'cause you've been wandering around with your head in the clouds, like all your brain molecules are still lost in Dean's dick."

"That is absolutely not true," Brody said.

Ramsey grinned and made a little bit motion with his fingers. "It's alright. He's hot. I can't blame you for picking him to 'experiment' on."

"I didn't *pick him*, it just sort of happened." Except that it hadn't really happened like that at all. Brody *had* been thinking about it—and specifically related to Dean. But Ramsey didn't need to know that, because he'd be insufferable about this, anyway.

"No? You sure about that?"

"Mostly."

"So," Ramsey said. He flopped back against his chair and shot Brody a knowing look. "You liked it. Liked him. Liked fucking around with men."

"Those are three things that are not necessarily true. I said it was an experiment, and that's all it was," Brody retorted, hating how defensive he sounded. Just like how he'd sounded the night it had happened.

He kept thinking he should apologize to Dean, but the first problem with that was he had to actually *see* the guy to do that, and the second was that he didn't actually know what he'd be apologizing for. Not the *during*, that was for damn sure. But the aftermath? That was a different story.

"Listen, we don't have to talk about it," Ramsey said, all casual and friendly, like he didn't care either way.

"Good," Brody said shortly, "because I don't want to."

Brody knew that neither of those things was really true—they *should* talk about it, and part of him *did* want to talk about it. And of course, he didn't really trust Ramsey to leave it alone, but he didn't know what else to say right now, either.

He had friends who were queer. Elliott. Mal. He had his suspicions about Finn, too. And then there was Ramsey. He was one of his best friends and he was out and proud and had probably never shirked from the truth in his whole goddamn life. *Ramsey.*

It had just never been *him*.

Brody squirmed in the booth.

Hating this. Kind of hating himself, right now.

How could he be such a fucking coward?

It was *just* sex.

Unlike some, his parents weren't going to disown him. And these days, if he *did* decide to go into pro hockey, his sexuality probably wouldn't destroy his career.

There were a number of "out" players in professional football now, and a few teams that it felt like were full of them, like the Los Angeles Riptide or the Miami Piranhas. Even the owner of the Charleston Condors was gay and dating an ex-player.

Hockey hadn't quite followed suit, but it would *probably* be okay. Ramsey certainly didn't seem worried about it. Neither did Elliott. And it was clear both of them were going to make it to the NHL. Ramsey had been drafted high and continued to perform as expected. Elliott wouldn't be drafted until next year but there was already chatter about the forward.

"Well, you wanna talk about what's had you so distracted on the ice, then? It was like you were in your own world out there today," Ramsey questioned, still casual and friendly.

Ugh.

"Classes?" Ramsey continued. "Your knee? No, you said your knee was just fine."

"It *is* just fine. You've been on the ice with me. You saw it for yourself."

"Then it must be your classes. You ready to give up on that ridiculous major yet?" Ramsey teased gently.

What would Ramsey say if he knew Brody was actually, in the dark of night, when he couldn't look at himself in the mirror and see the uncertainty in his eyes, contemplating doing more with his degree than just bragging about it?

"No," Brody said. "But yeah, it's tough right now." Not any tougher than normal, but then Ramsey didn't need to know that.

"Mine too."

Brody laughed. "What, now you're struggling with what to say to those hot twins you keep propositioning?"

"Ugh, don't remind me that they keep ghosting me. It's a real fucking ego killer," Ramsey said, his eyes twinkling.

"Uh-huh. Sure it is." Ramsey's ego was titanium-plated, and Brody couldn't help but envy him for that.

Maybe if he was more like Ramsey this thing with Dean wouldn't have thrown him the way it had.

"Seriously, though," Ramsey said, "*are* you okay?" His tone still held that friendly casual, *we're just chatting and bs-ing* vibe, but the words were unexpectedly serious.

Very unlike Ramsey.

"I'm . . ." Brody swallowed hard. Told himself it was just the last bite of his sandwich, but it was more than that.

He'd started this year a few weeks ago very sure that he'd figure his shit out sooner rather than later.

But he was as conflicted as ever about his future, and *now* there was this thing with Dean. Of course, it wasn't just *Dean*. Dean was just the person Brody had experimented with. It was the fact that he'd wanted to experiment at all.

He didn't feel found; instead, he felt more lost than ever.

"It's okay to not be okay, you know," Ramsey said, voice still even.

That was the one thing about Ramsey; he could be a remarkably judgment-free zone. He'd come here intending to not tell Ramsey shit, but the temptation to confess everything was strong.

"I'm going through some shit," Brody admitted.

"Yeah, you are," Ramsey said, and suddenly his hand was clasping Brody's, his grip a reassuring squeeze. "But you're gonna be okay in the end. I know it."

"I don't know it," Brody said and laughed because that was better than crying. Especially over the remnants of an Italian sub in Sammy's. "I don't know who I am anymore. What I want. I get on the ice, and it's good, but it's not the same. I feel . . .different."

"Your injury," Ramsey said.

"Yeah. Yeah, that's part of it. But then I go to class, and we're doing these medical case studies and I think, *God*, I could do that, too. I love doing this. I could get lost in it. Sometimes I think I want both—but we know that's not how it works, right?" Brody laughed again, because *fuck*, this rest-of-your-life shit was *hard*.

"I think you could be or do anything you wanted. Anything you decided on." Ramsey paused. "Are we still not talking about Dean?"

"No, we're not talking about Dean." Because Brody knew it wasn't really about Dean. He was a symptom of a larger situation. "We're talking about *me*."

"Your parents are gonna be just fine, and the rest of us are gonna be just fine, with whatever you want, with whatever direction you decide to swing. You know that, right?"

Brody nodded. He knew it. But the words burst out of his mouth anyway. "But am *I* gonna be fine with it? I don't know. I don't know fucking anything anymore." And there it was.

Everything he'd thought he was. Everything he'd thought he wanted. Everything he'd worked for. It was all a mess, shattered on the floor of his mind, and Brody didn't know how to put it back together again. Or if he even should.

"We all go through this," Ramsey said quietly.

"Not you," Brody retorted.

"Especially me," Ramsey admitted. His blue eyes were shadowed now, like he was thinking about it. Like Brody's confession had forced him to revisit it. Brody almost wanted to apologize for sending him there.

"Oh."

"Yeah, *oh*. And you don't gotta hide this shit, Faulkner. We're friends. We're teammates. We're there for each other. You know Mal's got his big four-year plan. Talk to him. Talk to Finn, who's only ever wanted to play hockey, even when the whole world seems either set against him doing it or waiting to see how fucking amazing he's gonna be. Nobody says you gotta take his path. Or your parents' path. Or that you gotta decide right now."

"Yeah." He knew Ramsey was telling the truth, but it still didn't help.

"I know you *know* all that though. So it's just . . .sometimes you gotta go through it before you get it."

"Did you?"

"When I kissed my first guy in high school? Yeah, I sure did. Didn't think that was me, but it is. Took me time to embrace it."

"Really?" Brody couldn't help the skepticism in his voice. Ramsey Andresen was the most unashamed person he knew.

"Really," Ramsey said warmly.

"Okay."

"And anytime you need to talk, I'm here. We're *all* here." Ramsey picked up his smoothie and sucked noisily on the straw. "Now, I'm sure you were about to tell me you've got some crazy hard bio shit you gotta do, so I'm gonna take off."

Brody rolled his eyes. Except Ramsey was right. "Yeah. And thanks, actually."

"Anytime," Ramsey said.

Except the "crazy hard bio shit" wasn't the only reason he was wanting to go home. Maybe he'd see Dean. This was usually the hour they *did* meet up, or at least they had pre-Friday night.

They'd sometimes sit on the couch in the living room, shooting the shit for a few minutes, sometimes reading in companionable silence as ESPN played low on the TV.

Brody knew Dean was avoiding him, but he *knew* it when he came home and the living room was empty.

Knew it with even more certainty when he looked at Dean's door and saw that sliver of light underneath it.

He'd already retreated to his room. Maybe if he hadn't gone with Ramsey for food after practice, he'd have caught him . . .

But did he really want to catch Dean if he didn't want to be caught?

No. No, he did not.

Angry frustration surged through Brody as he stared at the door.

Let Dean fucking hear him, just standing here in the hallway, not moving.

Let him hide and pretend that what happened the other night hadn't happened at all. That they hadn't been all over each other. That they hadn't kissed like the world was going to end tomorrow. That they hadn't gotten hard and come their brains out just from touching each other.

Brody's blood quickened again, just thinking about it.

Though frankly, it felt like he'd barely *stopped* thinking about it.

He glanced down at his half-hard cock tenting his gray sweatpants. He'd gotten off twice since the "experiment" and both times he hadn't had a fucking hope or a prayer of *not* thinking about Dean as he wrapped a hand around his dick.

It hadn't been as good. Not even close.

But he still knew what he'd be doing when his own door closed behind him.

Trying to recreate that fire that had surged through him.

He turned away, clearly heading to his room, but then Brody hesitated.

Why *should* he let Dean just keep hiding?

If he was going to drive Brody nuts, then he sure as fuck wanted to drive him nuts right back.

And after the way they'd come together on Friday, it *had* to be some kind of fucking mutual.

Brody waited a moment, until his erection died down a bit, steeled his nerve and knocked.

For a long second, there was only silence.

Then he heard the creak of a chair and Dean's footfalls as he walked across the room.

Finally, he opened the door.

"Hey," Dean said. His voice was a study in neutrality and if Brody had thought Coach's face tended towards blankness, then Dean's could give him a run for his money.

"Hey," Brody said back.

Before, when they'd just been hanging out—not friends but not really only roommates either—there'd always been this frisson of *something* in the air.

He hadn't known what it was, then. But now, after they'd kissed, after they'd touched each other, now Brody knew.

It was sexual tension, crackling in the air between them. In the way Dean's gaze dipped down, for a split-second, catching on Brody's lips. In the way his biceps in that tight, worn T-shirt, flexed.

Goddamn. Brody remembered what all those muscles had felt like. They'd been fucking devastating.

"Did you . . . uh . . . need something?" Dean asked awkwardly.

"Just wanted to make sure everything was okay." Brody paused. "You know, after the other night. Haven't seen you since then."

'Cause you've been freaking avoiding me.

"Oh yeah. Um. Sure. Of course. We're good."

"Good," Brody said, raising his chin. Maybe he'd freaked out a little bit during the aftermath but he wasn't the one freaking out now. He'd been the one to knock on Dean's door, after all. Make him face him again.

"You need something else?" Dean didn't say it rudely, but it was clear he wanted to be done with this conversation. And Brody wasn't sure he could blame him for that.

After all, the last time they'd seen each other, he'd been in full panic mode.

"Listen, I just wanted to say . . .uh . . .sorry if I freaked out a little bit."

Dean raised an eyebrow, but didn't say anything.

"I just haven't seen you since," Brody added, hating how petulant he sounded now.

"I've been busy," Dean said defensively.

He didn't have to say, *you knew I was super busy when you decided to hook up with me* because his meaning was clear enough.

Message received. Loud and clear.

Well, Brody had a message of his own to deliver.

He leaned in. Not quite as close as they'd been the other night, but close enough to bring all those memories, still red-hot, right back. Watched as Dean's breath caught and his knuckles gripping the edge of the door went white.

For a single moment, Brody remembered how it had all felt. Dean's mouth on his, fierce and undeniable, the firm grip of his big hands, and the way his hips had stuttered, searching for his, wanting more than either of them knew how to give.

It turned him on. And Brody was pretty goddamn sure he wasn't the only one.

"I've been busy too," Brody murmured. The arousal he felt, just thinking about how it had been, roughened his voice.

The wood under Dean's grip creaked ominously.

"Yeah?" Dean asked. His voice had softened, but he still seemed apprehensive.

"Yep," Brody said, nodding. "Have a good night."

But as Brody returned to his own room, shutting the door behind him with a long, heartfelt sigh, he realized the only problem with teasing Dean was the knife cut both ways.

Now he was really horny, with nothing to do but to take care of it himself and hope that his orgasm might even come close to how good it had been with Dean.

CHAPTER SIX

"You got my email then?" Ian, the agent that Dean had started chatting with this summer, leaned forward, his greenish-gray eyes intent on Dean.

They were sitting in Jimmy's, in one of the back booths, sipping coffee, and Ian had ordered a slice of Jimmy's famous apple pie, but Dean found he couldn't relax against the cushion because he was so tense.

He'd been dreading this meeting for a week now, ever since he'd gotten Ian's email.

Of course, the whole business with Brody had been a pretty decent enough distraction. If he wasn't agonizing over what had happened with his roommate on that couch, he was agonizing over the hard truths Ian had delivered.

"Yeah," Dean said. He'd read it probably a hundred times, and he couldn't say now that it was potentially any less true than it had been the first time he'd scanned through it.

Was he too tense? Too tightly wound?

Maybe.

But he was only that way because his life had forced him into that mode, over and over again. If he let go for a second, something bad could happen, could derail everything he'd worked for, and then what would he do?

Be *average?* Have an average life? Keep scraping away for every little thing?

He wasn't going to do that. He *couldn't* do that.

"You don't look happy about it," Ian said.

"Of course I'm not happy about it," Dean retorted.

"Right," Ian said sympathetically.

But Dean didn't want Ian's sympathy. He wanted his reassurance that these concerns weren't going to cost him a spot in the first round of the draft next year.

"Well," he said in a hard voice, "tell me what I can do to fix this."

Ian tilted his head and regarded Dean for a long, endless moment.

He'd come to this lunch hoping to smooth things over and reassure Ian—so that he could in turn reassure NFL teams—that he wasn't going to be a hot mess. But this thing with Brody had fucked him up so much, bringing all these frustrating hungers to the surface, hungers he'd never even noticed before. As a result, his temper was shorter than he'd hoped for.

Avoiding Brody for a few days had seemed like a good plan to return them both to the place they'd been in pre-hookup. And it had *mostly* seemed to be working, at least until Brody had shown up at his bedroom door last night, all soft sleepy brown eyes, warm with an emotion Dean didn't want to identify, and reminded him all over again of how good it had been.

Of how much his body craved a repeat.

Fuck my life.

Why hadn't he just told Brody he didn't want to be his experiment? That he didn't want Brody to be *his* experiment? Because he'd been relaxed in a way he never was, which was only partially the booze's fault—the rest lay entirely with Brody and also his goddamn curiosity.

He'd wondered and let those questions take the reins for the first time in his whole life, and now look at him paying for that choice.

"I'm not sure what to tell you," Ian said, and there was that blunt honesty again.

Of course, that same tendency to tell the truth was what had attracted Dean to Ian Parker in the first place.

He hadn't wanted polite platitudes. He'd wanted fucking *results.*

He'd wanted an agent who was going to fight for Dean as hard as Dean had fought for himself. Up until this point, it had been going well. He'd been ready to sign on Ian's dotted line the moment he could.

But now, ever since the email, he wasn't sure.

That wasn't the only thing he wasn't sure of these days.

Yeah, you were pretty fucking sure you were straight, too.

Brody had destroyed that with one kiss—and Ian had done the same with one email.

Was it any wonder he was reeling and fucking *hiding*? Maybe Brody had come to his door last night wanting a repeat, but with everything else shaky in a way that made Dean anxious, he wasn't willing to risk it.

Too much drama. Too much uncertainty. No matter how much his body craved what Brody had possibly been offering.

"I want to know the truth. I know I can fix this, but you have to tell me how," Dean said gruffly.

Ian sighed.

"Dean, I said it all in the email. I'm not saying that concern is gonna really scare any particular team away from drafting you, especially not if you keep playing lights out, this season and next. But it *could*. Especially if people start talking about it more—"

"You mean like the sports media." Dean glowered, just thinking of how he'd like to squeeze the life out of some of these bloodsuckers who'd never actually played a down of football yet felt like they could offer endless, pointed analyses of *his* play. Of who he was as a player. Of who he was as a person.

Ian nodded. "You can't listen to them, though, you know that. We talked about that."

They had. At length. And usually Dean was too busy to do it, anyway, but for a time, a whole stretch of his freshman and sophomore year, he'd had a Google alert set up with his name.

That had been one of Ian's first pieces of advice. Delete that alert. He'd done it, and it *had* helped him focus more on what was really important: his own performance, not what everyone else might say about it.

"I know, but—"

"No buts," Ian interrupted. He still had that easy, uncomplicated smile on his face, but Dean knew his future agent well enough to know that casual smile hid a sharp brain and a backbone of steel.

You like those things about him.

But not when Ian was using them *against* him.

"So there's nothing I can do?"

"Find some hobbies? Learn to smile on the sideline?"

"They should be happy I'm not having a fucking meltdown on the sideline," Dean grumbled.

Ian smirked. "They wouldn't like that either. Trust me on this one."

No, and he'd know better than anyone. Ian was famously with Carter Maxwell, a receiver in the NFL who had once been famous for those sideline meltdowns. He'd been even more famous for the methods he'd used to combat them: partying hard and fucking even harder, with anyone who'd have him. And since Carter Maxwell looked like a *GQ* model come to life, all golden hair and charming smile and ripped abs, there'd been a long, *long* line of takers.

But after Ian had come into his life, all that had stopped.

"I can smile. I *do* smile," Dean argued. "I just . . . I'm focused on the field. That's what they want, isn't it?"

It felt like every time he recorded another achievement, the nebulous powers-that-be moved the fucking goal posts, ensuring that he'd never be exactly what they wanted.

Guaranteeing that he'd stay Dean Scott, broke and from the wrong side of the tracks, with the boozy mom and the absent dad.

"Listen, Dean, nobody ever said this was right. *Or fair.*" Ian sighed. "I'm going to do what I can to get out what I do know of you, which is that you're maybe the most determined guy I've ever met. The hardest working. That counts for something. But you gotta do something for me, too."

"What? Anything, I'll do anything."

"Relax a little, okay? Don't just smile now, smile on the sideline. Enjoy what you've accomplished. You *should*, because it's a serious achievement to even have made it this far." Ian's voice was wry. He didn't call Dean on his desperate plea. He could have, but he didn't. Another tick in the column of *he is the right agent for you.*

"I can do that."

"Get a girlfriend. Or a boyfriend. Whichever. Or even a friend. Hang out with them. There's something besides just football and school. I know you're friends with Wes, but I'm thinking finding something outside football might be more reassuring."

Dean thought about Brody, but only for a split second. Then he dismissed him. He wasn't a boyfriend. He wasn't even a friend. He wasn't . . .well, he wasn't *anything*. Between Brody's panic over what they'd done and Dean's commitment to his future goals, they'd both made sure of that.

But he *could* tell Ian about Brody . . .

No.

No, he couldn't. What would be the point?

"I'll see what I can do," Dean said dryly. *Don't mention Brody, just don't do it, it's not anything. . .you're not anything.* "I . . .uh . . .I have a new roommate this year. Good guy. Plays hockey. Does that count? Yeah, he doesn't play football, but he's on the hockey team."

Why had he gone and brought him up?

"Hey, he's not in your normal path, that matters. Tell me about him," Ian's eyes lit up with approving pleasure.

He didn't want to talk about Brody, while also being literally unable to keep his name out of his mouth. It was a conundrum that Dean didn't fucking understand.

We kissed. It was hot.

"I . . .uh . . .he's a hockey player, like I said." What else did he know about Brody that wasn't part of what had happened on that goddamn couch? "He's a bio major. Super smart. Parents are doctors. He's goin' places."

"Sounds like it."

"Yeah," Dean said, but that was all. Because if he said more, he might keep word vomiting and that *couldn't* happen.

Him, word vomiting. Who most people had to freaking persuade to talk.

"Anything else? He's just your roommate who plays hockey who's a bio major?" Ian teased him gently.

"I guess . . .Brody's sort of a friend. A friendly acquaintance."

He sure didn't feel like just an acquaintance the other night, when your tongue was in his mouth and his hand was on your dick.

Ian rolled his eyes, but his face was still full of teasing delight. "This gonna be one of *those* roommate situations, Dean?"

"No. No. Definitely not." *Yes.*

"It would be okay if it was," Ian pointed out kindly.

"Funny how it doesn't matter if I'm fucking my male roommate now, but God forbid I care too much about my future and don't *smile* enough on the sideline."

"I know," Ian said sympathetically. "It's fucking nuts, isn't it?"

"It is," Dean griped.

"But if it's not like that—"

"It's not," Dean interrupted him before he could continue.

Ian just laughed. "Of course not. Well, keep me posted. And bonus points, if this roommate makes you smile and look like you *just* did when you told me about him . . .see more of him, okay?"

That was a fucking joke, considering that Dean had just spent the last few days making sure their paths literally *never* crossed. But before he could say anything else, their waitress arrived, two checks in hand.

Ian was scrupulous, making sure never to overstep the NCAA rules that forbade him from giving anything of any monetary value to Dean before he'd officially signed with him.

And Dean? Well he wasn't about to let some faceless organization that half the time felt like it was out for his youth and his blood all while it took in hundreds of millions of dollars *because* of guys like him do anything to fuck him over even more.

"I mean it," Ian said as Dean pulled a few dollar bills out of his wallet. "You actually looked like a *real* person the moment you brought him up."

"I don't want to talk about it," Dean grumbled.

"Sure. But I'm here when you want to." Ian shot him a knowing grin.

But Dean already knew that he was *never* going to want to talk about it.

About the easy way they'd begun to know each other over a dozen or so passing conversations they'd shared.

About Friday night's experiment.

About the heat and the knowing look in Brody's eyes when he'd knocked on his door yesterday.

About Brody, at all.

And definitely not about how he didn't know what the fuck to do about any of it.

CHAPTER SEVEN

Ian's words echoed through his mind through his two afternoon classes, and even though his attention span was usually great, Dean found himself unable to focus.

The thoughts followed him through the quick dinner he grabbed before practice.

Then to the gym, after.

And then, because fate was pointedly laughing at him, it dumped the very subject of his unruly thoughts right in front of him.

In the gym.

Shirtless.

Muscles straining as Brody worked his lats on one of the machines.

The sports teams at Portland U rotated use of the gym, each having their own scheduled time, but Tuesday night was always open, for anyone who wanted to use it.

Usually Dean avoided open gym because he hated having to share with a bunch of egotistical jocks who were sure that *they* knew best.

But he'd gone tonight, because Coach had taken it easy on them, this first practice after the bye week, and he'd felt too much crawling under his skin.

Too much *something*.

So he'd stopped by the gym, hoping that exhaustion might silence that feeling and also that he might continue to avoid Brody until he'd dealt with the former.

Until he'd managed to stop craving him, in this weird, painfully obsessive way that was totally unlike him.

Dean stared at Brody's figure. Remembering, in way too complete detail, exactly how his back had felt when Dean had slipped his fingers under his T-shirt.

How his breath had shuddered as he'd come apart.

The way his lips searched for Dean's. Had wanted to keep kissing him, even as he came.

According to everyone else, you're probably not being all that weird or obsessive.

Normal people probably wanted each other all the time and did something about it and then moved on, but Dean had long acknowledged that his singular drive had ruined normal for him, maybe even forever.

Of course that didn't explain Brody, but then anyone who was playing NCAA hockey and also getting a degree in biology probably wasn't normal either.

Maybe that was why he'd actually connected to the guy. Dean's weirdness had called out to Brody's weirdness.

Not for the first time, he wanted to call up Ramsey and tell him to fuck off. Interfering piece of shit.

Brody finished his set and looked up, sweat making the ripples of his back muscles shine under the fluorescent gym lights, and their gazes met in the mirror.

You're caught.

"Hey," Brody said, turning around to face Dean. His voice was normal, expression the same.

Probably nothing like how Dean looked, deer in the headlights at the vision of Brody's bare chest. The trail of golden brown hair that led down to the waistband of his shorts, hanging low on his hips.

One tug, and he'd get an eyeful of what he hadn't been lucky enough to see on Friday night.

Fucking snap out of it, man.

"Uh, hey," Dean said awkwardly.

"Don't usually see you here on a Tuesday," Brody said.

It was totally normal, totally friendly small talk.

"Yeah," Dean said. He did not say, *And you won't ever again, now that I know you come here on Tuesday nights.*

Brody ran a hand through his sweat-damp hair. "Not that you . . .uh . . .don't look like you spend plenty of time here."

At least he'd said *look* instead of *feel*. Because during their hookup, Brody's hands had been all over his body, like he'd been glorying in the firmness of it.

Like he couldn't get enough.

But he'd definitely gotten enough. That much had been clear right after it had ended.

Dean reminded himself of that particular fact. How anxious the aftermath had made him. How much he did not need this fucking drama in his life.

Relaxation, Ian had said.

Well, maybe he and Brody could at least be friendly. Surely he could conquer this craving to revisit their experiment, and if he could, then they could go back to the way they'd started to be before the whole damn experiment.

That Brody had relaxed him just fine.

"Yeah, I do," Dean said. He set his water bottle by the big mat on the other side of the gym. Originally he'd planned to do some ab work and then put in a hard run, because nothing wore him out like strengthening his core.

But he usually stripped off his shirt first.

Brody's shirtless. Are you gonna make this even weirder than it already is?

Forcing himself to stop overthinking, he lifted it up and off, tossing it down next to his water.

As he went down to the mat, he could feel Brody's eyes hot on his shoulders. Skimming down his chest.

His body was a tool, sure, a surefire way he was going to change his life, but he was proud of the way it looked too. How hard he worked to maintain it. To improve it. To make it the very best it could be.

And if Brody wanted to look and enjoy it too . . .well, Dean wasn't going to go out of his way to stop him.

On the other side of the room, he heard Brody moving around, changing machines. Then the inevitable sound of metal clunking together as he started another set.

But he didn't look. Didn't let himself. It was only his history of intense focus to the exclusion of everything else that kept his gaze locked onto the mat.

After a few warmup stretches, Dean picked up the medicine ball, took a deep breath and began.

Fifteen minutes later, sweat was dripping down his face, his core was burning and that was of course, the moment Brody reappeared in his line of vision.

"Hey," Brody said.

Dean swallowed hard, his abs aching, as he swiped a hand across his forehead.

"You're sure working hard over here," Brody said, the corner of his mouth tilting up in a teasing smile. Dean felt his abs twitch, and that was a good *and* a bad thing.

"Well, you . . .uh . . .know what they say," Dean said.

"What do they say?"

Dean wanted to kiss the tilt off that mouth.

But he didn't, because that would've been crazy, and he was trying very hard not to fall into crazy right now.

"Uh, yeah, that there's no point in working if you're not working hard," Dean said. Felt like apologizing. *Stupid. So fucking stupid.* "Or at least that's what Coach Stevens says to us."

"You must like him," Brody said, and when Dean nodded, he added, "'You know, since you're hard work's biggest fan."

Dean laughed, the sound startled right out of him, and he regretted that, because his abs were beginning to burn.

"I didn't know hockey players could make jokes," Dean said. If Brody was going to tease, to try to return them to the relatively easy acquaintanceship they'd occupied before the other night, then he wasn't going to let that opportunity pass him by.

"Oh, we're full of them," Brody claimed. "Haven't you ever met Ramsey?"

Dean rolled his eyes, but he was still smiling. He couldn't help it.

"Yeah, a few times, and he's sure something."

"Oh, so it's just me you didn't think was very funny," Brody teased. Dean opened his mouth to argue that no, he hadn't thought that at all, actually, but before he could, Brody continued. "I was going to do the bench press, but I didn't want to do it alone. You okay to spot me for a few?"

"Sure, if you'll do the same." Dean hadn't intended to work on his chest or shoulders, but if Brody was going to do it and he was going to be forced to watch, then at least he could return the favor.

Because that was what roommates slash friendly acquaintances did, right?

"'Course," Brody said, and he reached out a hand to help Dean up.

Dean took it before he could think better of it. Before he realized that this was the first time they'd touched since the couch.

Brody's hand was big and calloused. Strong. Sensation raced up his arm, and Dean ignored it, coming to his feet, trying to tell himself it was just remnants of his workout, even though he'd been focusing on his abs, not on his arms.

He squeezed his fingers into a fist and then released them, once then twice then a third time as he and Brody walked over to the bench press station.

Unsurprisingly, the weight was set to two hundred and twenty-five pounds.

"Ugh," Brody said as he gestured towards the weights, beginning to slide them off, "why is it *always* set to this whenever I come in?"

He pulled off fifty pounds, leaving the bar at a very respectable one-seventy-five.

Dean barked out another laugh as he moved behind it. "You don't know?"

"No?" Brody sat down on the bench and then leaned back, settling his back against it.

"Two-twenty-five is the weight we have to bench press at the NFL combine."

"So if you just bench two-twenty-five you're good?"

"No, no. You do as many reps as you can at that weight."

"Oh. Huh. Well. Our strength and conditioning guy is always telling us we've got to be strong, but agile. So less weight, more reps."

"Don't worry, I'm not judging your one-seventy-five," Dean joked.

Maybe at a different time and with a different person he might've. But he already knew Brody more than pulled his weight. That he was strong. It was impossible to look at his beautifully cut chest and arms and down lower, to his flat stomach, his abs rippling as he positioned himself underneath the bar, and think he didn't put a lot of work in here at the gym.

"Oh, thanks," Brody teased right back. "I'm flattered."

Brody had to know how gorgeous he was. Nothing too big or bulky, just fluid muscle, emphasizing the lines of his body, not hiding them.

"You should be," Dean said. Maybe they were trying to be only friendly now—an unspoken agreement between them to return to how they'd been before *that time on the couch*—but friends didn't hide the truth.

"Aw, you're such a softy underneath all that *hard work, hard body* mantra, Scott."

Dean's heart quickened at Brody's words, but instead of letting himself feel it, he chided himself to *focus*.

Even one-seventy-five wasn't chump weight, and Brody wasn't going to hurt himself, not on Dean's watch.

"You ready?" Dean asked. Not sure how to deal with Brody's admission that he had a hard body. Maybe it was just another truth. Or maybe it was something more. So he ignored it.

"Yeah," Brody said, getting set. He had great form, and even though it was second nature for Dean to always check for it when he was spotting in the gym, he didn't have a single comment to make about Brody's.

He lifted the bar, arms flexing in a way that Dean didn't want to admit was distracting—but *was*—and began his reps, breathing out and in steadily as he thrust the bar upward.

Five reps, and he set the bar back on the rack.

"Good," Dean said, even though it was probably useless, 'cause surely Brody knew how good he was.

So fucking good you can't get enough.

"Thanks," Brody said shortly. He wiped his face with a towel and tossed it back on the floor.

Some guys waited a freaking eternity between reps, but Brody wasn't one of those, and respect for his hard work bloomed in Dean's chest.

Brody settled back and began the next rep set.

On the fifth and final set, Dean could see he was struggling a little, muscles trembling with the effort, face glowing red, but he finished it with the same graceful, intentional movements he'd started with.

"Great job," Dean said, nodding with his approval.

"Thanks." Brody was breathless now, chest flushed, sweat trickling down to the waistband of his shorts, and Dean clenched his fists again.

He didn't want to be thinking like this. He didn't want to be so hyper-aware of Brody, not this way. He hadn't ever wanted to live a lie, but he also hadn't expected that *this guy* was gonna be the one to make him face these hard truths.

"You ready now?" Brody asked, after he stood and then wiped down the machine.

Ugh. He even wipes down the machines.

"Yeah."

Dean added the weight back.

"How many of these can you do?" Brody wondered as Dean settled onto the bench.

"A few," Dean said. "We'll start with thirty, six reps of five and go from there."

Dean couldn't see Brody easily, with him standing behind the bench, but he could practically *hear* his eyebrows rise.

"Alright," Brody said. "Whenever you're ready."

Dean sank into his place—a spot in his mind with laser-sharp focus, where he always went when faced with a physical challenge—and let the rest of the world fall away. Even Brody.

There was only the bar and its weight and his own body, and how he could not only move it, but control it.

His knuckles creaked with the strength of his grip, and he lifted the bar and began his first rep.

Breathe. In and out.

One down. Four to go.

Then there were three.

Two.

One.

Dean set the bar down on its rest and let out another big gust of air, clearing out his lungs and filling them with fresh.

His arms felt strong, invincible, but he knew this was the easy part.

After he hit twenty, that was when things were going to get hard. Or *harder.*

"You're really good at this." Brody's voice drifted over him.

"Yeah," Dean agreed.

He hadn't been, at first.

But once he'd learned the intricacies of the combine tests, he'd started working hard on getting as many reps as he could.

He did the second set.

And then the third. Fourth. Fifth. Sixth.

He was sweating in earnest now, his arms burning, but he still had some more in him. He wanted to push himself. *For the combine,* he lied to himself, *not because of who's watching.*

"Fuck," Brody exhaled sharply behind him as Dean set the bar down for the fourth time.

"I'm good to do some more," Dean said.

Last year, there'd been two linebackers at the combine who'd hit thirty-one.

He intended to be able to do thirty-five by the time it was his turn.

"Are you sure?"

Dean kind of hated the skepticism in his voice.

"Yeah." He needed to be sure.

"I wasn't wrong; you're crazy strong," Brody said. "Or maybe just crazy."

"I got shit to prove," Dean said stubbornly and then after centering himself again, picked up the bar and ground out three more reps, his muscles shaking with the effort on the final one.

"Shit," he said, when he finally managed to set the bar back on its rack. "I don't think I can feel my arms anymore."

"That was insane and impressive, and I'm real glad I didn't have to actually take it from you," Brody admitted. "I'm not sure I could've."

"Sure you could have," Dean disagreed. He wiped his face with the towel. Then wiped down the bench and the bar. "You're strong, too, Brody."

But Brody was side-eyeing him. "Not like you," he said.

And even though he should be totally fucking worn out with the exercise he'd done tonight, the image flashed in his mind.

His arms, strong and sure, pinning Brody to the wall, mouth devouring his. Then because that wasn't enough—it was *never* enough—him lifting him up, Brody's muscular thighs wrapping around his waist.

Dean trembled. And not because of the effort he'd just put in.

"Ah, well, we need to be," Dean stammered. He looked away, suddenly far too aware that at this late hour, they were the only ones here.

And with all the utilitarian decor and floor-to-ceiling mirrors reflecting the equipment back onto themselves, the gym shouldn't have felt private or intimate, but Dean realized suddenly that it felt like *both*.

"Right," Brody agreed. "Hey, you wanna grab a shower and then a smoothie? Sammy's is open late. We can hang out for a bit, too, if you have any homework left."

Normally, Dean would've had no issues deflecting the invite. He did it often enough. But he found himself wanting to accept, even though it was probably a bad idea.

He didn't need to spend more time with Brody Faulkner to realize that the other night probably hadn't been a fluke as much as an inevitability. But they were trying to be friends, right?

As Dean was internally debating, Brody added, with one of those irrepressibly charming lopsided smiles that he *had* to know were fucking lethal, "We're friends, aren't we? Friends hang out, Dean."

Dean hadn't been able to say before this moment that they *were* friends. They hadn't hung out that many times before the couch had happened, and then there was the couch. That had been very much *not* a friendly kind of occurrence. Then after, Dean had gone out of his way to avoid Brody.

So no, he wouldn't have counted them as friends. Even after tonight.

Of course, it had taken Wes at least a whole year to convince Dean that they were friends.

Maybe he was just too particular about the term.

"Yeah, they do," Dean agreed. He almost said, *but we're not friends, necessarily*, but he could at least see how Brody might find that offensive.

Especially since he'd so casually assumed it was true.

"So, you coming or not?"

"Sure," Dean said. He picked up his shirt. Then his water bottle, guzzling half of it.

The gym showers were fancy and had nice separators, unlike the locker room at the football field, so at least he was saved the undeniably arousing sight of hot water running down Brody's naked body. The body he hadn't even seen when they'd hooked up before.

But you wanna see it. That voice was insidious and didn't want to be denied, but still, Dean made an effort and squashed it like a bug, forcing it down and muting it. By the time he met up with Brody, he was clean and in control again.

Ready to just hang out.

Nothing like the "hanging out" they'd done on Friday night.

Sammy's was a sub and smoothie shop kitty corner from the athletic complex and the gym. Dean didn't go there as often as a lot of the guys from his team, because he could make smoothies and sandwiches so much more cheaply at home, and money was always a consideration.

Clearly, it wasn't for Brody, but it was hard for Dean to hold that against him these days. His resentment had melted away, like it had never existed at all.

How could he be resentful when the guy was so downright nice and friendly *and* charming, with no stuffy ego whatsoever?

Dean forgot more than he remembered that Brody's parents were rich and he'd probably never worried about where his next meal was coming from a single day in his whole life.

Even when he so adeptly maneuvered them so after they ordered, Brody just slipped the cashier a card, paying for both their smoothies and the sandwich they'd agreed to split.

Dean got mad at Wes whenever he tried to do the exact same goddamn thing, so he wasn't sure why his temper wasn't spiking now. Still, he didn't want it to continue. If he and Brody really were going to be friends, then Dean needed to pull his own weight.

"You didn't need to do that," he said as they took their seats in the corner booth.

"I know," Brody said. "But I wanted to. Call it a friendly gesture."

It was on a tip of Dean's tongue to ask if making out on their couch was also a friendly gesture, but Brody was being so pointed about not bringing it up that he decided he'd be dumb as rocks if he didn't follow suit. After all, he was the one who was sure it wouldn't be happening again.

"So you've decided that for me, then?" Dean asked, raising an eyebrow.

"I have a feeling you don't have many people you *call* friends, even if they'd feel differently. And I'm not patient enough to wait around for you to make up your mind." Brody shot him a teasing grin as he pulled out a massive textbook from his backpack.

"That's unfair," Dean grumbled.

"But true." Brody's very white, very even teeth flashed again.

"But true," Dean finally had to agree.

"I'll say this, you're a far better roommate than Ramsey would've been."

Dean chuckled. "No shit."

"He said I wasn't . . .um . . .practical. Good at school, bad at life." Brody made a face.

It was close, but Dean nearly nodded, agreeing with Ramsey. But then he remembered that he was trying to be *friends* and even though it was probably a bad idea, Ian's admonitions were still ringing in his ears, and he didn't have so many friendships he could just burn the ones he did have.

Dean had been educated the hard way, with a tough life that he was still trying to escape, clawing his way up with just his fingernails. Brody had never had to do that. But that also wasn't his fault. "You're one of the smartest guys I know," Dean finally said as diplomatically as he could.

Brody sighed. "That's a nice way of saying that yeah, Ramsey was right. I wasn't coddled, but I suppose I am lucky in that I didn't have to worry about a lot of the shit you did. That Ramsey did."

"Ramsey?"

Brody straight up laughed. "You really don't know him, do you? He was a foster kid."

"I think I've met him twice, so no, not really," Dean admitted with a wince.

"Seriously?" Brody's eyes widened. "You're serious. Oh my God, he met you *twice* and decided you were a better roommate for me than he was."

"From what you've told me about him, it doesn't sound like he was wrong, though," Dean pointed out.

There was a part of him that wanted to ask, *and what if we hadn't moved in together? Would you have conducted your experiment with some other lucky guy? Would you have kissed him the way you kissed me, like you couldn't get enough?*

But he kept his mouth shut, because they were trying to be friends, and Dean had always believed there was no room in friendship for jealousy or resentment.

"And that's the worst of it," Brody said wryly. "He wasn't wrong, not even a little. I hate it when Ramsey's right."

"He right that much?" They'd come here supposedly to study, and Dean *did* have pages to read, but neither of them had made any move to actually *open* their books.

"All the fucking time."

It *was* weird that while Dean hadn't grown up in foster care—though maybe he'd actually have had a *better* childhood if he had—he'd turned out like this: insanely dedicated to one goal and one goal only. To make sure he never worried about money or security ever again.

But unlike him, Ramsey seemed unconcerned about almost everything.

Hockey seemed to be the one exception. Brody had mentioned he'd been drafted a few years back, in the mid-rounds, and after he graduated, he'd likely move into pro hockey. But other than that, he seemed to not care about much. Relationships or school or his future position in life.

Dean couldn't really understand it, but then he supposed to even try, he'd have had to be a psychology major.

"He seems like an interesting guy," Dean said.

Brody just shrugged though. "I guess you could say that. He's like a duck, you know how they have those slick feathers on their back, and water just slides right off? That's Ramsey. Everything just slides off him. He's one of my best friends and sometimes I don't think I know him at all."

"Huh." Dean didn't know what to say. Even the few friends he had he wouldn't have said for sure he *knew*. There was Wes, of course, but he always felt like more the exception than the rule—and even then, Dean didn't know if he'd say that he and Wes *knew* each other, the way Brody seemed to take for granted.

"Just saying, he's like. . .opaque and all that shit."

"*Opaque.* Fucking hell. Maybe I shouldn't be calling you rich boy or pretty boy, but smart boy." Dean said it without thinking and then regretted it because of the flush blooming across Brody's cheeks.

"Brody!" a voice called out. "Your order's ready!"

"I . . .uh . . .I'll go grab it," Brody said as he slid out of the booth. Like he couldn't get away fast enough from the sudden awkwardness between them.

Dean hadn't *meant* to say pretty boy. Not when Brody had made it so clear they were going to be friends—and nothing else.

Shit. He was gonna need to get his head on straight.

With that in mind, he pulled out his own textbook and opened it up to the place he'd marked with a scrap of paper earlier.

When Brody returned with their sandwich, wrapped in its brown paper, and their two smoothies, Dean was attempting to read the first paragraph.

Of course, just because his eyes were reading, didn't mean his brain was comprehending. No, it was stuck on the way Brody leaned over, depositing his half of the sandwich next to Dean's textbook.

"Biology?" Brody asked, raising an eyebrow as he took in the page Dean was attempting to read.

"Well, yeah, physical education isn't all pushups and the rules of tag," Dean retorted.

"I guess maybe we should start calling *you* smart boy," Brody teased, and suddenly they were both grinning at each other and it felt, at least to Dean, like maybe he'd imagined the heat suddenly blooming between them when he'd called Brody *pretty boy*.

Yep, it was all in your own head, so get out of it, and be cool with what you've got now. It's better than what you might've imagined.

But the problem was that it wasn't *all* Dean had imagined.

CHAPTER EIGHT

It was third quarter in the game against USC, sun beating down on the team in the Coliseum, still hot in southern California even in the fall, when Wes brought the smiling up.

Dean told himself before the game that he'd smile more on the sidelines, even if they were losing—which they were not, not even close—and he was doing his best to remember, when Wes sidled over, already pulled from the game because they were up twenty-one points and said, "Why do you keep grimacing over here?"

"Grimacing? *What?*" Dean couldn't help his exclamation.

"Yeah." Wes pushed back his sweat-damp hair. "Every time I looked over here, you were standing on the edge of the sideline, like you always do, and you were making fucking faces. I thought it was the way I was playing—"

"No," Dean interrupted him. "No, you're playing great."

"I know," Wes said, his smile bringing out his dimples. "I couldn't figure it out, so I thought I'd ask you before you go back out there."

Coach Stevens had pulled Wes, probably because he was a very visible part of the offense—the *most* visible player on the whole goddamn team—and the media would rip him apart if Wes got hurt while the Evergreens were up three scores. But Dean was still out there, playing every down of the defense, because Coach had learned last year that when Dean's future was on the line, he didn't take being benched very well.

Even if it was supposedly for his own good.

"I'm not *grimacing*. I'm fucking smiling," Dean retorted.

Wes looked completely lost. "That's not how you smile, you idiot. And why are you tryin' to force yourself to smile?"

"Apparently I'm 'wound too tight' and a bunch of NFL scouts think I'm gonna bust up if I don't magically become happy and relaxed. Ian suggested the smiling, but clearly that was a stupid move."

"If you were *actually* smiling, sure, but you're . . .I don't know how to even describe what you were doing, man. But it didn't look like you were very happy *or* relaxed."

"Ugh," Dean groaned.

"It's just stupid noise. Those scouts always come up with the dumbest shit, you know that. It won't matter on draft night."

Dean knew all about the scouts and the way they liked to pick players apart. But he wasn't willing to let his whole future ride on the assumption it wouldn't matter. Maybe Wes didn't know him as well as he thought—or as well as Dean had believed—if he didn't understand that.

"But," Wes continued before Dean could say any of that out loud, "I get why you're worried. I wish I didn't have as many sleepless nights as I do, worrying about where I'm gonna end up." His gaze flicked towards the stands, where it was very likely Marcus was. "Where *we're* gonna end up."

"It's not your responsibility what happens to Marcus," Dean reminded him. It was easier to talk about Wes' baggage than his own.

Wes made a face. Probably not all that different than the ones Dean had apparently been making, while he was *trying* to smile. "Yeah, easier said than done." He slapped Dean on the shoulder. "Anyway, I get it. It's tough."

"Yeah," Dean agreed.

It occurred to him that *this* was why he and Wes were friends. Because they got it, both on this nearly impossible balancing act of a path they'd set for themselves.

On the field, the Evergreens' kicker set up for a field goal, and Dean grabbed his helmet. In a few minutes, he'd be back on the field, where he belonged. Where nobody gave a shit if he smiled or not.

Where they only depended on him to be what he was best at: a human wrecking ball.

"Give 'em hell, alright?" Wes said, patting him again.

Dean nodded and jogged onto the field, entering the loose circle of defensive players huddling up before the first play after the kickoff.

Jordan, his partner on the other side, was subbed out. When Dean asked Nick, the safety who was calling the plays, he just shrugged. "Coach pulled him, probably. You shouldn't be out here, either, Scott."

"They'd never be able to drag Dean off the field," Eaton, one of the corners, said with a snicker. "They'd have to fight him, first."

"Exactly," Dean said, not offended, because it wasn't of-fensive to want to play. To *need* to play.

"One quarter left," Nick said. He glanced over at Dean. "You still gonna keep rushing?"

"Like anyone's gonna stop him," Eaton said.

"Y'all could learn something from Dean," Nick said firmly. "He doesn't take a single fucking down off. He's fightin' for every single yard."

Dean nodded. Because he did.

Every time he didn't reach the quarterback or he didn't stop the Trojans' running game in its tracks felt like a loss.

And he didn't take loss well.

Nick clapped, breaking up the huddle, and the players arrayed themselves in front of the line of scrimmage. Dean moved to the right, leaning down and digging his cleat and his fingertips into the turf.

The offensive lineman who'd been trying, unsuccessfully, to block Dean for the whole game, looked winded.

Even more, he looked halfway to complete defeat.

Well, halfway wasn't enough for Dean.

They had changed their formation at halftime, moving to double team Dean in earnest, with the hope that this new plan might give their quarterback a precious few extra seconds to get the ball before Dean punched through the line.

It hadn't worked. Dean was used to being double teamed.

He'd just shucked the first guy and dodged the second, moving with the speed and undeniable strength that he'd been blessed with, and that he'd worked so fucking hard to hone.

The whistle blew, and Dean attacked, pushing his legs as hard as they would go. This was their fifth game of the season, and while he was always conditioned, he'd never been in better shape than he was right now. He could push forever, if he needed to.

And he intended to.

He came around the edge, shucking the offensive tackle with a stiff arm to the shoulder and then faced the tight end who was supposed to be helping the tackle with his impossible assignment—Dean. But the tight end, while big, wasn't as good at blocking as Dean was at destruction, and he gave him a quick step to the side and didn't even have to touch him. He went down, and Dean ran past him, legs churning, lungs burning.

The quarterback's panic was blatant even behind his helmet.

Dean only had a split second to decide—and while he almost never did this, because he didn't usually *have* to, he went for the ball instead of the player himself.

Marshaling his strength, he punched the ball with every ounce of it, and it popped right out.

Scooping it up, he tucked the ball away and dodging another lineman, took off for the Evergreens' end zone.

It was a good seventy yards away, and he wasn't sure he was going to make it. Good shape be damned, he didn't usually need to run for more than ten yards. His legs weren't conditioned to do long bursts—only short ones. But that didn't matter.

Like being born poor or unwanted had ever mattered.

Dean pushed all that bullshit to the side, dug deep and drove himself with every ounce of energy he had left in his system. Dodged one receiver, evaded another, and yet he could feel the group behind him, forcing him to move faster.

The crowd screaming in his ears faded away, and he had only one thought, crystallizing in his brain.

If you get a sack fumble touchdown, nobody's gonna say shit about your smile on the sideline.

Ten yards and all that shit they normally care about means less than nothing.

He knew it was true, and that was why when he heard the footsteps behind him, he tried to find one last burst, but it just wasn't there.

A hand shot out and a body followed, and Dean went down, six yards from the end zone.

A sack fumble, yes, but not a touchdown.

He lay there on the turf, black spots dancing across his vision, and didn't think he'd have it in him to even get up.

If he'd scored, sure, he'd probably be dancing around in the end zone, exhaustion be damned, but right now, six yards short felt like a million fucking miles.

A hand appeared over him, then a face. It was Eaton. "Shit, man, I never seen a big man run like that," he said, as Dean gripped his hand and prayed he wouldn't embarrass himself by puking all over the fucking field once he got upright.

He didn't.

But as he carefully jogged back to the sideline, so many back slaps and congratulations tossed his way, Dean only thought, *what would they be saying if I'd made it?*

"Shit, man," Wes said as Dean collapsed on the bench. So much for his normal spot, away from the team, all the way at the end of the sideline. He'd never be able to hold himself upright without his knees wobbling.

Someone thrust a water bottle into his hands, and he shot Gatorade down his throat, then the PT produced an oxygen mask and he took several deep, long breaths of it before pushing it away.

"Sorry I didn't make it in," Dean said, because that was all he could think about.

A roar went up, and then silence, and he had a feeling the Evergreens' offense had just punched the ball in for seven points.

Sure, he'd made that possible. But those seven points weren't *his* seven points. Not his touchdown, on his stat line.

"Are you fucking kidding me?" Wes exclaimed. He knelt in front of Dean, hand warm and reassuring on his knee. "Fuck, that was unbelievable. I didn't know you could run like that."

Dean's laugh was rusty. He squeezed more liquid down his gravelly throat. "I didn't know I could either."

"Shit, seriously. You don't gotta do it all yourself, you know?"

So everyone kept saying, but in the end, when everything went down, who was left? It was only Dean. Only ever Dean.

Maybe he shouldn't have dedicated himself so entirely to a *team* sport. But then, football was what he was good at.

Brody knew it would be late before Dean came home.

Too late.

But he stayed up anyway, ESPN still playing on the TV, but the sound turned down low, as Sportscenter showed Dean's unbelievable fumble return over and over again.

He hadn't really *meant* to turn the Evergreens' football game on, but his hand had picked up the remote anyway and navigated to the channel before he'd been able to totally talk himself out of it.

He'd watched the whole game while working on a lab report for his microbiology class, but by the time the third quarter rolled around and the Evergreens were up twenty-one points, he'd sort of tuned the game out.

Then the announcers had gotten very, *very* excited—shouting, nearly—and Brody had nearly fallen off the couch when he realized why.

Dean had the ball and he was running, faster than Brody had ever imagined a guy of his size could run, towards the Evergreens' end zone.

He hadn't gotten there, but the effort had been undeniable, and Brody had felt a thrill of both pride—he *knew* this guy, he watched him stumble out of the bedroom, sleepy-eyed, his hair sticking up on one side, with pillow creases across his face—and something else he was not entirely comfortable identifying.

Especially when Dean pulled his helmet off on the sideline, hair shiny with sweat, and Brody couldn't help but think of what his neck, just as damp, might taste like if he leaned in and licked.

You aren't licking him. Now or anytime, Brody reminded himself firmly. Dean had finally *mostly* relaxed, when Brody had returned them to the friend zone they'd just started to explore pre-drunken experiment.

He'd never said they wouldn't be doing it again, not explicitly, but he didn't need to. His awkwardness and avoidance right after had made that clear enough, and Brody had decided that there was no point in pushing him into something he clearly wasn't comfortable with.

Would it be easier if, every once in awhile, he didn't catch Dean staring at him like he could barely believe he existed? Yes, it sure would.

But Brody had dragged them across that line the first time, and fuck if he was going to do it again.

If Dean wanted it, he was going to have to say so. Maybe even lean in, one of these nights, and press his mouth—

"Goddamnit," Brody said with a sharp exhale, glancing down at his hardening cock.

The cock that, before the experiment, had seemed perfectly content with whatever crumbs Brody decided to throw it.

No longer.

He was just debating going into his bedroom to take care of it when Brody heard a key in the door lock turn, and he froze.

A second later, Dean filled the doorway and Brody had only a minute to yank a pillow over his crotch and try to look like he hadn't just been contemplating coming his brains out thinking of the guy in front of him.

Smooth, you idiot. Real smooth.

"Hey," Dean said, looking surprised to see him.

Or maybe he was surprised to see the pillow.

Dean dumped his bag on the floor by the door but didn't make a move to immediately leave. Instead he hovered, like what he really wanted was to join Brody on the couch—he just didn't know if he was invited or not.

Spoiler alert: as far as Brody was concerned, Dean was *always* invited.

Brody flushed and dug his fingers into the cheap cushioning. "Hey," he said. "I . . .uh . . .watched the game. It was amazing. *You* were amazing, that fumble return . . ." Brody trailed off when he realized he sounded *just* like the girls who always clustered around the athletes at the frat house parties. The ones who gazed at every athlete with a predatory, breathless awe.

And now that's you.

Dean frowned, and that was when he chose to collapse onto the couch. He looked tired, deep circles and lines under his eyes.

Not for the first time, Brody realized how much pressure he was under. *Empathized* with it. His own situation was bad enough, but he had so many ways he could land easily and softly, if the NHL fell through.

Dean didn't have those.

His only path was to move forward, inexorably.

"Yeah, except I didn't get in," he mumbled under his breath.

"What? No, you didn't, but like . . .seventy fucking yards, man." It had looked like a lot from Brody's perspective.

"Yeah," Dean said.

Brody couldn't say they knew each other *well*, but he'd already begun to figure out when Dean was shutting down.

He was doing it right now. Shutting down. Shutting Brody out.

And if Brody didn't *know*, intimately, how and why Dean felt the way he did, he might've let him.

"Listen, Dean, you can't do it all. Not every play, not every game, not every time you step onto the field."

Dean made a face. "Don't placate me. Do you *know* what I'm trying to do? What I'm trying to escape?"

Brody knew he hadn't meant to say it, from the way Dean's mouth flattened into a hard line.

"No, 'cause you haven't told me," Brody said quietly. But he'd wanted to know. Had almost asked half a dozen times.

"Right. *Right.*" Dean sighed. "You can probably guess though. Shitty small town. Shitty mom, too interested in drinking at the bar and dragging her flavor of the night home to worry about having a kid. Dad? Nowhere in sight, not ever."

"I'm sorry," Brody said, and he understood a lot better now why Dean had been a little guarded at the beginning. Brody had had the childhood Dean had never gotten. The parents he'd probably dreamt of, his whole life, that he'd never had.

"Don't be," Dean said. "Made me into the guy I am now. Made me work my ass off. But with that comes this anxiety shit. Makes me worried I'll screw it all up."

"You wouldn't." Brody believed it, more than he'd ever believed in anything, ever. Maybe even his *own* future.

Dean didn't say anything, just shrugged. Like he was helpless to that feeling, when the last person on earth who could ever be helpless was Dean Scott.

"You should listen to me. I'm the smart boy, remember?" Brody teased, and to his delight, the corner of Dean's mouth tilted up, like he was tempted to smile despite his mood.

"Thought you were pretty," Dean said, and he *was* smiling now, with his whole face.

Damn, Brody thought. And he almost regretted bringing it out of Dean. But not really. Not actually.

"See, you're smart where it counts," Brody joked.

"I try not to embarrass myself," Dean said with a self-deprecating grunt.

"You don't. You don't ever," Brody said, shifting to something more serious.

"Ah, well . . ." Dean looked uncomfortable. "I just wanted to get in, you know? A TD isn't just a fumble return. It's a different kinda stat. A *better* kind of stat."

It seemed unfair, but there were plenty of unfair statistics in hockey, too.

"Yeah, there's always gonna be something better, isn't there?" Brody said, and Dean nodded.

For a moment, they were both quiet.

Brody didn't know what Dean was thinking, but *he* was thinking that he liked this. This touching base with each other on the couch. Even if there was a respectable three feet between their thighs.

Then Dean said, "I didn't know you watched football."

Caught red-handed.

"I . . .uh . . ." Brody gave up. "I don't normally, but this lab report was kicking my ass, and I thought, why not put it on? See what the fuss is about?"

Dean grinned. "And 'cause your roommate was playing, right?"

Brody rolled his eyes, but he was not going to shy away from this. "Actually, 'cause my *friend* was playing."

Dean looked surprised by this admission, which was ridiculous. They were *friends*. Admittedly, friends who had an elephant in the room they were scrupulously ignoring, but friends nonetheless.

"Don't tell me we're gonna have to go over this again," Brody said with mock seriousness. "We covered this the other night."

Dean smiled again. Twice in one night. A new record! Brody mentally patted himself on the back.

Already Dean seemed lighter than when he'd come in, and if that was something Brody could do for him—take him out of his own head, a bit—then he'd gladly do it.

Because they were roommates. Because they were friends.

Or something like that.

"We don't. I . . .we're friends, yes," Dean took a deep breath and glanced over at Brody, and even that brief eye contact felt as good as a touch.

Under the pillow, Brody's cock stirred again, deciding it was time to rejoin the party.

"Good," Brody said, telling himself this was what he wanted. What they *both* wanted. But that didn't mean, deep down, it didn't feel almost like a lie.

A half-truth they were both telling themselves because it was easier and more comfortable.

"It was so stupid," Dean said, with a rushed exhale. "I spent the whole game trying to fucking *smile*, and I was so bad at it, Wes thought I was grimacing."

"Seriously?"

Dean legitimately grimaced now. "I can't decide which is worse: that I thought smiling on the sideline would actually convince an NFL team to draft me high, or that Wes thought I was fucking grimacing instead of smiling."

"I . . .uh . . ." Brody didn't know what to say. "You can totally smile." *Sometimes you smile and it takes my breath away.*

"Yeah." Dean chuckled humorlessly. He didn't sound convinced.

"Here. Try it right now." Brody reached over and gave his arm a reassuring squeeze before he remembered it was *way* better if they didn't touch.

Dean just stared at him, those unearthly light green eyes meeting Brody's own.

For a single moment, Brody thought that maybe he'd be the one to suggest another experiment.

But he didn't. Of course he didn't.

Instead Dean said, "How's this?" And then he cracked a smile. It was too rehearsed, too much teeth. Too much, Brody realized, like forcing it out actually hurt him.

That must've been what Wes had meant.

And if you knew Dean—and Wes clearly did—you knew the difference between that and his *real* smiles.

"Uh, well," Brody said, wincing. "No."

A single look of hurt outrage crossed over Dean's face before he buried it. But before he could get up and walk off to his bedroom, Brody reached out and latched onto his arm.

This time he didn't let go.

"No," Brody repeated, more gently this time. "You can smile better than that. A *real* smile. Not something that someone's forcing out of you. Let's try something . . .you love playing football, right?"

Dean frowned. "Yeah, I guess. It's a—"

"A means to an end, I know." This time Brody knew better than to let his wince show. It was fucking sad, almost, that the guy didn't even know what he loved anymore, because it was so tied up with all these plans he'd made for his future.

Brody might not know if he wanted to play pro hockey, but that didn't mean there wasn't something pure and beautiful about a stretch of untouched ice and blades underneath him that he was gonna use to carve it up. The sound as he did it.

He took a deep breath. "What *do* you like about it?"

But Dean was still frowning, a wrinkle between his dark eyebrows that Brody wanted to reach up and smooth away. It was bad enough that he was still touching his arm, though, and hadn't let go.

Hadn't *wanted* to let go. But he did now, because how awkward would it be if he just kept hanging on. That wasn't how *friends* behaved.

"How about this? I love when I come back on the ice after the Zamboni does its thing, and it's all clean and shiny and new and the possibilities feel endless. I love when we run a really good play, the exact way we set it up in practice. It doesn't even matter that we score or not—it's that we're all executing our roles perfectly, like we're folding into one player. There's no feeling that can match that."

Dean's face smoothed out, the lines disappearing. He thought for a second and then he said slowly, with more consideration that most people would ever believe of a football player best known for his destruction prowess on the field, "When Wes' shoulders relax."

Brody raised an eyebrow.

"Every game he starts out with a certain amount of anxiety. I'm not sure he can dismiss it entirely. It's the pressure—of how much each game means, that he's ultimately responsible 'cause he's the leader. But we score, and the defense holds, and slowly, it's like he can fucking relax. When he thinks he's got this—that *we've* got this—in the bag."

"What else?"

Dean rolled his eyes. "You gonna start moonlighting as a therapist, too, Faulkner?"

"Hey, it's helping, isn't it? At the end of that, you totally smiled a little. A *real* smile, just thinking about that moment."

And he had. Brody hadn't made that up.

"Fine. Uh . . .I really like practice, actually."

"Really? I *hate* practice. Not as much as Elliott, but enough."

"Who's Elliott?"

"He's a young guy on my team. A forward. He's about as anti-practice as they come."

"He's wrong," Dean declared matter-of-factly.

"Why?"

"Practice's the measure of an athlete. How dedicated they are to getting better. How determined they are to hone their skills. Anyone can show up on game day and be ready, but are you ready every single day? Do you bring it when there's no team opposite you?" Dean shrugged. "I approach every single practice like a game, and every game like a practice."

"Huh. I never thought of it that way before." He was going to have to use that line on Elliott sometime and watch as he made a face worse than any Dean had ever made.

"Well, now you have." Dean leaned forward. Set his elbows on his jean-covered knees. They were worn white in spots. Fit him like a glove. All that tightly coiled muscle.

Brody knew exactly what that muscle was capable of. He'd seen it the other night, in the gym, and this afternoon, when Dean had laid it all out on the field.

He wanted to lean over too and touch it.

Feel all that coiled strength for himself.

And yet, during the experiment he'd been unexpectedly careful. Gentle. Considerate.

Ramsey liked to talk about big dumb football players—not that hockey players were necessarily *any* kind of improvement in that area—but while Dean might be big, he wasn't dumb.

Not by a long shot.

"You gonna smile for me again?"

Dean's gaze was serious. Then he smiled, and it was real.

"There you go," Brody said, trying not to stammer as the impact of it hit him hard. Glad he'd still not let go of the stupid pillow, because his dick was just as affected by the smile as the rest of him was.

"Thanks to you." Dean's voice was gravelly rough.

Brody waved a hand, trying to underplay his contribution. "I . . .uh . . .it was just a bit of friendly assistance."

But he was beginning to think that wasn't true, at all.

Sure, he *did* feel friendly towards Dean. He straight up liked the guy. But it was more, too.

He'd wiggled right under Brody's skin when he hadn't been looking, and now he was there and wasn't going to let go.

It was just like Dean to be the source of the stubbornest crush in existence.

Dean got to his feet, like he was all-too-aware that Brody wasn't going to be moving from his spot—or without his handy pillow—until he did. "Right, pretty boy," he said as he was picking up his bag and moving through the living room. "See you tomorrow then."

It took an embarrassingly long time after Dean's bedroom door closed before Brody felt like he could move the pillow without exposing something about himself that *he* wasn't quite ready to face yet.

CHAPTER NINE

"I'VE HEARD THIS IS the best lab of the whole course," Gina said as Brody dropped his backpack on the floor underneath their shared lab table.

"Yeah?" Brody asked.

"Don't sound so excited," she teased. "I thought you liked this class."

He and Gina had been in a lot of the same classes for most of the last two years.

He liked her because she never hit on him. In fact, she'd have bust a gut at the thought of it. She had a high school sweetheart, a girlfriend who was a budding track star at the University of Oregon.

"I do, I'm just tired." Exhausted really. It was Tuesday. They'd had two games this last weekend and then of course, there'd been Saturday night—which he'd spent attempting to catch up on his lab work *and* staying up too late waiting on Dean—and then Monday, when he'd had a full morning of classes before Coach B had run them through a surprisingly brutal practice.

"Aw, didn't they tell you this year would get tougher—with the classes and your hockey stuff?" Gina looked sympathetic.

"Yeah." And he'd ignored them because he was Brody Faulkner and he was fucking invincible.

Or he *had* believed that.

He didn't feel particularly invincible this morning.

He felt lost and torn and *tired*.

"Well, it's a good thing that, at least, you've got the best lab partner in the whole section," Gina said brightly.

"I sure do," Brody agreed, giving her a smile. She was great, and even though he had every intention of carrying his own weight, having Gina as his partner would guarantee that he didn't have to do *more* than half the work.

"Okay, here's the instruction sheet," Gina said, pushing it across the desk. "Let's review it, and then we'll start."

It always helped Brody to sink into the work, into the technical minutiae of the process. It was one of the reasons he'd fought so hard to keep his biology major. He *genuinely* enjoyed science. Picking his way through things, discovering how they worked on a deeper level.

It helped today, too. Focusing on something he loved banished some of his bone-deep exhaustion, even.

His brain added, *and that used to be hockey*. But Brody shut that thought down hard and fast, because he didn't have the energy to deal with his bigger problems today.

Except it turned out that they came up anyway.

They were halfway through the lab—smearing their un-washed fingers across agar plates and doing the same after some intensive scrubbing with surgical soap—when Gina said ca-sually, "I didn't know you had a new boyfriend."

Brody nearly dropped the glass slide he'd just prepped. "What?"

"I saw you two in Sammy's the other night. Looked awfully comfy with him. And he's big, isn't he? I didn't know—"

Before Gina could say, *I didn't know you liked guys like that*, Brody interrupted her. "That's Dean. My new roommate."

"Oh. *Oh*. Sorry." Gina flushed. "You just looked . . .uh . . .very cozy with him."

They'd been on opposite sides of the booth, but Brody thought back to that night and he could see it. He'd probably been gazing at the guy like he was the answer to questions he hadn't even asked. All things considered, he really couldn't blame Gina for wondering.

"We're . . ." Brody stopped and started over. Gina was a friend, and queer, too. He could trust her. "I'm . . .I think I might . . ."

Of course that didn't really make it any easier to say out loud.

"Hey, you know it's okay, yeah?" Gina said softly, encour-agingly.

"Yeah. But I'm just such a mess . . .ugh, *such* a mess. This whole Dean thing. And then I know I'm gonna need to decide if—" Brody stopped again. He didn't want to say it *out loud* to *Gina*, who was already on the premed track, that he was seriously considering not playing pro hockey. That might make it real. He swallowed hard. "The only time it doesn't feel like a mess is when I'm with him, and I screwed it up, right after we kissed and hooked up, and now I don't think he wants what I want. It's all just a disaster."

Gina looked at him steadily then after his outburst, reached over and grasped his arm, squeezing it gently. "You don't have to have all the answers, you know?"

"That's what Ramsey said," Brody said. It still baffled him that Ramsey had been the one to give him good advice, but it was undeniable he had. Why hadn't he listened? Well, Brody *had*, but it was so much easier to hear the words than to actually take them to heart. To accept them for himself.

"Well, *God*, now I'm gonna lose my shit. Me and Ramsey agreeing on something. On *anything*," Gina said with a bark of laughter.

"I know," Brody said, and to his surprise, he was laughing too.

He couldn't believe it, but he actually felt better now—not even worse. It had helped to get that out. To admit, at least, that everything felt terrible and unsure and new and different—except when he was sitting with Dean and they were just talking. That with him, at least *some* of this stupid self-identity angst disappeared.

"How do you know he doesn't feel the same?" Gina asked when they finally stopped chuckling.

"I . . .well, he's straight." That was the easiest answer. Of course, it wasn't really true.

Dean hadn't had a big gay freakout; that had been *all* Brody.

"He told you that?"

"In as many words," Brody said.

He really didn't want to go into the experiment. He wasn't proud of how he'd acted after. Or how Dean had avoided him after.

You freaked out. Of course he avoided you, after.

But surely, if he *was* interested, it wouldn't have been so goddamn hard to convince the guy to even be friendly.

"Ah. Well, come on, let's finish this lab. And then you can run by the coffee shop. Maybe you can't have the guy, but you can have an iced latte with an extra shot," she teased.

Brody nudged her. "You gonna come with me?"

"I can spare a few minutes. Koffee Klatch?"

"Sounds good," Brody said. "So next week we need to check these under the microscope and examine for differences in the bacterial growth?"

Gina nodded. "Then we'll do the final lab report, with our findings. That'll be the most work, for sure." She winced. No doubt she was thinking of Brody's tight schedule, but even the prep work for the lab had convinced him that the sacrifices he was making to take his major were worth it.

He enjoyed the classes too much to call it quits.

"We'll make it work," Brody promised.

"Alright." But Brody could see the worry lingering in his friend's gaze.

"And in three weeks it's the midterm," Gina reminded him.

"Yeah, but we got this," Brody said, shooting her the cockiest smile in his arsenal.

She rolled her eyes, but he could see the rest of her concern melting away, and that was good enough for him.

If Gina thought he could tackle all this, surely he *could* actually do it.

They'd been skating for nearly forty-five minutes, Coach B rattling off formations and drills like he'd been a boot camp instructor in a former life, when Elliott missed the shot.

It was an easy pass from Mal, and should've gone right in, but Elliott juggled the puck a second longer than he should've, and instead of decisively taking action, he hesitated, and that was all the time Ramsey needed to steal it, skating quick and darting in between Ivan and Elliott then shooting it to Brody.

"Shit," Mal exclaimed loudly, a frown plastered across his face.

"Sorry," Elliott muttered, and the whole play fell apart, Coach B skating up and neatly plucking the puck away from Brody.

Rather, Brody *let* their coach take it.

Well, at least that was what Brody told himself. It was less of a blow to his ego, considering he was a player entering the prime of his abilities and Coach must be forty now, and a *coach*.

Now it wasn't just Mal frowning, but Coach too, Zach joining him and stopping next to him with an abrupt shower of ice from his skates.

"What's going on?" he asked mildly.

Coach B did not look mild at all. He looked frustrated, shoving a hand through his dark hair.

"Elliott, what the hell was that?" he demanded.

Elliott just shrugged. He famously hated practice. Brody got that. He hadn't really been enjoying it *himself* lately, which wasn't really fair, because the team was good and getting better. Probably because of all these brutal-ass practices. But with each practice, Brody felt himself sliding to the edges, struggling to give a shit about what was even happening on the ice.

He was existing in the space between the locker room and the rink, present but not as present as he should've been. It wasn't fair to his team. It wasn't fair to *him*.

So far nobody had called him on it, because he was making as much effort as he could to pretend on the surface that everything was normal.

But everything wasn't normal.

He wasn't normal. Not anymore.

It didn't help that Coach Blackburn was a stickler and demanded every ounce of effort from his players. So far, Brody had managed to slide under his radar—probably because he'd decided that Elliott, with his famously bad lack of practice dedication, had garnered most of his attention—but he had a feeling those days were numbered.

"Why didn't you take the shot?" Coach's voice softened a fraction, but considering the look on his face, it wasn't much of an improvement.

"I don't know," Elliott said, his jaw sticking out. "I'd have taken it in a game. This is just a practice."

"You should be treating every practice like a game, and every game like a practice." Brody hadn't even realized he'd said it out loud, until every eye on the ice swiveled in his direction.

He felt a twinge of guilt that everyone looked so fucking surprised that he'd spoken up. He should be better than this. He *used* to be better than this.

"Exactly," Coach said with an approving nod in Brody's direction. "You take that shot, Elliott. You gotta. If you don't, how will you be sure you'll do it during a game."

"I'd do it," Elliott said. He turned to Malcolm. "Come on, Mal. Back me up."

Elliott and Malcolm were sort of like oil and water, which was why it was so odd that they'd ended up on the same line *and* it was working out.

Mal took nothing more seriously than practice.

He always brought his A-game. He reminded Brody a little of Dean, with his single-mindedness.

But Mal didn't say anything, just scuffed his skate on the ice and didn't meet Elliott's entreating gaze.

Coach had to know he was pushing them all, and pushing them hard.

But Brody wasn't sure Coach cared how hard it was, not when he'd already said half a dozen times they shouldn't just want to get better, they *needed* to get better.

Same was true of most of the coaches in the NHL, too.

And that's what you're in for, a lifetime of this.

Brody knew he should've been enjoying the tough expectation that he play at a certain level, but instead, all he did was resent it.

This used to be fun.

The weird thing was that most everyone else seemed to be there. Even Ramsey, who Brody had never seen work so hard, was excelling.

He felt like the only one dragging his skates.

"Again," Coach said, waving around the ice. "And this time, take the fucking shot, Elliott."

Elliott made a face after Coach had turned, heading back to the boards to watch.

They ran the play again, but this time Brody made sure that Malcolm couldn't get the puck to Elliott in the same way, and then he stole it, passing it over to Ramsey, who cleared it easily.

Elliott made a frustrated noise, threw up his hands and his stick, and skated off, right as the buzzer sounded, indicating the end of practice.

Brody knew he should go after him—it had always seemingly fallen to him to counsel and mentor the younger guys, because he was good at it and before this year had actually enjoyed it—but this time, before he could, Ramsey grabbed his arm. "Let me," he said.

Brody raised an eyebrow. "You're gonna talk sense into him?"

"Better than Mal, who might kill him. Or Coach B, who doesn't understand him. Or you."

Brody didn't ask Ramsey why he would be a bad choice, because obviously Ramsey had seen the change in him, he just hadn't said anything about it.

Yet.

Trudging into the locker room, Brody shucked his gear, headed to the showers, and when he got out, Zach was leaning against the locker next to his. Ramsey's unoccupied locker. He must still be talking to Elliott.

"Hey," Zach said. "Coach wants to see you, if you've got a minute."

If you've got a minute was complete bullshit, because Brody couldn't imagine blithely telling their assistant coach that he was too busy to see Coach Blackburn.

Well, he *could* imagine it, but he didn't think it would go down well.

Or at all.

"Sure," Brody said. He still had a few hours of homework he had to tackle, but he'd make time to see Coach first.

Not that he wanted to. A sick feeling bloomed at the base of his stomach, sudden worry that Ramsey wasn't the only one who'd clocked his disinterest and subsequent forced interest.

You should be fucking grateful at how lucky you are. You know how many people would kill for this opportunity?

He knew. But it didn't seem to convince him any better that he still wanted it.

"Whenever you're dressed," Zach said, with a studied casual tone that made Brody's stomach tighten even further.

Maybe he was just hungry.

Or maybe he was actually terrified that Coach, whom he couldn't help but respect, even as he didn't precisely *like* him, would sit down across from him and expose all the weaknesses he'd been trying so hard to bury.

"Alright." Brody tried to match Zach's offhandedness, but he didn't think he quite got there, especially when Zach reached out and patted him on the shoulder and shot him one last empathetic look before departing.

Ten minutes later, he was dressed and sitting down in Coach's office.

Coach Blackburn was an undeniably intimidating figure. Still slim and still fit, he clearly possessed the same instincts he'd had when he'd been a player.

Before the season had begun, Brody had even been excited at how much better of a coach Blackburn was supposed to be than a player.

But that had faded, leaving feelings behind Brody didn't know how to identify.

"Brody," Coach said, steepling his fingers in front of him as he leaned back in his chair. "I'm glad you spoke up out there, with Elliott."

The funny thing was that Brody was actually regretting saying it. At least saying it like that. He should've been the one to defend his teammate and then pull Elliott aside after practice, like Ramsey was doing right now, and talk some sense into him.

"You haven't been as much of a team leader as I was promised, when I came in," Coach said bluntly.

Brody's stomach clenched.

Definitely not just hunger.

"Who told you that?" Brody asked.

That seemed—not *safe,* exactly—but *safer.*

Coach leaned forward, eyes intent on Brody. "It doesn't matter who said it or why. What matters is that you're detaching from this team and I'm not sure why." He paused. "I'm not sure *you* know why."

Brody told himself firmly not to squirm under that intense gray stare.

"This year just hasn't been what I expected." But before Coach could remind him that they'd only lost three games this year and won the rest, Brody plowed ahead. "Which isn't anything to do with you. Or the team. Just . . .I'm adjusting to the new vibe."

His dark eyebrows slanted. "Vibe?"

Brody laughed nervously. "I mean, just . . .not that there's anything *wrong* with how you're running the team, of course not, it's just very different than how Coach Nichols ran it."

"Here's the thing, Brody." Coach's face, so hard and craggy, suddenly softened, surprising the hell out of Brody. He'd been sure he was in for a shitty lecture after he'd said that. "I'm not only trying to win games, I'm trying to prep you for a career in the pros. You were drafted? That's fucking great. But it takes a lot more than that to make it. I know what it takes. Zach knows what it takes. That's partly why we're here. Why Zach wanted me to come back."

The door opened and Zach walked in, worry creasing his face. "You didn't wait," he said under his breath to his boss, but Coach just shrugged. "He was here, I was here," he said, tilting his head up and meeting Zach's eyes. "You didn't miss much."

Zach smiled. "Alright," he said, leaning back against the wall behind Coach's desk. "So, you wanna talk about it, Brody?"

"I was telling him how getting drafted and getting onto an NHL roster are two very different things," Coach said.

Zach nodded. "They are. That's what we're trying to do here. Do you know I was the last Evergreens player to sign an entry level contract? To make it onto a roster? And do you know when I left college?"

Brody shook his head. He hadn't realized this. But now that he did, it made more sense why Zach was brought in, and then he convinced Coach B to return, as well.

"Seven years ago. Seven years since the Evergreens have seen someone make it. If we're hard on you, that's why," Zach said. "We want to change that pattern."

"Not that we're gonna try to change it, but we're gonna actually *do* it," Coach echoed. He glanced back at Zach, and Zach nodded in agreement.

It was clear they were on the same page—and it was also clear that goal for the team and for the season was possibly the opposite of what he wanted. Or really, what he wasn't sure he wanted anymore.

He wasn't convinced enough he wanted to give up on a lifetime of goals and all that hard work and throw in the towel on hockey. And he wasn't convinced he wanted to spend the rest of his life in a lab or in a hospital. Would he regret walking away? He didn't want to be that person, full of bitter resentment.

"Brody," Zach said carefully, "you gotta think about what you want."

"I'm trying," he retorted. Annoyed that they were putting him on the spot.

"You say the right things, and you're out there every day on the ice, putting the work in, but I gotta wonder if your heart's in it," Coach said. His tone was gentle, but the admonition was there. *You gotta do more than just show up, kid.*

He didn't say anything for a long moment. He didn't know *what* to say.

"I want to keep my options open," he finally said. "The truth is, honest to God, I don't know what direction I'm gonna take, so the last thing I wanna do is close the door on something I might actually want."

"Good. Actually, I was hoping you'd say that." Coach looked approving, and then to Brody's surprise, he glanced behind him again, at Zach.

Zach's pose was relaxed, but Brody realized as he stared at the guy that was all surface level bullshit. He wasn't tense, exactly, but he was glancing over at the back of Coach's head, all the time. Like he was keeping an eye on him.

Maybe it was that Coach Blackburn had been *his* coach, when he'd played hockey for the Evergreens. Or maybe he was worried about Coach B cracking up again, since this was his first job after the death of his wife had left him grieving and lost.

Brody didn't know *what* those looks meant, but he did know they were at least a distraction from the something in his stomach that still felt like crawling away from this whole conversation.

"Were you really?" Brody couldn't help the question.

"Actually, I try *not* to be a tough guy," Coach said, his tense expression cracking neatly in half to reveal a surprisingly kind smile. "Right, Zach?" He glanced back at him *again*.

"Of course not," Zach said, and he was gazing right back. Did all assistants and head coaches look at each other this much and he'd missed it? Brody didn't think so. The only time he ever looked at someone like this . . .

Brody cut that thought off hard and fast, though he did think, and consider saying, *Just come and stand next to him, it'd be easier than giving your neck a cramp by turning to look at him every five seconds.*

But he didn't, because while Coach Blackburn might've revealed himself as sympathetic, he wasn't necessarily soft or the joking kind.

Zach they could poke fun at, a little, because he was still in his twenties and very much still a hockey bro.

But Coach was different. The whole team knew that.

"Yeah," Zach agreed. "You've got the skills, Brody. You've got the raw material, and even more than that, I'd argue. You're skating well. Your instincts are getting better. Other than the slight setback of the knee, you're right where the 'Canes want you, and in a few years, who knows? Maybe you'll end up on their roster. Maybe sent down to the developmental league for a year or two. But the potential's there."

"But not if you don't want it. Not if you don't put that extra effort in, the kind of effort that doesn't come from your brain," Coach added, shooting him another one of those hard-ass looks.

Brody didn't ask where it came from, because he already knew, and he wasn't sure yet if he had it.

But he'd find out, because it was looking like he didn't have much of a choice.

Either he dedicated himself, or he should call it quits.

"Listen, though, Brody . . ." Finally Zach walked around the side of the desk and put a reassuring hand on his shoulder and squeezed it. "Take the year. Figure your shit out. You were always gonna come back for your senior year, right?" When

Brody nodded, he continued. "Then spend this year figuring out if you want to be a pro hockey player, and then next year, all you'll need is to take that last little step up and you'll be there. I do expect though, that you'll keep working like you *do* want it. We don't accept less here, in Portland. Alright?"

Brody looked over at Coach, who didn't seem either surprised or bothered by Zach's declaration.

"You're okay with this?" he asked, because he couldn't help it. He needed to know.

Could he take the year?

He'd thought he'd have weeks, maybe, not months. And that didn't solve the problem, but it sure made it a hell of a lot easier to deal with.

"Zach wouldn't have said it if I wasn't," Coach said, his voice steady. "But if you phone it in—"

"I wouldn't," Brody interrupted.

"But if you *do*," Coach continued with a suddenly grim tone, "then the next conversation won't be so easy, okay?"

Brody nodded. "Okay." He could accept that—or at least, he was gonna have to.

Dean debated with himself for a full ten minutes before sending Brody the text.

It's what a friend would do, he argued with himself.

I got a great table in the library, he finally sent, before one side of his brain could point out to the other that all these things he was feeling weren't *only* platonic, **if you wanna join me.**

He knew Brody's practice had ended half an hour ago, and after he almost always studied somewhere. If not their apartment, then Koffee Klatch, or the library.

He'd not tried to memorize Brody's schedule, but he'd done it accidentally. Or at least that was the argument he continued to make.

They'd already met up twice this week for more study sessions, and even though the desires he couldn't quite deny kept pressing on him, insistent and undeniable, he was getting better at ignoring them in favor of just enjoying Brody's company.

If friendship was what Brody wanted to offer him, he'd take it—even if sometimes it felt like fate was playing the world's biggest cosmic joke on him.

Ha, guess you're not straight after all.

Ha, guess you're into the idea of sex way more than you ever wanted to be.

But not with just anyone.

Just one person. Just one *guy*.

One guy who doesn't seem interested in you. Not that way.

Dean shoved his phone away before he spent the next half an hour of important study time staring at the screen, waiting for Brody's reply to pop up on the screen.

And then, suddenly, it didn't matter, because he was right there, all Brody's pretty boy-ness on full display in a pair of gray sweatpants and a blue hoody that made his skin glow.

Jesus, you're a fucking wreck. Skin glow, my ass.

"Hey," Brody said, slipping into the seat opposite Dean without an invitation—and without an explanation of how he'd known exactly where Dean was without Dean telling him.

"Oh, uh, hey," Dean stammered.

"You're right, this *is* the best table in the library," Brody said with a teasing grin. Dean felt it lick right along his skin.

He took a deep breath and then let it out.

"Yeah, it is," Dean agreed. "That how you found me?"

Every time he didn't see Brody for hours—sometimes even for a day at a time—he always thought, *I can control this, I can overcome this*—but whenever Brody appeared in his proximity, it was clear just how deeply he'd slipped under his skin.

Dean wasn't even mad about it; only surprised, each and every time.

Okay, he was a *little* mad about it.

He'd be a lot *less* mad if somehow Brody made his way into his bed.

Even if he wanted that, even if by some miracle he landed there, you've got no fucking clue what to do with him.

"Yep." Brody grinned. "Close to the bathrooms. Close to the vending machines. And in the quietest corner. Means we won't be bothered."

Dean swallowed hard. "Yeah."

He, who so rarely even formed friendships, wanted to hoard every moment with Brody, holding them close, treating them like precious gems he secreted away for a bad day.

Wes would tell him he was fucked, which was why Dean hadn't told Wes about any of this, yet.

Dean tried to return to his textbook, but the words swam in front of his eyes. When he glanced up at Brody, Brody was staring at him, a puzzled expression on his face. And he hadn't gotten out his own books or the notebook he took class notes in yet.

You're something past fucked, if you know what kind of notebook he uses for notes.

"Everything okay?" Dean asked.

"Yeah, I just . . ." Brody didn't do almost anything awkwardly, but he was shrugging awkwardly now.

"You just what?" Dean asked.

"I had a weird meeting after practice with my coach. Coaches, actually." Brody made a face.

"You wanna talk about it?"

Brody made *another* face. "Not really, no. We're here to study, aren't we?"

"Are you gonna be able to study if you don't lay it out there? Talk it over?" Dean wanted to know.

Brody shrugged, still looking unsure.

And normally, *yeah,* Dean would be the first fucking guy to say, *leave me the hell alone,* but Brody hadn't done that to him, ever. Even during his whole pity party after the last game. He'd sat there and listened, even though it was crazy late at night. He'd, Dean realized later, *stayed up* for him. Waited for him to get home.

Even watched his football game even though he didn't give a shit about football.

But Dean was beginning to realize, that was what being Brody's friend meant. He gave a shit about *him.*

Other people did too—Wes was the most obvious example Dean could think of—but he'd never felt such a strong desire to turn it around and give that consideration right back.

"Come on," Dean said, "tell me about it." He wasn't the most persuasive guy in the universe; words had never been his thing. Actions were. And he knew action wouldn't work here, even as he felt the pull to reach under the table and just touch Brody.

"Coach figured out that I've been feeling . . .unmotivated," Brody admitted.

"I didn't realize it had gotten that bad."

Brody looked away. "I was hoping that nobody had realized it," he said. "I keep thinking it's gonna come back—the way I felt about hockey before I got injured—but it just *won't*."

"What did you do when you got hurt last year?" Dean asked. Because he didn't know what else to possibly say.

"I don't know, rehabbed the knee after I got cleared by the surgeon. Did everything I could in the gym to stay in shape—get in *better* shape."

Dean had had a front row seat, a glorious three-dimensional view, of how fit Brody's body was, just the other night. But he wasn't going to say it, so he nodded instead.

"And I guess . . ." Brody paused. "I did other stuff, too. Focused a lot on my classes, in a way I can't, really, when hockey's happening. Did extra reading. Dug into some lab stuff that interested me."

"So you filled that time with your science shit," Dean said.

Comprehension was dawning on Brody's face. "Yeah, I think so. I can't just . . .despite what you might think of me, I'm not just gonna sit on my ass and do *nothing*, just 'cause I can."

Dean heard the unspoken end of Brody's sentence. *Just 'cause my parents are rich.*

Yes, maybe he'd thought that once, but he hadn't believed that was true in at least a month, now.

"I know," he said. "And I'm sorry I ever thought that was true."

"Oh." Brody looked even more surprised.

"Yeah," Dean said, nodding. "You work hard. It shows."

"I must, if you're willing to be friends with me," Brody teased lightly.

"So, you had time last year to really dig into something that interested you. And it only interested you more, and now you come back, and you're playing hockey again but you're . . ." Dean didn't want to put words in Brody's mouth so he trailed off. Hoping that Brody might finish his thought for him.

And he did.

"Torn," Brody said. "I feel torn. But Coach also talked about how he and Zach are pushing us all to get us to that next level, and that's a lot of work we weren't doing before. And I don't dislike it, not exactly, but it's a lot to commit fully to a program like that if I'm having doubts."

"What else did your coach say?" Dean wondered.

"He gave me the season to figure my shit out, which . . .I'll give him this. It was more than I expected."

"More than I'd give you," Dean said, his tone deadpan.

Brody looked downright shocked for a moment, then he realized Dean was joking and he smiled and then even started laughing.

"Oh my God," he said, "Dean Scott makes an actual fucking joke. I should put it on the goddamn calendar and commemorate this day for years to come."

"Hey, I'm not *that* bad," Dean retorted lightly.

"Close, but yeah, you're pretty good, anyway," Brody said. He leaned across the table and patted Dean's hand. Or at least that was what he'd attempted to do, before Dean lost the rest of his mind and actually took his hand in his own, bigger one, and squeezed it.

And then didn't let it go.

His callouses rubbed against Brody's callouses, electricity running up his arm from the feel of their skin touching.

Brody's light brown eyes dilated and he caught his breath. Dean's own was pumping faster, like his lungs couldn't quite get enough air.

He'd been pretty sure that Brody's freakout and then his subsequent insistence that they be friends had been meant they'd *only* be friends.

But the way Brody was staring at him now didn't feel only platonic.

It felt loaded. Weighty. Like any moment Brody might lean over and kiss him again, obliterating that particular fallacy.

But then Brody tugged his hand away, and the moment disappeared.

Dean told himself he wasn't disappointed, but he was. He felt it, deep down, in his bones.

The craziest thing was that he hadn't even decided that *he* wanted Brody, though it wasn't like he thought the lie he was telling himself about being unsure was all that convincing these days.

The story he'd told himself about Brody being dramatic, about being too much trouble, too much distraction, had faded away in light of them becoming friends and hanging out more often.

The truth was, he'd found out that Brody was level-headed and nearly as focused as Dean was. Maybe he didn't know what the goal was, exactly, but he kept pushing forward. Kept striving, anyway. Made it impossible not to respect the hell out of the guy.

"I . . .uh . . ." Brody's hand was his own again, but Dean didn't miss how he stammered, still.

"Something else," he continued when Dean nodded. "There were some weird vibes in that meeting."

"What do you mean?"

"Like, I don't even know. Something off, or different, in the way Coach and Zach talked and even just freaking looked at each other."

"Like how?"

Brody met his gaze for one burning second and then glanced away. "I don't know. Like they were on a different wavelength, almost. Like they had a deeper connection. Maybe it's 'cause Coach used to be Zach's coach, too, back in the day. But it felt different even than that. More than just a coach or even a mentor. Like Zach was worried about him, and *aware* of him."

Dean tried to figure out exactly what Brody was trying to say without actually saying it.

"You mean he . . .he *likes* him, like that?"

"Maybe. Or he's . . .I don't know. Aware of him. But it goes both ways." Brody frowned.

"You didn't like it?"

"It . . .it worried me," Brody admitted. "Coach went through it when his wife died. Everyone knows that. Maybe he's vulnerable still, even though he tries to be a hard-ass."

"Maybe they're friends. Like we're friends." It was all Dean could think of to say.

Friends who might want more than to only *be friends.*

Brody looked shaken, like he'd thought it, but hadn't anticipated that Dean would actually say it out loud. *Dean* hadn't expected that he'd say it out loud, but then he had.

"I mean, *yeah*, sure. I . . .I guess," Brody said.

"Come on, let's get some studying done," Dean said, and Brody let out a breath. "You feel better, yeah?"

"Yeah," Brody said, but there was something else in his eyes, as his gaze met Dean's, right before he glanced down towards his books, that said the opposite.

That maybe Brody had asked more questions than he'd answered.

CHAPTER TEN

It was hot.

Okay, it wasn't *actually* hot. It was Portland in the fall, which meant it was drizzly and mid-forties and Brody spent most of his time bundled up in sweatshirts and sweatpants, trying to get feeling back into his toes.

No, it was just Brody. Just Brody, *right now*.

He'd been sitting in his room, trying to focus on writing up this homework assignment for his psychology class, when he'd heard the front door open and close and a few minutes later, the shower flip on.

The sound of the water went on and on and on, and the longer it did, the more distracted Brody got.

He didn't have a particularly good imagination—he was a fucking scientist, alright?—but ever since their first hookup, it felt like Brody couldn't stop thinking about it.

About Dean's hard body and water cascading down it.

What he could be doing for so long in the shower.

His hand sliding down ridged abs. He'd have a big cock, because Brody was all too aware of how big the rest of him was. And Brody, who hadn't ever thought he'd be interested in one that didn't belong to him, found himself grower hotter and hotter at only the thought of Dean's.

That one night, he'd barely touched it. Hadn't gotten to explore more. Of course, at the time, he'd been so shocked at the thought of how brilliant the whole experiment was that he probably wouldn't have been ready to. Not the way he wanted to, now that he'd had time to adjust to the idea. To accept it.

He wanted Dean.

He wasn't sure Dean wanted *him*, though.

Brody let out a deep breath, feeling unbearably hot under the collar. He'd already stripped off his sweatshirt and now he did the same with his T-shirt, tossing it onto the bed.

It didn't help. Not enough. Sweat still prickled along his skin, like it was suddenly too tight, and his cock? It was half-hard in his sweatpants, and he nearly stripped *those* off, too, but if he did, he'd only end up getting himself off.

And if he'd learned anything about jerking off in the last few weeks, it was that ultimately, it just wasn't satisfying. Not anymore. If he did it, in an hour he'd be hot and hard again, ready to go.

He'd gone out of his way to become friends with Dean, because it turned out not only did he definitely lust after him, he just plain fucking *liked* him. But all this hanging out and liking had only made his lust burn so much hotter.

You're not a fucking coward. Go knock on his door and ask him for a repeat. He didn't have a bad time. You definitely didn't have a bad time. Why can't you just experiment again?

What would Dean do if he did it?

Shut the door in his face?

Or welcome him in?

"Fuck this," Brody said, and he stood, shoving his chair back and headed out into the hallway.

But instead of turning in the direction of Dean's room, he went into the kitchen.

A nice cold drink. That was what he needed. Or maybe to hold an ice pack to his crotch and cool himself down once and for all.

But as soon as he walked into the dimly lit kitchen, he stopped in his tracks.

"Fuck me," Brody muttered under his breath.

Dean was in the kitchen, in front of the open refrigerator, only wearing a pair of tight black boxer briefs clinging to his shapely ass and his muscled thighs. His arms were braced on each side of the open door and his back was a fucking work of art, all smooth rippling muscle.

He turned.

His hair was still damp from his shower, and there was at least two days of thick black scruff dusting his jaw.

He looked wild and rough and Brody *burned*. His body so hot, it was amazing his bare feet didn't sizzle against the linoleum.

So much for cooling down.

Dean's gaze swept over him, head to toe, and not for the first time, Brody swore that he wasn't the only one currently suffering from this standoff. Because that was what it *had* to be, right? Brody couldn't possibly be the only one feeling this way. Caught between desire and restraint.

Then Dean pushed off from the fridge and prowled closer. Brody's breath caught in his chest as he stopped right in front of him.

Neither of them had said a word yet. Brody because words had permanently dried up. Dean . . .well, it wasn't like he was a man of many words, anyway.

"You're bruised," Dean finally said, voice low and rough. Reaching out, Brody swore he wasn't fucking breathing as he gently traced the edges of the bruise on the curve of his torso that he'd gotten during the last game, when one of the opposing players had shoved him a little too hard into the boards.

"Uh, yeah," Brody said, barely managing to unstick his tongue.

Saying something brilliant and/or witty was a fucking pipe dream, especially with Dean touching him like that.

"Does it hurt?"

He'd already established there was no blood in his goddamn brain, and so it wasn't all that much of a shock when he laid out the blunt truth. "No, that's not really what hurts."

A dark eyebrow quirked upward. "Yeah?" Dean asked. He was close enough that it would be so easy to just reach up and *take*. But Brody had enough of his mind left that he wasn't going to do it if he wasn't positive Dean wanted it, too. They were friends, now, after all, and he was pretty sure you weren't supposed to go around kissing your friends, uninvited.

But that gentle, purposeful touch sure as hell *felt* like an invitation.

Tilting his head back, Brody took in those light green eyes. Piercing and intense. It felt like they could see all the way through him. Through all his pretenses. All his bullshit.

And pretending he didn't want Dean was a fucking *ton* of bullshit.

"You gonna tell me what hurts?" Dean asked again. His lips curled up into a knowing grin.

Brody took a deep breath and then another. Every bit of the air smelled like Dean. *Felt* like Dean. "Every bit of me, every second I don't do this," he said and settled a hand on all that bunched muscle on Dean's shoulder.

Their lips met at the same time.

If the first time had been a hesitant experiment, this was a conflagration, burning out of control from the first brush of their mouths together.

Brody knew what *he* wanted, and it was pretty damn clear Dean wanted the same thing. At least now that his mouth was on Brody's and he was kissing him fiercely, tongue slipping into his mouth, hands curled around Brody's waist, digging into his skin like he wanted to leave his own marks.

They stumbled across the little kitchen and Brody's hip hit the edge of the back counter as he panted into Dean's mouth, trying to give as good as he was getting.

It was the wildest kiss he'd ever had, full of intense longing, and Brody realized, with a hard clanging realization, that he hadn't been the only one wanting this. Craving this.

He pulled his mouth off Dean's, breathless. Dean's chest was rising and falling just as hard as Brody's own. "Why didn't you say?"

Dean chuckled, but he didn't look upset. In fact he looked . . .

Brody swallowed hard.

He could feel the ridge of Dean's hard, muscled thigh against his and that wasn't the only thing that was hard, either.

If Brody had been hot before, he was scorching now.

"Why didn't *you* say?" Dean retorted lightly.

"I . . .uh . . .well, that's a damn good question," Brody admitted.

"You said we were just gonna be friends, but here's the thing, I don't usually want to strip my friends naked and explore every inch of their bodies," Dean said.

The top of Brody's head blew right off, and the only appropriate response he could come up with was to kiss him again, hard, pouring everything *he'd* thought about into it.

Dean's hands slid up, cupped his cheeks, and it wasn't tender, not exactly, but it was full of . . .*something*. Not just heat, not anymore.

But there was plenty of heat, too, if Dean's hard cock was any indication. Brody knew he had to be feeling his, too, and he nearly said *fuck it* and just rubbed it against Dean's muscled body, openly chasing pleasure.

"You can't say shit like that," Brody said, after he broke the kiss. "You really fucking can't say it."

"Why not?" Amusement—and arousal—glinted in Dean's pale green gaze.

"'Cause that's gonna make me just hump your leg and not feel an ounce of shame."

It was only the truth, but it was wondrous what Brody's confession did to Dean.

His brows slammed together, pupils dilating even further, and Brody swore he felt his cock twitch against his thigh.

His fingers itched to explore it, to feel what that hard ridge was like.

But he held back.

It wasn't really fear or uncertainty. It was clear they both wanted each other. Instead it was a foolhardy desire to prolong this moment as long as possible.

Because Brody knew the moment they touched each other, it was going to be game over. He was too hot and worked up, and he had a feeling Dean was the same.

"Well, don't let me stop you from doing it," Dean teased in a low voice. "Maybe I want you to do it."

"Kiss me," Brody half-moaned, half-begged, and then he was, the two of them wrapped up in each other, Dean's bigger body pressing him into the counter.

Brody couldn't help himself. Not when the pressure of Dean's thigh was so delicious, exactly the pleasure he wanted so desperately, the kind of feeling that he couldn't stop himself from chasing any longer.

"Come on, take it," Dean groaned into his mouth, and Brody did what he was told.

Took everything he wanted, their tongues stroking, his body thrusting against Dean's, his thrusts becoming more and more uncontrolled because of the need coiling hard and insistent at the bottom of his belly.

He needed just a little more. Pressure. Or *something*.

Then Dean slipped a hand down his stomach, those calloused fingers sending shivers up his spine, and he cupped his cock in his palm. Two strokes later, that was all it took, and Brody's whole world was rocked to its foundations as he came and came and came, shuddering hard with the power of his orgasm.

Brody came down from what he could only describe as a fucking *high*. And he'd only been humping against Dean's thigh and then his hand.

Imagine what it would feel like if they did *more*.

Heat spiked through him at just the thought. It wasn't the insistent blaze of before, because he'd finally gotten some relief, but it was hot enough that he knew this orgasm wouldn't be enough to forestall it forever.

He was going to want a hell of a lot more.

Speaking of more . . .

Dean was still, unnaturally so, as he watched Brody come back down to earth—and Brody realized then that *he* hadn't come.

This is your chance, his brain whispered. *You wanted to see. Then see.*

"Is this okay?" Brody asked, reaching down and cupping Dean's cock, much the same as he'd done to him only a minute ago.

Dean nodded, face tense with need.

"How about this?" Brody steeled himself—reminding himself exactly how much he wanted this exact thing—and slipped his hand inside those tight black boxer briefs.

Dean was big and hot against his hand, twitching against the pressure he was already giving it.

"Yeah," he ground out, head tipping back, wonder filling his whole face.

Brody had never done this to anybody but himself, but surely it wasn't so hard to just copy what *he* liked and try it on Dean.

A second experiment, of sorts.

His cock was wet at the tip, and Brody spread the moisture down, making his movements a little smoother, a little easier.

"Fuck," Dean groaned, his Adam's apple bobbing.

It was glorious to bring a guy like this, big and powerful with so much self-control, to his metaphorical knees. It was intoxicating, like the best high in the whole goddamn world. Better than any drink that Brody had ever tried.

"You want more?" Brody asked.

He wasn't ready to get to *his* knees and try a blowjob, but he could at least give himself a little more room to work. With his other hand, he slid Dean's boxer briefs down his thighs and couldn't help but look down. To watch as his hand wrapped around Dean's cock and gave him an experimental stroke.

"Harder. Faster." Dean was lost to it, and Brody wasn't even sure he was aware he was giving orders.

But Brody didn't mind. He *liked* doing what Dean liked.

He squeezed harder, giving it to him a little rougher, like he liked when he got close, when he just needed a tiny bit more stimulation to tip right over the edge.

It must've been the same for Dean, because a second later he was falling apart, breath sawing out of his lungs in big gulps of air, his cock going rock-hard in Brody's hand and then spurting come between them.

Brody tried to catch it all, but he missed some, a few drops falling to the floor.

He worked him through the pleasure, and only once Dean began to flinch he moved his hand, reaching for a paper towel from the holder.

He cleaned his hand and then dipped down to the floor, to clean up there, too.

When he rose back up, Dean was staring at him.

He'd looked at him like that before. Like he was a problem Dean couldn't quite solve.

But now it was ever so slightly different. Like Dean was finally beginning to figure him out.

Well, Brody didn't think it was all that complicated. He had a major hard-on for the guy, *and* he liked him as a friend.

"That was good," Dean said.

He was not quite as awkward as he'd been the first time, and Brody had to say *he* was handling it a hell of a lot better. No freakouts here. He'd touched a dick that wasn't his own and jerked Dean off to what seemed to be a pretty damn good orgasm, and he wasn't panicking at all.

In fact, he was already wondering when they could do it again. Maybe they'd actually make it to a bed this time.

"Just good?" Brody teased.

Dean's eyes fluttered. He had surprisingly long, surprisingly pretty eyelashes. Spiky and dark, framing those light eyes beautifully. "Okay, you caught me. Best orgasm I can remember."

"Let's not fuck around anymore," Brody said.

Dean raised an eyebrow. And okay, *fair*, that was not really what he'd meant.

"I *mean*," Brody regrouped, "let's fuck around some more. A lot more, actually."

"Yeah?"

"Do you want that?" Brody had noticed Dean liked to answer questions with other questions. It was annoying, but not surprising.

Still, he'd thought he'd managed to get under those walls at this point, at least for a little while.

Dean didn't say anything for a long minute. And this time, there was no awkwardness. Dean was standing there, in the dim light of their kitchen, pants around his ankles, dick hanging out, and he wasn't looking away from Brody or looking like he wanted to run away.

And Brody had to wonder if last time, a lot of that awkwardness he'd felt had actually come from *him*. If he'd been so shocked and so floored and so overwhelmed by his world expanding around him in that dizzying rush that he'd imagined Dean felt the same.

But maybe Dean hadn't felt the same.

From the way it was looking now, he hadn't.

"Listen," Brody said when he couldn't take that long, slow perusal of Dean's gaze any longer, "I know I didn't react very well the last time we did this."

Dean raised an eyebrow again.

"Okay, I reacted like total shit. Ran off like a complete asshole," Brody retorted.

"It was a big thing."

"Not just for me," Brody pointed out dryly.

"We're all gonna react to the news that we're not always what we thought we were differently," Dean drawled. "So, yeah, no, you didn't. But it's alright. I just thought . . .you wouldn't want to do it again. Then you were so insistent on being friends . . ."

"That's a lot of words for you," Brody teased.

Dean shot him a look that seared him all the way to his toes.

"I don't want there to be any more confusion. I liked it. I liked it then. I liked it tonight. I'd do it some more, if you wanted."

"And you want to, too?" Brody asked, hating how insecure he sounded.

Dean shook his head, a glimmer of a smile emerging on his face. "Pretty boy, I thought it was plenty obvious what I wanted."

"Alright, then," Brody said, smiling, because it turned out he couldn't hide his delight at this—or his incredulity. They'd been dancing around each other these last few weeks, when they could've been doing *this*.

Whatever *this* was.

Maybe they couldn't put a name on it—maybe *Brody* couldn't put a name on it, yet—but he knew he wanted to keep doing it.

Wasn't sure he could *stop* doing it.

"Anytime you want me, you just gotta say," Dean said, and Brody could appreciate how both of them were making an effort to avoid the same kind of misunderstanding that had plagued them these last few weeks.

"And what about you?" Brody slid closer and didn't stop himself from doing what he wanted, which was to put his hands back on that amazing body. Right onto those broad shoulders, curling his fingertips into the muscle there.

Dean laughed. "Oh, you don't gotta worry about me."

"No?"

"Trust me, I'm gonna be bothering you," Dean said lightly, leaning down and brushing a quick, reassuring kiss across his lips.

"Good," Brody said, nodding. "And you know what else? I didn't tell you we were gonna be friends just because I wanted . . ." *You. This.* "Uh . . ." He gestured between them.

"You're not that kind of guy, Faulkner. Never imagined you were. Don't worry. I get it. Friends with benefits?"

Brody hadn't known what label he wanted to put on it, but he supposed that worked as well as any other. And *Dean* had been the one to suggest it.

"Works for me," Brody said. "You ever done this before?"

Dean shot him another of those disbelieving looks, and he'd *just* come, so it shouldn't have heated him up the way it did.

"You know I haven't," Dean said.

"No, I mean . . .like a casual friendly hookup," Brody said. He'd never imagined he was good at this, but he was worse than he'd expected.

"No, not really. But we'll figure it out." Dean paused, his loose grip around Brody's waist tightening. "But no more bull-shit, okay? I don't do drama."

It was a warning. Brody knew it.

"No worries. I've definitely worked through my gay freak-out," Brody said lightly.

"Well, next time, text me and we'll do it together."

"Oh my God, you made *another joke.*"

Dean rolled his eyes, but he was smiling, eyes crinkling at the corners.

"I do that, sometimes."

Brody reached up and patted him on the cheek. "I'm sure you do, big guy."

"I . . .I," Dean stuttered a bit, and oh *hey*, here was a little of that awkwardness. But instead of letting it turn him off, Brody was only amused and enchanted.

"Use your words. I know you can, now," Brody teased.

"I've got to do some homework, still," Dean admitted. "I want to hang out, but . . ." He shrugged.

"I get it. Me too. I just came in here because I was thinking about you in the shower—"

"Hey, guess what, I was thinking about *you* in the shower." Dean grinned.

Brody made a face. "Don't even tease me like that. I was sure that was what you were doing, and I got . . .well, *hot* thinking about it."

"Was pretty hot. Hot enough that I was ready to go again, just now."

Brody laughed. He hadn't been entirely sure, but *yes*, they could have this easy friendship that they'd been building *and* indulge in that undeniable heat between them.

"Too bad that shower's too small for the both of us," Brody said.

"Yeah," Dean agreed.

Brody knew this was his cue to disentangle himself from Dean's body. But it was so big and warm and he didn't want to let go.

But a hookup would let him go. Especially because he said he had homework, still.

So he did, moving away, hating how his pulse eventually returned to normal. Detouring to the fridge, even though he wasn't particularly hungry or thirsty, figuring it would be a good cover.

It was. Dean righted his clothes and then leaned against the counter.

"We're home on Saturday," he said. "Wes invited me to a party and I told him I'd pass, but maybe you'd want to go."

Brody almost asked, *with you?* But that would make it sound like a date, when really it was just two bros hanging out. Two bros who'd probably be hooking up after.

"Sure," he said instead. "Our game's Saturday afternoon, same as yours, yeah? So sure, I'm free. Might as well."

Dean gave a sharp nod. "Sounds good," he said and then gestured towards his room. "I better get going or I'm not gonna want to study at all."

Brody grinned. "Better do it then."

"You're really coming tonight?" Wes asked as he flopped down in the big chair in the football common room.

Their game was in six hours, and even though the team had done their walkthrough the night before, the coaches always wanted their players at the facility long before warmups started.

Some of the guys did homework. Others played the games in the common room—foosball and pool and half a dozen pinball machines against the back wall.

In an hour or so they'd have their team meal, and Coach would give them one last pregame speech before they headed to the locker room to get dressed for warmups.

"I said I was," Dean said.

He hadn't seen Brody yesterday—he'd had classes and then a game of his own—but when he'd texted him asking him if he was still coming after his second game of the weekend, Brody had sent him a thumbs-up emoji.

"Yeah, but you've been impossible to pin down lately. Even more impossible than normal," Wes said.

"Don't know what you mean," Dean said, but he knew. Even before a few nights ago in the kitchen, he and Brody had been spending a lot of time together. Studying. Working out. Hanging out.

You're friends. That's allowed.

'Course he's also a friend you desperately want to kiss.

"No, you wouldn't." Wes chuckled. "But seriously, man, what is going on?"

Dean knew he should be able to tell his *other* friend, his other friend who also happened to be queer, too, about Brody. But he hadn't, yet. Didn't know how to even begin.

If he did, it would probably make things easier, because Wes was always harassing him about being such a lone wolf.

Of course, if he did tell Wes, he'd probably make more of it than there was. Assume they were going somewhere other than the bedroom.

Dean was a realist; maybe Brody had made it past his gay freakout, but they were headed in two very different directions. Dean would, God willing, get drafted to the NFL and Brody would have to decide between the science shit he loved so much and a pro career in hockey.

There wasn't a future here, no matter how Wes might want to dress it up.

"Nothing much," Dean said. He didn't like lying to his friend, but he wasn't sure what else he could say. But naturally, that didn't really stop him in the end. Brody's name was in his mouth before he could even help himself. "Been hanging out with Brody some."

"Your roommate Brody? Hockey player Brody?"

Dean nodded.

"And that's good? You like him?"

"Why wouldn't it be? He's a good guy. A friend."

Wes smacked a hand across his heart and exclaimed, "Oh my God, so you *can* make friends."

Dean rolled his eyes. "We're friends, aren't we?"

"Yes, but I had to practically badger you into it," Wes said.

And yeah, that was probably true. Two years ago, Dean could admit that he'd been even worse about it, insistent on being painfully focused to the exclusion of just about everything else.

"So did Brody," Dean said. Though it wasn't like he'd put up much of a fight, either. He'd liked Brody almost from the very beginning. Even before he'd really begun to let go of his resentment of their very different childhoods.

"I'm glad he did." Wes paused. "You shouldn't be alone so goddamn much."

"If I'm alone, it's 'cause I chose to be," Dean reminded him. "Not everyone has got to be some social butterfly."

"No, but there's a happy medium, too. You know that. And I'm glad you're finally doing something about it. So you're bringing Brody to the party. That's good."

"Not *bringing* him," Dean retorted, and he knew the moment the words were out of his mouth that he'd gotten too defensive. That he'd exposed something he hadn't been ready to share.

Wes smiled slow and easy. "No?"

"He's . . ." Dean considered continuing pretending otherwise, but maybe this was inevitable. And maybe he could use a little advice. He felt out of his depth, with this thing with Brody. Technical knowledge he could glean from an internet search, but it was so much more than that.

"He's what?" Wes was still smiling, knowingly.

"He's a good guy, that's all. A nice guy."

"Attractive, too."

"I noticed that."

Wes raised an eyebrow. "Oh, you did?"

Dean told himself firmly not to flush bright fucking red. "I called him pretty boy, from the beginning."

"You got a crush," Wes guessed. "I don't want it to seem like I'm dissuading you from having one, because it's a fucking *amazing* thing that you're finally looking at *anybody* and thinking about more than just your future, but based on a few things Ramsey's mentioned, he's not gonna swing that way."

"Well, about that," Dean said and then hesitated again. Not that he thought Wes was gonna go around talking out his ass about Brody's sexual preferences, but it wasn't his place to say.

"Oh, he *does*," Wes said. And it was him guessing, not Dean admitting it, so he nodded.

"But it's not . . .not common knowledge."

"About you either," Wes pointed out. "Not that I didn't think if the right guy caught your eye, you wouldn't do anything about it. You're remarkably free from that kind of angst. But the catching your eye part was going to be toughest part of that whole thing."

Brody caught it alright.

"Yeah," Dean agreed. Because it was true.

"So you're what . . .dating now?"

"No, no," Dean said hurriedly. He should have led with that. "Just . . .just friends. Friends and hooking up. And it's good so don't try to convince me to overthink it."

Wes shot him a fond look. "Like anyone could get you to overthink *anything* if you didn't want to."

"You're not bothered by that?"

"By you being friends with benefits with the hockey player? Why would I be?"

"I don't know. Maybe you'd want me to be like . . .madly in love with him, or something," Dean muttered.

Wes just laughed. "No, I'm thrilled you're doing just *this*. Something you've picked for yourself."

"Sometimes I think Brody picked *me*," Dean said. After all, he'd been the one to suggest the initial experiment on the couch. Of course, Dean could have not been interested. Could have said no. But he'd thought, *what the hell* and then *what the hell,* again.

"Well, he's got good taste," Wes said approvingly. "Anything you need to know? Google and lube are your friends, but then you're not stupid."

"Figured those." Dean could hear how gruff his voice had gotten. He was already thinking about it. About everything he and Brody had done. Everything they hadn't. Things they'd need that lube for. He cleared his throat.

"No questions, then?"

"Well, uh . . ." Dean had thought he could ask about this easier than he could, but in the end, it turned out this was more nerve-wracking than he'd imagined.

"Just ask me, Dean. I promise. No judging." Wes shot him a quicksilver smile. "Not like you haven't learned more about me and Marcus than you ever wanted to know."

"That's true," Dean retorted. He'd even walked in on them more than once.

"Well, there's nothing stopping you, then," he said.

Nothing except his pride.

"How do you . . .you know . . .*decide* who's gonna do . . ." Dean trailed off, not sure if he hated himself more for asking this or Wes for convincing him to ask in the first place.

"Oh come on, I'm dying of anticipation here," Wes said. "I'm practically *begging* you to ask me now."

"How do you decide who . . .uh . . .does the butt stuff?"

Dean couldn't help his face from flaming bright red when Wes threw his head back and laughed and laughed and laughed.

"I'm sorry, I'm so sorry, but you should see your *face*," Wes said, still cackling.

Dean nearly got up and left. It hadn't been easy for him to ask, and Wes finding his question hilarious had been almost the last straw. This was why he hadn't wanted to talk about it.

But Wes knew him—knew him better than anybody, probably—and right before he hefted himself out of the chair, Wes leaned over and put a hand on his arm and his expression softened from hilarity to empathy.

"I shouldn't have laughed, I'm sorry," Wes repeated, but this time he genuinely looked like he regretted it. "I just wasn't expecting that or for you to say it like that."

"How else am I supposed to say it?" Dean demanded.

Wes shook his head. "It was fine. It was perfect. I'm just saying—you don't usually talk about sex."

"I'm not usually having sex," Dean retorted.

"Exactly. But I'm glad you are. I'm glad you're exploring this part of you, and without shame, too. That's a big thing. I . . .uh . . .truth be told, there isn't a right answer. It's what you two decide together. Maybe it's one of you, maybe it's both of you, maybe it's *none* of you."

"None?"

"What have you done so far?" Wes asked.

Dean's face went bright red again. "Uh. Barely anything. Honestly. We both get so worked up just from kissing we just . . ."

Wes' expression softened even further. "I'm happy for you, you know that?"

"It's not . . .it's not like that," Dean stuttered. But he was thinking, even though he'd been the one to label it, telling Brody that they were going to be friends with benefits, that it was already more than that for him.

He didn't let people in close. But he'd let Brody in.

And it definitely wasn't a platonic thing, because Brody made him sweat like nobody else had, ever.

Still, it made sense to try to keep it casual. In two years, he'd be drafted, and Brody would be doing something brilliant. Science or hockey, it didn't matter which, 'cause he was good at both.

They'd probably end up on opposite sides of the country, and well, Dean already knew it was better to not get too attached.

"But it *could* be like that," Wes said softly, earnestly.

Dean shrugged. "I don't know. I like the guy, as a friend. As . . .as . . .as more, I guess. But you know the situation. Better than most."

"Yeah," Wes agreed. "You know how guilty I feel, making Marcus wait around on me, his future being determined by *my* future."

"But he chose that," Dean reminded him.

"Yeah, and neither of you are choosing that, I get it. And you shouldn't. But this is *still* a real good thing, Dean. I can still be happy you have it."

It was not very hard to agree. "Yeah, me too," he said.

"About the butt stuff—"

"Oh my God," Dean interrupted.

"I *mean* it. It can be one of you or both of you or *none* of you. You like what you've done so far?"

Dean could only nod, helplessly. They'd barely touched each other yet. Never even made it to a bed. And yet even the thought of Brody had him in a chokehold.

"Then, keep doing whatever feels good. There's no obligation to ever go there. Not if you don't want to. I'm going to make a suggestion that you're going to veto—"

"Then don't make it," Dean inserted before he could continue.

"No, 'cause if you're not gonna talk nuts and bolts . . ." Wes paused, chuckling under his breath. "Then this *really* isn't a bad idea. Watch some porn. Decide what you like. What you don't like. And then *talk* about it with him."

"I'm really not sure I can," Dean said. Not like he didn't occasionally watch porn now, but he'd never watched it with the primary aim of discovering what he wanted to do.

"Oh come on, you can watch regular porn, you can watch gay porn," Wes teased.

"That isn't the problem." Dean wasn't going to admit he'd already done it once, in the week after his first hookup with Brody. When he'd thought Brody wouldn't be willing to do it again, and he'd been going out of his mind with how much he needed some kind of relief.

He'd gotten thirty seconds into the video—they'd still only been kissing and petting, nobody had even touched anybody's dick yet—and he'd blown his load.

It had been embarrassing, and also illuminating.

"Then what's the problem?"

He couldn't say, *I want so many things, so badly, I can't even get to the good stuff.*

"I . . ." Dean found himself flustered now. Just talking about it. By *thinking* about it. "I'll try it."

Wes raised an eyebrow. "I guess this was always inevitable," he conceded.

"What was inevitable?"

"When you finally found someone you wanted enough to have sex with, I could've guessed you'd become obsessed with it. The way the rest of us are."

"I'm not—"

But this time Wes didn't let *him* finish. "You are, and it's alright. It's a perfectly human thing. As long as it doesn't distract you on the field."

"Do you really think I'd let that happen?" Dean asked dryly.

"No way," Wes agreed with a smile.

CHAPTER ELEVEN

BRODY DIDN'T KNOW WHAT to expect from the party.

He knew he'd surprised the hell out of Ramsey, who'd been all ready to drag him to it, forcibly if necessary, but then he'd just said simply that Dean had already invited him.

"Dean invited you and you just said yes, just like that?" Ramsey ripped the tape off his hands, shedding it like skin into the trash can in front of him.

"Yeah, I said yes, just like that," Brody retorted.

They'd won by a goal today, squeaking by a very good Eastern Washington team one to zip, and while Brody thought he'd played decently enough, he knew his focus hadn't been everything it could be.

There'd been more than once their sly, fast forward had slipped right past him, making a break for it, and he'd had to push hard, skating as fast and as nimbly as he was able to catch up with him. Ramsey had shot him a look or two, and Zach had leaned down, during one of his breaks, and asked him if he was alright.

He was—and he wasn't.

What he was, was fucking hanging in there, by his fingernails. Trying to get used to living under this cloud of uncertainty.

Ramsey shot him a look. Not dissimilar to the looks Brody had gotten during the game. "If only it was always that easy with you," he said.

After the conversation with Coach B, Brody had finally understood that nothing was going to go back to normal. This was the new normal, and the only way to deal with it was to go right through it.

'Course that didn't mean it was particularly enjoyable.

Brody sure as hell wasn't having a good time.

Ironically, the only thing about his life that felt free and easy and relatively straightforward was Dean.

"I'm not some kind of dramatic, complicated guy," Brody argued, but these days, he kinda was, wasn't he? He felt like a garbage fire, in human form.

"So you say," Ramsey said. He finished with the tape and began to shuck his equipment next.

Brody had already dumped his into the big bin for the equipment manager to clean and repair and get set for the next game.

He turned to head to the showers, but Ramsey's hand on his arm stopped him.

"What I want to know," Ramsey said, still casual, the opposite of his grip on Brody's arm, "is what's going on between you two."

"Me and Dean?" Brody knew his voice went high and squeaky, like it always did when he was lying.

"You and Dean," Ramsey repeated steadily.

"I . . .I told you, we're friends," Brody stuttered.

"Such good friends, all of a sudden, that you're gonna go to a party just because he asks you. *You*, who's being even cagier than usual?"

"I'm not being—"

"Yeah," Ramsey cut off. "That's bullshit. Don't blow me off with bullshit. I let you get away with not talking about it before, but it's gone further than that. *Obviously.*"

Brody took a deep breath. Ramsey was one of his best friends. "I like him. We're . . .uh . . .hooking up."

Ramsey raised an eyebrow. "You're welcome," he said.

"What is that supposed to mean?" Brody had imagined Ramsey reacting a bunch of different ways when he finally came out. Incredulity. Shock. He'd been sure that one of Ramsey's immediate responses would've been something like, *if you were gonna experiment with a guy, why not do it with me?*

But none of those turned out to be right.

Instead, of course, Ramsey was going to take credit for the whole fucking thing.

"I mean, *you're welcome* for calling him up and suggesting he move in with you."

Brody rolled his eyes. He grabbed his bag, slid his feet into his slides, and headed towards the showers. "You're ridiculous."

"And you're the one hooking up with him." Ramsey paused. "Is that all it is? A hookup?"

"Yeah of course. What else is it gonna be?" Brody challenged.

Ramsey shrugged. "You're the one who isn't sure he wants to play hockey anymore."

"How do you know that?" *Nobody* knew that. Just Coach B, Zach, and Dean. And Brody never would've thought *any* of those guys would've blabbed about it.

"It's not that hard to tell," Ramsey said bluntly. "You're all up your own ass lately, more broody than usual."

Brody wanted to tell Ramsey his assessment was not only totally unfair, but totally fucking wrong, but well . . .it wasn't really either of those things, was it?

"Do you think everybody knows?" Brody asked in a soft voice as he flipped the shower on. Ramsey took the one next to him and shook his head.

"Everyone else is all up their *own* ass, trying to impress Coach B. Elliott's trying to lone wolf it out. Finn's a mess, one goal away from breaking down. Mal's trying to keep it all together. Ivan's just trying to stay out of it."

"And you?"

Ramsey's pale blue eyes were intent on Brody. "You know I don't miss a thing, Faulkner."

He knew it.

Ramsey patted him on the arm. "You're gonna be fine."

"No admonitions that I'm going to eventually pick the right thing, AKA hockey?"

But Ramsey didn't say anything. Just stared at him.

It was frustratingly both a non-answer and an answer, at the same time.

"Yeah, thanks," Brody muttered and shoved his head under the spray.

The party was in full swing, people spilling out of the frat house not only onto the Gamma Sigma lawn but all of them, up and down frat row.

There'd been a home football game today, *and* the hockey game, and with both Evergreens teams winning, the students of Portland U were ready to celebrate.

"There's Dean," Ramsey said, gesturing to where Dean stood in the corner of the living room, in a T-shirt and worn jeans, fitting him like a fucking glove. "You gonna go jump in his arms?"

Brody smacked him in the chest. "Don't be an ass."

Ramsey just grinned. "But that's my natural state."

"Exactly."

But it turned out that Dean walked over to *him*, ditching the guys he'd been talking to. They looked like football players, too, but then *nobody* looked the part as much as Dean Scott did.

Brody's throat went a little dry as he tilted his head back, taking in Dean's impressive body.

He knew what that body felt like. Maybe tonight, he'd discover what it tasted like.

"Hey," Dean said. They didn't touch or hug—and definitely they didn't kiss—even though Brody wanted to. Instead he shoved his hands into his jean pockets to help him better resist the urge.

"Hey. Heard you guys won today."

"By two touchdowns," Dean said, nodding. "And you guys won, too."

"Yeah," Brody said. He wanted to say, *though I'm not sure I had anything to do with that.* But he didn't. This was a party.

He didn't need to be a depressed sad sack, angsting, like Ramsey said, about all these things he couldn't change.

"Come on, let's get a beer," Dean said, and even though he didn't reach out and touch Brody, Brody swore he could feel his hand ghosting across the small of his back as they walked towards the back of the house.

Even though neither of them was publicly out—Brody didn't even know what he'd label himself, honestly, only that he *liked* Dean—he wanted him to do it anyway, damn the consequences.

He didn't know what that said about him, except that he was down bad to the man behind him.

Ramsey had already found his way behind the bar and was eyeing the two of them with interest. "You guys want shots?" he asked. "Or something else?"

"I'm just gonna grab us some beers," Dean said, reaching into the cooler and pulling two out with only one of his big hands. He popped the tops off and handed one to Brody.

Dean didn't say, *I want to remember this night, every single technicolor moment of it*, but maybe he didn't need to. Because Brody was thinking it anyway.

"To winning," Dean said, clinking his bottle with Brody's. Brody nodded and they both took a sip.

"You do anything else freaking unreal and completely inhuman today?" Brody asked, because that was easier than talking about his own game, where it felt like he'd barely been hanging on.

Dean blushed. It was adorable. "Just the usual."

Wes approached and draped an arm around Dean's shoulders—not the easiest thing in the world, considering his height—and said, "If you call the usual two and a half sacks and like half a dozen pressures. The poor QB opposite me barely had time to set his feet the whole game."

"I'm not sure why you know my stats," Dean said.

"It's 'cause he's your friend," Brody said. "You know his, don't you?"

Dean glanced over at Wes. "What, three hundred some-odd yards, and three touchdowns, right?"

Wes smiled. "Exactly."

"Yep, you two are definitely unreal," Brody said.

"Like you're not killing it too," Wes scoffed.

But Dean didn't say anything. Just met Brody's eyes, and there was a hidden concern—a hidden question—in his gaze. *Was it okay? You doing okay?*

He nodded briefly, and Dean smiled, the corner of his mouth tilting up.

"I'm doing my part," Brody said.

"Eastern has got this slippery asshole," Ramsey chimed in. "We had our hands full today."

"But we handled him." If Ramsey hadn't been there, Brody didn't know if he'd have been able to, but Ramsey was playing the best hockey of his life and that was bailing Brody's ass out.

It was a reminder—both good and bad—that even as Brody flailed, his future suddenly up in the air, some of his teammates were finding the new coaching direction a positive change.

"Yep," Ramsey said with a firm nod. "You guys go out and have fun. Enjoy the party."

Dean glanced in the direction of the living room. "Yeah? Should we?"

Brody didn't want to go back to the crowded living room, full of people he didn't know and didn't give a shit about. He'd come to the party tonight because Dean had asked him.

Because Dean was going to be there.

"Let's go sit outside. It's quiet and there's some back steps . . ."

"Yeah," Dean agreed with a decisive nod, and like he was familiar with them too, he led the way out the back door.

Brody wasn't surprised not many people were out here and the steps down the back porch were empty. He sat down on the top one, and Dean dropped down next to him.

"You want to talk about it?" Dean asked into the silence.

"Not particularly," Brody said, sipping his beer. "It's just depressing."

"How so?"

Brody took a deep breath. "Some days it feels like I'm gonna be stuck in this in-between purgatory forever. And it fucking sucks."

"That's not true." Dean touched him on the knee, a fleeting touch that still lit him inside. "You're gonna figure this shit out. You're too smart not to."

"You don't gotta be nice and supportive. You can tell me pretty lies instead."

Dean's mouth quirked up. "Pretty lies for a pretty boy?"

"Why not? I'm already a sure thing."

Dean leaned in. "Are you?"

Brody's palms were sweating, slipping on the condensation dripping down the side of his beer bottle. "You know I am."

"Maybe," Dean conceded, not looking disappointed by this fact, "but you're not just a sure thing in bed. You're my friend too."

Gah. Brody didn't want to keep discovering what a goddamn good guy Dean was.

A goddamn *great* guy.

"But," Dean added, fingers beginning to pick at the label of his beer, "we *should* talk about this."

"I thought we already did." Was Dean going to tell him nevermind? That he didn't want to do this after all? Brody's stomach sank right into the fucking ground.

"Not about uh . . .the particulars. All the particulars. Wes said—"

"You told Wes?" Brody didn't think he was mad, necessarily. After all, he'd told Ramsey—or Ramsey had guessed—but he hadn't really expected that Dean would tell anybody. That he'd want to keep his public straightness intact, even when it came to his friends. His *queer* friends, even.

"I did, I'm sorry. I didn't know—"

Brody interrupted him again. Put a hand on his arm and squeezed. Tried not to get distracted by all that muscle under his fingertips. "It's alright, I'm not mad. I told Ramsey. Well, Ramsey *guessed*."

He didn't move his hand, and Dean didn't seem to mind as he curled his fingers around it, stroking the underside of his forearm, appreciating it like the work of art it was.

Even long after this was over, and they'd gone their separate ways, Brody would remember this.

"Yeah, so did Wes. Are we not very good at this?" Dean seemed like he genuinely wanted to know.

"Neither of us do this very often, so yeah, probably."

Dean nodded. "That's more what Wes meant, I think. We just need to . . .uh . . .keep communicating."

"Can we 'communicate' later, when we get back to the apartment?" Brody asked, barely able to keep a straight face.

He hadn't needed to. Dean started to laugh, and then Brody couldn't help it either, chuckling as they leaned into each other, their shoulders bumping.

"I think he meant more if you want something, or I want something, we need to be honest about it," Dean said, his gaze growing serious.

Serious *and* warm, skimming over the lines of Brody's body.

He knew he was good-looking. He'd known it even before Dean had ever called him pretty boy, but he'd never felt it as viscerally as he did right now.

Like the strong bones of his face and his thick, wavy hair actually had a freaking purpose.

If it was to entice Dean, he was totally okay with that situation.

"What do you want, then?" Brody asked, because he *was* curious, and the more they talked about this, the hotter the anticipation rose in him.

He'd thought quenching that thirst was the sexiest thing in the world, but he'd been wrong. The sexiest thing in the world was drawing it out, teasing each other with it, until one of them couldn't take a single moment more and caved.

"I don't know if I want anything *specifically*," Dean said, and he was flushing now, and it turned out that was sexy too.

No wonder Brody felt obsessed by this feeling. No wonder *everyone* felt obsessed by this feeling. He'd always wondered why people lost their minds over sex, but no longer.

"No?" Brody could hear how low and rough his voice had gotten as he leaned in closer. They were practically intertwined now, his fingers still stroking Dean's arm and his other arm tucked behind Brody's back. He could feel the heat of it, the possession of it, even though it wasn't technically touching him.

Dean's eyes flicked down to his lips, and Brody knew exactly what he wanted.

Because he wanted the exact same goddamn thing.

Why had they agreed to go to this party?

They could be home, now, on the couch, or in one of their *beds*, finally naked together.

Fuck restraint. Fuck teasing.

Brody was just about to suggest they get out of here when a noise behind them made Dean move back a fraction and then Ramsey's voice called out, "There you two are. We're gonna have a big beer pong tournament, and you guys have to team up."

Dean looked at him. "Do you want to play beer pong?" he asked.

Brody didn't. Not really. He was shit at it, and what he *actually* wanted was to drag Dean back to the apartment, to do things he was probably *also* shit at, but craved all the same.

"Come on," Ramsey entreated. "One game. Then y'all can go do what you want to do." Ramsey was behind them, and Brody couldn't see his face, but he knew the kind of knowing grin his friend was wearing.

"Fine," Brody said, rising from the step, Dean following behind him.

"You good at this?" he asked, dipping his head low so he could murmur in Brody's ear. He shivered at the feeling of Dean's warm breath against his neck.

But before Brody could answer, Dean's hand was latching onto his, and he was tugging him away. "One second," he called out to Ramsey. "We'll be there in one sec."

Then Dean was practically dragging him around the frat house, to a dark corner by the trash cans. Not exactly the most atmospheric conditions, but Brody didn't even have a moment to comment on it, before Dean was crowding him up against the house.

"I had to do this first," Dean admitted and then, after framing his face with his hands, kissed him.

It was like a shot of pure adrenaline to his system.

Brody understood now why people got addicted to this give and take. Why they'd do anything to get another hit. Because he'd do the same. His fingers dug into Dean's shoulders and he hung on for the ride, and it was a *ride*.

Dean's mouth was hot and eager on his, tongue brushing against his own, and for a second everything disappeared. The frat house. Ramsey and his friends waiting. The beer pong tournament.

Even the uncertainty that had dogged Brody these last few weeks.

Brody almost sank into it, lost himself to that feeling, but before he could, Dean pulled away.

"Sorry," he mumbled, sounding a little embarrassed, face shadowed. "I'd been wanting to do that since you showed up and I *couldn't*, and I sure as fuck couldn't wait to do it through a whole beer pong tournament."

Brody smacked him lightly on the side. "Don't apologize. I liked it. I liked it enough that I wish we could do it again."

"We could always escape, tell Ramsey and his beer pong to fuck off?"

They could. There was a part—currently pressing into Dean's thigh, hot and hard and throbbing—that really wanted to do exactly what Dean suggested.

But if they couldn't keep their hands off each other for even a few hours, what did that mean?

Brody wasn't sure he wanted to look too closely at the answer.

So, better to just hold on. Hook up at the end of the night, as he'd expected they would.

That was what friends with benefits did, right?

That was his assumption, anyway.

"We should go play," Brody said, making sure it was clear just how regretful he was about it.

"Alright." Dean pushed back from the house and Brody immediately felt the loss of him. "We can do that. You any good?"

"No," Brody said, chuckling. "Maybe I should be apologizing in advance for that."

"Well, I'm okay, so we'll probably even out."

Except that it turned out that Dean wasn't just *okay*. Unsurprisingly, he was fucking brilliant, and even with Brody pulling down his skill level considerably, they spent the next hour and a half laughing and playing, and to Brody's surprise, he actually had a pretty good time.

Dean seemed to, as well, and even though they didn't do more than casually touch, in celebration and in commiseration a handful of times, it didn't matter, because underneath, Brody's blood was simmering.

Waiting.

More than once, he looked over and Dean's gaze met his own, and he knew Dean was thinking the same thing.

This is fun. And we're gonna have fun later, too.

After beating Finn and Elliott, then Ramsey and Ivan, and then finally Marcus and Wes, they made it to the semi-final, and with Brody up to play next, he knew they'd probably lose. He didn't know if he was sad or happy about it.

This *had* been an unexpectedly pleasant evening, and if Brody had to chalk it up to anyone, it was going to be because of Dean.

Not just because of the kiss earlier—or their promises of more, later—but because he just genuinely enjoyed spending time with the guy.

He was quietly supportive, openly proud, and an easy person to be around.

Brody was setting up for his final shot when Dean leaned in. His fingertips brushed the small of his back and Brody wanted to moan and lean into that touch, but he didn't.

"Hey, you got this," Dean murmured.

Brody glanced back, and their eyes met.

"Or," Dean added, the corner of his mouth quirking up, "if you wanted to miss, I wouldn't be too torn up about it."

"You're telling me to throw this game?" Brody teased.

Dean shrugged. "Up to you."

"Hey, stop flirting and start playing," Ramsey called out.

"You're one to talk," Ivan retorted.

"Yeah, seriously," Elliott complained. "Every time I go to take a shot you say something about Mal very loudly."

"Hey, it's not my fault you're so worked up about him," Ramsey teased.

Elliott crossed his arms over his chest. "I'm not worked up about him. He pisses me off. He was supposed to come tonight, and the fucker bailed."

"Exactly," Ramsey said. "You're worked up about him."

Elliott didn't say a word, just walked off, probably in the direction of the kitchen, to find something else to drink.

"You gonna take the shot or not?" Ramsey challenged.

Brody rolled his eyes but he straightened and tossed the ball.

He hadn't known until right as it was leaving his hand what he'd decided.

The ball glanced right off the lip of the cup and for a split second, Brody was sure it was gonna go in, but then it bounced off, onto the table and then onto the floor.

"Ah, sucks," Dean said, sounding not very disappointed at all. "That was a good shot, though."

"Nearly brilliant," Ramsey said, and he was laughing. Probably because he was laboring under the assumption that Brody had missed on purpose.

"Hey, it's alright," Brody said and leaned over, shaking their opponents' hands. Dean seemed to know them, and he'd said Rand and Ty played on the football team with him. "Great game, guys. Go out and destroy Ramsey for me, okay?"

Rand grinned. "You got it, boss. And Dean, good to see you."

"Yeah," Ty added. "Not just on the field, for once."

Dean flushed and brushed it off, giving them both a handshake that of course, evolved into one of those complicated hugs.

"See you at practice Tuesday," he said. "We're taking off."

Brody didn't know how he felt about being part of a *we*.

No. That wasn't true at all. He knew exactly how it felt. Intoxicating, more so even than the beer they'd drunk as part of the tournament.

"You good?" Dean asked as they walked out of the house.

He didn't need to be specific about his question for Brody to understand what he was asking. *You sober? You sober enough to hook up, still?*

"Yeah," Brody said. "But the walk home will do me good."

And not just because of the beer. His stomach was still fluttering over the *we* Dean had used—even though Brody knew there hadn't exactly been another pronoun he *could* have used.

"Same," Dean agreed.

They walked for another minute before Dean broke the silence. "That was a pretty decent shot there, at the end."

Brody grinned. "You asking me if I missed on purpose?"

"You wouldn't ever throw a game on purpose. That would be poor sportsmanship," Dean said firmly.

"You suggested it," Brody reminded him. "Maybe I wouldn't have considered doing it if you hadn't."

"Maybe I wanted to properly motivate you."

"To win or to lose?" Brody teased in a low voice. He stopped just outside a pool of light from one of the streetlights. There were still a few pockets of students wandering around, but it was getting late and they were far between. He felt comfortable enough reaching over and tucking a hand into the belt loop of Dean's jeans, tugging him a little closer.

"I'm still tryin' to figure that out," Dean said wryly. "That's why I asked."

"Honestly, I'm not sure. I told you I was crap, and I am. I wanted to make it—and I didn't want to make it. We'll never know what the truth really is. I *think* I tried but maybe not all that hard."

Dean grinned. "I like it."

"Do you?"

Say it. I like you.

"Yeah."

Of course Dean didn't, because that wasn't what this was, even though this whole evening felt like that phrase, repeated over and over, echoing in his head so insistently that Brody couldn't have dismissed it even if he'd wanted to.

He didn't.

Even if it was a mess, even if it was hard. Impossible, really.

We're friends. And more, too. That's what we said. You're not thinking anything different than he is.

But it *felt* different than Brody had heard people talk about when they described friends with benefits.

"Well come on, we don't want to waste this chance my missed shot gave us," Brody said, tugging on Dean's belt loop and they started walking again.

Their apartment was only another block, and a minute later, Dean was unlocking the door, tossing his keys onto the coffee table as Brody closed the door behind him.

They were alone.

Only once had he felt awkward tonight, and that had been when he'd first seen Dean. When he'd wanted more things than he was allowed to take.

And it was awkward now, as they stared at each other.

Awkward *and* tense, but not an ugly kind of tension, but the best kind. Full of promise and anticipation.

"Come 'ere," Dean said gruffly, and that was all the invitation Brody needed to fall into him, tilting his face up as their mouths met.

The kiss earlier tonight had been undeniably hot, but this one burned him up from the inside out.

"I didn't know," Brody gasped as Dean broke the kiss, tugging his T-shirt over his head and tossing it onto the couch.

They weren't even going to make it to the *couch*.

"Didn't know what," Dean said, and maybe he hadn't ever undressed a guy before, but his fingers were confident and sure on Brody's jeans, unbuttoning and unzipping them. They sagged around his waist, and Brody felt the ghost of Dean's touch against his lower abs, making his cock twitch with need.

Brody took a step back, trying to get his breathing under control.

"Didn't know it would feel like this," he admitted.

"Yeah," Dean agreed, and from the earnest look on his face as he took in Brody's body, he wasn't just giving him lip service either.

"We should . . .uh . . ." Brody motioned to his bedroom. "We *could* . . .here . . .but . . ."

"I like the way you think, pretty boy," Dean said gruffly and then just fucking *picked him up.*

Brody squawked. First, because he'd never expected that and second, because he was heavy, right? He was not a light person. He was strong and muscular and six foot, and here Dean was picking him up like he weighed fucking nothing.

Except—Dean could probably bench press more than Brody weighed.

And *that* was insanely fucking hot.

"You good there?" Dean asked, barely breathing hard as he nudged open Brody's door and deposited him on the edge of the bed.

"I . . .*no*," Brody said with the strongest emphasis he could. "*No.* You can't do that shit. I'm gonna . . .I'm gonna blow my load right now if I think about how sexy that was."

Dean grinned. "Yeah? You like me manhandling you around?"

"Yes. *Yes.* Put a pin in that though," Brody said. Because he meant it. This was going to be over before it started if Dean kept going with that shit. "Take your clothes off."

He leaned back, toed his shoes off and decided he was going to enjoy the show.

Dean raised an eyebrow as he lifted his T-shirt up, discarding it on the floor. "You don't wanna take them off for me?"

"Someday, yeah. But right now? I've barely gotten to see you naked and I want to *enjoy it.*"

Dean flushed again, the color deepening down his chest, and Brody was curious just how far down it went.

"Don't tell me I'm the first person to bring up that you're seriously hot," Brody added in a teasing voice, leaning back on his elbows.

There was only a slight dusting of dark hair on Dean's pecs, and a trail leading down to his jeans.

Brody wanted to know how soft it felt, so he sat up and reached out, pressing a palm to his chest. Slid it lower. Felt Dean's sharp intake of breath as he stroked his lower abs.

"No," Dean said, voice low. "But I didn't give a shit before."

"You give a shit now," Brody stated—didn't question. Because the look in those light eyes of Dean's made it clear that he did.

"You keep touchin' me like that, yeah," Dean said, swallowing hard.

"Like how?" Brody asked and pulled his hand away.

Dean made a noise full of disappointed disbelief.

Brody chuckled and waved his hand at the rest of Dean's clothes. "Those need to go, still. Then I'll show you."

"You'd better." Dean's fingers were trembling as he unbuttoned his jeans and shucked them down. It was impossible to miss his cock, hard and straining against his dark green boxer briefs.

Yeah, Brody might not have been into cocks before this, but it was undeniable that he was into *this* cock, now.

"Trust me, I don't want to be hands-off," Brody teased.

Dean tucked his fingers under the waistband of his boxer briefs and tugged them down.

Brody's pulse accelerated.

"Now, this is a view I like," he said, trying for casual but unable to help the way his tone wavered at the heat in Dean's gaze as the last piece of his clothing fell away.

"You like it?" Dean eroded much of Brody's studied nonchalance as he wrapped his hand around his dick, stroking it himself. "Like how big and hard I am for you?"

"Come 'ere," Brody said roughly, the last of his pretense disintegrating, leaving only hot, fierce desire surging through him.

"Not yet." Dean even moved back half a step, right out of Brody's reach.

Maybe it should have annoyed Brody that Dean had more self-control than he did, but he was too turned on to give a shit.

"Why not?" Brody was aware he was whining, even.

Dean grinned and made the same hand motion that Brody had. "It's *your* turn to get undressed. Come on, get naked, pretty boy. I wanna see it *all*."

Brody did not scramble. That would be undignified and a little too desperate. Definitely unsexy, especially right now.

But he wasted no time, sucking in his stomach as he braced himself on his forearm to slowly slide his pants down. He cupped his cotton-covered cock, hissing at the pressure of his hand. Dean's eyes darkened, the pupils dilating even further.

"Don't tell *me* nobody's ever called you hot, pretty boy," Dean said in an intoxicatingly low voice that pulled at Brody, right where all his arousal was building in the base of his stomach. Sparking him up.

"Didn't give a shit before," Brody said, tossing him his most confident, charming smile. Ramsey always said he could get anyone he wanted, if he ever chose to. The problem was he'd never really wanted just *anyone*. And now? There was only one person he wanted.

"Now you do," Dean said, grinning too. "Come on, pretty boy, show me what you got."

"So hard." *So hard for you*. Brody groaned a little as he shifted, pulling his boxer briefs down, over his cock.

It bobbed out, probably as hard as he'd ever been in his whole goddamn life.

He tried to reach for it again, but Dean moved fast, so fucking fast, considering his size, and slapped his hand away.

"That's mine," Dean said, and then he covered Brody's body—and his mouth—with his own.

Brody moaned into his mouth, the impact of their skin-to-skin connection rocking his world to its foundations.

Dean's hands were everywhere, slow and steady, like they had all the time in the world. Between those sweet, tantalizingly sexy touches and the passionate press of Dean's mouth against his, Brody was panting, desperate and needy, by the time Dean broke the kiss.

"Shit, this is so good." Maybe Brody shouldn't have been so blunt about it, but his easygoing, offhand veneer was gone, totally stripped away by the intense look in Dean's eyes.

Dean leaned further as Brody's fingers scrabbled against his shoulders, his back, trying to pull him in.

"Yeah?" he asked. His hand dipped lower, Brody's cock twitching at the promise of something more than just the pressure of Dean's body.

"Yeah, yeah, *more*," he begged. He was past giving a shit about how desperate he sounded.

Then Dean casually licked up and down his fingers, wetting them, those eyes never leaving Brody's. Brody's mind just plain fucking whited out as he reached down and wrapped that spit-slick hand around his cock.

Brody dug into the comforter, bracing himself for more as the pleasure surged through him.

"Oh yeah, that's even better," Dean murmured, like he was talking to himself. He gave Brody a stroke and then another, and *Jesus*, it was almost too much to look at the big bulk of him, wide shoulders and all that fucking muscle, and then experience the careful, gentle way he was touching Brody.

But even though it wasn't rough, it wasn't hesitant, either.

Dean wanted this. Dean wanted to do this *to him*.

"Should've known you'd be so goddamn pretty like this," Dean murmured, and *wow*, that had not been on Brody's bingo card either. Dean, the man of few words, being so good at dirty talking that Brody was sure he was going to come way before he wanted to. Just from the rough-edged reverence in Dean's voice.

"Should've known you'd be good at this."

"You like it slower?" Dean's movements slowed to a crawl as he made it last with long, gentle, even strokes that made Brody's pulse spike. "Or a little harder?" He nearly sent him over the edge then, gripping his cock harder, letting Brody really feel those big calloused fingers as they worked him over.

"I like it any way you're gonna give it to me," Brody admitted. "But come 'ere. Kiss me."

He heard a rumble of approval in the back of Dean's throat and then he was leaning over him again, kissing him hard, and it only took a minute of losing himself in slick press of Dean's tongue against his own and he was right on the edge, so close it almost hurt.

But Dean seemed to know that, seemed to want to draw it out, because every time he got so close to coming Brody could nearly taste it, he pulled back. Went even slower. Gave him just enough pressure to feel so good, but not to shove him over into ecstasy.

"You fucking tease," Brody gasped out, pulling back from Dean's mouth for a breath. Then two.

"You love it, pretty boy," Dean murmured and leaned in to kiss him again. Then his mouth was slipping lower, tongue wet against his skin, every inch of it electrified.

He slid lower and then lower still, mouth moving over the sensitive ridges of Brody's abs, and he knew there was sound coming out of his mouth. Prayerful grunts or gasps or moans—he'd long lost the ability to control or dignify the way Dean was wrenching this orgasm out of him.

Then Dean sucked a deep bruise nearly into the crease between Brody's thigh and his stomach, the pain sharp and beautiful. His hand tightened right then, and Brody gave a shout of warning before he was experiencing the best orgasm of his whole life.

The aftershocks felt like they went on forever, Dean drawing them out with those easy, gentle strokes, Brody continuing to shudder on the bed.

"Oh yeah, pretty boy, you liked that just fine," Dean said, grinning.

Like his own cock wasn't bobbing in front of him, hard and red and wet at the tip, shining in the dim light of Brody's bedroom.

"Now. Come here *now*," Brody said breathlessly and didn't even wait for him to follow orders—because it wasn't like he even *expected* Dean to do it—he just took what he wanted. Scrambled across the comforter, slid to the floor, and didn't think.

Just put his mouth right over that big, hard cock and sucked.

Dean yelled, then a gentle hand—Brody hoped it was at least a little clean, but he was at the point where he didn't give a fuck anymore—fell to his head, stroking him.

Brody didn't know what the fuck he was doing, but then Dean didn't seem to mind. He licked, he sucked, he let his tongue trail up and down his length. Did whatever he thought might feel good, things he'd experienced before that he thought he could possibly replicate, all while the remnants of his own orgasm were buzzing inside him right alongside new sparks of arousal at the thought that he was doing this. He was sucking Dean Scott's cock and he was loving every moment of it.

"Goddamn, pretty boy," Dean groaned as he took him a little too deep and tried not to choke. How did people do this, easily? Brody wasn't sure. *Practice*, he could imagine Ramsey saying in a knowing voice.

And yeah, he'd definitely be willing to put some practice hours in to sucking cock, if it was always this good, this overwhelming.

Brody let saliva pool in his mouth, easing his slide, and reached down, brushing Dean's balls. Dean gave another shout, and then there was a hand tugging Brody off. It was over, nearly before it began, as he used his hand to jerk Dean through his orgasm.

Dean was wavering above him and Brody rose, using his own weight to pull them back into the bed. Then he used Dean's T-shirt to wipe his hand clean.

"Shit," Dean said, flopping over and grinning. "Did you just use my shirt? Right after I used it? That shouldn't be hot—"

"But it is?" Brody laughed. "Maybe we're just both weird."

"Maybe." Dean didn't seem fazed by this possibility, just turned over onto his back.

Brody decided that was an invitation and followed him.

He didn't usually hook up, and he didn't usually cuddle with his hookups, but this felt good. *Right.* Especially when Dean's arm wound its way around him and tugged him close.

He rested his chin against Dean's pec, feeling the slight abrasion of hair, and thought he'd genuinely never felt more like himself.

It didn't make sense, because he'd never thought he'd wanted this before. He hadn't been denying it to himself. But at the same time, this felt like the answer to a question he'd simply never asked before.

"Well," Dean drawled into the quiet. "Guess that resolves a lot of things."

"Yeah?"

Dean's fingers tightened on him. "You're the one who asked. I hadn't really thought about it, and I guess I should've."

Brody realized that Dean was referring to the first time they'd hooked up, on the couch, that Friday night weeks ago.

"I was a little drunk, that night."

"But not drunk enough to not know what you wanted," Dean said. "Me either."

Brody nodded. "I wondered if it was just the franticness of it. Like the shock, the first time, and then the second time, just . . .I don't know . . .maybe just being super horny."

"Oh, you were super horny alright," Dean said wryly.

Brody laughed. "I was. But it wasn't just that. And tonight? Ugh. That was really, really good." He didn't want to specify which bits, though he was fairly certain Dean thought he was just talking about everything after they'd gotten naked and finally ended up in a bed together. But the truth was, he was talking about the whole thing. From the moment he'd spotted Dean in the frat house, to their talk on the steps, to the kiss, to the beer pong, to *this*, lying together in bed, just because they could.

"Yeah," Dean said, and Brody noticed he hadn't specified either. But surely, yes, the only thing Dean was agreeing to was the sex. Because it had been really, really good. No question.

"Next time, I'm gonna figure out how to do that better," Brody said. They'd agreed to do this, and it had gone spectacularly well so surely there would be a repeat, but he wanted to make sure he locked down that it wasn't just a possibility, it was *happening*, one hundred percent, for sure.

"You do that any better, my head's gonna blow right off."

"Well, that's kinda the idea," Brody teased. He turned and set his forearms on Dean's firm chest, letting his gaze drift up and down and finally meet Dean's eyes.

They were no less intent than normal, but also sweet and sleepy, glazed a bit from his orgasm. It was a good look. But then just about anything was a good look on Dean.

"You did good, pretty boy," Dean said.

"Another thing that should not be hot, but is," Brody pointed out in a dry tone.

"Me calling you pretty boy? Sure is," Dean agreed. "What else do you think fits that category?"

"That we didn't think would be hot, but is? I'm not sure. Like, blowing a guy? A guy taking off his clothes real slow? A guy giving me a hickey practically on my dick?"

Dean rolled his eyes. "It was just a little nip, and it wasn't on your dick. Plus, I don't think you can bitch when it made you come like that."

For a minute, Brody was quiet, thinking. Considering the things he could say, and all the things he wasn't sure he was ready to say, yet.

"Honestly, I don't know what else fits. I guess we're gonna have to find out," Brody said.

"I got something," Dean said. Because of course he did. This man had never been afraid of honesty in his whole damn life.

Brody didn't know whether to be envious or appreciative.

"Okay," Brody said.

"Next time, I wanna lay you out, on your stomach. You got such a pretty back, pretty boy, and lick all the way up and down it, and then . . .lick you lower. Get you nice and wet for my fingers. Feel you come around them, just from them inside of you, and you humping against the bed because you can't help it any longer."

"Jesus," Brody said, his throat suddenly tight and dry. Okay, he was *definitely* falling on the appreciative side of this, tonight.

"Just something I thought about," Dean said modestly.

"That sounds like a pretty advanced maneuver," Brody said, but his cock was already stirring against his thigh.

Dean just shrugged. "Might not be any good at it. Doesn't mean we shouldn't try it."

"Alright, twist my arm," Brody said.

"Next time," Dean said.

"Actually—" Brody paused and then straightened up, hand straying downward and *yep,* Dean was getting hard again too. He wrapped his hand around his cock, giving it an experimental stroke as Dean hissed. "Actually, I think it's gonna be the *next* next time."

"I think you're right, pretty boy," Dean groaned.

CHAPTER TWELVE

It wasn't like every game wasn't important.

They were.

Coach B and Zach—plus all the many, many coaches Brody had had over the years—had always impressed on him that every single minute on the ice mattered.

But this one loomed even larger. The Evergreens' main conference rival, the Sabretooths, were in town, and this was the second game they'd played against them in as many days.

In preparation for this weekend's games, Coach and Zach had them working really hard all week, especially the defense, because the Olympia Sabretooths were considered to have one of the best offensive lines in all of NCAA hockey. Practices had been so long and grueling this week, he'd barely had time to see Dean.

Definitely they hadn't had time to fool around. Disappointingly.

Brody shoved those thoughts away. Trying to focus on today's challenge.

Yesterday, they'd narrowly lost, with the Sabretooths scoring a goal in the last five minutes of the third period. Finn had been despondent after, not letting anyone talk to him, and then disappearing.

But today, Brody knew, was a new day. A new game. A new opportunity to make his mark and be part of the team that stopped Olympia.

Right now? They were doing it. They were up 2 to 1, and Brody felt like he was playing his best hockey of the season. Frankly, the Sabretooths had required it. He'd had no choice but to give this challenge everything he had.

"Ten minutes left. Let's not let them tie it up," Coach said, during one of the last TV timeouts of the game. He met each player's eyes, but Brody didn't miss how his gaze settled on Brody and Ramsey. They'd be spending a lot of this last ten minutes on the ice, hoping to prevent Olympia from tying it up.

"No mistakes," Ramsey echoed.

"Don't let them bait you into anything," Coach added.

They'd only let the Sabers have the power play once this game. And during that one power play, despite his and Ramsey's best efforts, they'd set up and scored a fairly easy goal twenty seconds in.

Coach turned to say something to Finn, who had a particularly determined tilt to his jaw.

If Brody knew him at all, he'd bet that Finn was already beating himself up for missing that goal.

"Hey," Ramsey said, nudging Brody. "They're gonna get aggressive out there, with you. With all of us."

"Oh, they're gonna *get* aggressive?" Brody questioned. They'd already been pushing him hard, into the boards and getting into his face what felt like every moment of the game so far.

Olympia's game plan tonight seemed to be to put their most physical line onto the ice, and then wait to send their ace scoring power play team.

It hadn't worked so far, and Brody—and clearly Ramsey—expected them to push harder.

They'd want to take both of these games and go home to Olympia as the sole leader of the conference. But Brody was determined, in a fierce way that he hadn't been since the season started, to not let that happen.

"I'm just saying, don't lose your shit, no matter what they throw at you," Ramsey reminded him.

"I won't."

The TV coordinator lowered his arm, indicating the timeout was at an end, and they set up at the Sabretooths' side for the face-off.

Ivan took the puck and passed it to Elliott, but he was getting swarmed as he tried to work towards the center of the ice, and Brody skated over to assist, trying to draw some of the attention off.

It worked a little too well, drawing their defenders over, one big burly guy whose build resembled Dean's. He slammed Brody right into the boards, but he barely blinked. This guy had been a pain in his fucking side—*literally*—for the last two games.

But Brody wasn't going to let a twinge of pain stop him. He pushed back and then took off again, not letting the guy slow him down for more than a few seconds.

His gaze narrowed, taking in where Mal and Elliott were trying to get the puck centered, Ramsey playing interference, and Brody skated in, too, still back enough in the zone where he could respond if Olympia's players decided to make a push to their side of the ice.

Elliott went in, skating hard, and took a shot, the puck barely glancing off the goalie's pad, and Mal was there for the rebound, trying to punch it in higher.

But he missed, the goalie grabbing it out of mid-air and passing it to one of his players.

Brody only had a moment to react.

But before he could skate after the guy, along with Ramsey, the big burly guy checked him into the boards again, and this time, he ground him in, trapping him with one huge arm.

Brody tried to wiggle out, hoping that any second the ref would at least be calling roughing, but nobody did.

Brody's temper spiked as the guy shoved his gloved hand hard into his stomach, but they were close enough Brody guessed the ref hadn't even seen it.

It was semi-dirty, and also not surprising.

But it still pissed him off.

"Cut the shit," Brody told him, but the guy only kept grinning and kept coming, no matter how Brody tried to wiggle out of it.

Where was the fucking ref?

Finally, annoyed that if he wasted one more second, he'd be leaving Ramsey and the rest of the line to deal with the Sabretooths' potent offense, he elbowed the guy hard, hoping it would be enough to release him.

It wasn't. So he did it again. And again, and until finally he was able to skate off, but not before he heard the ref finally blow his whistle.

Brody's stomach dropped as the ref pointed his direction and finally called the roughing.

"Shit, that wasn't me," Brody yelled. "I was just—"

But before he could, Ramsey was skating over, taking him by the arm and pulling him away from the ref. "You needed to trust we could handle that shit," he muttered to Brody.

"I did—"

But before he keep arguing, Ramsey was skating away, leaving him to enter the penalty box on his own.

Fuck.

Sure enough, he saw Olympia's power play team, famous throughout the conference—frankly they were fucking famous throughout the country, at this point—come over the boards onto the ice.

Ramsey had already been on for the last minute, and he was coming to the end of his time, but he saw him motion to Coach B to keep him in.

It was foolish and risky, but Coach nodded.

What else could they do?

The rest of the Evergreens' team couldn't hold them.

He and Ramsey were barely able to fucking hold them.

Brody slammed his gloves onto the bench, anger rushing through him in a hot, dizzying wave. He hadn't been the one to fuck up. He'd only been trying to pry himself loose. Maybe a little more forcefully than he'd needed to, sure, but what was it they always said?

It was always the second guy who got caught.

It took them a little over thirty seconds this power play.

They slipped right past Ramsey, who Brody could tell was exhausted, and flicked the puck in only a split second before Finn dived for the empty space, and the crowd erupted.

"Fuck, fuck, fuck," Brody cried out, as the penalty box door opened.

"Bench," Zach called, even though he'd just been *on* the bench.

Brody made a face but he retreated over to the bench, lifting himself over the boards and collapsing next to Ramsey, who was breathing hard.

"I—"

"I don't want to hear it," Ramsey said, not letting him even get the apology out. "I told you not to fuck with them."

"I wasn't," Brody claimed. But he'd hit the guy harder than he'd really intended. And more times than he'd probably needed to. He'd felt the frustration bubbling up inside him, and he'd just reacted.

Instead of focusing, instead of being the needle, slid in exactly as deep as needed, he'd become the hammer.

"It's not how you play hockey," Ramsey pointed out.

It hurt, but it was also fair.

"Focus," Coach B barked out. His stern expression promised that they'd be talking about this at the end of the game.

Brody wanted to say, *I don't know how I play hockey, anymore,* but he didn't, because this definitely wasn't the right place to be having *that* conversation.

"I'm subbing Greene for Faulkner with Ramsey," Coach said, when Brody went to get up.

Fucking shifted to the second defensive pair at the end of the game. Brody wanted to howl about how fucking unfair this all was, but he'd been the one to nab the penalty that had led to the tying goal.

Part of him got it. Part of him understood it.

While the other part of him screamed in protest.

Two minutes before the end of the game, Elliott grabbed the puck on a breakaway, and took an insane risk, deking the goalie, and slapped it in with a nice little shot up above his right shoulder.

Brody celebrated with the rest of his team, but by the time they trudged into the locker room, elated but exhausted, he didn't feel much like patting himself—or anybody else—on the back.

He was sure someone was going to corner him and read him the riot act. Coach B, definitely. Ramsey, for sure.

But nobody did.

Until Brody wanted to lash out, pound his fists at anyone who kept smiling at him, like he'd fucking done anything to win the game.

Along with the rest of the team, he showered, dressed, and dutifully headed out to the victory dinner that Coach had told them was waiting at Jimmy's if they pulled this win off.

But still, nobody said a word.

Everyone acted, Brody realized, like his fuckup hadn't even happened. Like it wasn't even worth commenting on.

He lingered in the doorway of Jimmy's, watching as the team piled into a dozen booths.

There was his normal spot, right next to Ramsey, but he was afraid to take it.

He didn't feel like he deserved it, or the victory fries that they'd share together.

"Come on," Zach said, patting him on the shoulder. "Let's celebrate."

Brody grimaced but dropped down next to Ramsey, who was staring at the menu like he hadn't been eating here for three plus years.

"Listen, I went too hard. I know that," Brody said. "I'm sorry."

"I warned you," Ramsey said, not looking at him.

Brody felt the snub like a fist to the face.

This was *Ramsey*. One of his best friends.

"Maybe you're not taking this shit seriously," Ramsey continued quietly, before Brody could try to argue—or apologize—again. "But the rest of us fucking are, Brody."

"I'm taking it seriously," Brody argued. He wouldn't be here if he wasn't.

But even as he told himself that, this was still the biggest goddamn slam to his ego.

Ramsey telling *him* to take something seriously.

But this Ramsey was a new and improved Ramsey. Still the same Ramsey on the surface, sure, easygoing and fun and the life of every party, but underneath? There was a steel to him that Brody had never seen before.

He *wanted* this in a way Ramsey never had before.

In a way Brody recognized, because he used to feel this way about hockey.

"Not seriously enough," Ramsey said.

Brody stood. "I'm good," he spat and marched out, letting the door slam behind him.

Dean couldn't say he wasn't disappointed that he and Brody had only managed to share a single pair of rushed hand jobs this week. Or that Brody had already texted him and said he'd be late getting home tonight, too, after the game, because if they won—and Brody had added that they *were* gonna win, no questions—they'd be going out after.

And a few minutes ago, he'd checked the scores and sure enough, the Evergreens hockey team had beaten the Olympia Sabretooths.

Dean was happy for Brody. He shouldn't be disappointed.

Brody *should* be out celebrating with his teammates.

But he was. Disappointed. And restless. And horny.

Their plane had gotten in from their Saturday game, and he was by himself in the apartment, wishing more than he felt comfortable admitting to, just how much wanted to not be alone tonight.

Dean flopped back on the couch.

Considered putting ESPN or a movie on.

But he was alone. Totally alone.

You could watch anything you fucking wanted to. Anything at all.

Dean's fingers twitched on the remote, but finally, instead of clicking on something innocent like Sportscenter, he hit the power button instead.

He shouldn't.

It felt wrong to do this without Brody, even if he was thinking about Brody.

A few days ago, Wes had sent him a link to a porn site—specifically a *gay* porn site—hosting a free two-week trial period, and had added, *in case you need any extra info. Or any additional inspiration.*

He didn't need any, as long as Brody was around. But after last Saturday, Brody hadn't been, not really. Their schedules, which they could usually massage into meshing, had clashed instead.

Dean couldn't even say he'd gotten used to regular orgasms, because four in approximately four weeks didn't make a pattern, not even close. But his brain—and his dick—and gotten used to the concept that they might start happening more regularly.

Except that they hadn't, and Dean was tired of just using his right hand and his imagination.

What would be the harm of at least *looking* at the stuff Wes sent?

Guys watched porn. It wasn't *that* unusual, even if it was sort of unusual for Dean.

After all, he'd confessed one of his fantasies to Brody and he'd said, *that sounds like an advanced maneuver.* Shouldn't he be learning enough that maybe he could pull that kind of move off?

That was what convinced him.

Dean pulled his laptop out. Checked that the door was locked. Not that it mattered. Brody had a key, even if he wouldn't be home for hours, and even if he did come home, what Dean was doing was hardly shameful.

After all, he was *learning* for Brody, right? He and Brody, both, would benefit from this.

As he navigated to the site and clicked the free trial, his palms were already sweating and his dick was already half-hard in his sweatpants.

A whole string of videos popped up on his screen.

Most of them sounded semi-terrifying.

Guy gets railed by two guys.

Hot dude delivers a pizza—with extra sausage.

Deep throat orgy.

But finally there was one that sounded promising: *two guys experiment for the first time.*

Maybe it wasn't the learning experience that Dean had told himself he was gonna watch, but there was enough of a kernel of truth in that title that he couldn't stop himself from clicking on it.

After he did, and the video started playing, he realized it was more than just a little kernel of truth. It was a whole fucking popcorn bucket full.

Two guys, one smaller than the other, who even looked a little like Brody, were sitting on a couch in a way that was *so* similar to the way they'd been sitting that first night.

Then one of them leaned over, put a hand on the smaller guy's thigh, and Dean let out a gust of hot air.

He'd never been this turned on by watching porn before. But then again, he'd never been as turned on as he was regularly with Brody.

On screen, the thigh touch had led to kissing, then one guy, the smaller one, naturally, sliding into the other guy's lap.

Dean's fingers clenched, spasming near his hard, aching cock. He didn't want to touch himself, but he desperately did, too. But he was afraid if he did, he'd come before he could stop himself. Because that was him and Brody on screen. Those were his hands, cupping Brody's perfect, shapely ass, running up and down his gorgeous back, his mouth claiming Brody's until he was moaning and squirming.

That was *his* look of unbelievable bliss, the face of a man who'd just gotten everything he'd never even thought to want, but now didn't know how to live without.

Dean leaned forward, hearing his harsh pants in the quiet of the room mingling with the sounds from the screen.

On the screen, the smaller guy scrambled down off the bigger man's lap and then licked his lips in anticipation as he pulled the other guy's cock out.

Dean had to close his fist around his own, because he didn't want to come right now, thinking about how Brody had gone to his knees for him. How eager he'd been, even if he didn't know what he was doing. How fucking incredible it had felt, because it wasn't just some random mouth, but *Brody's*.

He'd never thought that would make any difference. One blowjob had to feel about the same as any other. They always felt good.

But Brody, who stupidly claimed he needed to get "better," had systematically destroyed all of Dean's assumptions about pleasure.

Dean was squeezing his cock, eyes glued to the screen, trying not to come, which felt like an irony, because wasn't that the point of porn, when he heard a noise.

A noise like a key in a lock.

Like a key in the lock of the front door.

He only had time to think, *but Brody's not supposed to be home yet,* before Brody was undeniably there, striding into the living room.

He stopped right in his tracks, clearly not expecting to see his roommate with his cock hanging out, porn playing on his laptop.

Well, Dean hadn't expected to see *him*. Or else he wouldn't have bothered with the porn. It was hot, but there was nothing hotter than the real thing.

"Are you . . .you *are*," Brody said. Dean realized then that what he was seeing was pure frustration clearing off Brody's face, replaced by a combination of wonder and arousal.

"I . . .yeah," Dean admitted. Because how was he supposed to deny it, when the guys were currently moaning up a storm on the screen, and he was sitting here, with his cock out.

He hadn't softened at all from the interruption, but he could probably thank the source of the interruption for that.

"Huh." Brody cocked his head. Regarding Dean, eyes flicking from the laptop to his dick and then back. "Are you watching two guys hooking up on a couch?"

Dean flushed. This could not possibly get more embarrassing than it was, and yet he felt they were plumbing new depths.

The only way it would've been worse was if he and Brody weren't actually hooking up.

"Yeah," Dean admitted.

"Hot," Brody said and then grinned. "You want some company?"

Dean fumbled for the stop button, but before he could, Brody put his hand out and stopped him. "That wasn't me telling you to pause it," he said and sat down right next to Dean, palming the bulge in his jeans with no shame whatsoever, only a bright, cocky grin shot in Dean's direction that somehow made *him* even harder.

"You wanna watch it . . .uh . . .together?" Dean didn't think he had air in his lungs any longer, but nope, that was when Brody nodded.

"Uh . . .alright," Dean stuttered. He kept thinking, every single time he and Brody hooked up, that he'd never been harder in his life. But he was practically fucking aching with how hot this was.

Especially when, completely matter-of-factly, Brody shed his jeans, shoving them around his thighs, followed by his boxer briefs.

His cock bobbed out, almost totally hard now. Dean wondered if he should look somewhere else, but he couldn't tear his eyes off it as Brody gave himself an experimental stroke and moaned.

"You're supposed to look at the porn," Brody teased him.

It probably wasn't very friends-with-benefits-y to say, *you're hotter than any porn I've ever seen. Including this one. Which is practically me and you, together.* Dean knew it. It was like holding up a flashing neon sign that said, *I'm in this deeper than we both expected I'd be. What should we do about it?*

Nothing, that was what they should do about it.

Still, it wasn't a habit of his to hide the truth. It was his habit to lay it out, unvarnished and ugly, even if it pissed everyone off.

"I don't want to," Dean said simply.

Brody smiled. "Kind of defeats the purpose," he said.

"No, it doesn't." Dean stroked himself again, more insistently this time, even as pleasure muddled his senses, just to prove that it definitely didn't.

Every inch of Brody was gorgeous. Outside, for sure, no fucking question about that, and Dean was beginning to suspect inside was similar. Even like this, so turned on and tense with it he could barely breathe, he'd never felt as *safe* as he did with Brody. As completely fucking free.

"Oh," Brody said suddenly as his gaze flicked to the screen, and Dean *had* to look now, because anything that could cause Brody to make that noise had to be worth seeing. And repeating.

The guys had gone back to other guy's lap, but this time, the bigger guy was circling the smaller guy's ass with his fingers, damp with lube, and then he slid a thumb in.

"You like that?" Dean could hear the gruffness in his own voice. Because he was thinking about it, now.

He wasn't the only one.

"I don't know," Brody said. But his eyes were glued to the screen, his hand moving on his cock. He looked as into this as

Dean imagined he'd looked earlier, when these two had started kissing on the couch.

"Come 'ere," Dean said.

Brody looked over at him. "You don't want—"

"I want *you*. Don't care how it happens," Dean said. But he did know Brody was too far away, even though he was right there, next to him on the couch. Dean couldn't touch him. Not the way he wanted to. Couldn't kiss him, and suddenly that was the crime of the century.

He wasn't stupid enough to think they'd have a million endless opportunities to kiss, and he was going to steal every single fucking one.

Brody leaned over, first with his head and then his whole body, climbing right where he belonged, which was Dean's lap. He tangled a hand in Brody's hair as their mouths met.

"How," Brody panted between long kisses, "did you know I needed this?"

It was a stupid question; Dean needed this all the time, so surely Brody had to feel even a tiny fraction of what he did.

By the time Brody slid off his lap, boneless, eyes so bright with pleasure and joy, the bigger guy was two fingers deep into the smaller guy's ass and his moans had grown increasingly desperate.

"Do it," Brody demanded, gazing up at Dean with those hero-worship eyes. Those soft, sugar-sweet eyes that Dean never wanted to deny.

"Do—"

But before Dean could get the question out, Brody was scrambling off the couch, shedding the rest of his clothes, and suddenly finding a new gear of speed as he tore through the apartment, returning only a second breathless moment later with a bottle of lube.

"Do it," Brody demanded again. "Finger me."

"But you don't know if you like it." Dean never wanted to do anything Brody wasn't into. But he also couldn't deny his cock was twitching, leaking now at the tip. He'd never been so turned on at just the thought of mirroring exactly what the pair was up to on screen.

"I'll like it," Brody said, panting. He put the lube in Dean's palm, not giving him any more opportunities to argue. Then he settled back on Dean's lap, gave his cock a stroke, and then Dean's. Dean groaned, deep in his throat.

Dean knew the general thought behind this. Go nice and slow. Find the prostate. Lots of lube.

But he still hesitated.

Brody ran a hand through Dean's hair. It was shorter, cropped close to his head, and Dean wondered if Brody kept this up, he'd want to grow it out. Give his man something to hang on to.

Focus, you fucking idiot.

"Do you . . .do you not think you'll like it?" Brody asked, suddenly hesitant. "You said—"

"I'll like it." Dean repeated Brody's own claim. "I'm gonna fucking love it. So much that I'm afraid I won't make it good for you. And that's all I want, for *you* to like it."

"You're gonna do it amazing. Promise," Brody said, seriously, earnestly. Then leaned in and kissed him again, and there was nothing Brody could do to better convince him than to seduce him with that amazing mouth.

Dean broke the kiss a minute later. "Okay," he said and, wetting his fingers, carefully slid them back, definitely not missing the opportunity to get a nice handful of Brody's incredible ass with his dry hand as he spread his cheeks.

"Fuck, you feel so good," Dean said. He wasn't the most vocal guy in the universe—he knew that, already—and he knew Brody was taking a risk here, trying this, and even if it didn't come naturally to him, Dean was going to encourage him every step of the way.

"Yeah?" Brody's voice had gone high and breathy as Dean's thumb brushed his hole.

Gentle, he had to remind himself, because he wanted to bury his whole fucking hand in that hot tightness. Not just his hand. His *cock*. He throbbed with the desire, but he pushed that down. If he didn't make this good for Brody this time, there'd never even be a possibility that he might want more.

"Tell me if this is too fast. Too hard. Too anything," Dean ground out. He dug the fingertips of his other hand into the meat of Brody's ass. Trying to control himself. Brody squeaked.

"What if it's too good?"

"That, *definitely*," Dean said. He felt winded, like they'd been running sprints for hours.

That was all Brody. He stripped away all his defenses, his control, simply everything. And unlike anyone else, Dean wanted to thank him for it.

"Get on with it," Brody demanded, writhing against his bigger body. "I'm so fucking horny I think I might explode."

"Why am I not surprised you're a bossy bottom?" Dean teased as he slid his thumb farther in.

"You said it." Brody panted. Pressed a kiss against the corner of Dean's mouth. "I'm a pretty boy."

"*Fuck*." Dean felt so close to the edge, so close to losing it. He gripped Brody's ass and tried not to just thrust up, into gorgeous oblivion.

"God, you're so hot like this," said Brody, the undeniably hot one of the pair of them.

"Like what?" Dean gave an experimental thrust and then another, feeling Brody's body beginning to open to him, like a fucking miracle.

"Like you're barely hanging on to your control."

"I *am* barely hanging on to my control," Dean admitted. "And you're trying to push me right over, and that shouldn't be hot, too, but it is."

"Something else to add to the list." Brody's reminder was punctuated with a little desperate moan as Dean pulled back and then thrust again. And again.

"More," he added, with a hard groan. "Goddamn it, give me more."

"Tryin' to be careful here," Dean argued, but he pressed a second finger in next to where his thumb was buried.

"Fuck careful and *fuck me*," Brody begged.

But Dean had no intention of doing the first, and every intention of the second.

He thrust in and out, carefully working that second finger in, and then Brody was kissing him hard and fast, tongue in his mouth moving in the same rhythm, and he was shouting, cock rubbing against Dean's abs.

A second later, he gasped into Dean's mouth, and he was shaking apart in his arms, ass gripping his fingers like Brody's ass was determined to squeeze the life out of them.

"Shit, shit, shit," Brody cried out as he came back down.

He glanced at Dean's cock, and he only had to put his hand on and give it one or two strokes before Dean's own orgasm overtook him.

"That," Dean said with a gasp, "was the hottest fucking thing I've ever seen in my whole life."

Brody slumped down, head resting against his chest. "The porn?" he asked in a teasing voice.

"You know it wasn't the porn," Dean said as sternly as he could with his whole body as relaxed and happy as it was right now.

"Yeah," Brody agreed.

"Guess you *did* like it."

Brody chuckled. Dean felt more than heard the sound.

"Obviously, me too," Dean said. He didn't know why he kept talking. He *never* wanted to keep talking. But the truth was, he didn't want this moment to end. Mess and all.

"Yeah, that was so fucking hot. You coming like that, when I barely touched you?"

Dean laughed, this time. "I was pretty fucking worked up."

"Me too," Brody said and then sighed. "Not just horny. Frustrated. Upset. That's why I was home early. I skipped out on the 'victory' celebration."

"But you guys won."

Brody didn't say anything for a long moment. Then another.

Dean waited him out, because he knew that Brody *would* eventually tell him.

"I got into it with Ramsey," he finally said.

"*You* got into it with *Ramsey*?" Dean couldn't believe it and wouldn't have, if Brody didn't have that look on his face that promised this was the truth.

"He's . . .he's becoming different. More serious. Especially on the ice. And me . . ." Brody trailed off. Then sat up. Pressed a last kiss to Dean's mouth and scrambled off his lap, before Dean could grab his arm and convince him to stay, any way he could.

Dean waited a second and then said *fuck it* and followed Brody, into the bathroom.

He'd grabbed a washcloth and was cleaning up. When he was done, he handed it very matter-of-factly to Dean so he could do the same.

Dean figured this was the point where they were supposed to be separating the *friends* from the *benefits*. But fuck that. This was important.

Brody might be trying to hide it, to mask it, but he might be the most upset that Dean had seen him since they'd met.

"And you what?" Dean asked. He finished cleaning himself and tossed the washcloth into the laundry basket in the corner. Brody was leaning over the sink, eyes squeezed shut. Like now that the lust wasn't fogging his brain anymore, he could think again, and he didn't really want to.

"I lost my temper. I got pinned by an asshole on the other team and I fought back and I shouldn't have. I knew I shouldn't, but I did it anyway. Then of course *I* got penalized, and well, we'd been trying to keep them off the power play—"

"Olympia *is* really good on the power play," Dean inserted gravely.

Brody looked up and met his gaze in the mirror. He looked confused—and also, weirdly pleased. Which was exactly the reaction Dean had been hoping for.

He shrugged. "I've read a few articles," he said. An understatement. Between homework and practices, he'd been binging everything he could about hockey and Evergreens hockey specifically, wanting to understand exactly what Brody was going through. Hoping that maybe when he needed it, he could be a friend.

Though that was kind of delusional, wasn't it? Because friends didn't do anything they'd just done. Or want to do it again. Or want to hold their other friends close, after, and make sure they were okay.

"You're reading about hockey?"

And watching some of your highlight packages on YouTube. I might be more embarrassed if you came in and saw me watching those than what you actually *caught me watching.*

"Uh, yeah, a little." *Don't ask me why. Please don't ask me to fucking explain.*

"Huh." But Brody didn't.

Dean didn't know whether to be relieved or disappointed.

"So, to make sure I understand," Dean said, returning the subject to what had happened during Brody's game, "you fought back, were the one who got the penalty, and then the Sabretooths went on the power play."

Brody nodded. Their eyes met in the mirror again. "And they scored, almost immediately." He sighed, then added wryly, "It sure didn't help that I'm usually on the penalty kill, and I couldn't exactly help out."

"Probably not," Dean said.

"Anyway, Ramsey chewed my ass out for it. *Ramsey.*"

"That's why you fought."

Brody's jaw took on a stubborn tilt. "I didn't need him to remind me not to get penalized in the first place. I didn't do it for shits and giggles. And I sure as fuck didn't need him to lecture me about it after."

"You still won, though," Dean reminded him.

"Yeah, thanks to Elliott. No thanks to me."

Dean considered the problem. Maybe if he'd known all this happened and this was why Brody had come home early, he wouldn't have been quite so eager to have sex. Maybe he'd have asked Brody if he wanted to talk about it first.

But then he realized the sex had actually helped Brody work some of that frustration off. It had been the best kind of distraction.

But like all distractions, eventually it was going to end.

"So, last time I checked, hockey's a team sport."

Brody looked startled, and turned, pinning Dean with a hot glare.

"Yeah. And?" he retorted.

Dean knew him well enough now to know what he was thinking. *Oh, think you're so smart now, huh?*

But if Brody was pissed at him, he couldn't be pissed at Ramsey—or at himself.

"And you didn't fuck it all up, just the same as Elliott wasn't the guy who saved it all. Y'all work as a team. Today it was Elliott who saved your asses. Next time, it'll be Ramsey. And it'll be you. It's *been* you."

Brody made a frustrated noise.

"I know, it sucks when I make so much goddamn sense," Dean teased.

"I liked you better when we were fucking," Brody said bluntly.

"No, you didn't," Dean said calmly.

And that made Brody smile. "Well, it's *sort* of true. Nobody's ever made me come like that before. Didn't even know it could feel like that."

Dean almost reminded Brody that he wasn't exactly experienced in this area, but then he didn't. If Brody wanted to think he was some kind of sex god, who was he to dissuade him? If it kept Brody coming back to his bed, Dean would be whatever he needed.

"You feelin' better?" Dean asked instead.

Brody considered the question for a second, and that was how Dean knew he was going to get the truth and not some pretty brush-off.

"Not entirely. Won't until I talk to Ramsey. Get to the bottom of this," Brody said. Paused. "Actually, probably won't feel completely better until I figure out all this future crap."

"That's what you and Ramsey are really fighting about," Dean said.

Brody nodded. And then to Dean's surprise, Brody pushed off from the counter and wrapped his arms around him, kissing him briefly on the bare shoulder. Dean felt his lips like a brand. Like Brody wasn't just expressing appreciation for the sex and the conversation, but claiming him, *owning* him. And the really shocking thing was how much Dean wished that was really true.

That Brody was his, and he was Brody's.

Not just for these few fleeting moments of pleasure and companionship, but *more*.

He wanted to be by Brody's side as he figured his stuff out. Wanted to stand right next to him, supporting him, as he kept on this path—or as he tore the whole path up and forged a new one. Whichever one, it didn't matter to Dean.

He didn't care if Brody was a hockey player; only that he was Brody.

"Thanks," Brody murmured into his shoulder.

Dean had a feeling he'd intended the embrace to be quick, fleeting, even casual. But he was also beginning to feel like nothing between them could be casual. Not now. So he held on, wrapping his arms around Brody's body and holding him close. Comforting him the only other way he knew how to do.

"You got it," Dean said, after a long moment and then reluctantly, finally let him go.

"Maybe . . .uh . . ." Brody didn't usually stumble over his words, so Dean wondered if he was uneasy about this. Awkward, even. "Maybe we could meet up this week for uh . . .homework? In the library?"

Dean nudged him, chuckling. "We do that anyway." It had seemed crazy at first, but he kept making sure of it—that they met up either at the gym or the library or at the apartment at least two or three times a week.

"Homework *and* sex, then?" Brody asked, an undeniably hopeful light in his eyes.

"Yeah. I think I could deal with that," Dean said. Wes would probably tell him to stop trying to play it cool, because he wasn't any good at it, but it was too much of ingrained habit to stop now.

"Uh, and next week my parents are coming. I wish they weren't."

"No?" Dean didn't bring up that his mom hadn't come to visit him once, since he'd moved to Portland. And his dad? Well, he'd never even *met* the asshole.

"They're gonna want to talk about *it*," Brody said.

Dean nearly choked. "They're gonna want to talk about your sex life?"

That was finally the thing that made Brody laugh, long and loud, tossing his head back as he did. He elbowed Dean. "No, *no*, God no. All this future bullshit."

"Why would they?"

"Because I was stupid enough to text my dad and ask him about prereqs for medical school. I should've asked anyone else—or googled it or something—but it was a weak moment."

But Dean knew there was more to it.

"And?" he asked.

Brody sighed. "And I'm worried if I go to my advisor, word will get around. I don't want to talk to anybody about it on campus."

"Didn't your coach tell you to take this year to think about it? To explore your options?" Surely that would've helped Brody feel more settled about it. That he had *time*. That he had *options*.

Dean didn't have any fucking options. It was make the NFL or go back to his shitty little hometown and grind out a living for the rest of his life.

"Listen," Brody said as he walked past him towards the kitchen, Dean following behind him. He grabbed two bottles of water from the fridge and tossed one to Dean, who caught it. "You know exactly what it's like. This culture. This attitude. You're on it, you're either making it, or it was all a waste. You're a failure. Nobody understands you *choosing* a different path."

"Yeah."

Brody waved his arms, clearly passionate about this argument. "It's like a fucking cult. Like they've all been brainwashed to believe that *this*—playing pro hockey or getting drafted to the NFL or whatever it is—is all there can be. There's nothing else. You either make it or your life's over."

Dean froze, the water bottle halfway to his lips. He'd *just* had that thought. *But for me, it's true. I didn't come from money or a secure home. Brody's got options I never had.*

But Dean wondered, for the very first time, if that was really true.

He'd made himself into a football player; couldn't he make himself into something else? Anything else? The only thing it required was a base of skill and then a shit ton of hard work.

"I see it, in your face." Brody's voice overflowed with frustration. "You buy into it, too. It's either *this* or nothing."

"I don't know . . ." Dean hated how he stuttered, but this was radical fucking thinking for a kid who had only had *this* as a goal for the last ten years.

Make it and get out.

Or fail and live a hard, pointless life.

"You know," Brody said, crossing his arms over his chest. "You know because you've been brainwashed, too."

"Realizing it should help you, yeah?" Dean managed to say.

"Yeah, except I think I'm still partially brainwashed," Brody said wryly. "And everyone around me still is. You think if I decided to say fuck it to pro hockey and go to medical school, everyone wouldn't think I was nuts?"

Dean wanted to say no. But that wasn't fair to Brody, who was asking the hard questions—even if they were hard—and deserved some hard answers.

"Everyone would think you're nuts, especially if you *could* play pro hockey," Dean admitted.

"Exactly," Brody said heavily. "Even my parents, who you'd think would be fucking thrilled at the thought I'm considering going into medicine, are freaking out."

"Yeah?" Dean couldn't even imagine his mom raising her head from her routine of work and partying to give what he did a second thought. But Brody was making him *think*, and once he'd started, he couldn't stop. It wouldn't necessarily be easier to have parents who were that invested, like Brody's parents, either. A different kind of hard, maybe, but hard all the same.

"They're here Thursday night and we're going to dinner." Brody paused. "You should come with us."

"What?" Dean couldn't help the flat exclamation that came out of his mouth.

"You should come with us." Brody paused. Reached out for Dean, and to Dean's shock, tugged him back into his arms.

Brody tilted his head back, those sugar eyes sweet and undeniably persuasive. "I want you to come with us."

"You want me to meet your parents?"

"Yeah." Brody didn't say why, but Dean could imagine more than a few reasons. Some casual-ish. Some that were quite a bit more serious.

"I . . .I'll look at my schedule," Dean said, but he already knew that he'd be moving heaven and earth to do it. Same way he'd fit in meeting Brody at the library and the gym. Same as he'd found the time to read up on hockey.

"Good," Brody said and brushed a final kiss across his mouth. "I'm gonna go do some reading."

And then he was gone, leaving Dean wondering what the fuck had just happened to their casual benefits arrangement.

CHAPTER THIRTEEN

"Hey, wait up," Brody called out, chasing Ramsey down outside the rink.

It had been four days since the game they'd nearly lost because of that stupid power play goal and their argument after. Ramsey had ignored multiple texts, and whenever they were at the rink and at practice, he made sure there were other players and coaches around. Brody hadn't been able to pin him down to talk since.

Except now.

He'd seen Ramsey ducking out, and he'd grabbed his bag, barely dressed, and chased after him.

His parents were in town, and tonight they, and *Dean*, were going to dinner. But first, he needed to clear the air with his best friend.

The guy he'd *thought* was his best friend. Lately, he was beginning to think that that particular position—and so much more—belonged to Dean, now.

Ramsey finally turned around. He had that blank look on his face. The one he seemed to wear around Brody a lot, lately. The one Brody hated. The one Brody was semi-tempted to punch off. "What?" he asked.

"Listen, I'm sorry, again, about the penalty," Brody said, thinking that starting off with an apology and not an accusation like, *You're being fucking weird and it's not helping my own weirdness about everything* might make Ramsey more willing to listen.

It didn't.

Ramsey's face closed down even more. "I know," he said. "You're so fucking sorry."

"That's not fair," Brody said. He refused to look away. Stared right at Ramsey, at the guy who'd taken him under his wing the moment he'd shown up on campus. Who'd been a mentor, but even more than that, a *friend*. And now seemingly had abandoned him, because of one stupid mistake—and a whole lot of questions.

"Nothing's fair," Ramsey said. "We were supposed to be unstoppable this year. I wanted us to be unstoppable. Instead, half the time it feels like you wanna be someplace else." He paused. Made a face. "With someone else."

"Wait. Are you *jealous*?" Brody could barely believe it. Was he jealous of Dean? Had he . . .*no.* There was no fucking way Ramsey had felt that way about him. He'd have known. He'd have sensed it.

But then, in the last two months, it didn't feel like he really knew Ramsey anymore.

"Not the way you think," Ramsey said. "Trust me. Dean's welcome to you, that way. I just . . .after last year got fucked up with your injury, this was supposed to be *our* year, Brody.

You know it. I know you do. We fucking talked about being *that* team on the ice. It was gonna propel both of us to the NHL. And when Coach B showed up and he wanted the same thing, to get us there, I thought it might actually happen. I really wanted it. I *want* it. And suddenly, you just fucking don't. Not anymore. It wasn't supposed to be like that."

"I know," Brody said.

Ramsey shot him a look full of frustrated venom, and the worst part was that Brody couldn't even blame him for it. This whole thing of Brody's probably really fucking sucked for his teammates, for Ramsey specifically, but then it also sucked for him, too.

It wasn't like he'd *chosen* this sudden, pervasive doubt. All these undeniable questions.

"And that's supposed to help?" Ramsey challenged. "That you know? That you feel so fucking bad, too?"

"No," Brody said. He wanted to cry. He wanted to hug Dean. He wanted Dean to remind him again that this was allowed. That he was supposed to do what he wanted. Not what everyone else wanted from him.

Before Ramsey could rail at him again for things he couldn't prevent, couldn't change, Brody continued, "If it's not you and me together anymore, you being pissed off about this is part of it. If I want to be around other people, it's because they *don't* judge me, don't sit around waiting for the old Brody to show again. They accept that I don't fucking know anymore. If I'm choosing *them*, that's why."

And because of everyone I fucking know, you're the most brainwashed, all of a fucking sudden—and that's saying something, because I know Dean. And I don't think anybody's ever want- ed to make it as badly as Dean does.

"Oh." Ramsey looked suddenly deflated. Like Brody had unexpectedly pricked him in a soft, undefended spot, and all his anger just whooshed out. "I'm being an asshole, aren't I?"

"Kinda, yeah. And me, too, frankly. We're both being . . .well, *assholes.*"

Ramsey grinned, and it was only a shadow of his former carefree grin, but even the shadow was enough. Was better than the on-purpose blankness of before.

And maybe that was all the carefree that Ramsey had any- more. While Brody had been changing, evolving, Ramsey had been doing it too.

They'd just been doing it in opposite directions.

"Listen, I'm sorry, too," Ramsey said and reached for him, and a second later, they were hugging tight and hard. "I'm here for you, if you need it. You know that, right?"

"Now I do," Brody said as he pulled back. He was feeling better than he had in days. Weeks, maybe. Of course, just in time for his parents to roll into town.

Ramsey winced. "Thanks for reminding me I was an ass- hole."

"I promise to *always* be there to remind you of that."

"Thanks," Ramsey said, chuckling. "You wanna grab a smoothie or something?"

"Actually . . ." Brody hesitated. "My parents are in town. I think they're worried about me."

"They should be," Ramsey said. It was weird, still, to hear that serious, earnest tone in his voice. Weird, but kinda nice, actually.

"We're going to dinner, and I roped Dean into going with us," Brody said, because he didn't want to touch, *they should be worried about you* with a freaking ten-foot pole.

"You're bringing Dean to meet your parents?" Ramsey's mouth fell open.

"Not like . . .not like *that.*" Except that Brody wasn't sure it wasn't *not* like that.

Ramsey shot him a look that said he agreed. "You sure about that?"

"No," Brody admitted. "But he said he'd come, help me play interference a bit, with them."

"I'd think they'd be thrilled you're considering doing something with your life and your degree besides playing hockey for a living," Ramsey said.

"You'd think," Brody muttered. And he wouldn't say they weren't cautiously interested or optimistic, based on the handful of texts they'd exchanged, since he'd asked his dad about medical school—but the truth was, they were brainwashed, too.

He fully expected them to ask something like, *but if you just wanted to be a doctor, what was all this for? The early morning practices, the special camps, the one-on-one coaching, the college recruiting?*

Brody wasn't sure. Not anymore.

But if he was going to move forward, he knew he needed to be sure.

As sure as Ramsey was.

"If he's willing to go, and deal with you *and* your parents, he must really like you," Ramsey said.

"I . . .we're not like that, we're friends."

Ramsey shot him a knowing look. "Don't bullshit yourself, Faulkner. You know he does. And you like him, too."

"We're friends," Brody repeated, even though he could admit to himself—maybe not to Ramsey, or to anyone else, *especially* Dean, yet—that the term didn't quite fit. Not anymore.

"Sure," Ramsey said, and of course now was the time he chose to find that casual, devil-may-care grin, and *now* was the time he chose to shoot it in Brody's direction.

Brody rolled his eyes, but it was a palpable hit.

Maybe he wasn't doing a very good job of lying to himself *or* a very good job of lying to everyone else.

"But have a good time. Give your mom a hug for me," Ramsey said.

"They'll be around for the game tomorrow, so you can give her one yourself," Brody said.

"Good." Ramsey smiled. "How 'bout you give *Dean* a hug for me, then?"

"You're being an asshole," Brody retorted.

"Yeah, a little. But it's fun to tease you about this. I've never gotten to before."

Brody nearly told him it was for a reason. Because he didn't *do* this. But whatever he wanted to call this thing with Dean, whatever comfortable, convenient label they were plastering over it, it was happening. Brody couldn't deny that.

"Yeah," Brody agreed.

And maybe that wasn't much, but Ramsey smiled, softer this time, because he clearly knew it *was* something, too.

"Alright, well, have fun. Don't let your parents freak Dean out too much."

"You think they could?" Brody hadn't worried about that.

"Bro—he's clearly crazy about you if he's willing to go to this dinner. But he's still a human and a clueless guy, because we're all sort of clueless. Add in that your parents can be a lot, and well . . .all I'm saying is that it *could* happen."

"Alright. Yes. I know. Okay." Brody took a deep breath.

"Don't worry. It's all gonna be fine." Ramsey patted him on the shoulder.

Brody hoped that he was right.

Dean was waiting for him at the apartment, sitting on the couch, wearing what Brody had already figured out were his nicest pair of jeans and a dark green button-up that did unbelievable things for not only his eyes, but his shoulders, his chest, his torso, his . . .

As Brody stood in the doorway, staring at him, he realized that Ramsey was right.

Dean *was* a friend.

He was more, too.

And he wondered, because he couldn't help it, if Dean felt the same as he rose, his gaze never leaving Brody.

"You ready to go?" Dean asked, his voice low and rumbling.

"No," Brody said.

Dean raised a dark eyebrow. "No?"

"I need . . ." Everything was suddenly pushing in on him. This new thing with Dean—untested and unspoken and possibly fleeting, to boot—and the thing with his parents, the pressure they were going to exert on him in the next few hours, even though they wouldn't mean too.

It helped that his friendship with Ramsey was no longer a jagged hole in his chest but the rest was a lot, too, and he just needed—

But Brody didn't need to ask. Didn't even need to say it.

Because Dean knew, and he was already rounding the coffee table and tugging Brody into his arms, hugging him tightly, fiercely.

He'd just hugged Ramsey outside the rink, and that had felt good, undeniably, but this felt *great.*

How had this happened? It felt like Brody had blinked and woken up and suddenly, he had *feelings.*

You have a crush on Dean. A big fat freaking crush.

"You're gonna be fine. They seem like nice enough people."

"You met them for probably five minutes before," Brody said into his shoulder.

"Yeah, but they raised you, so they can't be all bad," Dean said, pulling back. His green eyes were intent.

"And don't," Dean continued, "bring up my mom here, because I know it doesn't always work out that way."

"It's your mom's loss," Brody said. He *didn't* bring up Dean's dad, who he knew had been little more than a sperm donor. That they weren't in Dean's life was both of their losses.

"Yeah, yeah," Dean said, brushing him off, but Brody hoped he'd believed him, anyway.

"Can I ask you something?" Brody said, suddenly thinking of what Ramsey had insinuated. When Dean nodded, he plunged ahead. He didn't want to do this without Dean, but at the same time, he didn't want to fuck this up. Whatever *this* was. "Are you worried at all about uh . . .going to dinner with us? Like making things weird between us?"

Dean didn't answer immediately. "I can't say I'm comfortable with it. I don't have a lot of experience with parents. At least parents who *parent*. But you need someone there, who's there for *just you*, that's clear, and if you want me to be that person, I'm happy to do it."

Brody noticed he didn't really answer the question. He should let it go, take the easy win, but instead he found himself wanting to press on it, like a bruise.

"And you don't think it's gonna make anything weird?"

"You sayin' this is like a date? A double date with your parents? Then yeah, that might be weird."

Brody wanted to ask if it would be weird that it was a date or if it was because it was with his parents, but smartly shut his mouth this time. Maybe because he wasn't sure he *wanted* to know the answer.

"Okay, yeah." Brody nodded. He didn't really know what he was agreeing to, but at least they'd gotten *some* of the awkwardness out of the way. "We'd better go actually. We're meeting them, there, at the restaurant."

It was not that far, and normally Brody might just walk, but it was drizzling, and so he pulled out his keys.

Dean's eyebrows skidded up. "Oh, we're gonna take your fancy car, huh?"

"It's not fancy, it's just new."

"Fancy to me," Dean said, pulling his door open and sliding in. "Nice leather seats, even."

"Am *I* fancy to you?" Brody wondered.

Dean's gaze slipped over his form. And yeah, he'd dressed up a little. His nicest jeans, too, in a dark wash, and his button-up was a deep purple. Helped his summer tan look a little less washed out than it actually was.

"Yeah, but I like you anyway," Dean said gruffly.

"Reassuring," Brody teased. But he smiled all the way to the restaurant and even into the front.

The hostess led them back to the table and his parents stood up as they approached.

"Oh, Brody," his mom said, wasting no time and embracing him immediately. "It's so good to see you."

"It's good to see you too, Mom," he said, and he turned to where Dean had finished shaking hands with his dad. "And you remember Dean. My roommate." He and Dean exchanged a little loaded glance. He hadn't intended to say more, but he added, because he wasn't sure he could help himself, *and*, besides, it was true now, "And a friend."

His mom let go of him and pulled Dean, so much bigger and broader, but still as helpless in the face of her affection, into a hug. Gentle, too, with her, like she was something he could break and didn't want to.

"I'm happy you could come tonight," Tish said, directing one of her brightest smiles in Dean's direction.

"Well," Dean said, looking surprised by this, "I was happy Brody invited me. Not often we get a nice meal like this one."

"And you order whatever you want, our treat," his dad said as they sat down at the square table. Brody's knee brushed Dean's under the table, and it felt intimate, even though he was pretty sure it had been accidental.

"Thanks, sir," Dean said.

Maybe he didn't meet parents very often—and probably never under these circumstances—but Brody had to say he was doing an exemplary job.

He'd have to give him a real nice thank you, later.

The waitress appeared, took their drink orders. He ordered a Coke. Dean stuck to iced tea. His parents each got a glass of red wine. And then, before Brody could even decide if he wanted the New York strip or the filet, his mom started in on the interrogation.

"What's this about you asking about medical school pre-reqs?" she asked, turning to Brody, a worried crease appearing between her brows.

Brody shot his dad a look, who just raised his hands in mock surrender. "I didn't realize it was a secret," he said.

"It's not," Brody said, even though it kind of was. There was a reason he hadn't felt comfortable asking his advisor.

He was already sick of people saying, *but what about hockey?* even though it hadn't happened yet.

But it would.

"I'm just exploring my options," Brody continued defensively, when nobody said a word.

"Well, of course you can't play hockey forever," Tish reasoned.

"What if—" Brody broke off.

And then there was that touch again, against his leg. This time Brody knew Dean's touch wasn't accidental, but entirely on purpose.

It was just a single reassuring brush of his fingers against his jean-covered knee, but it gave him the courage to keep going.

"What if I don't want to play hockey after college?"

Brody had half-expected his parents to come around to the notion fairly easily. After all, they were *both* doctors. They'd encouraged him to take the biology major, even though most of his teammates thought he was crazy for attempting it.

His mom took a very long sip of wine. "Let me make sure I understand you," she said softly, but directly, "you want to go to medical school instead of playing pro hockey?"

"Is it your knee? I know Hauser was supposed to be the best, but—"

But Brody didn't let his dad get the rest of the question out. "It's not my knee. My knee is fine." That was the simple answer, at least. The more complicated answer—the answer he wasn't sure they'd understand, was that his injury last spring had opened doors in his mind that he'd never explored before.

Without hockey, he'd felt himself looming over a black hole of depression. Not wanting to get out of bed. Wanting to let the frustration swallow him whole. He'd had to find something else he really loved that wasn't hockey, and it had been so easy for that to be school and science because he'd already loved them, and it turned out that love had only needed air and room to grow, to really blossom.

"Then what is it?" Tish asked, clearly mystified.

Dean bumped his knee again, and that was the only warning Brody had before he spoke up. "I think it's cool that Brody's exploring his options. He's such a smart guy. Caring and thoughtful. And he's lucky, too, that he *has* options." Dean didn't need to say that *he* didn't. The subtext was clear enough.

Brody gave his parents credit. They both listened to what Dean said, nodding in understanding, but then Tish turned to him again. "But you *love* playing hockey."

"I do, but I think I don't love it quite enough." He didn't love it to the exclusion of everything else. Not anymore. His world had opened, he'd gotten a peek at another future, and he didn't want to just shut the door on it.

Dean's hand brushed his knee again, but this time it didn't move away again. It stayed. A firm, welcome pressure, grounding him. Reminding him.

You want different things than you did, and that's okay.

"Huh," Roger said. "Well, if that's true, then I'm glad you're talking to us, Brody."

"I wouldn't talk to anyone else," Brody said wryly.

"We support you no matter what," Tish added.

The waitress arrived back, and they ordered, Brody not even paying attention to what he picked out. He was too edgy, even with Dean's hand on his knee.

"Well, about med school." Roger sighed, and Brody had a feeling this wasn't good news. "You're probably about a year behind on the prereqs. You'd need to take another year of school, at least. Some additional classes."

That jived with the rudimentary research Brody had done on his own, late at night when he was feeling wild and free, like he could do *anything* and it wouldn't come back to bite him in the ass.

"Okay," Brody said, nodding.

"Or, possibly some kind of gap year. Taking a few classes to supplement your application. Studying for the entrance exams." His dad shot him an apologetic look. "There's no question if you're smart enough, Brody, or if we think you'd be a good doctor or not. It's just surprising. Feels like this is coming out of left field."

"Probably because I've been afraid to bring it up," Brody admitted.

"And that takes guts. To buck what everyone assumes you're gonna do," Dean said, those green eyes steady and supportive as they gazed at him.

"I'd ask if you'd ever considered that," Tish said to Dean, "but I have a feeling you haven't."

"Next year, I'll be drafted into the NFL and if God's willing, I'll have a nice long career before I've got to figure out what else I'm doing," Dean said.

"I saw that fumble return you had against USC," Roger said, with clear admiration in his expression, "so it doesn't feel like much of a prayer, and more of a certainty."

"No certainties, but I feel good about my chances."

"Dean's the most determined person I've ever met," Brody said.

"Sounds like it was a good thing that Ramsey bailed on living with you."

"Actually," Brody said, smiling, "I think Ramsey was playing matchmaker."

Tish's wine glass, halfway to her lips, froze.

"Uh, *roommate* matchmaker," Brody clarified.

But the knowing look in his mom's eyes was hard to miss.

She'd guessed. Maybe even before tonight.

Well, Brody was beginning to think they weren't all that subtle, actually. He definitely wasn't.

"I'll make sure to tell him I'm thankful for his intervention tomorrow night," Tish said firmly.

"How's he feel about his chances after graduation?" Roger asked.

And thankfully, his own interrogation was over. At least for now. There was no way they wouldn't discuss this again, but he'd made his feelings clear, and his parents had at least appeared to accept them.

"Honestly, I've never seen Ramsey work so damn hard," Brody admitted.

"Good for him," Tish said.

"He's really improved since that draft spot where the Oilers took him, a few years back."

"Yeah, I know he's pushing to make it right onto a roster, after dev camp and then the regular preseason camp," Brody said. "And Coach B is good for him, that way. He's pushing all of us hard."

His mom shot him a look, and Brody didn't need her to say it out loud for him to understand it. *Even you?*

"Even me, Mom," Brody added, rolling his eyes. "You can say shit out loud, you know?"

"Language, Brody," Tish said sternly, but she was smiling. "I'm sorry, this is just such an adjustment for me. The way I think of you."

"He's growing up," Roger said, glancing over at his wife. "And for the record, *I* think that's a very good thing."

"I do too," Tish agreed, then she sighed. "It's just . . . different. That's all."

"It's only less weird to me because it's been on my mind for awhile," Brody admitted.

"Awhile?" his dad questioned.

"Some this summer, but I thought when I got back, it would be different. The same, I guess, as it always was. At first, it was easy to tell myself I was uneasy about my knee, but I know now that it's not just that."

"As long as you're not forcing yourself to do something you don't want," Tish said firmly. "If you're worrying about not making it—"

"I'm not," Brody said, cutting that thought off hard and fast. "It's not that I hate playing hockey now or that I don't think I'm good enough. It's just not what I think I want to do for the rest of my life."

"Alright," Tish said, smiling.

Dean's fingers tightened on his knee, and even though he didn't say anything, Brody had a feeling he knew what he was thinking.

You got this. You did it, baby.

"Well, I'm really fucking glad *that's* over," Brody said, as the door shut behind his parents.

After dinner, his mom had not very subtly insisted on coming by to see the apartment, by claiming she had a load of stuff in the car for him.

They'd stayed for at least ten minutes longer than Brody wanted, chatting on the couch about his classes, about the game tomorrow night, even about Dean's game this weekend.

"It wasn't so bad. I got a free steak out of it," Dean said, leaning back on the couch, stretching his long legs out to their full length. "Besides, your parents are nice. Normal, even."

"What even is normal?" Brody wondered.

What he really wanted to ask was how long his parents had to be gone for him to lean over and kiss Dean.

"Good question." Dean grinned at him. "You got any others?"

"A suggestion," Brody said.

Dean raised an eyebrow. "My bedroom, now?" he asked.

Brody laughed. "Okay, that mind reading was sort of freaky."

"Freaky *and* hot, I hope?"

"Add it to the list," Brody said and stood, reaching out for Dean's hand, and he took it, squeezing it.

"If I didn't say it, you did good," Dean said, low and earnest as Brody paused in the doorway of Dean's room.

He'd suggested *his* room, but he'd only been in here a handful of times. It was neat, not surprisingly, and the bed was covered in a blue comforter.

"Thanks," Brody said.

"I know it wasn't easy."

"You didn't say it, but I felt it anyway." But before he could say more, Dean cupped his cheeks and tilted him up for a kiss.

It was sweeter, gentler. Less fiery than he'd expected.

It was the kiss version of that touch on his knee.

But they couldn't kiss, not when it felt as good as it did, and not have passion flame between them, hot and undeniable.

Brody groaned into his mouth as Dean captured it, their bodies stumbling back towards the bed.

"I *know* I didn't say this, but you're goddamn hot," Dean growled as his fingers made quick work of Brody's shirt, tossing it on the floor, those big, calloused hands pushing him down on the bed.

"Thought I was pretty," Brody teased, gazing up at him. There was nothing like the way Dean's gaze fired when he pushed him.

"Hot, pretty, all I know is I can't look away from you," Dean said, and the confession sounded wrenched out of him. He leaned in, ghosting a hand over his cock, hard in his jeans.

"Trust me, the feeling's mutual," Brody said, arching into his touch. "You gonna make me feel good, baby?"

"Gonna do even better than that." Dean pulled Brody's jeans off, then his underwear, sliding them slowly down his legs, straightening as that intense gaze took in every single inch of his bare skin.

Dean was still dressed, and that was another turn-on Brody hadn't considered before, but apparently worked for him anyway.

Also that look in his eyes . . .Brody's cock twitched.

"Turn over," Dean said.

"No *please*?" Brody asked, raising an eyebrow.

"Trust me, you're gonna be the one begging me before this is over," Dean said gruffly. "Turn over."

Brody wanted to keep arguing, keep teasing, but *that* look promised so much pleasure that it was hard to resist Dean's order any longer.

He turned over, stretching out against the bed, pushing his cock against the soft roughness of the comforter, reveling in the pressure of it.

"None of that," Dean said and smacked him lightly on the ass.

They both froze.

"Is that . . .is that another one of those things?" Brody wondered, even though he already knew it was.

Things that shouldn't have been hot, but were.

Maybe at the top of that whole fucking list.

"Yeah," Dean said, but his next touch was softer as his rough fingers traced the lines of Brody's back, down lower. "You gonna be good for me, pretty boy, let me do the things I want to you?"

Brody's back arched, involuntarily. He wanted more. He wanted this endless arousal inside him to spike and then explode.

If he'd ever thought sex could feel like this . . .

But it didn't. Not with anyone else. Only with Dean.

"Yeah, I thought so," Dean said, smugly.

Then his lips were replacing his fingers, and they were unexpectedly soft, reverent, the scratch of his stubble lighting up every one of Brody's nerves as Dean made his way down his back.

"You've got the prettiest fucking back I've ever seen. So gorgeous," Dean murmured into his skin.

Brody, whose mind was already half-dead with lust, realized then what Dean was doing. Just as he'd promised.

Next time, I wanna lay you out, on your stomach. You got such a pretty back, pretty boy, and lick all the way up and down it, and then . . .lick you lower. Get you nice and wet for my fingers. Feel you come around them, just from them inside of you, and you humping against the bed because you can't help it any longer.

Brody moaned, because he couldn't hold it back any longer. He already wanted it so bad he couldn't imagine Dean working him up even harder, but then maybe he could, as Dean's mouth dipped lower.

"You want this?" Dean asked, spreading his cheeks.

Brody had never heard him sound like that before. Voice rough and full of worship, full of awe.

It felt so real, so right Brody's heart squeezed and his cock twitched.

"Yeah," Brody said. Moaned against the fabric as he felt Dean's tentative brush of a wet fingertip against his hole. He'd really liked it the last time Dean had done this.

"You said this was an advanced maneuver," Dean murmured into his skin. "If I do something you don't like, you gotta say."

Brody gasped as he slid that finger in, next to something warmer, wetter. "Fuck, fuck, *yes*." His skin felt too tight, too small, as Dean kept gently fingering him. Kept licking him, right there, his tongue soft and rough, the pressure too perfect to stand.

He was barely holding himself back from rubbing against the mattress and exploding, but Dean had asked him if he was gonna be good, if he wanted this. And he'd said yes, to both.

So he'd trust Dean to give it to him, when he couldn't stand it anymore.

"This is definitely on the list," Dean said, and Brody could hear the desperation in his voice. It was all he was hanging on to as a second finger slipped in. They crooked, big and inescapable inside him, and Dean rubbed against something that lit him up. Brody cried out.

"That's it," Dean soothed, his other hand swiping up and down his back in reassuring strokes. "You can take it, pretty boy. Yeah, you can. Just like that."

"I . . .I can't . . ." Brody groaned. "I'm so fucking close. You keep doing that and I'm gonna—"

"Exactly," Dean said. And he thrust not necessarily harder, but more insistently, faster and better, right against that spot, over and over, until Brody was hanging on to control by his fingertips, and they were slipping.

"You wanna come?" Dean asked.

Brody half-laughed, half-sobbed. "Yes."

"Fuck, you're so hot like this, so goddamn pretty."

"I gotta . . ." Brody panted. He couldn't fuck against the mattress. But he could against Dean's fingers, so he did, pushing back, until Dean was groaning too.

"Touch yourself," Dean finally murmured, "I'm touching myself."

Brody craned his neck, right before he put a hand on his aching cock and saw that Dean was telling the truth. He'd opened his jeans, shoved them around his knees, and had his hand, big and rough, around his own cock, stroking it hard, face twisted at the pleasure, as Brody fucked his fingers.

Brody froze then exploded, barely getting a hand around himself before he was clenching hard in orgasm.

"Shit, *shit*." Brody heard Dean's exclamation, feeling hot stripes of come falling over his back.

For a second, Brody just floated along in inescapable pleasure.

Heard Dean murmur, as he leaned over him, "Don't move, I'm gonna clean you up."

Then there was a damp cloth, wiping off his back.

Dean turned him over and he wiped his front, and they both looked down at the wet patch on Dean's comforter.

"Don't you dare apologize," Dean said.

"Okay, I won't," Brody said. He patted the bed next to him. "We can work around the wet spot." He nearly suggested they move over to *his* bed. And spend the night there, too.

They hadn't done that yet—spend the night together.

Dean or Brody had always retreated to their own bed, after their experimenting.

But Brody didn't want to leave. Even if they had to work around the wet spot.

He wanted to lie here, forever, with Dean gazing at him like he wasn't wrong, wasn't losing his mind, like he was perfect and shiny and amazing.

Like he really was that pretty boy Dean liked to call him.

CHAPTER FOURTEEN

It was drizzling and cold, a typical November day in Portland, which was why it was bizarre that Brody was sweating, practically right through his T-shirt. He'd already shed his sweatshirt, and when he had, Ramsey had shot him a weird look.

"What is your deal?" Ramsey asked when they took their seats.

Brody told himself, firmly, to stop squirming. He shoved his fists into the balled-up sweatshirt on his lap.

"Good seats, huh?" Brody said. He gazed out onto Harrington Field. It was his third year here, yet he'd never gone to a football game. But then he'd never had a reason to, before.

Ramsey still looked concerned. "Yeah, though I don't know why we couldn't have just sat in the student section."

"You know how hard those tickets are to come by? Besides, this way we didn't have to fight for a spot, or deal with all that rowdy shit," Brody said.

Ramsey's dubiousness deepened. "Yeah, 'cause it's not gonna get rowdy around here." He glanced around them. And yep, the whole section was full of bros and their wives in their mid-twenties to early thirties, most of them flushed like they'd spent the last four hours "tailgating." Brody had learned that was mostly a polite euphemism for drinking a lot, because you couldn't buy booze at the stadium itself.

"It's okay to be enthusiastic about your alma mater," Brody said, not even sure why he was defending these guys who were clearly only here to try to recapture even an afternoon of what their youth had felt like.

"You're gonna end up like one of these guys," Ramsey said.

It was harsh. But then Ramsey rarely varnished his truths.

Brody rolled his eyes. "You think I'm gonna regret not playing if I decide not to."

"Look at these guys. They're all trying to remember what it feels like, even for a minute. It's pathetic."

"Don't sugarcoat it or anything," Brody tried joking. But he *was* afraid of that. Would he wake up at twenty-seven or thirty-one and wish he'd made different choices?

"Okay, this isn't me sugarcoating it," Ramsey said. "You spent God knows how much money on these fucking seats so you can get a better view of your boyfriend's ass in those tight white pants, so enjoy it."

"He's not my boyfriend—"

Ramsey raised an eyebrow and Brody stopped.

"He's *not,*" Brody restarted. He didn't know if he wanted a boyfriend. Of course, if he did, then there was only one person he'd be interested in occupying that position, and he *was* on the field below them, wearing those aforementioned tight white pants.

Brody had seen him totally naked, not a stitch of clothing in sight, and yet those white pants still made his heart beat a little faster.

"If he's not your boyfriend, then you're stupider than I thought you were."

"What if we just want to hook up? Don't *you* do that?" Brody retorted. "Why can't I want that?"

Ramsey shot him another one of those looks that said, explicitly, *you're a fucking moron.* "Because you're Brody Faulkner," he said with exaggerated patience. "You want the picket fence and the white house and the two-point-five children."

"I never said I wanted any of those things. Picket fences are stupid—pointless, really. They can't even keep a dog in. And two-point-five children are gonna be harder for me, if . . ." Brody trailed off. He wasn't thinking that way, he *wasn't.* And yet he'd still *almost* thought, *if Dean and I could go the distance.*

They couldn't fucking go the distance. Their paths might be aligned right now, but in a year or two, they'd diverge radically.

They both knew that, which was one—but not the *only*—reason they were keeping this thing between them casual.

"If what?" Ramsey demanded.

Brody glared at him.

"If you and Dean end up together? Wildly in love? If you follow him to whatever city he's drafted to? Is that what you're gonna do, Brody? Follow him like a good little WAG? Do exactly what Marcus is gonna do with Wes?"

"WAG's an offensive term," Brody said stiffly.

"And so is puck bunny, and lots of idiots still use it." Ramsey took a deep breath. "I don't want to fight with you again, but here's the thing, you idiot, the longer you pretend this isn't serious, that you don't have big fat feelings for each other, the tougher it's gonna be to figure out what to do about it."

"Trust me," Brody muttered, "we're doing *plenty* about it."

"And believe *me*, I'm fucking thrilled you've finally discovered sex. But that's not what I'm talking about."

"Oh, look, the game's starting," Brody said, attempting to change the subject.

Ramsey elbowed him. "You know what I *just* said about regret? About you waking up in ten years and wondering what you did with your fucking life, when you could've been playing in the NHL? Well, same thing with Dean. You wanna wake up in a year or two or five and wonder what happened to him? Wonder why you never felt this way again?"

Brody opened his mouth and then snapped it shut again.

He didn't know what to say.

"It's complicated," was what he finally settled for.

But Ramsey only rolled his eyes. "It's *always* complicated."

"If I knew you were gonna ride my ass the whole game, I'd have invited someone else." Brody sniffed.

"No, you invited me, 'cause you wanted to prove something. Well, I'm here, aren't I?" Ramsey teased.

"I was actually surprised you agreed," Brody said. It *had* been a little bit of a test, asking Ramsey to come with him to the football game. Ramsey was notorious for disliking football. And yet he'd agreed, and he was here.

"Me too," Ramsey said. "Maybe I wanted a front row seat to you mooning over your boyfriend."

"He's not—"

Ramsey held up a hand. "Don't even argue. We both know you want him to be. And if you'd just find some balls and *talk to him*, I'd bet you'd discover he'd be very fucking good with that idea. Your mom told me you two were *very* coupley at dinner."

"Ugh, you talked to my mom about Dean?"

"*She* brought *him* up. Wanted to know what was going on with you two. Said you kept playing footsy under the table during dinner."

"We were not!" Brody exclaimed. He couldn't believe his mom would ask *Ramsey* about Dean and not him. He said so, emphatically, and Ramsey patted him on the shoulder reassuringly.

"If you want my honest opinion, she's going to. But she was doing some advanced reconnaissance first."

"I guess it would come as kind of a surprise to them, me with a guy." Brody could admit that, at least. Maybe he'd have told her—told both his parents, actually—if things with Dean were more serious.

"You with *anyone*, and to be honest, not really, actually."

"Oh."

Ramsey patted him on the knee again. "Exactly. Tell her. But before you do that, talk to Dean, okay?"

"We *do* talk," Brody grumbled.

"Listen, if I had that in my bed, I wouldn't be doing much talking either, so I get it," Ramsey said, gesturing to where Dean stood on the sidelines, separate from everyone.

"We *do* talk," Brody said. He didn't add that sometimes it was *in* bed. After they'd worn each other out, and it felt like they were more honest with each other in those moments than they'd ever been with anyone else.

"You tell him you were coming to the game?"

"Actually, no. I wanted it to be a surprise."

Ramsey groaned. "Oh God. You are *such* a boyfriend, Faulkner."

Brody wanted to deny it again, but it was becoming hard to. "Watch the game, Ramsey. Do you need me to explain the rules to you?"

Ramsey cocked his head. "I think I'll be able to figure it out."

"Alright." Brody focused back on Dean, who was about to jog onto the field. During one of those late nights, Brody's head on Dean's chest, he'd confided his nerves about this game.

They've got a good line. And they'll double team me. Maybe triple team me. If I can't prove I can still stop the play then... He'd hesitated, then. Brody had heard the unmistakable worry in his voice and what he hadn't said. *I might not make it after all*, was his unspoken fear.

He'd almost said, *then maybe we can be together. Like for real.*

But as much as Brody was afraid he wanted that, he didn't want it at the cost of Dean's dreams.

If he didn't end up in the NHL, then it was because he'd found something else he wanted more. But Dean didn't have a backup plan. Dean's plan was to make it, and he'd devoted himself with an intense single-minded focus to that one goal.

But Dean shouldn't have worried, Brody realized, as the first play unfolded on the field.

Dean gained the edge with a neat little side-step, then stiff-armed the second lineman, and was around behind the quarterback, not even letting him get rid of the ball before he tackled him to the ground.

The stadium erupted as Dean popped back up, kicking his leg out, his muscular arms straining as he yelled in triumph.

"Shit, I can totally see the attraction," Ramsey said, nudging Brody, who could barely tear his gaze off the guy on the field.

The only guy on the field who mattered.

"Are you checking out my boyfriend?" Brody teased.

"Fucking finally," Ramsey teased right back, grinning.

"He's not yet, we still need to talk, but . . ." Brody gazed down at him. "Yeah, I'd like that, I think. If we could figure out how to make it work."

"You're fucking brilliant and he's no slouch himself, despite his major. You'll get there."

"Did you just say something supportive?"

"I say plenty of supportive shit," Ramsey retorted, but he was still smiling.

"Next, you're gonna be taking credit for all this," Brody said.

Ramsey raised an eyebrow. "Shouldn't I?"

"No," Brody said, smacking him in the chest.

"I don't know. I kinda think I'm sort of responsible for you two. If I hadn't bowed out, you'd be miserable, going through this bullshit alone."

"I wouldn't have been alone," Brody argued, but he knew what Ramsey was saying. Dean did make him feel less alone. He didn't want to go through this crisis at all, but the only thing that made it even remotely bearable was Dean.

Dean's support.

Dean's smile, gentle and bright.

Dean's touch, his expression full of awe.

Dean when he called him pretty boy. He wasn't just saying he was pretty, he was saying a million other things, too, and Brody could feel each and every one.

"Yeah, you're so fucking gone," Ramsey retorted fondly.

"Shut up and watch the football game," Brody said.

"You mean, shut up and watch your boyfriend play some fucking killer football."

Brody wanted to tell him he was full of shit, but *well*, that was the truth, wasn't it?

⋙ ⋘

"Great game," Wes said, clapping Dean on the back. "I'd say you killed it, but you kinda do that every week."

"Thanks," Dean said. "You too."

"Eh, I barely need to go out there and throw the ball around when the defense is playing like it is."

"We can't win if you don't score," Dean argued.

"Yeah, but you make it a hell of a lot easier." Wes paused. "Take some fucking credit, you've earned it."

"Yeah," Dean said noncommittally. He'd been worried about this game. He hadn't told Wes, though maybe in an alternate universe he might've. Instead, he'd told Brody. And now, with the game over, he just wanted to get back to the apartment and tell him all about it.

How he'd faced down those double and triple teams and still owned their asses.

How he'd beaten the senior offensive tackle who was poised to be drafted in the first round, who was considered one of the best tackles in the whole country.

He'd done it, and the whole time, in the back of his mind, had been Brody.

Brody smiling. Brody laughing. Brody gasping as Dean wrung every last ounce of pleasure from his gorgeous body.

Dean grabbed his phone from his locker and scrolled through the messages of congratulations. Most of them were from people he didn't really know. Admirers. Agents who weren't Ian who wanted a chance at signing him as a client when he finally declared for the draft.

But there was a message from Ian. **Killer game,** he'd written, **if you want to grab something to eat, let's do that. Also I found a friend of yours, he's gonna come with us.**

Dean didn't know who the friend could possibly be, or how Ian would've known about him or her.

He was dreading it, as he walked out of the locker room, but to his shock, there was Ian, his auburn hair bright in the dark corridor, and standing next to him was Brody, his smile possibly eclipsing Ian's hair.

"There's the MVP," Ian said, teasing him and patting him on the back as he turned to Brody.

"You came to a game?" he asked stupidly.

He'd come. Dean had assumed Brody's presence had been in his own head, but he'd actually been there, in the stands, wasting one of his rare Saturday afternoons off, to go to a game for a sport he didn't even particularly care about.

"It was so great. *You* were so great," Brody said and tugged him into a hug.

It was *mostly* platonic.

But the way Dean didn't want to let go of him, wanting to hold him close forever, definitely edged it nearer to non-platonic territory. Unfortunately kissing Brody was way off-limits, but Dean wanted it anyway. Wanted to press his lips to Brody's and prove once and for all who he was, and that this wasn't a casual thing. Not anymore. Not at all.

Ian must've known too, because he was smirking when they finally broke apart.

"I ran into Brody waiting for you, too," Ian explained. "And I recognized him."

"You looked him up," Dean said.

Brody was smirking, now, too. God, he was going to get a big head, from everything he was probably imagining that Dean had said about him to his prospective agent—and his friend.

Well, Dean was ready and willing to take him down a peg. Or two. Or ten.

In fact, he was looking forward to it. Had been, from the last orgasm they'd shared.

"Yeah," Ian admitted. "I did. There aren't many Brodys on the hockey team who also have a bio major."

"Guilty as charged," Brody said, not sounding upset at all that Dean had been telling Ian about him. "Come on, let's get some food and talk about how fucking awesome you were today."

"I'm still stuck on the fact that you *came*," Dean murmured as they headed out of the athletic complex.

"I wanted to surprise you," Brody said, smugly.

And well, it wasn't unearned because he sure was fucking surprised.

"Yeah, it was a good one," Dean said. Wanted to say more, but they were still surrounded by fans and players, streaming out of the area around the football stadium, and then there was Ian.

He had a feeling Ian already suspected what was going on, but he wasn't going to say a word about it unless one of them did first.

Brody suggested Jimmy's, and they all nodded, switching directions.

"I'll tell you this," Ian said, glancing between them as they walked over to the diner, "you keep playing like this and I'm gonna get a fucking unreal number of calls wondering if you're gonna declare for the draft *this* year."

"He can do that?" Brody asked, and Dean could tell he was trying to ask casually, but he knew Brody, and the way his gaze sharpened wasn't casual at all.

"Oh, he can, if he wanted to," Ian said.

"But I don't want to. I want to get my degree."

"He wants it *all*," Ian said, smacking Dean fondly on the back. "I admire that about him."

"I do too," Brody said, with an approving nod.

Dean felt himself flushing, warm blood rushing to his cheeks. "I just . . .it feels wrong to come to college, the first one in my family to make it here, and *not* graduate."

"Well, the good news is if you continue to play like a demon, it won't matter if you declare for the draft this year or next year," Ian said.

"Guess I've been smiling on the sideline enough," Dean said wryly.

"What?" Brody sounded confused.

Ian shrugged, the corner of his mouth tilting up. "It was kind of stupid advice, but what other kind of advice do you give a guy that's got the whole package? There *was* a concern Dean was too focused, his whole self tied up in football, with nothing else to support him if anything went wrong. A first-round pick is a lot to spend on a guy." Ian hesitated. "But I can see he's doing better. Maybe your doing?"

Brody beamed. "Totally my doing." He glanced over at Dean, like he wasn't sure how much he was supposed to say. "We've been sorta helpin' each other out."

"Is that what we're calling it?" Dean teased.

Brody's smile widening even further proved that his hunch had been correct. Brody felt okay revealing to Ian what was going on.

Of course, that would mean *Dean* would have to know what was going on. Lately, the last week or so, it felt like this thing going on between them had shifted, and Dean didn't understand what new ground they'd landed on.

He only knew he was fucking thrilled—and a little terrified—about it.

They walked into Jimmy's, grabbed the last booth in the back, and ordered.

"So, Brody, you play hockey."

Brody nodded, taking a sip of his Coke. "This is still on the DL, but not sure for how much longer. I'd like to finish out my college career, but I'm considering going to med school instead of trying to make it in the NHL."

"Smart, too." Ian shot Dean an approving glance.

It didn't matter if his future agent—and friend—approved of Brody. It wouldn't change a fucking thing when it came to how Dean felt. But it felt good, anyway.

"He's brilliant," Dean said gruffly. "Got a lot of options."

Brody smiled and glanced over at Dean, sitting next to him, his gaze as intimate as a touch. "I'm a lucky man."

Well. There was no way they were keeping this under wraps, now. At least in front of Ian.

Dean cleared his throat—because suddenly it was clogged with emotion.

Nobody had ever really been proud of him like this before. They'd thought he was amazing on the football field, of course. They wanted him for what he could do. But they'd never just wanted him for *him*.

But there was no question in Dean's mind that Brody did.

The only question he still had was if Brody's feelings had blossomed from friendship and sex to something else, the way Dean's had.

Let's fucking face it. You're head over heels, crazy ass in love with this guy.

Dean choked on his Dr. Pepper. He wanted to tell that insane squirrel part of his brain that had just had the *nerve* to suggest it that it was wrong.

But he didn't think it was.

After all, he'd never felt like this before. And he'd never been in love before.

So . . . logically . . .

"Are you okay?" Brody was briskly whacking him on his back. "You just went white and then red. Ian here thought he was going to have to break out his high school CPR skills."

"No, no, I'm fine." *Mostly. My whole world just shifted.*

He didn't know if Brody felt the same. Maybe he didn't. Maybe he *wouldn't*.

And that didn't even touch on what the fuck they were going to do about it besides enjoying the year and a half they both had before they inevitably went their separate ways. Brody to whatever amazing thing he decided to tackle next, and Dean to the NFL.

"Okay good." The concern melted off Brody's face and it softened. Dean felt his fingers brush against his knee, then move away, like he needed to reassure both of them that he was actually fine.

"Seriously, though, I've been getting a lot of interest," Ian said. He paused, grinning. "So you can't inhale Dr. Pepper and die now."

"Wasn't planning on it. Good interest?"

"I'd say just about every team," Ian said.

"That's fantastic, Dean," Brody said enthusiastically, like he didn't mind at all if Dean took off and chased his NFL dreams.

It didn't necessarily *mean* that, but that enthusiasm dimmed his own perspective, and a little bit of the hope he'd been holding on to.

"Yeah, it's great news," he said slowly. He wanted to hang on to the way it had felt when he'd realized Brody had come to his game.

Then do it, that stupid squirrel voice insisted. *Nothing has to change, even though you've caught feelings. It's been good between you. Keep it good.*

Even though it was the stupid squirrel part of his brain and Dean would've assumed totally clueless, that was actually pretty decent advice. He could do that.

Truthfully, it was way fucking easy to keep it good with Brody. Because it *was* so goddamn good.

"I think the only thing I've got to say is keep annihilating those offenses, and keep doing whatever else you're doing," Ian said, the sly glance he gave Brody giving away exactly what he meant.

"I can do that," Dean said.

The waitress came with their orders and they shifted into small talk as they ate, Ian telling a story about some of his boyfriend Carter's shenanigans at their local bar.

"Wait," Brody said, chewing some of his Reuben and swallowing, "the bar you go to is called the *Pirate's Booty*?"

Ian grinned. "Yep. Funny isn't it?"

"It's hilarious. What team does Carter play for again? I can't remember. It's the Piranhas, right?"

Ian chuckled and Dean didn't hold back his eye roll. "It's the Condors, and you'd better not say that around them. They take that kind of stuff personally."

"The Condors and the Piranhas are division rivals," Dean explained and Brody's eyes lit up.

"Oh! Like the Rangers and the Canes?"

"You hockey guys are so weird," Dean teased.

"Oh yeah, like we're *any* weirder than you football guys," Brody dished right back, grinning at him.

For a second, it felt like the whole world fell away. There was just that bright smile on Brody's face and the affection in his honey brown eyes, and *more*, Dean hoped. He was going to enjoy what he could, while he could, but there was no way not to hope that maybe someday, Brody might feel the same.

Ian cleared his throat and the moment broke. Brody looked away, back down to his sandwich, and Dean fished around on his plate for a few leftover fries.

"Well, I think as a third-party arbiter, I'm gonna say you're *both* weird, but I'm gonna give the edge to football," Ian said.

"That's only 'cause you're dating a football player," Dean objected.

Ian raised an eyebrow. "Yep, I get a front row seat to all that weirdness. And then Carter's got his own idiosyncrasies."

"Making him one of the best receivers in the NFL," Dean pointed out wryly.

"But probably not any easier to live with," Brody said.

Ian nodded, but this sweet, gooey look crossed over his face. Love, that was what it was, Dean realized. Ian was wildly in love with Carter, the same way he—

No. He wouldn't let himself finish that thought.

He wasn't going to let himself get too carried away.

"Not easy, but worth every minute," Ian said. He looked over at Dean. "Carter's actually looking forward to meeting up, on the field."

"I wouldn't be playing against him." That would be the corner's job, for whatever team he ended up on. A thankless job, because Carter was damn good.

"Oh, he knows. But that's the thing about Carter. He always wants to be the best, and that means going up against the best."

"Well tell him to give Flynn two years and I'll be tackling his ass to the ground." Dean referred to the Condors' quarterback, Riley Flynn.

"Oh, he knows," Ian said with amusement. "I think the whole NFL's holding their breath, waiting for you to come in and be the wrecking ball we all know you can be."

"Damn straight," Dean said, nodding. He glanced over at Brody, and the pride shining in his eyes there meant the world—but it also meant that Brody was perfectly okay with sending him off to wherever.

Damn it.

They finished up their meal, Brody shooting Dean a quick glance before he paid the check for the whole table. "I know," he mentioned under his breath to Dean after they'd said their goodbyes to Ian, "that you've got to be super careful about money and him."

"Yeah." Dean nodded. "Can't even take a bottle of water from the guy."

"It's stupid," Brody said.

"Yeah, a little." They lingered outside Jimmy's. Dean wanted to suggest going back to the apartment, but he didn't want to be the first one to suggest it, either. Still, he had homework to do. Even on a Saturday night. Even on a Saturday night after winning a football game.

But first, Dean wanted to tell Brody—even if it was only in words—how much it had meant to him that he'd showed up today.

"I'm real glad you came," Dean confessed. "Didn't even know I wanted you in the stands until there you were, waiting for me to get out of the locker room."

Brody smiled. "I hoped you'd feel that way. I even got Ramsey to go with me."

"You brought Ramsey?"

"Yeah, he ducked out right after, to go to some party, but he's real proud of you too," Brody said.

"Even if I play football?"

"I think it's actually growing on him a bit, but I didn't tell you that," Brody said with a low chuckle that lit up all of Dean's nerves. God, he wanted to feel that sound against his bare skin. He was so gone for this man. And it wasn't even surprising that it was a man; it was only surprising that he'd fallen for *anyone*.

"'Course not," Dean said.

"Actually, I've got to go to the library. Meet Gina, my lab partner, and work on one of our reports." Brody shoved his hands into his jean pockets and Dean had an inkling that maybe this was as awkward for Brody as it was for him. The difference was that Brody made everything look so coolly effortless because he looked like *that*.

Brody hadn't invited him, but he said anyway, "You mind if I join you? I'll just stick my headphones in. I've got a lot of reading to do, and a paper to write."

Dean had half-expected Brody to say no, but to his surprise he nodded, looking unexpectedly pleased that he'd invited himself.

"Oh yeah, sure. I'm sure . . .uh . . .Gina would love to finally meet you."

Dean raised an eyebrow. "You told your lab partner about me?"

Now, Brody looked *really* flustered. "Well, you told your prospective agent about *me.*"

"Yeah," Dean admitted.

"Just, you've been stealing me away for homework time. Usually that's what Gina does. I had to tell her who it was."

"Right." Dean bumped Brody's shoulder. "That's all it was."

"It was," Brody retorted, but the pleased look in his eyes told the *real* story.

They detoured to the apartment, grabbing their bags and then heading out into the darkening drizzle towards Hazel Hall, the library.

They'd both pulled their hoodies up, sheltering them from the rain.

For a split second, Dean had wondered if Brody would suggest a quickie when they returned to the apartment, but he just picked up his backpack and said he was ready to go.

You could always suggest it, Dean reminded himself as they approached the library. *Nothing saying you can't proposition him.*

They neared the stairs leading up to the main doorway, but before Dean could take the first step, Brody's hand closed around his arm, and he tugged him away, leading him around the corner, between Hazel and Clark Hall, one of the dorms. Just after dinner on a Saturday night with the rain coming down, nobody was around, and Brody tucked him under a little awning, pressed Dean's body to the wall, and kissed him.

Dean fell into it immediately, cupping Brody's cold cheek, rough with stubble, against his palm, and said everything he hadn't been able to earlier. *Thank you for coming. Thank you for being proud of me. Thank you for being a friend. And more. But mostly, thank you for being you.*

There wasn't a way for a kiss between the two of them to not be passionate, and it was, but it was sweet, too, Brody ducking his head as he pulled back.

"I just had to do that, before we went inside."

"You could've done it when we were at the apartment," Dean pointed out wryly.

"Yeah, and then it wouldn't have stopped at a kiss," Brody retorted.

Dean had to give him that. "True."

He knew friends who were enjoying benefits didn't want to kiss each other like this. It was on the tip of his tongue to ask Brody if that had changed, if his *feelings* had changed, like Dean's had, but what stopped him was the worry that Brody would just shake his head and smile lightly, like that was still all he wanted.

Like it didn't really matter that Dean craved Brody's whole self with his whole body.

And he'd had enough experience with rejection in his life that he wasn't sure he wanted to risk it. Not now. Not from this person. Dean could take a lot and *had* taken a lot. But he wasn't sure he could take that.

So he didn't ask.

"Maybe keep that in your back pocket as a promise for later." As he said it, Brody tucked a hand into Dean's back pocket, his hand warm against the chilled fabric of his jeans. Cupping him and squeezing. "I know *I'll* be thinking about that."

"You keep that up," Dean said roughly, "and that's *all* I'll be thinking about."

Brody grinned. "Good."

Then he turned and walked off.

Dean chased after him, following him up the stairs, willing his erection to die as they approached the big open room with its rows of study tables.

There was a girl with dark brown hair, a bright pinkish-purple streak weaving from the crown of her head, sitting at a table near the back, and that was the direction Brody took them in.

She glanced up. "There you are!" she said. She tilted her head, glancing around Brody and looking straight at him. "And you must be Dean, the roommate. Brody said you were big but I think he—"

"Yep," Brody interrupted her.

Dean was a little disappointed. He wanted to know what else Brody had told Gina, but Brody's glare made it clear she wasn't supposed to say anything else and predictably she clammed up.

"Well, it's real good to meet you," she said.

Dean inclined his head.

"Even," she added, the corner of her mouth lifting into a smirk, "if you've been monopolizing Brody's study time."

"Sorry. I didn't know he'd been bailing on you. We could've invited you."

Brody flushed. Like he'd just been caught out.

"Uh, yeah, we should've," Brody said. He nudged Dean under the table, and Dean wasn't sure he understood.

Didn't understand until he'd slipped his headphones on and was a few paragraphs into his reading. His phone dinged, and he glanced down at it.

It was a message from Brody, just across the table, supposedly deep into a discussion with Gina about their lab report. But he'd sent him this anyway.

Maybe I didn't want to share you, Brody had texted him.

Brody glanced up at him, and Dean could still see the remnants of that red flush on his cheeks. They didn't say anything, but Dean hoped his look spoke volumes.

Me too. I want to hoard you right back.

CHAPTER FIFTEEN

Brody felt different.

This whole time he'd expected that one day, he'd wake up, tie up his skates, and take his first smooth slide onto the ice or he'd even look over at Ramsey and *know*.

But there hadn't been one moment when he'd known more than any other. It had been a slow, gradual slide into acceptance.

A hundred tiny things had decided him.

How much he loved bending over the microscope in labs with Gina.

Writing lab reports, which everyone else hated, and he found he actually kind of enjoyed.

His parents' acceptance. His dad sending him a list of good medical schools he might want to apply to.

Watching Dean on his field of play, the relish and joy he took in tackling every single down as a new challenge.

Brody wanting his *own* new challenge.

The funny thing was with his decision solidifying in his mind, slowly taking shape and form with each game of his own, he actually found himself getting his groove back.

The ice felt cleaner, his blades sharper, his senses more attuned to the action on the ice.

Ever since he'd taken that penalty and he and Ramsey had argued about it, Brody had realized that his attitude was morphing, shifting.

And today, during this game? Brody realized midway through the third period that it had never felt better to play hockey.

He'd never enjoyed each and every second more.

The love he had for it had never been an issue—but now, it was sharper and deeper, more well defined, and it didn't make him want to *keep* playing hockey. He just wanted to play it now, to enjoy every moment.

Ramsey looked his way and then tilted his head in the direction of the ice. Zach barked at them from behind, and Brody vaulted over the boards, joining Ramsey as they skated where the Napa Buccaneers' center was heading—Finn and the goal he protected.

The Evergreens were up two goals to nothing, and there wasn't much they needed to do except to remain vigilant, of which Coach B and Zach had both reminded them during the last TV timeout.

With that lead, Coach B had also been letting some of the younger, less experienced defensive pairs take the bulk of the second and third period ice time.

But they'd all seen the Bucs pushing to score, notching a number of shots on goal during the third period, and Coach B had obviously decided that it was time for their defense to stiffen up again for the final five minutes of the game.

"Come on, come on," Ramsey crowed as they circled around the back of the net. He went on the attack, shoving the center against the boards, and they nearly went down with the force of it as they battled for the puck, sticks clashing.

Brody took advantage of the slowing of the action, skating into a slightly better angle in front of the right winger, who'd been a fucking pest the whole game. On the off chance that Ramsey lost this, he wasn't going to let the guy grab the puck.

Ivan joined in, apparently deciding he'd had enough of this bullshit, and of course it was his interference that made the center go down.

Brody was already moving fast towards the knot of players when the ref blew the whistle, calling roughing on Ivan, who made a face.

"Wrong-ass call," Ramsey called out, popping up with an assist from Brody as the ref led Ivan to the penalty box.

"You good for penalty kill?" Brody asked.

Ramsey shot him a dirty look. "I'm gonna pretend you didn't ask me that."

Brody rolled his eyes. "I'm *allowed*."

"You're skating really fucking well," Ramsey said, as they circled up for the faceoff. "By the way." Like it was nothing. Like this was something they should be discussing right now, down a player for the next two minutes.

"Thanks," Brody said dryly. He could feel it though. Not just a little, but literally surging through him. His growing certainty allowing him to finally enjoy playing in a way he hadn't all season long.

He wasn't going to stupidly make this decision quickly, but the more he leaned into the shining kernel of truth inside him, the better he felt.

The more like *Brody* he felt.

Mal took the faceoff, but he lost the puck and that smug fucking center from Napa took it, circling around the back of the goal before passing the puck to one of his wingers, Ramsey skating in front of him to try to take it away.

This year Ramsey had become easily the best defensive man on the team, and so he usually let him take the lead on penalty kill. It had been working for them. They had one of the best penalty kill rates in the conference. But today, Brody met Ramsey's eyes across the ice, and when the winger passed to the one by Brody, he went after it. Nicked the puck right out from underneath him, and he realized out of the corner of his eye that there was a big, wide-open sheet behind him.

It was risky, but they were up two goals, and another quick glance told him they had only four minutes left in the game.

Maybe in an earlier game, he'd have let the opportunity go, his confidence and his joy diminished. But today, he took it and grabbed it and made a quick cut, gaining the speed that was why he'd been drafted in the third round, crossing across the midpoint, Ramsey shouting his encouragement.

Brody could feel the rest of the players breathing down his neck as he sized up the goalie and the shot he wanted to make.

He'd only get one chance, but he was gonna make it a good one.

The Bucs' goalie had not been prepared for an aggressive push like this, and Brody made another split-second decision and went low instead of high, slipping to the right suddenly and sliding the puck in between the goalie's lower pad and the goal post.

He watched it go in, no disbelief because he'd taken his shot and he'd *known* it was going to go in.

The horn sounded and he was overtaken by Ramsey and the rest of the team, shouting in his ear and smacking him on the back.

"Shit," Ramsey said when they collapsed back on the bench a few moments later. "You fucking lunatic."

"Hey, can't let you have all the fun," Brody said lightly, but he already knew this wouldn't just be probably the best game of his career, but the game he remembered. The one where he gotten his groove back.

"Didn't know you were worried about that." Ramsey grinned, fully aware because he'd only mentioned it offhandedly a million times that he was the leading defensive scorer in the conference this season.

"I'm not." *I'm not now.*

"Great play, Faulkner," Coach B said, leaning down by his helmet. "Fucking great vision."

Brody already knew Ramsey was gonna ask after the game.

And inevitably, after he'd showered and was sitting on the bench in front of his locker, Ramsey dropped down next to him, wearing only a towel around his waist.

"You wanna tell me what that was about?" he asked.

Brody raised an eyebrow. "I took a reasoned chance and scored. Don't you do it all the time?"

"No, you're playing like . . .like you used to. No." Ramsey stood and began to pace. Clearly he wasn't worried about giving the whole locker room an eyeful because his towel was flapping, barely hanging on for dear life. Brody rolled his eyes. "*No*, you're not playing like the old Brody, you're playing like a *new* Brody. You weren't this good even last year, before you got hurt."

"From the way you're looking at me, I'd think you were pissed about it."

"I'm not pissed. I'm fucking confused." Ramsey stopped in front of him, a frown creasing his face. "What the hell is going on, Bro? You decide to stick with it?"

Brody knew what he was asking. He hesitated. He should tell Ramsey the truth, but Ramsey was weird about this, weirder than he'd ever expected he'd be, and he suddenly didn't know *how* to say it.

"Not sure yet," Brody said, even though he was pretty fucking sure, at this point.

But the right time to tell Ramsey wasn't now, when they were flush with the win and Brody hadn't ever been prouder of how he'd played.

He was on top of the world right now. And telling everyone—telling *Ramsey*—was going to be understandably really fucking hard.

He decided he was allowed to want to wait so he could savor this moment just a little longer.

"Alright, well, just know . . .that was a fucking sick move out there. You keep skating that well, you're gonna give Elliott a run for his money."

"No, I'm not," Brody said, laughing. "But I appreciate the thought, anyway."

Ramsey smacked him on the shoulder. "Proud of you, Bro."

For a split second, Brody wondered if his reaction would've been the same if he'd told Ramsey the whole truth, but he shoved that thought away before he could consider it.

It wasn't fair to Ramsey. And it definitely wasn't fair to Brody, who was on top of the world right now.

"Thanks," Brody said.

"Let's go grab a celebratory drink at Darcelle's," Ramsey said, and Brody shrugged in agreement.

Then he grabbed his phone from his locker, scrolling through the messages he'd gotten. His parents had both sent congrats, a bunch of friends had, too—even Gina had.

But the text that stopped Brody, fingers frozen over his screen, was Dean's.

What a fucking goal, Dean had written. **We need to celebrate it.**

Brody's heart beat a little faster.

He wouldn't say that either of them had gotten better about being honest and laying out when they wanted each other—though that was beginning to seem like all the fucking time, anyway—but Brody knew this was an invitation because he'd been learning Dean.

"Hey, I'm gonna take a rain check on that drink," Brody said.

Ramsey shot him a knowing look. "Dean booty call you? Oh *wait*." Ramsey slapped himself on the thigh. "It *can't* be a booty call cause you two are head over heels crazy about each other. It's never just a booty call."

"Ramsey," Brody chided.

"I mean it. You two are nuts about each other and just won't talk about it. I don't know what makes me more insane, that you fell for a football player, that you fell in love at all, or that you won't actually *do* anything about it."

"Trust me, I'm doing something about it." He was gonna fucking pin Dean to the bed and demand he fuck him, finally. That was what he was gonna do about it.

"Not sex." This time Ramsey smacked *him*.

Unfair.

"What's wrong with sex?"

"Absolutely fucking nothing, I'm so glad you're finally doing it, but *Jesus*, read that boy's mind. It's not very hard. He went to dinner with your *parents*."

"Because I asked," Brody objected.

"Exactly. You *asked*." Ramsey paused. "Maybe you can deny he's caught feelings, but you can't deny you're there. I saw your face when I said the big *L* word. You're super there and loving every moment of it."

"I don't know about that," Brody said. But he *was* loving every moment of it, wasn't he? And if he couldn't get enough just of Dean's body and his touch, but his very *presence*, wasn't that . . .

Well.

"You think about it," Ramsey said, patting him on the back with a sly smile blooming across his handsome face. "Maybe *after* you get him into bed."

Brody didn't want to think about it, but he was, inevitably, as he walked home to the apartment he and Dean shared.

"Ramsey's wrong," he said out loud.

But he didn't *feel* very wrong.

"It's just sex . . . it's just . . ." But it wasn't. It hadn't been for awhile. Brody was beginning to wonder if it had ever been "just sex."

Maybe for Dean.

But not for Brody.

He paused in front of the door, keys in hand.

Damn Ramsey. He'd just wanted to take Dean up on his thinly veiled offer, enjoy *this* night, without worrying about anything for once.

Without wondering for five fucking seconds if he knew his own goddamned mind.

But it's not your mind in question now. It's your heart.

Brody swallowed hard, keys still in his hand as he couldn't make himself move.

Then his phone dinged again.

He pulled it out of his pocket, and this time Dean hadn't just sent a message. There was a picture, too. A selfie, of him, shirtless, abs rippling, the trail of dark hair Brody was becoming so intimately familiar with exposed. Brody recognized his blue comforter underneath him, but he wasn't looking at that. He was looking at the hard ridge of his cock, trapped in the dark fabric of Dean's boxer briefs.

Brody's mouth watered.

Okay, I was probably too subtle before. Come home. I've got all the celebration you need, right here.

Brody's uncertainty and all those fucking questions washed away with the wave of heat that crashed over him.

Shoving his phone back into his pocket, he nearly fumbled and dropped the keys in his eagerness to get the door unlocked.

He found Dean in exactly the same position as the picture he'd sent. Lying on his bed, cock hard, dark hair spread across the pillow.

"You weren't subtle, not even close," Brody said, shoving his shoes off and pulling his sweatshirt and then his T-shirt off.

Dean smiled. "No?"

"No, I knew exactly what you wanted. And what *I* wanted."

"Yeah?" Dean was so hot like this, everything Brody craved, it was hard to keep his hands to himself as he shoved his sweatpants down his legs. Socks last, and finally, he was naked enough to approach the gorgeous fucking man in his bed.

Our bed. The thought wove its way through Brody's mind before he could chase it away.

Before Dean reached for him, hand cupping his hip, and the electricity of his touch chased it away for good.

"I know exactly what I want." Brody licked his lips and then bent down, giving Dean's mouth a brief kiss. His fingers dug into his hip. "You gonna give it to me?"

"I want what you want," Dean murmured.

"What about you?"

Dean shot him a look full of disbelief. "You think I'm not getting what I want? You're here, in my bed. That's everything—"

Brody didn't let him finish. His heart was swelling too much, the words Ramsey had said earlier echoing through him with every breath he took. But he wasn't ready to even *think* the words, nevermind say them, so instead he took Dean's mouth with his own, kissing him fiercely.

Dean tugged him over onto his body and Brody came easily, stretching out on top of him. It was amazing; he wasn't exactly small, but Dean made him feel small.

Not vulnerable. Not helpless or weak.

But treasured.

They'd done their share of making out, but they'd never kissed like this before, over and over again, like they couldn't get enough of just their lips colliding together, hot and wet, tongues slipping into each other's mouths.

Dean's hands were rough and sweet along his back, stroking and touching him everywhere. Then he dug his fingertips into the meat of Brody's ass, and Brody groaned.

But it was loud enough—Brody's mind stuttered over the realization that *actually*, that wasn't *just* him groaning. It was Dean, too.

He pulled back, panting, barely resisting the urge to thrust his hard cock against Dean's big meaty thigh.

It would feel so good and he'd lose himself in it.

But he stopped himself, with the last remnants of his self-control.

"God, *you*," Dean murmured roughly.

Brody curled his fingers into Dean's biceps. Loving the way they flexed and tightened. Dean liked to call *him* pretty boy, but Dean was a hot as fuck man, with a body that just didn't quit. It was a weapon and a tool. Maybe he normally used it for sheer destruction on the football field, but it was just as effective here, in bed.

"You want me?" Brody teased, fluttering his eyelashes.

Dean thrust up, and yeah, he was just as hard as Brody was. "Yeah, I sure do, pretty boy," he said, voice gravelly.

Brody pinned him with the most earnest, bossiest look in his arsenal. "Then fuck me, okay? I want it. I know you'll take good care of me—"

But he didn't get the rest out. Because Dean was covering his mouth with his own again, kissing him hard and relentless, but sweet, too.

He was such a bundle of those contradictions. Intense and determined, maybe the most stubborn man Brody had ever met, with the hardest will, entirely unrelenting. But he was sweet and soft, too, thoughtful in ways Brody never would've imagined could be possible if he hadn't witnessed them for himself over and over again.

Dean flipped them, in a move so effortless Brody's cock grew impossibly harder. His hand was still cupping his ass and he squeezed. "God." Dean's voice had gone from gruff to guttural.

Reaching up, Brody dug his fingers into Dean's hair, tugging him down. "Yeah, you gonna get on with it? I'm *dying* here."

"Like I'm not? You ask me for that, and I'm *weak.*"

His confession wasn't wrenched out of him, like he'd never wanted to admit it. It was confided, instead, soft and so intimate, like Dean believed that weakness made him strong.

Stronger than he'd ever been before.

Is it any wonder you're in love with him?

Brody pushed that thought away, the voice that sounded just like Ramsey's.

"I want you," Brody repeated, *pleaded*. If he said it enough times like that, maybe he'd stop mentally substituting another word for *want*.

"I've got you," Dean said, and then he was rising to his knees, rummaging in the drawer, pulling out the lube bottle that now seemingly shifted from bedroom to bedroom to living room once they'd figured out how much Brody enjoyed being fingered.

Then he was kneeling between Brody's knees, and Brody cried out as Dean leaned down, mouth burning hot as it brushed across his aching cock. His fingertips, wet with lube, slid lower.

It wasn't the first time Dean had sucked his cock, but it didn't matter how many times it had happened, Brody didn't think he'd ever get used to it. This big strong man, brought to his knees, more powerful on them than he was standing up.

He definitely hadn't expected the hot suction of his mouth along with the inevitable push of his fingers. Brody clenched around the first one and moaned when the second joined the first.

He shouldn't have been surprised at how slow Dean was, how sweet him dragging it out was.

Pleasure kept cresting through him in one hypnotizing wave after another. Just when he thought he'd taken as much as he could, Dean would pull back and then he'd lean in and give him a little more.

More than Brody thought he could take and then more still.

"Come on," Brody groaned.

"You can take it, pretty boy. You're so fucking tight," Dean said, his voice equally tight. Was he nervous? Wasn't Brody the one who should be? But he wasn't at all. Instead, he was a bundle of exposed nerves, desperate and panting.

"You gotta," Brody slurred, trying to fuck himself back on Dean's tongue, on his fingers, on *anything* that would send him over the edge.

But Dean wouldn't give him enough, even as he gave him everything.

He could tell though, when a third finger joined his other two, carefully stretching him, Dean's movements slowing to practically a crawl.

"Gah," he groaned. "I *need* you."

"Just a little more." Dean was panting now, too, and Brody knew if he looked down—well, *he'd* probably come, just from the sight of his man like this—he'd see just how hard Dean was.

But before he could argue more, Dean pulled his fingers free and scrambled for the condom packet, lost in the covers that Brody had mussed with his clenching hands.

Brody squeezed his eyes shut, sure that Dean rolling the condom on would be enough to make him lose it entirely.

"Brody, baby, you gotta turn over," Dean murmured, leaning down, kissing him between each word. "It'll be easier."

Brody choked out a noise somewhere between a laugh and a sob. "You an expert now?"

"Did my research," Dean insisted. "Wanted this to be good for you."

"It's so good already," Brody argued, but he was weak enough that he didn't fight Dean as he moved him. Turning him over, pulling him up, and *oh God*, there was his cock, hot and heavy, pushing right up to his hole, and he thought he was going to die if Dean put it in him and he was going to die if Dean didn't.

Maybe Dean felt the same, because his hands were shaking, digging into his hips, and Brody could hear, loud and clear, every single one of his huffed breaths.

"You gotta be still, just let me," Dean begged.

It was funny, because Brody had always imagined being in this position would feel powerless, but he'd never felt more the opposite, like he was bringing Dean to his knees, instead of the other way around.

"Then do it," Brody insisted.

The first slide hurt, burned a little, but Brody forced himself to relax into it. To embrace it.

"Tell me you're okay," Dean demanded. He must've felt him tense.

"I'm . . . okay." Brody realized he was. And then he realized there was more, still. "More, just give me more." Reaching down, he stroked his cock, flagging now, surprisingly, but it didn't take much for him to be hard again. Especially when Dean's hips hit his own.

They both exhaled at the same time.

"Fuck," Dean groaned. "That's so fucking good."

Brody tested out squeezing around his cock. But before he'd entirely finished, Dean was pulling out and sliding in again, thrusting gently this time.

And *shit*, yes it was. So good, so much better than just Dean's fingers—as insanely fucking good as those were.

Brody's hand dropped from his cock, because if he touched himself, he'd come. Especially now, especially now that Dean was thrusting over and over, angling his hips so he was sliding over that spot inside him each time.

Giving Brody so much pleasure he didn't think he could take it.

He must've been mumbling or groaning or begging, because Dean laughed, a deep guttural sound, wrenched from inside him, and then he thrust harder.

Brody dug into the mattress and wailed. "More," he cried, and he couldn't just take any longer, he had to move too, and he gingerly thrust backward.

Muttering under his breath, Dean's fingers were leaving bruises on his hips, and Brody didn't even give a fuck anymore. He wanted more. *Needed* more.

And then they were suddenly moving hard and fierce, chasing after the feeling with every bit of their strength.

Brody's cock bobbed in front him, and every few thrusts it brushed against the mattress, and he knew that was all it was going to take. He was going to come, inevitably, and he wanted nothing more than to drag Dean over the edge with him.

Brand him with this moment, until he couldn't even look at Brody without remembering how good it had been.

Dean muttered, and Brody heard something crack, and he shifted downward, suddenly. That was all it took, because his face and his cock pushed firmly against the comforter that smelled just like Dean and he shuddered his orgasm, wailing with every additional thrust Dean gave, and then Dean's hips were stuttering too, and it was over.

It was over, Brody realized blurrily as he collapsed onto the bed, but nothing would ever be the same again.

Dean's hand was reverent on his back as he stroked him.

After finding this, how was he supposed to live without it now?

"I think we might've broken the bed," Dean said, carefully sliding out of him. He settled next to Brody, neither of them apparently giving a shit about the wet spot this time.

"Oh?" Brody chuckled, gasping as the last little bit of pleasure escaped him. He realized then that they were lying together, but tilted.

"It was worth it," Dean said. He was touching Brody everywhere, again, hands coasting across his skin like he needed to know for sure that he was okay. That he was still in one piece.

Well, Brody had to tell him his head had just blown clean off, and that was entirely *his* fault.

Maybe *both* of their faults, if Brody was being generous.

"Yeah," Brody said, and then he started to laugh and couldn't stop.

Dean joined him. "We definitely did that."

"Next year, we're gonna have to get a metal bed frame," Brody said. "Especially if I ride you the way I want to."

Dean's hand froze on his back. Didn't move. Brody steeled himself and rolled over so he could see his face.

He hadn't really *meant* to say it, hadn't meant to assume that they'd be doing this next year, that they'd be sharing both an apartment *and* a bed next year.

But he knew he'd want to.

Emotion flickered in Dean's eyes. "You want that?"

"The riding? Hell yes. Have you seen that porn where—"

Dean chuckled again and shook his head, kissing Brody to shut him up. Then he pulled back. "You'd want to be with me next year?"

"I don't know about the year after that"—though he was beginning to have an idea—"but yeah, I do." *As much time as you'll give me. Might not be enough, but it would be better than nothing.*

Dean smiled. "Guess we're pretty shitty at friends with benefits."

Something tangled unwound in Brody's chest, but before he could say anything, Dean kept going. "Not sure how this looks. Or works. Or anything. But I don't want to give it up, either."

It wasn't a confession of eternal love—*and*, that voice added in Brody's mind, *you're not ready to make those either, by the way*—but it was enough, for now.

It meant that Brody could stop worrying that the next time this happened would be the last time.

That they meant something to each other, whatever that something was.

It's love, you two fucking morons, that Ramsey voice added.

But Brody shook his head to clear it. "I'm not giving it up. Giving you up," he said.

A long moment of quiet silence later, Dean said, "I gotta get up. Clean up. Figure out how fucked the bed is."

"Does it matter?" Brody paused. "We can just share mine."

Dean gazed at him. "You'd want that?"

"I want you," Brody said, and that had to be enough, for now.

Even if the alternate version was echoing through his head, unspoken.

CHAPTER SIXTEEN

"I can't believe you talked me into this," Dean said dubiously. He stared out across the ice. It looked different than it did for Evergreens' games. No goals. No players. The lights were low and bolstered by banks of soft colored lights flashing across the glistening surface.

Music was playing, and it wasn't the Evergreens' goal song. It was bright, happy pop music. Taylor Swift maybe? And the ice wasn't crowded with hockey players, but Evergreen students, laughing and falling down and skating around in slow circles.

"Oh, you wanted to come, I know you did." Brody shot him a dimpled smile. "Secretly, maybe."

"It's for charity, that's why I'm here," Dean said gruffly. Though that wasn't entirely true, either. He was here because Brody had asked him to come. He hadn't understood exactly what that meant until they'd arrived and seen the many, many couples together on the ice.

This was totally a date. Or a date-ish kind of thing.

Dean didn't really do dates, which was probably the reason it hadn't even occurred to him.

But even though he was new to this—new to *all* of this—he still wanted to take Brody's hand. Make sure everyone knew the gorgeous guy they kept eyeing next to him was here with *him*. That when Brody left, it would be with him, and he'd be coming home to *their* bed.

But instead of reaching for Brody's hand, Dean shoved his own into his pockets. He didn't give a shit what anyone thought of him and he *really* didn't care if they figured who he was, but Brody should get to come out to their classmates and his teammates the way he wanted to, on his own timeline.

"Right. No other reason whatsoever," Brody teased, giving him a sideways look that made it very clear he knew exactly why Dean was here.

"You said it would be for charity, and a good time," Dean said. "You didn't say there'd be ice skating."

"Ice skating's not so scary," Brody said reassuringly. He gestured towards where they'd set up a skate rental in front of the Evergreens' locker room. "Come on, let's get you outfitted."

"You're going to regret this," Dean warned again. He'd never been on the ice before, and while he was good on a field, ice was very different. Slippery. And wet. And requiring coordination that Dean was almost one hundred percent sure he did not possess.

"Oh, no, no, I'm definitely not," Brody said, smiling.

Dean huffed. Worried he was going to humiliate himself. That wouldn't be so terrible, but what if Brody *laughed* at him humiliating himself? Enjoyed this evening because he did?

That would be pretty freaking terrible.

But then Dean reminded himself that this was *Brody*. He wouldn't do that.

As they approached the skate rental, Brody suddenly grabbed his arm and tugged him to the side. "What?" Dean asked. "Am I going to have to do this on one leg now, or something?"

Brody laughed. "No. No. Actually, I wanted to say . . .if you don't want to do it at all, we don't have to."

"But you have to be here."

"It's *our* fundraiser, for the hockey team, so yeah," Brody said, nodding.

"And if I want to be with you . . ."

Brody's smile grew. "Oh, you wanna be here with me, huh?"

Dean hadn't known for sure that he'd do it until this moment, and now he knew he would. Because he loved this man and he was pretty sure they didn't have unlimited time together. If he wanted to take advantage of what they *did* have, then he'd have to strap those skates on and almost definitely humiliate himself.

"I'm going to ice skate with you, aren't I?"

Brody nudged him. "You're the worst. Always answering my question with a question."

Dean didn't even know he did that, but he was, wasn't he? Deflecting, because at the heart of it, he worried that Brody didn't feel the same bone-deep desperation he did.

He wanted Brody forever. Even if it was insane. Even if it was impossible.

"I . . ." *You can do this. Put yourself out there.* After a lifetime of holding everyone at bay, it was hard. Impossible, almost, but if anyone could push him out of that holding pattern, it was the man in front of him. "Yeah, I want to be here with you. All the time, if I'm being honest. I'd do way worse than ice skating." Dean paused as Brody's eyes lit up. "But don't do it, okay? Just . . .take it easy on me."

"Oh, don't worry. I'm gonna." Brody nudged him, softer and sweeter this time. "And I want to be here with you, too."

"You invited me." Dean cleared his throat. "I kinda assumed you did."

Brody gazed up at him, and it felt like his heart was in his eyes. Just like how Dean felt.

But he'd already said enough, so he said, gruffly, "You ready to skate now?"

"And here I thought I'd have to forcibly drag you onto the ice," Brody teased as they went over to the skate rental.

Ten minutes later, Dean glanced over as Brody finished tying his own skates on. They were pretty different than Dean's. Real hockey skates, unlike whatever Dean was wearing.

Brody's warm brown eyes met his. "You ready to go?" he asked.

Dean sighed, glancing back down at his skates. They felt wobbly, loose, but it also felt like he'd done the best he could to lace them up. He didn't know what was wrong, only that he should ask Brody for help. But before he could, Brody saw what was wrong.

"Oh no, *no*," Brody said under his breath, and before Dean could stop him, he was down on his knees in front of him, re-lacing his skates with quick, expert motions.

There was no time Brody being on his knees in front of him that wouldn't get him worked up, and today was no exception.

His cock twitched as Brody's hair, mussed and longer than it had been since they'd met, shone under the lights, calling to him, asking him without words to tangle his hands in it. Pull Brody in closer.

Dean resisted the urge, but when Brody glanced up, he could tell from the heat in his eyes Brody knew just what he'd been thinking.

"There. Now you're all set," Brody said, tightening his lace one last bit. He patted him on the knee. Anyone might think it was just a friendly touch, but Dean knew different from the way Brody's eyes flashed with an undeniable heat.

"Thanks," Dean said. He reached out, helping Brody to his feet. When he got to his own, unlike Brody, he wobbled a little.

Or a lot.

Okay, definitely a lot.

"You alright there, big guy?" Brody asked under his breath. He was taking advantage of Dean's imbalance to lean close, to tuck a hand around his waist, holding him firmly.

"Yeah," Dean said. "Don't tell me it's gonna be easier on the ice."

"But it will," Brody promised, and slowly they made their way to the rink.

"Now," Brody said, "I want you to promise me one thing."

"Anything," Dean said, feeling a bit more desperation as the wide expanse of ice stretched out in front of them, shining and undeniably slick. "Just don't abandon me, okay?"

"See? You got it already. Promise me you won't try to be a hero. Hang on to me if you need to. You might be a big boy, but I'm strong enough to keep both of us up."

Brody took the ice first, moving better on it than he had off, if Dean was being honest. He ground his teeth and took his first cautious movement onto it, and *damn*, it was slick. Like stepping onto a freshly polished linoleum floor, wet with rain.

He was sure he might've just ate it then, but Brody hung on to him tightly, making sure he didn't, as Dean took one hesitant step and then another.

"No, no, like more of a glide, or a slide," Brody murmured into his arm. "Like this."

He demonstrated, moving like he'd been born to move on the ice—and frankly, maybe he *had*—and there was no way Dean was going to be able to match his innate grace, but he tried to duplicate the movements anyway.

He didn't get close, but it *was* easier to move like that. Long strides versus short, uncertain steps. A minute later, they were moving, not *fast* but just fast enough to keep up with the flow of traffic around the rink.

"This is . . .nice," Dean allowed as they neared the end of their first rotation.

Brody chuckled. "Yeah?"

"I'm not gonna lie. I like having the excuse of hanging on to you."

He did. Feeling Brody pressed against him was wonderful, and he never wanted it to end, even if they had to keep ice skating to do it.

"You can do it anytime you want," Brody said, and there was that look in his eyes again as he gazed up at Dean. That warm gooey look he'd worn the other night and tonight, too. Often, now, once Dean thought about it.

"But—" Before Dean could stutter out what that could mean—exposure, for both of them, adding another layer of seriousness and intent to their relationship—Brody waved a hand.

"Yeah, yeah, I know," he said, and Dean was far too aware of the way Brody's body tensed against his own.

Dean wanted to let it go. He'd let Brody inside, hadn't he? He'd tried his best to stop deflecting, and wasn't that going to be enough? But even as he thought it, Dean knew that couldn't be enough.

Brody wouldn't just want his non-deflections, but he'd want his truths, too.

"I didn't mean that I wouldn't like it if meant people knew," Dean said. "I don't give a shit what people think of me, or what kind of opinions they have of who I want in my bed or holding my hand."

"Even the NFL?"

Dean shrugged. "If you can play, they don't seem to care the way they used to. There's lots of queer guys, living openly now, who play in the pros. I'm not going to worry about it."

Brody grinned. "Dean, you worried about how much you were smiling on the sideline."

"Yeah, that was fucking ridiculous." Dean could see it now. Could feel it. But he also understood where Ian and some of those scouts had been coming from. He could look back on the Dean of the beginning of the year and see how tensely wound he was.

"But you worried about it," Brody said, loyally.

"I'm not worried about it now," Dean said. Hesitated, but plunged forward anyway. "If it meant . . .if *you* wanted . . ."

Brody smiled, soft and tender. There was no way else to describe it and Dean felt floored that *he'd* put that look on Brody's face. That he made him feel . . .well, however he felt.

Maybe even the way you feel.

"Noted," Brody said, nodding. And he slid his hand down from around Dean's waist and tucked it into his, squeezing it once.

"Don't go too far away, though," Dean warned. "I'm still half a breath away here from wiping out completely."

"Nah," Brody retorted. "You're good." He leaned in. "So fucking good, Dean."

Dean completely missed his next slide, toe pick catching on the ice, and he went down, *hard*, and to his embarrassment, he dragged Brody right down to him.

But Brody was laughing the whole way, even as his ass hit the ice. "Whoops. Note to self, don't turn you on while we're skating."

"Too late," Dean said, still chuckling, as they tried to untangle their legs and get back to their feet.

A minute later they were back up, and skating again, but this time Dean wasn't going to take a fucking thing for granted. Damn toe picks.

"Hey, look," Brody said, gesturing across the ice, "it's Wes and Marcus."

Sure enough it was them. There were other players there, too. The whole hockey team, for sure, even Brody's coaches, who were settled at one end of the rink, Coach Blackburn, arms crossed, leaning down as Zach said something to him.

"Who's that guy?" Dean asked, pointing to an older man with dark auburn hair and broad shoulders, cutting through the crowd with easy, quick strokes that spoke of a history of familiarity on the ice.

"Oh, that's Jacob Braun. He played in the NHL for a few years. A goalie. Knew Finn's dad. But he retired near here. Comes in sometimes to give Finn and Nick some tips." Brody shot him a look. "He's weird, though. Like a lot of goalies. Keeps to himself, now."

Brody pointed out Mal and Elliott, both forwards on the Evergreens, names that Dean recognized from following Brody's games this year. They seemed to be deep in the middle of a discussion, verging on an argument.

"They okay?" Dean wondered as they passed by them.

Brody just shrugged. "They're always arguing. Very different approaches to the game. And life, honestly."

"Ah," Dean said.

If he had to guess, there was more going on there than just conflicting opinions, but he wasn't going to say anything if Brody hadn't picked up on that, yet.

"Didn't Ramsey say he was coming by too?" Dean asked.

"Yeah, where *is* Ramsey?" Brody wondered. "He's supposed to be here."

Next rotation, they slowed near where Elliott and Mal were skating. "Where's Ramsey?" Brody asked them.

Malcolm shook his head. "No idea." He glanced over at El-liott. "Though this idiot here might know. He's plugged into every opportunity at this place to cause trouble. Same as Ramsey."

"Unfair," Elliott complained.

"But *true*," Mal stressed.

"Hm, alright," Brody said. He looked concerned, the crease between his brows deepening. Dean wanted to reach over and smooth it out. Tell him everything was going to be okay, but it was hard to when there were no guarantees Dean could make.

"You're worried," Dean said as they skated away, Brody digging in his pocket for his phone. Dean could never have pulled that move off, but then Brody was a damn fine skater.

"Yeah. I'm gonna text him." But then before he could, his phone blared out, ringing. Brody stared, uncomprehending, at the screen and then answered it. He cut sharply over to the boards, leaving Dean to fend for himself, which he did. Barely.

Then he could only watch as Brody's frown grew more and more pronounced the longer the phone call went on.

Finally it ended, and Brody looked up at him, and Dean realized he was more than worried. He was upset.

"That was the hospital," Brody said, panic rising in his voice. "Something's happened to Ramsey. He was riding here on his bike and something happened. An accident? He's hurt, and in the ER."

Dean put out a hand. "Tell me where and we'll go, right now."

Brody looked shaken, and Dean knew that as much as Brody had been there for him, now he could return the favor. "Come on," he coaxed him. "We'll get our shoes, and I'll drive."

"He's just this way." The nurse motioned to them.

Brody's heart was in his throat and had been ever since he'd answered the phone, about half an hour ago.

It had taken time to get their shoes and for Dean to lead him to his car and to take the wheel himself, driving them to the hospital. Then they'd had to find out where Ramsey was.

It had all taken time. Time Brody was worried he didn't have. Nobody would give him a straight answer about what had happened. Only that Ramsey had been hit, while riding his bike to the rink for the fundraiser.

He'd gotten the call because apparently *he,* Brody Faulkner, was listed as Ramsey's emergency contact.

He knew Ramsey didn't know his parents and had spent years in foster care, but he didn't realize that out of everyone Ramsey knew—and that was a *lot* of people, both in the naked *and* clothed sense—he was the one Ramsey trusted the most to have his back when it counted.

And how had he paid Ramsey back? By taking half an hour to get to the right spot in the fucking hospital.

"It's gonna be okay," Dean soothed next to him, his voice pitched low for only Brody to hear him. "It's gonna be just fine."

Brody wanted to retort he didn't know that, but he also couldn't help but be incredibly grateful for Dean's calming, supportive presence. Without it, Brody was pretty sure he'd have flown apart into a million pieces.

When the nurse had told Dean that he wasn't Ramsey's emergency contact, he'd stared back implacably at her, and

Brody had added, hurriedly, that he wasn't going anywhere without Dean. To the point of reaching out and grabbing his hand.

The nurse had finally nodded and led them back to where Ramsey was supposedly being treated.

She pulled the curtain back, and there was Ramsey, a small bandage above his left eye, a woozy look in his expression, and then he smiled, like nothing was fucking wrong.

Brody wanted to throttle him.

For scaring him this way. For being alright, in spite of it.

"He's got a mild concussion," the nurse said. "He'll need to be watched, after release. But he's fine otherwise."

"I've been promised this won't scar, but I'm holding out hope," Ramsey said, touching the bandage. "I think it'll give me a real devil-may-care, rakish look to have a scar."

Brody did smack him now, on the arm. "You fucker, you freaked me out."

"Sorry, I told them not to call you, but they wouldn't release me to my own devices." Ramsey rolled his eyes. "I've got a headache, but I'm fine. Really."

"You have a concussion. You are not fine," the nurse retorted, but she was smiling, like even in this short time, Ramsey had charmed her.

This was Ramsey so it was entirely possible that he had—*and* that he'd grabbed her number, while he was at it.

"Here's his care instructions," the nurse said, turning to Brody. "He'll need to be checked every few hours. There's a list of sample questions in the paperwork, but mostly anything works. Anything you both know the answer to."

"Am I the most handsome, intriguing man you've ever met?" Ramsey said, in a singsong voice.

"You're the worst," Dean said. "And *no*."

Ramsey slapped a hand over his heart. "I think you actually mean the *best.*" Ramsey's gaze dropped to where Brody was still clutching Dean's hand. "Especially now."

"This isn't *because* of you," Brody retorted.

"Sure it's not," Ramsey said, grinning.

The nurse went over what he could take for the headache—ibuprofen, and if he needed something stronger, he could call in, but he'd need to come in for that, again—and how long he'd need to be observed.

"As for hockey," the nurse said with a reluctant sigh. "He'll need to pass whatever protocols you have for the team."

"Damn," Ramsey said, sounding upset for the first time since Brody showed up.

"Will you contact the team?" Brody asked. Realizing that he was going to need to speak up, make sure that Ramsey followed the doctor's instructions.

"The doctor will, yes,"

"Could I talk to him?"

The nurse looked surprised at the question, but Ramsey said, hurriedly, before she could respond, "Why do you need to do that? They're gonna talk to each other. I promise. I'm not gonna—"

"I know what you're gonna do," Brody retorted, shooting his friend a firm look. "And what I'm gonna do is talk to the doctor."

"Let me just get her," the nurse said.

"Why is this necessary?" Ramsey asked after she ducked out.

"I want to talk to him about specifics. Specifics that aren't on this." Brody shook the packet of paperwork. "And specifics that might not get communicated to Dr. Robison."

"God, you're practically already a fucking doctor," Ramsey complained.

"I'm a friend," Brody insisted.

A minute later, the nurse returned with a middle-aged lady, hair shoved onto her head and anchored with four or five different colored pens.

"Hi," Brody said, extending his hand. She shook, her expression blank but expectant. "I'm Brody Faulkner. I'm Ramsey's teammate."

"His emergency contact," the nurse inserted.

"I wanted to know what exactly you did to diagnose him."

Her expression softened. "We didn't do the CT scan, if that's what you're asking. But that might be something Dr. Robison from the hockey team might still want to do. He lost a minute before the accident, and a few minutes after seemed blurry too, when I questioned him. But other than the headache, he didn't seem to have any significant trauma."

Brody nodded. "That's why you're having him go home with me. To observe."

Her chin raised, and there was undeniable approval in her gaze. "If anything changes, if you feel like any of his brain function is slipping, you know to call us."

"I will. Thanks."

"I *will* be sending Dr. Robison the full report," she said.

"You're gonna have to forgive him. He's got doctorate envy," Ramsey inserted.

Confusion creased the doctor's forehead.

"I'm thinking about going to medical school," Brody explained. "But that's not why I wanted to talk to you."

"Well, you're definitely one of the more detail-oriented athletes we've gotten in here. So . . .might be a good path for you," she said with a smile.

"Thanks," Brody said, pleased, even though he had to admit he wasn't thrilled it had been under these circumstances.

With the way Ramsey was playing right now, he wasn't going to want to follow the protocols. He'd have to keep an eye out. Make sure Ramsey didn't bend the rules or bully Dr. Robison into letting him on the ice sooner than he should be.

"Come on," Dean said to Ramsey, after both the doctor and the nurse had left. "Let's go."

Ramsey slid off the bed, and Dean caught him as he wobbled a bit.

"Did I crash a date? Oh, man, you brought him to the fundraiser, didn't you? Did you at least get some extra super-duper romantic skating time in first?" Ramsey questioned as they walked through the hospital towards the front door.

"We did," Dean said.

"Sorry." Ramsey made a face. "They weren't supposed to call you."

"I'm *glad* they called me," Brody retorted. "But it was fucking terrifying, too, because I didn't even know I was your emergency contact."

"Who else would it be?" Ramsey's voice was light, but Brody knew he was fronting.

"Glad about that, too. That it was me." Brody unlocked the car door. "Come on, get in. Do you need us to swing by the frat and get some stuff for you?"

"I'll just borrow some sweatpants. Between the two of you, you've probably overflowing with them."

"Alright," Brody said.

This time Dean took the front seat without a word, even when Ramsey made an offhand comment about being a passenger princess. But other than that, the drive home was quiet.

Brody finally pulled into the parking lot of the apartment complex and realized, as they climbed up the stairs, that they were going to have explain to Ramsey why Dean was in his bed every single night.

Besides the fact that hopefully he *wanted* to be.

After the bed had broken, Dean had said he'd talked to someone about fixing it, but then the next week had gone by and there hadn't been any more talk of it. Every night Dean came to his bed and they woke up every morning together—and Brody never wanted it to change.

But now, they were going to have to explain this situation to Ramsey.

Ramsey, who had been giving him a boat load of shit about Dean being his boyfriend. And sharing a bed? That was undeniably boyfriend-y. Maybe they hadn't used the word yet, but Brody didn't think it was that far off from the way they'd been talking to each other.

"Uh," Dean said under his breath as Brody unlocked the door. "I can take the couch, if you need to monitor him . . ."

"What?" Ramsey questioned. "Why wouldn't you use your own bed?"

You've been doing it, you can own it.

"We had . . .uh . . .an unfortunate incident with Dean's bed. So it's currently . . .ah . . .out of service. So we've been sharing mine."

Ramsey looked from Brody to Dean and back again. "You broke his bed?"

Brody shoved his hands into his pockets. "Don't make a big deal out of it, okay?"

"It *is* a big deal. And sharing—"

Dean growled under his breath.

"Okay," Ramsey said, throwing his hands up. "*I'll* be fine on the couch. I already deprived of you of your romantic date night, I'm not gonna deprive you of your even more romantic bed-sharing. Besides, Brody kicks at night."

"I do not," Brody retorted.

Dean winced.

"Do I?" Brody couldn't believe it. "You didn't say anything."

"You're too cute in the morning," Dean said, lowering his voice and tucking his head down, near Brody's. "It's alright. I don't mind it. It's . . .it's worth it."

Brody's heart melted, right there in front of Ramsey.

"If I leave you on the couch, are you going to sneak out? Avoid me in any way?" Brody asked Ramsey in the sternest voice he could manage with his heart currently in a puddle at his feet.

"Swear to God I'll be good. I won't even sneak over and press my ear to the door. Hope that I can hear some of your antics for myself."

Dean rolled his eyes. "There aren't going to be any antics."

"Guess I should apologize for that, too," Ramsey said.

"No need," Brody said, clearing his throat. "I'll go grab you some sweatpants. The couch is pretty comfy."

Ramsey glanced from Brody to Dean. "Do I want to know the sexual history of this couch?"

"No," Brody said and hoped Ramsey would leave it at that. And *finally,* he did. In fact, as Brody glanced over at him, he looked tired.

"I'll grab you some blankets. A pillow," Dean said, slipping out of the living room.

Brody made sure Ramsey was all settled, couch made up as best he could, and after leaving him with a bottle of water and a pair of loose sweatpants, he ducked into his own bedroom, and sure enough Dean was there, stretched out on the bed as he scrolled through something on his phone.

"He all good?" Dean asked.

Brody nodded. "Not happy about staying here. Not happy about the concussion. But he'll stick around. He knows if he doesn't, I'll report him to Dr. Robison."

"Did you get out of him what happened?"

"Some fucking fool in one of those pedi-cabs ran a stop sign, and Ramsey had to swerve to avoid getting hit. Fell over the curb and smacked his head on the sidewalk. A faculty member saw it happen and insisted on taking him to the hospital. The idiot wasn't wearing his helmet. He got lucky, but *ugh.*"

"Could've been worse," Dean pointed out.

"Could've been better too." Brody let out a frustrated breath. Sat down on the bed, and took Dean lifting his arm as an invitation, nestling his body against Dean's bigger one. "You know how easily a promising career can be derailed."

"I do know," Dean said.

"And here I am ..." Brody trailed off. He didn't even want to say it. But that didn't change it. It was still true. *And here I am, thinking I'm gonna throw away perfectly good prospects. Prospects anyone else would've killed for.*

"You can't think like that," Dean said firmly.

"It's hard *not* to think like that," Brody retorted.

"You're *you*, not anyone else. You know what you gotta do, what you believe is right, more than anyone else."

Brody knew Dean was right, but that didn't make it easy. Or *easier*. He didn't say anything else, just sighed, the sound muffled by Dean's T-shirt-covered chest.

"Besides," Dean said, "if she'd been worried, she'd have done the CT scan."

"Maybe you should be the one going to medical school," Brody teased, because it was easier to make the joke than it was to think about if the doctor *should* have done the CT scan, checking for deeper and more pervasive brain damage.

"Nope. Think the best one of us is."

Brody considered what he'd said. How he'd taken it as a fact. And how there'd been a complete lack of judgment in Dean's voice. How he'd just taken it for granted.

"How'd you know?" He hadn't told a soul yet. Was still adjusting to the idea that he'd made his choice.

"I know you," Dean rumbled.

Brody relaxed against him. In more ways than one. "Yeah," he agreed. He knew he should say more. But before he could, Dean settled a hand, heavy and warm, on his hip, stroking him there. It was arousing but also strangely soothing.

"Go to sleep," Dean said gruffly. "I set the alarm for two hours from now. You can go check on him, then."

It was the second time Brody checked on Ramsey that he said it, sleepily as he gazed up at him.

"You've made your mind up, haven't you?" Ramsey asked.

Brody, settling down on one of the couch's arms and trying to force his tired brain to conceive of a question to ask Ramsey, froze.

"What do you mean?"

"I mean, you've decided. You're going to medical school."

Brody opened his mouth and then snapped it shut again.

"It's alright, you know?" Ramsey continued. He wasn't looking at Brody. Instead he was gazing down at his bare feet. "You're gonna be a fucking amazing doctor. Maybe not as amazing as you'd have been as a hockey player, but you want it more."

"I do," Brody admitted. He considered asking Ramsey how he'd known, but probably he'd get the same answer Dean had given him. They knew him.

He hadn't imagined that anyone would ever know him as well as Ramsey or his teammates, but then Dean had come along, and he'd not only changed Brody's perspective, he'd altered his whole fucking world.

Now there'd be no world without him in it.

"I figured," Ramsey said with a sigh. He glanced up, met Brody's eyes. "Can't imagine anyone deserves you to chase after them, but he gets close."

"I'm not—"

"I know," Ramsey interrupted. He yawned. "That came out wrong. I know you're not doing it *for* him, but it's part of it, it has to be."

"I tried to not let him be part of the choice," Brody argued. But he knew the truth. Of course Dean had been part of it. "It wasn't just about following him, Ramsey. It was about me wanting a *life*."

"Yeah," Ramsey said. "You gonna ask me your question now?"

Brody patted him on the arm. "You're good," he said. "I don't think you'd have been able to have a conversation of such emotional complexity and depth if your brain was irrevocably broken."

Ramsey grinned, teeth flashing in the dark. "You fucker."

"You love me."

"Yeah, yeah, yeah," Ramsey said, and Brody stood up, ready to go back to bed.

"You're gonna be okay," Brody said, pausing in the doorway.

"Shouldn't I be saying that to you?" Ramsey asked.

Brody swallowed hard and kept walking. Afraid that if he stopped—if he responded—he'd give all his emotions away.

When Brody finally returned to his bed, Dean, big and warm and perfect on the other side, opened one eye. "Everything okay?" he asked.

"Yeah." Brody paused. "Yeah, it really is. It's gonna be okay."

Dean slung an arm around him and dragged him over onto his side. "Yeah, it is," he agreed.

CHAPTER SEVENTEEN

"Hey, Coach, can I see you for a sec?" Brody asked, ducking his head into Coach B's office, twenty minutes before practice was set to begin.

He'd planned this meticulously. Giving them enough time to talk it through, but not so much time that things got awkward.

Coach B looked up from his laptop. "Oh, Brody, sure, come on in."

Though he'd wanted to, Brody could admit that he'd never gotten as close to Coach Blackburn as some of the other guys. Ramsey, for one, and both Mal and Elliott, even though they seemed so fundamentally different in every other way.

Coach B had seemingly tried to get close to Finn, but Brody had noticed that instead, Finn kept to himself, resisting any-one's outstretched hand.

Maybe Brody should've done more with him. But he hadn't, too caught up in his own struggles.

"Everything alright?" Coach asked, taking his glasses off, rubbing his eyes.

He looked tired. But still less worn out than he'd looked when he'd arrived in Portland a few months ago.

"Yeah, I just wanted to . . .uh . . .talk about my situation." The moment had arrived and now that Brody couldn't focus on the comfortable minutiae of how to time the meeting, he found himself tongue-tied and frozen.

"Yeah?" Coach B leaned back in his chair. "You want me to call Zach in?"

"No," Brody said, with certainty. There was a . . .well, he could call it an "air" around the two of them that didn't make anything easier, but instead, the opposite. A tension that wouldn't dispel, and Brody was currently full up in the tension department because of this conversation.

"Alright."

"You said if I didn't want to make the NHL my future, I could still play—"

"And I stand by that. This team is a launching point for that, sure, but Brody, I'd hate to lose you. You're a great skater, really a natural out there, and I can tell you love it. There's something to be said for that too."

"Even though you came here to send as many of us as you can to the pros?"

Coach chuckled. "I did, sure, but I came for other reasons, too. There's more to life than just hockey."

"Sir!" Brody gave a faux shocked gasp.

Coach laughed now, not even bothering to hold it back. "Don't tell anyone, alright?"

"My lips are sealed."

"You've decided then?" Coach asked.

Brody barely held back his eye roll, but he did ask, "Did you figure it out, too?"

"I had a hunch. A week or so ago, you took the ice and you seemed different. Less hesitant. Like you were wanting to enjoy every second. That's not someone who's going to play forever."

Brody sighed. "No, it's not."

"There's plenty of rec leagues." Coach grinned. "You'd skate circles around them."

"I'm sure I will," Brody said. Maybe he should be looking forward to that, but he wasn't. He'd miss the intense competition of NCAA hockey, but he'd still get to skate.

"You gonna tell anyone?" Coach asked.

Brody was surprised. "You're not going to tell them?"

"Son, you're going to finish out this season and play the next, right?" When Brody nodded, he continued. "Then I appreciate knowing your future plans. It helps me understand how I can help you—and how you can help me, to win hockey games. But it's not their business what you're doing in a year and a half. If you're gonna end up heading to Carolina, to their camp, or to medical school. That's *your* business. All that matters is that you're their teammate, on and off the ice."

Brody was surprised. He didn't know why because what Coach said made sense. What did it matter what he was going to do after he graduated, as long as he committed himself to the team now?

He'd told Ramsey—or Ramsey had told *him*—because Ramsey was more than just a teammate or a line partner. He was a friend. One of Brody's best friends.

"Okay," Brody said, nodding. "I worried . . .I worried they might not take me seriously. Or treat me different, if they knew."

"Brody, you've earned their respect. If they don't, then that's on them. And if you choose to tell them *and* they choose to disrespect you because of that, then you let me know, okay?"

Brody nodded, though he didn't have any intention of squealing about anyone being shitty to him.

But Coach B leaned forward, his gray eyes intent on Brody. "Don't pawn me off with that bullshit, Faulkner. Anyone's shitty to you because of this choice, you come to me, okay? Promise me that."

"I . . ." Brody hesitated. He didn't want to promise, not verbally anyway, if he didn't intend to.

"I get not wanting to be a tattle. But this is important. I'm not just teaching you to play hockey, but how to be men. What you're doing is brave and impressive."

"I haven't done it yet, not officially." Even though he knew he needed to let the Hurricanes know his decision. "And anyway, it doesn't feel brave. More stupid, if I'm being honest," Brody protested. But that didn't mean he was going to do anything differently.

"Hockey's never a sure thing, but you'd be excused from believing it's more of a sure thing than med school," Coach said. "It's brave to look at your future and see a different path than everyone else. So you've got to promise me, if anyone gives you shit, you tell me."

"I will." Brody caved. What Coach said made sense. And he couldn't deny it felt good that he'd continue to have his back, *and* that Coach didn't seem to respect him any less for the decision he'd made.

"Besides," Coach said as Brody stood, "do you think I thought any less of Zach for deciding he was done in the pros?"

"No," Brody said. He hadn't even had to hesitate before he'd declared it. Of course Coach hadn't thought less of Zach for that, and Zach was here, wasn't he? In grad school and yet still helping Coach B coach this team. It proved that there wasn't just *one* path to loving hockey and having a life.

"Of course I didn't. Everyone's journey is different. And if you want to talk to him about it, you always can, too. He'd be a good resource."

"He would be," Brody said. He wondered why he hadn't considered talking to Zach before. Maybe because in his head, he'd seen Zach as an ex-pro player. A guy who'd made different choices than Brody. Not as someone who'd picked something else they loved over hockey. But Zach had made a way to have both in his life, and Brody could see that was a pattern he might want to emulate.

"Good. Think on it," Coach said, rising to his feet. "I'm honored you still want to play on my team, Brody, and we're lucky to have you."

He knew if he'd been smarter, he'd have made *this* year his last, with the difficulty of balancing the demands of NCAA hockey and all his homework, but just for another year he wanted it all. After all, he'd done it this far, hadn't he?

Brody went to the locker room to get ready for practice feeling lighter than he had in weeks. Maybe even lighter than he'd felt since the beginning of the season.

Even though the decision hadn't been easy, the aftermath sure felt easy.

Ramsey was sitting on the bench in front of his locker, a grumpy expression on his face.

"You feelin' alright?" Brody asked as he passed him.

"Ugh," Ramsey said. "Fucking protocols."

"They're for your own safety," Malcolm said from across the room.

"Ugh," Ramsey repeated. "Did you hear that? A fucking parrot in this fucking room."

"Ramsey," Brody warned.

"If you want to play, they should just let you play," Elliott chimed in.

More, Brody thought, because it would bring a frown to Mal's face than because Elliott actually thought it was a good idea to duck the concussion protocols that Dr. Robison put into place.

But *that* was a whole different-ass problem.

It was weird how two people on the ice and then off the ice could be so different.

On the ice, the Evergreens' first line was a well-oiled machine.

Off the ice, though, it was an entirely different story and it felt like half the shit Elliott said and did in the locker room was to rile Mal up.

Brody wanted to say it didn't work, because Malcolm had always been a pretty level-headed guy, but with Elliott, he *always* rose to the bait.

It was baffling, and more than a little frustrating.

"No way, if you're not passing, you need to stay on the bench," Brody stressed to Ramsey. "Coach wouldn't even put you in, anyway."

"Believe me, I know that," Ramsey said. "I practically fucking begged him earlier today."

"Well, I know you're frustrated, but I can't say I'm surprised. You gotta sit this week out. Heal, right?"

"Right," Ramsey agreed reluctantly. "But it's fucking bullshit! I hate watching you skate with Greene." Ramsey glanced up and saw Nate Greene watching them, and he added, quickly, "not that you're doing a bad job. I swear. It's just . . .Brody's *mine*."

"Think Brody's man might have something to say about that," Elliott teased.

Brody froze, eyes glued to Ramsey's.

But it seemed nobody in the locker room was even slightly bothered by this or even really *noticed*. Everyone else kept moving along, taping up and gearing up, Finn doing his warmups on the other end of the cavernous room.

"Ell, you can't fucking say that shit," Malcolm hissed at him.

"Why not?" Elliott looked genuinely confused. "Aren't they together? But at the fundraiser—"

Brody found his voice and cut this speculation off. "Yeah, you're right. Dean's my man," he said, with a casualness he knew sounded studied. He couldn't quite make it sound natural, but maybe that was okay. Maybe it was fine because coming out to your teammates *was* a big deal.

"Thought so," Elliott said, shooting Mal a smug look.

"I didn't say they *weren't*," Malcolm hissed back at him. "I only was saying you can't go around outing people without their permission."

"Does he look bothered?" Elliott demanded. Mal shot him a look full of frustrated annoyance.

"Children," Brody said, even though Mal was actually older than he was. "Let's get along, okay?"

"Oh, so you're finally gonna say something to these two, huh?" Ivan said, rolling his eyes. "Where you been all year?"

Brody pulled off his shirt and tugged down his sweatpants. "I've been here, I just thought they might work it out on their own without interference."

"We're not fighting," Malcolm objected. "We're fine."

It was Brody's turn to roll his eyes. "Uh-huh, sure."

"Maybe you should fuck it out," Ramsey suggested, and Brody leaned over, elbowing him in the side.

"They should *not*," Brody said under his breath.

"Agreed," Zach said, striding into the room half a second too soon to miss Ramsey's suggestion.

"Don't worry, I have good taste. I wouldn't ever," Mal said, shooting Elliott another one of those daggered looks.

Elliott just shrugged. "I think you've got more like *non* taste, myself."

Zach's gaze went from one to the other. "Enough," he said shortly. "We've got practice to prep for." He turned to Ramsey. "I know you can't do any cooperative drills, but you can drill some basics. Anything non-contact."

"Joy," Ramsey said, not exactly sounding enthused at the prospect.

"Maybe give Finn some shots to block," Zach suggested.

Ramsey glanced over at Brody and Brody could tell they were both on the same page. Maybe Finn didn't need any more testing. He felt brittle enough, already. The last thing they wanted was to test him right out of the net.

"Sure, can't hurt to work on that," Ramsey said.

"Good," Zach said, nodding. "As for you, Brody, I'm gonna work with you and Greene on your communication. You're way too used to skating with Ramsey."

"For good reason," Ramsey said mournfully.

"Hey, it'll be over soon," Brody said. "I stopped by Dr. Robison's office today, on my way in, and he said your scans were clear."

"You asked the doctor about my scans?" Ramsey sighed. "Why am I even surprised?"

"You shouldn't be?"

Ramsey's frustration broke into a fierce grin and the next thing Brody knew, he had his arms full of his best friend.

"You know, I'm gonna fucking miss you," Ramsey said under his breath.

"You aren't even going to be on the team next year," Brody reminded him, after clearing his throat a bit.

Ramsey pulled back, and he was grinning that old carefree Ramsey grin. The one that Brody had seen the first day he'd skated onto the ice at Hossa Rink and knew he'd found the right place to play hockey.

The path Brody was taking might be different now, but it still felt like reassurance, like he was coming home.

"Yeah, still," Ramsey teased. "Guess you're gonna have to come visit me, once I'm a big shot hockey player."

"Try and keep me away," Brody said. And that was a promise.

"Shouldn't have let Wes talk me into this party," Dean said as he and Brody walked up to the frat house.

"Why not? You had a free evening. Our game was earlier, so it worked out." Brody grinned at him. "What, are you not feeling social this evening?"

Dean shot him a look. He knew it was full of heat and full of promise. "You know I'm not. Except when it's you."

"Except," Brody retorted, grinning over at him, "we wouldn't be doing much talking."

Dean leaned in, feeling his blood quickening. Brody was potent tonight. Hot as fuck—all smug and cocky—knowing just the effect he had on Dean. "Oh, I'd be talking alright."

Dean could give it right back, because he watched as Brody's pupils dilated, his body angling closer, like their two bodies were magnets and he was inextricably drawn in and couldn't fight it any longer.

"Yeah?" Brody's voice had gone gruff as they climbed the stairs up to the front porch.

"Later," Dean promised. He shot Brody a grin. "You dragged us to this party, after all."

Brody rolled his eyes but he was still glued to Dean's side as they walked into the living room, crowded with people.

"You still happy we came?" Dean teased.

He actually wasn't *that* disappointed he was spending part of the evening at this frat party. As long as he was with Brody, he was practically guaranteed to have a good time.

"Yeah," Brody said, and Dean followed his gaze. There were some of his football guys on the other side of the room—Wes and Marcus, of course, and Damian, the starting running back—but Brody was looking at the other side, where a knot of hockey players had gathered.

Ramsey was there, holding court. Dean recognized Elliott, too, one of their young forwards, and an older guy, with dark hair and dark eyes, glowering over at him. The goalie was there, too, Dean only realizing it was him because they'd played him in beer pong during the last party they'd been at.

His hand had shook, with nerves or pressure, and he'd actually gotten more intense when someone had brought up his dad, who was apparently some big shot famous hockey player.

Dean didn't know; he'd barely given hockey a second thought before he and Brody had moved in together.

Before he'd fallen for Brody.

"I'm gonna go over there, you want to—"

"I can talk to those guys any time," Dean said, not wanting to leave Brody's side. "I don't mind slumming it with the hockey guys."

Brody elbowed him, but his eyes were glowing as he gazed up at Dean. "You wanna grab us some beers?"

Nobody watching them would think for half a second that they were just two platonic bros, hanging out at a party. This felt like a date, and Dean discovered he *liked* that.

"Yeah," Dean said and let his hand brush against the small of Brody's gorgeous back. Felt Brody relax into his touch. "I'll be right back."

It would be so easy to lean down and brush a kiss across Brody's mouth.

He knew, from the way Brody's gaze flicked to his lips, that he was thinking about it.

But they hadn't even had the conversation about how serious this was. Or how Dean was head-over-heels, fucking-wildly-in-love, yet.

Dean figured they had time for that. Maybe if he gave it enough time, gave *Brody* enough time, by the time it came up, Brody would feel a fraction of what he did. He wouldn't just shake his head, regretfully, as Dean bared his heart and his soul.

"Okay," Brody murmured. He reached up, curling his fingers into Dean's T-shirt, like he wanted one last touch to ground him, to remind him Dean was real. "I'll be right here."

It hurt to move away from him, but Dean made himself do it, heading into the kitchen and its makeshift bar. Dean made quick work of grabbing two beers from the cooler while making bland small talk with a guy and a girl, her mentioning he was impressed by a sack during Dean's last game, and him gazing up down at her like she was saying something life-changing.

Did he and Brody look at each other like that?

Dean was pretty sure he looked at *Brody* like that. Every time he opened his mouth, Dean probably stared at him like he was spouting the mysteries of the universe.

Well.

He'd never promised to be subtle. Or discreet.

Brody hadn't seemed to mind at the fundraiser that they were pressed together in an entirely unplatonic way. And he hadn't been shy about touching him tonight, either.

Maybe he wouldn't have minded if Dean *had* kissed him.

Maybe he should've.

Maybe Dean was already disappointing him . . .

Shut up, he told that annoying voice. *Brody likes me just fine.*

But you love *him.*

He did.

With the kind of dedication he'd previously reserved for his football career.

He returned to the living room, and to Brody, handing him the other bottle, and Brody clicked it against Dean's own. "Hey, everyone this is Dean," Brody said, and the few people Dean hadn't met yet nodded back at him.

"My . . .uh . . .roommate," Brody clarified. He glanced over at Dean, and Dean knew all his expressions well enough at this point that he could see the apology in it.

He knew not everyone in this group played hockey. Some were friends of players. Which would explain why even after Brody had told his team about them, he was still being circumspect here and now.

Dean told himself that he wasn't disappointed. That they were still figuring this thing out, and that Brody didn't need to tell everyone. Not when they both knew the truth.

"Heard your dad was in town," Ramsey said, blissfully changing the subject, directing the question to Finn. Who looked up, surprised. He downed the rest of the drink in his red plastic cup and lifted it up, like he was toasting an imaginary person.

"Yeah," Finn said in a dry voice. "He sure is. Wanting to make sure his investment is paying off."

Dean understood a little of Finn's bitterness. *His* bitterness was different, of course. More of a *why do my parents both think I'm worthless* flavor, but he imagined that having an overly invested parent would be hard, too.

"Hey, if my dad was a famous hockey player, I'd fucking love it," one of the guys Dean didn't recognize said. One of the guys Dean was pretty sure wasn't a hockey player.

Ramsey and Brody exchanged a knowing glance.

"You don't know anything," Brody said slowly, as Finn's gaze drifted back to the ground.

"All those genes and the money and the exposure," the guy kept arguing.

Ramsey cuffed the guy on the back of the head. "Hey, you," Ramsey said, turning to the guy with his most flirtatious smile, "why don't you go get me another drink?"

"Me?" the guy squeaked. Looking downright floored that anyone who looked like Ramsey would trust him to do any kind of errand involving Ramsey's mouth.

Brody rolled his eyes and Dean stifled a laugh.

"Yeah, you," Ramsey said.

"Sure, be right back," the guy said. Leered one more time and then left.

"Sorry," Ramsey said to Finn, who just shrugged. Like he didn't want to be bothered. But Dean could tell he was bothered.

"We know it sucks," Elliott said.

Finn shrugged again. Clearly he didn't want to talk about it, and that much was obvious to everyone, so why had Ramsey brought it up in the first place?

"You need anyone to take some of his attention, you just say the word," Ramsey said.

"You couldn't walk for days after his last private lesson," Finn said, barking out a laugh.

"Drills are all I can do anymore. No contact til I'm cleared."

"Soon, right?" Dean asked, deciding that he might as well join in the conversation. He was here, wasn't he? And he was dating, whether or not they used the actual word in public, a hockey player.

Ramsey nodded. "Next weekend I'll be clear, for sure."

"Good. I missed you," Brody said.

"Oh, I just bet you did," Ramsey said, and to Dean's surprise, he sidled closer to Brody. "Bet I could do a few other things you'd miss too."

Dean hadn't been very far away from his guy, but he'd been at least trying to keep a respectful distance that said, *we might be dating but I'm gonna make everyone speculate*. Ramsey split the distance and gathered Brody close.

Everyone knew when Ramsey turned on the charm—it was like he flicked on a spotlight—and he was grinning at Brody now, hand stroking up and down his side.

Brody didn't look surprised or bothered or *anything*.

"Yeah?" He laughed. Like Ramsey wasn't serious. Like it was normal. Like it was *okay*.

Dean wanted to howl.

Put a fist right into Ramsey's smug, handsome face.

He didn't, because he was possessive but not crazy. Besides, Ramsey and Brody were friends, weren't they? Dean wouldn't say he was this touchy-feely with his friends, but he and Wes touched plenty, and it wasn't like Marcus ever wanted to punch him.

Right?

Suddenly Dean wondered.

He glanced back at where Wes and Marcus were laughing together with Damian.

Maybe he should have asked, before this.

"Come on," Ramsey said to Brody. "I wanna talk to you about something." He was tucking his head close, like he wanted to tell Brody a secret, and Dean hated it—not the fact that Ramsey was doing it, but the fact that Brody wasn't leaning away.

Maybe his closeness with Dean wasn't special. Maybe it was something he did with everyone, and Dean was just now noticing this.

There's certain things you know *he's only done with you*, that voice inside Dean reminded him.

"I . . .I'm gonna go talk to Wes," Dean said, hating how uncertain he sounded.

And how Brody just gave him an absentminded nod as Ramsey dragged him off to God knew where.

"What's going on?" Wes asked Dean as he wandered over, probably looking something close to blindsided.

"Yeah, you look weird. Like someone just stole your favorite toy," Marcus pointed out.

"Someone did, I think," Damian teased.

And okay, maybe nothing about this was subtle.

He hadn't been subtle.

But what about Brody? Was he not . . .

Dean didn't let the thought out, but it was hovering in the back of his mind, still. Ugly and poisonous and potentially life-destroying.

"You should just tell him you're in love with him," Wes said bluntly.

"Now? But—"

"He's probably thinking this is kosher because you *haven't*," Marcus pointed out.

Dean stared at the doorway they'd disappeared through.

He didn't think Brody would do anything with Ramsey. He *trusted* Brody.

But Ramsey was Ramsey. He could have anyone in his bed. All he had to do was give them a come hither glance and they were *his*.

Dean was not nearly that smooth. Or charming. Or skilled.

"We did talk," Dean said, hating how defensive he sounded. How defensive he felt. "We're . . .I thought we were getting there."

"And why didn't you drop the big L then?" Wes wanted to know.

God, why hadn't he? Maybe he should have. The night they'd broken the bed. Or any other night after that, when he'd woken up next to Brody, so fucking in love and unsure what to do about it. He should have, the night he'd guessed the truth about Brody. He'd thought, earlier that evening, at the fundraiser, when Brody had made it clear he didn't care if people knew, that maybe Brody was beginning to really care about him.

"I . . .I thought it might be too soon," Dean said.

"Please. You've been practically inseparable for months now. Ever since he moved in." Marcus looked like he was gearing up for a closing argument, and Dean let his certainty wash over him. "He's crazy about you. You're crazy about him. You're the only two who don't realize what you look like together."

"Like a couple," Wes said, finishing his boyfriend's argument.

Dean let out a heavy sigh. "What if he . . .what if he doesn't feel the same?"

Wes shrugged. "Then he doesn't. But I'm thinking he does. Sometimes, we all have to risk something to get something in return. Did football ever give you any guarantees?"

"No." Dean could acknowledge that.

"There's no guarantees at all, in life," Wes continued. "You've got to take the hand you're given and play it the best you can." Marcus nodded his agreement and gave Dean a little shove. But Dean had about six inches and about a hundred pounds of muscle on Wes' boyfriend so he didn't really budge.

"Come on. Go play that hand," Marcus added.

Dean was beginning to realize he needed to.

He didn't want to go to another party and have Brody introduce him as his roommate. He wasn't just his roommate. He was his best friend and his lover and the person he wanted to wake up every morning to and whisper every secret to at night.

The only person he'd ever trusted to have his back the same as he himself did.

"Okay," Dean said.

"What the fuck are you doing?" Brody played along until they were out of sight and then he pulled away from Ramsey's grip and crossed his arms over his chest.

"Helping you two, because God knows you can't help your-self," Ramsey said.

"What do you mean?" Except that Brody had a pretty good idea what he meant, and he hated it. "I just fucked it all up, didn't I? God, I did. I fucked it up." He'd known, the minute the word *roommate* exited his mouth he'd fucked up, but now he knew, one hundred percent for sure.

"You just told your friends and teammates that you're dating Dean, but tonight, with a few other randoms, that Dean is your *roommate*. Not even your friend. You're pushing him back into the bro zone, and I don't have to tell you that was shitty to do. You don't gotta come out all at once, guns blazing, but *geez,* give that guy a little consideration."

"I . . . I know I should have said something else." The moment the word had come out of his mouth, Brody had regretted it. But Ramsey was right; he could have fixed it. He could have at least added, *and a friend. And, by the way, a guy I happen to be wildly in love with.*

But he hadn't.

"Yeah, you fucking should have." Ramsey leaned against the wall. "I shouldn't have to flirt with you—which was *gross,* by the way—to get your boyfriend to tell you he loves you. Or for you to tell him back. For God's sake."

"It was *gross*?" Brody was stuck on that.

"You're my best friend. We don't . . . it's not like that between us. Just . . . *ew*. Gross."

"I'm not gonna argue with that," Brody said. "And we did talk. We're together."

"He tell you he wanted to stay in the closet?" Ramsey challenged.

"No," Brody said, shaking his head. "In fact...he told me the opposite."

"And I know you don't give a fuck about it either, so what are you doing, Brody?"

"I'm ..." Brody didn't know. He only knew that the further he got into this with Dean, the more he didn't know how he'd live without him. "Did you really mean what you said, that I'd end up chasing after him? Dropping all my dreams for his?"

Ramsey's eyes bugged out. "Is that why you're pulling this shit?"

"Yes. No. I don't know. I have a plan ...I decided on a whole fucking plan, and the moment it came to me telling him, I freaked out. I chickened out. And I'm still fucking chickening out. What if that's what people think? That I'm dickmatized or something. Or that I think he's my fucking meal ticket?"

"Brody Anderson Faulkner. Your parents own three houses and *gave* you a BMW for your twenty-first birthday. Nobody is gonna think you're chasing after Dean's coattails for his NFL money."

"True," Brody said morosely. "Maybe only that I'm dickmatized."

"Let's face it, you *are* a little dickmatized. But as an expert in that state, I can tell you, that's not all it is. You genuinely like that guy. You *love* that guy. You light up when you're together. And also being an expert on *you*, I can promise you that's what it is. Sure, the sex is good. The sex is great. But you'd want him anyway."

Brody thought about this. "Yeah," he agreed and then looked down at the dusty floorboards, scuffed by so many pairs of feet. "At the end of next year, Dean'll be drafted, but I'll take a year off. Get all my prereqs out of the way, and then I can apply to med schools wherever he's at."

"Have you told *him* this yet?" Ramsey challenged. His blue stare was hard as ice chips.

"You know I haven't. I've barely decided it myself. We're .. .we're still figuring things out. We talked about the rest of the year, about *next* year, but . . ."

"You don't want just a nice college hookup. You don't want just a college boyfriend. You want a future." Ramsey gestured towards the doorway they'd just come through. On the other side, Dean was probably confused, wondering what the fuck had just happened. Why Ramsey had flirted with him. Even though Ramsey flirted with everyone with a pulse, he'd never done it to Brody. "The truth is when you decided you didn't want to play hockey, sure, you wanted to go to medical school. You love that science shit. And you want a life. But even more than that, you want a life with *him.*"

It was true. Brody did.

He wanted to help himself. He wanted to help others. And he wanted to help Dean be the best version of himself, too.

"Don't be ashamed of wanting that," Ramsey said in a low voice. He pushed off the wall he'd been leaning against. "Embrace it, okay? Because it's special. It doesn't come along all that often."

Brody nodded.

"Brody."

He looked over and Dean was standing there in the doorway. His heart lifted. Had Dean come looking for him? He was frowning, too, like he hadn't *liked* Ramsey flirting.

And Brody got that. Because if anyone else put hands on his man, he'd have been fucking furious.

Because Dean was *his*, and goddamnit, he was Dean's.

"I need to talk to you," Brody said, and Dean nodded.

This time he didn't hesitate. He took Dean's hand and led him out the kitchen, down the stairs, and they settled there, same as they had the last time they'd come to a party here.

Dean hadn't said a word, but the moment Brody sat down and looked over at him, it all spilled out of his mouth.

"I love you, you know? I didn't think I could love anyone. But I do. I love you. And if you love Ramsey or want Ramsey . . .well, I don't know how okay I'll ever be with that. But I want you to be happy, however that happens. If that's not with me, that's going to fucking suck, no lie, but I . . ." Dean's voice cracked. "I love you."

Brody reached out and gripped his hands, squeezing them hard. "I love you, too. And I don't want Ramsey. Not now. Not ever. I want *you*. I want you so bad I . . .I don't just want you this year and next year. I want . . .I want us to build something together."

"You do?" Dean looked surprised by this, and Brody kicked himself, a little. Or a lot.

God, he'd called Dean his *roommate*. And that was so far from the truth, it was a fucking cosmic-sized joke.

"*Yes*, you idiot," Brody said and leaned in, kissing him firmly.

The kiss was just getting good—though frankly every kiss with Dean was pretty fucking amazing. Still, this was pretty high up on the scale, considering Dean had just told him he loved him and Brody had said it back.

"What do you mean?" Dean said, trying to clear his head and wrap his head around what Brody had just said. "How can we even build something? I'm gonna get drafted. You're gonna get accepted to like every medical school you apply to, cause you're so fucking smart."

"Oh, you're cute, I like you," Brody said, patting him on the cheek. "I *love* you."

"I *still* don't know what that means," Dean said.

"It means, if it works out the way I hope it will, I'll take a year after we graduate and get some pre-requisite classes out of the way. Set myself up so every medical school *will* accept me. After you get drafted, I'll know where all those are gonna be."

"Wait, you're gonna come *with* me to wherever I go?" Dean didn't look dismayed by this possibility but thrilled by it.

"If you don't mind," Brody said. It was stupid to still be hedging his bets at this point. After all, Dean had just said, *If that's not with me, that's gonna fucking suck*, and it wasn't like that it would suck less in two years.

Probably it would suck more.

"If I don't *mind*," Dean retorted. Then he was being pulled into his big boyfriend's even bigger, beefier arms and held so tightly Brody wasn't sure he could breathe.

Or maybe that was the joy rushing through him, one thrilling wave after another, leaving him breathless.

Brody wiggled, trying to get a real breath out. "I take it you like that idea," Brody said.

Dean's face told him everything he needed to know.

"I love you," Dean said, "and I fucking love that idea."

He kissed him again, and the first time they'd ever done it, on that dirty, dingy couch, had felt like a beginning, but this felt so much more like one.

Like the rest of his life.

Like the rest of *their* life.

EPILOGUE

Eighteen months later

"Did it feel like this when you got drafted?" Dean asked, glancing over at where Brody sat kitty corner to him on the other couch. He'd wanted Brody next to him, but the TV crew who'd set up in his house had insisted that he be in the shot by himself.

Annoyingly.

Dean knew there'd been plenty of draft night shots with girlfriends but apparently boyfriends was a step too far. So much for the NFL not giving a shit anymore. His anxiety spiked again, even though Ian had personally assured him that his sexuality being an open secret wouldn't change a thing.

"Do you mean, was I a freaking mess? Barely able to sit still? Hopping up every five seconds to pace?" Brody raised an eyebrow. "No."

Dean wiped his sweaty hands on his slacks. Even though he'd decided he didn't want to do the whole going to draft night thing, climbing up on stage with the commissioner—because what if he *didn't* go in the first round?—Ian and Brody had both insisted he be dressed in a suit for the occasion.

Even if the occasion was just a camera crew, standing by with thirty-two NFL hats in bins at their feet, filming in their tiny apartment, waiting for the call Dean was theoretically going to get.

Not theoretically, Ian would tell him firmly, *it's reality.*

"I'm just nervous," Dean explained, even though that was most definitely something Brody was already aware of.

"You did everything you could do. Set some records your last year. Set more at the combine. I think half the teams in the NFL are falling over themselves in their excitement at even the *possibility* you might be on their roster next year." Brody sounded so proud. He shifted over onto the couch next to Dean and gave a hot glare to anyone who might argue. Not surprisingly, nobody argued.

Brody pressed a kiss to Dean's trembling mouth. "You're gonna kill it, and whoever gets you is gonna be the luckiest team in the NFL."

"You're just saying that because you're the luckiest guy," Dean said weakly.

Normally, he'd say that and *mean* it, but he felt a little like puking right now.

Brody seemed to understand though, tucking a hand into his and squeezing it, hard. "I *am* the luckiest guy," he said. "And you know what else? We're gonna be lucky together. I just know it."

"You ready?" Ian said, walking in, tucking his phone into his pocket.

"We're ready," Brody said, and Dean agreed, nodding.

When the producers had asked him who he wanted to be there—if there'd be a big party they'd be capturing on camera if he went, as predicted, early in the first round of the draft, or if their apartment would be crammed full of family and friends and well-wishers—but Dean had very firmly shaken his head.

Still, it wasn't as empty as it might have been, once.

His mom *was* here, tucked away in the back, like she didn't really want to be on camera, and he supposed he couldn't blame her for that. The spotlight wasn't something everyone wanted. Fuck, Dean wasn't sure how *he* felt about it, yet.

Brody's parents were here, and since it felt sometimes like they'd actually adopted him into the family, that felt right.

Ian was here. Ian's boyfriend, Carter Maxwell, too. Dean could hear his big booming laugh echoing in the walls of their small place.

Brody's hockey teammates had come too. Elliott and Malcolm. Finn. Even Ramsey had flown in. They were gathered around the edges of the living room, spilling into their tiny kitchen.

This last year he and Brody had finally converted their second bedroom into an office of sorts, a study lounge they went to when they *actually* needed to focus on their homework.

Wes and Marcus weren't here because they'd gone to the big draft party in Miami, even though there was a lot of talk the quarterback wouldn't get drafted in the first *or* second round.

"Maybe it doesn't happen, but at least I was there," Wes had told him, the last time they'd seen each other, about a week ago. The next time they saw each other, everything would be different. They'd be professional football players.

Dean couldn't say this life was what he'd expected. He'd planned on being head-down, singularly focused on this one goal. The goal he was about to achieve.

But life had gotten in the way, like he was beginning to understand it always did, and that was okay too.

Whatever happened tonight was how things were meant to go.

"I'm so proud of you," Brody murmured as they watched on the TV as the NFL commissioner walked onto the stage for the first time. "Whatever happens."

"Even if I fall out of the first round?" Dean almost didn't want to say it. What if it came true? But he had to voice it, because he'd spent too much time in the last few months dreading the possibility. Doing everything he could to avoid it, but it was there, all the same.

"Don't be ridiculous," Brody said. "It could happen, sure, but we know how much like at least a dozen teams want you. The Riptide *traded up* in the draft. They're now sitting at number three. You don't think that was for shits and giggles, do you?"

Dean nearly giggled now. The pressure inside him was mounting, to an almost unbearable level. The only thing that kept it bearable was sitting next to him. Hand in his. Never flinching.

Ian leaned over, murmuring. "I told you, they want you to replace Spencer Evans. He retired two seasons ago, and the backup they had last year, he didn't work out so well."

Spencer Evans was one of the most famous defensive ends in football. Out and proud. An inspiration on and off the field.

It was mind-boggling, even after all his hard work, that anyone could look at him, Dean Scott, and think he could be even a fraction of what Spencer Evans was. But the Riptide had looked at him and then kept looking.

"Besides," Brody continued, smirking at him, "I think I'd like LA, don't you?"

Dean looked over him. He was gorgeous, so fucking gorgeous, in slacks and a clingy green knit polo shirt that Dean was already fantasizing about removing with his teeth. He'd love LA and LA would love him right back.

Maybe Brody wouldn't be playing hockey professionally, but he'd hardly let himself go. In fact, one of their favorite things to do was go to the gym, egging each other on, until they lost the thread and usually ended up fucking in the gym bathroom.

Dean wasn't proud of it, but he couldn't deny he loved every second of it.

"I think you'd fit in anywhere," Dean said.

Brody had that easy manner to him, the way he'd fit in so effortlessly with Dean, when Dean himself had never felt comfortable anywhere. Not until he'd walked out the door and seen Brody for the first time.

"I just want you to know"—Ramsey leaned over the couch, head between theirs, because of course it was—"that anything that happens in the next few hours is ninety percent because of Dean being a monster on the football field and ten percent because I hooked you two up. Not just once, but *twice*."

"I'll concede the roommate thing. But if you're talking about how you sort of flirted with him, *no*," Dean said firmly.

"I knew you were still bent out of shape because of that," Ramsey crowed, like Dean wanting to punch him in the face was something to be proud of.

"I wasn't then and I'm not now. I didn't think for a second that Brody would even look at you," Dean said.

Brody wiggled closer to him. The producer looked like he was about to say something but it was Ramsey who shot him a look, and he smartly shut his mouth. "It *was* kinda hot," Brody said. "My big man, getting all possessive."

"Anytime you need a repeat, you just ask. I've always heard the sex life palls a bit after two years. After you're . . .uh . . .*settled*. And I know Brody is real interested in that picket fence."

"Brody," Brody said firmly, "still thinks picket fences are very stupid, thank you very much. Now get out of our shot, Ramsey. You got your say, and we think you're still full of it."

Ramsey grinned. "Ten percent! I get ten percent!"

Dean rolled his eyes. On the TV the commissioner was about to read out the first card. His phone had not rung. Ian's eyes met his own, and he gave an imperceptible shake of his head.

Well, they'd not expected him to go number one, anyway. Defensive players rarely did.

Besides, the two teams holding the first two spots in the draft were both sorely in need of a quarterback. Dean might be a lot of things, but he was no quarterback.

The five minutes to the next pick was interminable. Dean's phone stayed silent. So did Ian's.

Next to him, Brody made soothing noises, and Dean felt like he'd been reduced to grunts by the immense force of the pressure bearing down on him.

Then Brody apparently decided it was a good idea to make him hard, right before they might both be on national television.

"Hey," he said casually, "do you remember the first time we sat on this couch together?"

It was not the same couch.

Though it *was* a couch in the same place, and it wasn't like they hadn't had sex on this couch before. Brody had insisted on having it steam cleaned before tonight, because there'd been one rather insistent stain neither of them could get out, from a memorable night about six months ago . . .

Dean yanked his mind out of the gutter and out of that memory.

"It's not the same couch," Dean reminded him.

"Oh, but it *feels* like it, doesn't it?" Brody's hand slid to his knee. Squeezed. Dean knew he was trying to distract him, and even though he *knew* it, it was still working.

"It doesn't feel like anything," Dean lied.

What it felt like was Brody was going to seduce him, right here in front of fucking everybody, right before Marisa Lyon, the daughter of the owner, might call his phone and tell him the Riptide were taking him with the third pick of the draft.

And Dean? Well, he wasn't mad about it.

Except for the erection. That was a problem that nobody, least of all Ramsey, would probably let him forget.

"You're lying," Brody teased. "I can feel you tense up right here." Brody's hand moved up another inch. Almost to his thigh. "Same as you did that night."

Dean felt drunk on Brody. On possibilities. On the thought of them in Los Angeles together, Brody's skin golden in the sunlight.

"It wasn't even the *first* time we sat on this couch," Dean argued.

"First, second, third . . .it was easily in the first half dozen times," Brody countered sweetly.

"I didn't know you'd be so into going for my dick that night," Dean said.

"Oh, but deep down you wanted me to," Brody said.

A hit. Dean couldn't even deny it.

He'd wanted it then. He wanted it now. He wanted it as much as he wanted to take his next breath.

"I love you," Dean said and then grabbed Brody's hand, squeezing it firmly but insistently. "But you gotta stop making me hard."

Brody grinned at him. "But you quit angsting, didn't you?"

"I love you," Dean said again, because no other words felt sufficient to explain this goddamned miracle of a man he'd found and somehow managed to keep.

"Love you more," Brody said.

"Okay, you two lovebirds, we're going on air in five," the producer called out, and then, on the coffee table in front of him, his phone rang.

It was California area code.

Ian looked at him, and Dean smiled, heart skipping a beat.

He leaned forward and picked up the phone.

"Hello?" he said.

And the rest of their life—not just *his*, not anymore—began.

How does Ramsey end up picking Dean to be Brody's roommate? Find out here!

-

To preorder *Cold as Ice*, book two in the Portland Evergreens series, click here.

-

Malcolm and Elliot. They're fire and ice. Bad boy and virgin. They shouldn't work at all.

-

But the more time they spend together, the more desperate Mal becomes for Elliott to tutor him in bed, and the more determined Elliot becomes to win Mal's heart.

INTERESTED IN READING MORE OF
BETH'S BOOKS?

CHECK OUT A FULL LIST OF TILES
BY SCANNING THE QR CODE
OR VISITING HER WEBSITE

WWW.BETHBOLDEN.COM/BOOKLIST

WANT TO FOLLOW BETH?

MAKE SURE YOU NEVER
MISS A RELEASE?

SCAN THE QR CODE BELOW
OR VISIT HER WEBSITE
FOR A SOCIAL MEDIA LIST,
NEWSLETTER SIGNUP,
AND SO MUCH MORE!

WWW.BETHBOLDEN.COM/ABOUT